BOOKS BY TED DEKKER

*Boneman's Daughter*
*The Bride Collector*
*Adam*
*Thr3e\**
*The Priest's Graveyard*


WINNER OF
**THE CHRISTY BOOK AWARD**
BEST MYSTERY THRILLER\*

# TED
# DEKkER

## BLINK OF
## AN EYE

CENTER
STREET

NEW YORK   BOSTON   NASHVILLE

Copyright © 2002, 2007, 2011 Ted Dekker
Excerpt from *Forbidden* copyright © 2011 by Ted Dekker

Published in association with Thomas Nelson and Creative Trust, Inc. Thomas Nelson is a trademark of Thomas Nelson, Inc.

Center Street
Hachette Book Group
237 Park Avenue
New York, NY 10017
Visit our website at www.centerstreet.com.

Center Street is a division of Hachette Book Group, Inc. The Center Street name and logo are trademarks of Hachette Book Group, Inc.

The publisher is not responsible for websites (or their content) that are not owned by the publisher.

Printed in the United States of America

First mass market edition, July 2011

10  9  8  7  6  5  4  3  2

**ATTENTION CORPORATIONS AND ORGANIZATIONS:**
MOST HACHETTE BOOK GROUP books are available at quantity discounts with bulk purchase for educational, business, or sales promotional use. For information, please call or write:

**Special Markets Department, Hachette Book Group**
**237 Park Avenue, New York, NY 10017**
**Telephone: 1-800-222-6747  Fax: 1-800-477-5925**

# BLINK OF
# AN EYE

# 1

MIRIAM SWEPT THE purple velvet drape to one side and gazed through the window at the courtyard. The marble palace had been completed just last year and was easily the grandest of her father's residences. She hadn't visited all of them, but she didn't need to. Prince Salman bin Fahd had four wives, and he'd built each of them three palaces, two in Riyadh, and one in Jidda. All four wives had identical dwellings in each location, although to say his wives had the palaces was misleading. Father had the palaces, and he had wives for each.

This, Salman's thirteenth palace, he'd built solely for special events such as today's, the wedding of Sita, one of Miriam's closest friends.

Outside, the sun glinted off a spewing fountain in the center of a large pond. Bright red petals from two hundred dozen roses flown in from Holland blanketed the water. Evidently the groom, Hatam bin Hazat, had heard that his young bride liked red roses. Upon seeing the extravagant display two days earlier, Sita vowed never to look upon another red rose in her life.

Dozens of Filipino servants crossed the lawn, carrying silver trays stacked high with every imaginable food, prepared by eighteen chefs brought in from Egypt. Roast almond duck, curried beef rolled in lamb flanks, liver-stuffed lobster—Miriam had never seen such an extravagant display. And this for the women only. As at many Saudi weddings, the male guests would never actually see the women. Custom required two separate ceremonies for the simple reason that women attended weddings unveiled. The traditional path of the Wahhabi sect forbade a man from seeing the face of a woman unless she was a family member or tied closely to his family.

Sounds of music and drums and gaiety drifted through the window. The world mistook the prevailing cultural practices in the Arabian Peninsula as unfair to women, Miriam often thought. She'd studied at the University of Berkeley in California for three months two summers ago and had first heard there the misconception that a Saudi woman dies three times during her span on earth.

It was said that she dies on the day of her first menses, when she is forced to don the black veil and slip into obscurity; she dies on the day of her wedding, when she is given as a possession to a stranger; and she dies when she finally passes on. She'd been tempted to slap the woman who uttered the words.

Perhaps if the Americans knew Saudi history better, they would hold their tongues. True enough, a woman was traditionally forbidden from some of the activities accepted by the West—driving, for example. Or giving testimony in a dispute. Or walking about freely with her face uncovered.

But all of these practices advanced Saudi culture in ways the West did not see. Saudis understood the value of strong families, for example. Of loyalty to God and his word. Of respect for an order that supported both families and God.

Miriam let her mind drift over the events that had placed her and her friend Sita here, in this magnificent palace, where they awaited the ceremony that would change Sita's life as she knew it.

The kingdom's first king, Abdul Aziz ibn Saud, conquered Riyadh in 1902. He was in his early twenties then. The four kings who had ruled since his death in 1953 were all his sons. But when Miriam looked down history's foggy halls, she decided it was the first king's women, not his sons, who shaped the country. He'd taken over three hundred wives, and it was these women who gave him so many sons.

"I can't believe it's actually happening," Sita said from the sofa.

Miriam let the curtain fall back in place and turned around. Sita sat like a small doll dressed in lace and pink. At weddings, all the women, from bride to servants, shed their black abaayas and veils for colorful dresses. Her eyes were round and dark—so very insecure. Miriam and Sultana had rescued Sita from a flock of aunts busying her for the final ceremony and brought her here, to this room they'd dubbed the piano room for the white grand piano sitting to their right. The carpet, a thick Persian weave with a lion embroidered at the center, swallowed their feet. Evidently the designer Salman hired liked big cats; the walls of the room formed a virtual zoo of cat paintings.

Sita's lips trembled. "I'm frightened."

Sultana, the third in the inseparable trio, ran her hand over the younger girl's hair. "Sh, sh. It won't be the end of the world. At least he's wealthy. Better to marry into palaces than into the gutter."

"He's old enough to be my grandfather."

"He's younger than my sister's husband," Miriam said. "Sara's husband was sixty-two when he took her. I understand that Hatam is no older than fifty-five."

"And I'm fifteen!" Sita said.

"And Sara was fifteen too," Miriam said. "And what about my new mother, Haya?"

That got silence from both of them. A year earlier, Miriam's father had taken Haya as a bride when Miriam's biological mother died. Haya was only thirteen at the time. As was customary, the girl took over the duties of the wife in their household, even though she was younger than those under her charge. Miriam had been nineteen then.

At first Miriam resented the child. But one look at Haya's nervous eyes after the wedding changed her heart. Haya slipped into her role of submissive wife with surprising grace.

But Sita was not Haya.

Miriam looked at her friend's frightened face. Sita was still a child too. A small part of Miriam wanted to cry. But she could never cry, especially not now, just minutes before the ceremony.

Sultana looked out the window. Of the three, she was perhaps the boldest. She was twenty-three and barren. But she was married to a good man who treated her well and turned a blind eye when she spoke out against the marriage of young girls. Sultana's frequent trips to Europe had given her a somewhat Western perspective on that particular practice.

"Haya was two years younger than you," Miriam said.

"I saw him," Sita said softly.

Miriam glanced up. It was unusual for anyone to see her betrothed before the actual wedding.

"You saw the groom?" Sultana asked. "You saw Hatam?"

Sita nodded.

"How?" Miriam asked. "What's he like?"

"Two weeks ago, at the souk." She looked up and her eyes flashed. "He's very large. He'll kill me."

Miriam knew she should say something, but words escaped her. Though she'd made inquiries, she'd been able to learn only that Hatam was a wealthy oil mogul from Dammam on the Persian Gulf.

Sita sniffed and wiped her nose with a frail, shaky hand. She spoke quietly. "I make a vow," she said. "I make a vow today to refuse my husband. He will not touch me while I am alive."

Miriam reached out a hand. "Please, Sita, he'll be kind. Today you'll find your life enriched beyond words, you'll see."

Sita rose to her feet, red in the face. "I'm not ready to marry!" She trembled, a child about to have a tantrum. Miriam felt her stomach turn.

"I swear it," Sita said, and Miriam did not doubt her. "You're almost twenty-one and you're still not married. And you have this secret love with Samir. I hate you for it!" She turned away.

"You don't hate me, Sita. You better not hate me, because you're like a sister to me, and I love you dearly."

Twenty and not married. Rumor had it that dozens of suitors had approached Father for Miriam's hand, and he'd turned them all away. His denial was a sore subject for her.

Sultana placed a hand on Miriam's shoulder. "You can't know how she feels. Salman protects you."

"Both Haya and Sara were married—"

The door flew open and they turned as one. "Sita!" Sita's mother stood in the doorway, white as the desert sand. "Where have you been? They are ready!"

Then she saw Sita's tears and she hurried in, face softening. "Please, don't cry, child. I know you are frightened, but we all grow up, don't we?" She smoothed Sita's hair and looked at her lovingly.

"I'm afraid, Mother," Sita said.

"Of course. But you must think beyond the uncertainty that you feel and consider the wonderful privileges that await you as the wife of a powerful man." She kissed her daughter's forehead. "He's a wealthy man, Sita. He will give you a good life, and you'll bear him many children. What else could a woman ask?"

"I don't want to bear his children."

"Don't be silly! It will be a great honor to bear his children. You'll see." She paused and studied her daughter tenderly. "God knows how much I love you, Sita. I am so proud of you. Just yesterday you were still a child, playing with your dolls. Now look, you've grown into a beautiful young woman." She kissed her again. "Now, come along. The drummers are waiting."

She slipped Sita's veil over her face. And with that Sita's fears were hidden.

Miriam joined a thousand women in the great hall and watched as the drums announced the groom's arrival. The only men present were the bride's father, the groom (whose father was dead of old age), and the religious man who would perform the marriage.

Hatam walked out alone, and Miriam nearly gasped aloud. Blubber sat like a bloated tube around his stomach, sloshing with each step under a tent of a tunic. The fat under his chin hung like a reservoir of water. To say the man was large would be a horrible miscalculation. He was an obese mountain.

Beside Miriam, Sultana groaned softly. Several women glanced at her, but she ignored them.

The drums beat again. Sita's mother and her aunt led the bride out. Hatam smiled and lifted her veil. Sita stared at him, and in her cloaked defiance, she looked more beautiful than Miriam could remember.

The ceremony lasted only a few minutes. The actual marriage had been performed hours earlier, first with the bride and then with the groom, separately, signing documents that affirmed the agreed upon dowry and terms of marriage.

Now the religious man looked at Sita's father and spoke the token words that confirmed the union. After a nod, he glanced at the groom, who replied that he accepted Sita as his bride. A thousand women broke the silence with joyful ululating. Today the noise sent chills down Miriam's arms. Hatam walked past his new bride, tossing coins to the women. Sita hesitated, then followed.

Hatam led Sita from the room, and Miriam saw that her friend walked like a newborn lamb still searching for its legs.

The women began to move outside, where food, music, and festivity awaited. They would celebrate for another two days after the groom departed with his new bride.

But Miriam wasn't sure she could participate. Not with Sita's oath ringing in her ears. She quietly begged her friend to come to her senses so that she could enter her new life with joy.

# 2

IT WAS THREE o'clock in the afternoon and Seth Border, although arguably one of the most popular men on campus, was lonely. Popular, because he possessed both the sharpest mind the university had seen since its inception and the kind of all-American face the media loved. Lonely, because he felt oddly disconnected from that popularity.

If he'd learned anything at Berkeley, it was that when academia put you on a pedestal, it expected you to perform as advertised. If it wanted you to grow green skin, you'd better paint your skin green, because if you came out onstage with blue skin, it would resent you. Ironic, considering the freedom preached by those in this neck of the woods.

Seth stared out the small windows that ran along the high wall of the lecture hall, thinking he was a blue person in a green person's world. Blue, like the sky outside—another cloudless California day. He ran a hand through his shaggy blond mop and released a barely audible sigh.

He glanced at the complex equation on the whiteboard behind the professor, solved it before he finished reading it, and let his mind drift again.

He was twenty-six, and his whole life had felt like a long string of abandonments. Sitting here listening to graduate lectures on quantum physics by Dr. Gregory Baaron with forty other students only seemed to reinforce the feeling. He should be doing something to lift himself out of this valley. Something like surfing.

Surfing had always been his one escape from a world gone mad, but the last time he'd seen the really good side of a wave was three years ago, back at Point Loma in San Diego, during a freak storm that swept fifteen-foot swells along the coast from Malibu to Tijuana. There was nothing quite like catching the right wave and riding in its belly until it decided to dump you off.

Seth first experienced the freedom of surfing when he was six, when his mom bought him a board and took him to the beach—her way of helping them both escape his father's abuse.

Paul loved three things in life and, as far as Seth saw, three things only: Pabst Blue Ribbon. Baseball. Himself. In no particular order. The fact that he'd married a woman named Rachel and had a kid they'd named Seth barely mattered to him.

His mom, on the other hand, did love her son. They had, in fact, saved each other's lives on more than one occasion, most memorably when his dad confused their bodies with baseballs.

It was during the worst of those times when Seth asked his mom if she would take him to the library. She took him the very next day in the Rust Bucket, as she called their Vega. From age six on, Seth's life was comprised of a strange brew of surfing, reading, and being kicked around the house by his dad.

"You're special, Seth," his mom used to say. "Don't let anyone ever tell you any different, you hear? You ignore what your father says."

Her words filled him with more warmth than the California sun. "I love you, Mom."

She would always swallow, pull him close, and wipe at the tears in her eyes when he said that.

As it turned out, Seth was more than special. He was a genius.

In any other setting his unique gift would have been discovered and nurtured from the time he was two or three. Unfortunately or fortunately, depending on perspective, no one really understood what an exceptional young boy Seth was until he was older.

His mother was a hairdresser, not a schoolteacher, and although she made sure all the other beauticians knew about her boy's quick wit, she wasn't equipped to recognize genius. And because Rachel would just as soon take him to the beach or the library as to the school, his reputation as a student languished.

He was nine before anyone in the academic world even noticed Seth's brilliance. A surfer named Mark Nobel who attended the small Nazarene university on Point Loma had watched him surf and insisted Seth give his surfboard a spin. By the time Seth washed back to shore, the student had left for class. Seth wandered onto the campus looking for Mark.

Half an hour later Seth found him in the math department, wading through a calculus equation with twenty other students and a professor who seemed to be having difficulty showing them just how simple this particular equation really was.

Seeing Seth at the door, the professor jokingly suggested that he come forward and show this band of halfwits how simple math could be. He did.

Then he solved another, more complex equation that the professor scribbled on the board. And another. He left the stunned students twenty minutes later, not quite sure how he knew what he knew. The equations just came together in his mind like simple puzzles.

The teachers at his grade school learned of his little adventure the next day, and their attitude toward him brightened considerably. He agreed to some tests. They said that less than 1 percent of humans had an IQ greater than 135 and that Einstein's was estimated to be 163. Seth's IQ was 193. They told him he couldn't dare waste such an exceptional mind.

But Seth still had to find a way to cope with reality at home, which meant losing himself in books and riding waves off the point. School simply wasn't a meaningful part of his world.

Life improved when his dad left for good after discovering just how effectively an angry thirteen-year-old boy could fight back. But by then Seth had lost his taste for formal education altogether. It wasn't until he was twenty that he began responding to pressure that he pursue a real education.

He'd selected Berkeley in part for its proximity. It wasn't in his backyard, where he was the local curiosity who could count by primes in his sleep; it wasn't two thousand miles away either. He thought he'd be a blue guy in a green world at Harvard or Yale or any of the other half-dozen universities that begged him to attend. Berkeley seemed like a good compromise.

The three years that followed failed to challenge him. As much as Seth hated to admit it, he was bored. Bored with academia, bored with his own mind.

The only real challenge to this boredom came from an unlikely source: a recruiter from the NSA named Clive Masters.

Berkeley's dean of students had summoned a gathering of drooling recruiters exclusively for Seth during his freshman year. They came from IBM, NASA, Lawrence Livermore National Laboratories, and a bunch of Japanese companies. Sony Pictures sent a rep—evidently movie magic took brains. But Clive was the only recruiter who captured Seth's attention.

"You have a gift, Seth," he'd said. "I've been watching you for ten years because it's in my job description to watch people like you. Your disinterest in education just might be a crime. And I've given my life to fighting crime, first with the FBI and now with the NSA."

"FBI, huh? Were you born wrapped in a flag?"

"No. I was born to be challenged," Clive said.

"Locking heads with fugitives," Seth said. "With the dregs of society. Sounds like a ball."

"There are two kinds of bad guys. The stupid ones, which make up about 99 percent of the lot, and the brilliant ones—each single-handedly capable of the damage done by a thousand idiots. I've gone up against some of the sharpest." He paused. "But there's more to the thrill than raw intelligence."

"And what would that be?"

"Danger."

Seth nodded. "Danger."

"There's no substitute for the thrill of danger. But I think you've already figured that out, haven't you?"

"And the NSA is all about danger."

"I split my time between being called in on the head-scratching cases and finding that rare breed who can do the same. We have something in common, you and I."

"Which is why you're interested in convincing an inno-cent impressionable that pursuing the life of James Bond is far more attractive than sitting in a basement of some laboratory, breaking complex codes," Seth responded.

"I hadn't thought of it in those exact terms, but your summary does have a ring to it. Still, solving mathemati-cal challenges has its place. The NSA's Mathematical Sciences Program is the world's single largest employer of mathematicians. Cryptology isn't easy work. The halls down in Fort Meade are lined with some of the world's brightest."

Actually, the thought of possessing the casual confi-dence of this man who faced him struck Seth as refresh-ing. Unlike the other sycophant recruiters, Clive seemed more interested in Seth's psyche than in what he could do for the organization.

"All I'm suggesting is that you finish here. Get your doctorate in high-energy physics and wow the world with some new discovery. But when you get bored—and the best always do—you think about me."

Clive smiled enigmatically, and Seth couldn't help thinking he just might.

"Do you surf, Clive?"

The man had chuckled. "Seth the surfer. No, I don't

surf, but I think I understand why you do. I think it's for the same reasons I do what I do."

Clive reappeared every six months or so, just long enough to gift Seth with a few tempting morsels before disappearing into his world of secrecy. Seth never seriously thought he would ever follow the path Clive had taken, but he felt a connection to this man who, despite being no intellectual slouch, applied his brilliance to thrill-seeking. The possibilities were enough to help Seth slog through the months of boredom.

Seth received his bachelor's in his second year at Berkeley. He skipped the master's program and was now in the second year of his doctorate. But four years of this stuff was wearing thin, and he was no longer sure he could stomach all the nonsense required to finish after all.

If the graduate dean, the very fellow lecturing at this very moment, Gregory Baaron, would allow him to write his dissertation and be done with it, that would be one thing. But Baaron had—

"Perhaps you'd like to tell us, Mr. Border." Seth blinked and returned his mind to the lecture hall. Baaron was staring over bifocals. "How do you calculate the quantum field between two charged particles?"

Seth cleared his throat. Baaron was one of the leading lights in the field of particle physics and had taught this basic material a hundred times. Much of his work was based on the equation now written on the board. Unfortunately, the equation was wrong. At least by Seth's thinking. But because of Baaron's stake in the matter, the dean would hardly consider, much less accept, the possibility that it was wrong. Even worse, Baaron seemed to have developed a healthy dose of professional jealousy toward Seth.

"Well, that would depend on whether you're doing it by the textbook," Seth said. Watch yourself, boy. Tread easy.

"The textbook will suffice," Baaron said after a moment, and Seth felt a pang of sympathy for the man.

He paraphrased from Baaron's own textbook. "Solve the Lagrangian field equation. That is, apply the principle of least action by defining a quantity called the Lagrangian action, the integral of which is minimized along the actual observed path. The easiest way to set the equation up is to use Feynman diagrams and to insert terms in the action for each of the first-order interactions." Seth paused. "You studied with Feynman, didn't you? I read his Nobel-winning papers when I was fifteen. Some interesting thoughts." He paused, thinking he should stop there. But he couldn't. Or just didn't.

"Of course, the whole method is problematic on both conceptual and explanatory levels. The conceptual problem is that the equations seem to say that the reality we observe is just the sum of all possible realities. On an explanatory level, you have to apply the renormalization factors to make the numbers come out right. That's hardly the sign of a really good predictive theory. Putting both problems together, I'm inclined to think the theory's misguided."

The professor's face twitched. "Really? Misguided? You do realize that the calculations of this method accord well with reality, at least in the world most of us live in."

"The calculations may work, but the implication bothers me. Are we really to believe that of all imaginable futures, the real one—the one we actually experience—is simply the weighted sum of all the others? Is the future merely the product of a simple mathematical formula? I don't think so. Someday this theory might look as out-dated as a flat-earth theory." That was too much, Seth. He felt his pulse quicken.

Baaron stared at him for what must have been a full five seconds.

"The principle of least action is widely accepted as a basis for calculation," he finally said. "And unless you think you've outwitted a few hundred of the most brilliant mathematical minds in the country, I don't think you've got a leg to stand on, Seth."

The condescension in Baaron's voice, as if the dean were his father commanding him to stand in the corner for questioning his recollection of baseball history, pushed Seth over a foggy cliff. He'd been here before, jumping off the same cliff. Without fail, the experience proved not only unsatisfying, but painful.

The knowledge of this fact didn't stop him.

There were over two hundred stadium seats in the hall, sloping from the podium up to a sound booth, and although only forty were filled, the eyes of every occu-pant turned Seth's way. He slipped his hands into his pockets and palmed the Super Ball at the bottom of his right pocket.

"To have doubted one's first principles is the mark of a civilized man," Seth said.

"So now I'm not only outdated, but I'm uncivilized?" Baaron walked to the podium wearing a smirk. "This from a man who hardly knows the difference between a dinner jacket and a tank top. From where I'm standing, your reasoning looks ugly."

"Nothing has an uglier look to us than reason, when it's not on our side," Seth said. "Big ideas are so hard to recognize, so fragile, so easy to kill. People who don't have them can't possibly understand."

Baaron turned his head. There might have been a barely audible gasp in the auditorium. Seth wasn't sure. Maybe the air-conditioning just came on. You're digging yourself a grave, Seth.

"Watch your tongue, young man. Just because you have a natural talent does not mean you've conquered ignorance."

Well, he was already in a hole. "Ignorance. To be ignorant of one's ignorance is the disease of the ignorant. And we all know that nothing is more terrible than ignorance in action—"

"You're stepping over the line, Mr. Border. You have a responsibility that comes with your mind. I suggest you keep your wits about you."

"Wit? He who doesn't lose his wits over certain things has no wits to lose."

Someone coughed to cover a chuckle. The professor paused.

"This is quantum field theory, not psychology. You think you're cute, flaunting your questionable wit? Why don't you engage me on the point, boy?"

"I've learned never to engage in a battle of wits with an unarmed person. Sir."

Baaron's face went red. He'd lost his cool with Seth once, when Seth came to class barefoot, dressed in surf shorts, and toting a surfboard. He'd hollowed out the board and cemented his laptop into it so that the whole contraption became his computer. The exchange got ugly when Seth expounded on the superiority of surfing over education before a howling class.

Nobody was howling now.

"I am not someone to toy with," Baaron said. "We have standards at this institution."

"Please, sir, don't mistake my simple review of literature as disregard for your authority. I'm merely saying what our most brilliant scholars have said better before me."

"This has nothing to do with literature."

"But it does. Rather than tackle your noteworthy intellect with my own, I'm afraid I've stolen from others. In fact, not a word I've spoken has been my own."

He paused and Baaron just blinked. "The first quote was from Oliver Holmes. Then George Savile from the seventeenth century. Then Amos Bronson Alcott and Gotthold Lessing and finally Johann Wolfgang von Goethe." Maybe that would bail him out. "Perhaps you should file a complaint against the lot of them. They are far too imaginative to associate with the tiny minds of this institution anyway."

Seth took a slow breath. Then again, maybe not.

Graduate Dean Gregory Baaron turned and walked out the side door without another word. No one moved. Seth glanced at the clock on the wall—five minutes to the hour.

He regretted his words already. Why did he do this? Why hadn't he just answered Baaron's stupid question?

A book slammed closed. One of the students vacated the back row and slipped out the rear entrance. The rest just sat there. Matt Doil, a forty-five-year-old engineer from Caltech, twisted in his chair near the front. He flashed a grin and shook his head.

"You're not serious about the least action principle being outdated, are you?"

The others were looking at him again. He cleared his throat. "Shut up and calculate—wasn't that what Feynman told students who wanted to know what his method really mean?"

They all knew it was.

"Show us," Doil said.

"Show you what?"

"An alternative."

Seth considered that. Why not? He'd done as much damage as he could possibly manage already. He might as well redeem himself in some small way.

"Okay."

He stood, walked to the stage, and picked up a white-board marker. It took him thirty seconds to complete a complex calculation he knew they would all understand. He finished the last stroke, stabbed the board with the marker, and turned around. To a student they were glued to him.

"What does this equation tell me about the forces at work on this marker?" He held out the pen between his thumb and forefinger, as if to drop it.

"That when you drop it, it'll bounce," someone said.

"Or that when you drop it, it'll roll," Matt said.

"But that's meaningless, isn't it?" Seth said. "What if I decide not to drop the marker? The numbers on the wall behind me tell us that the future is calculable as the sum of all possible futures. But I don't think it is. I think the future's beyond our calculation. And I think the future's singular. That there's only one possible future, namely the future that will happen, because it's known by a designer."

They looked at him with blank stares. Trying to com-municate some of the ideas that popped into his head was often more complicated than the ideas themselves. Lan-guage had its limits.

"What if I did this?"

He turned, changed several numbers on the board, erased the solution, and extended the equation by eight characters with a new solution. He dropped the marker in the tray and stepped back. It was the first time even he had seen the new equation actually written down.

He cleared his throat. "Makes the world much simpler, but also much more interesting, don't you think?"

"Does that work?" It was Matt.

"I think so," Seth said. "Doesn't that work?" Of course it did. He turned to the class. They were wide-eyed. Some were writing furiously. Some still didn't get it.

Matt rose, eyes fixed on the board. "You're . . . that does work! That's amazing."

Awkwardness took Seth by the throat. He'd just rewritten a small part of history, and for some reason he felt naked. Abandoned. He had no business being here on this stage for everyone to look at. He belonged in a basement somewhere. Back home in San Diego.

He turned and walked out through the same door Dean Baaron had used.

# 3

MIRIAM FACED MECCA and dropped to her knees in her room while the muezzin's noon prayer call still wavered. It was said that Muhammad disliked the church bells of his day, so he insisted on a vocal call to prayer. Miriam thought he was right—a bell was far too harsh.

She recited the first sura of the Koran without thinking about the words. She had taken a keen interest in the holy book, at one point thinking to become a hafiz, the coveted title of one who'd memorized all 114 suras of the Koran.

Of course, that would have been impossible: She was a woman. But the poetic nature of the Koran was like music to her mind and she found it pleasing. The word Koran meant "recitation." Her faith wasn't compelled to understand the words of the Prophet, but to repeat them. So then, if she could recite as well as a man, couldn't she be a great theologian?

She stood and rearranged the pillows on her bed. Her room was decorated in purple because her father had decided many years ago that it should be, despite Miriam's vocal dislike of the color. Her declaration that he best leave decorating to women with good taste earned her a slap.

Miriam headed for the main living room, where her mother, young Haya, was instructing the servants' preparations of Salman's breakfast. Like many men with multiple wives, Salman rotated villas every day, so that he was with each woman only every fourth day—a blessing or a curse for the wife, depending on her view of him.

Haya slid across the room toward Miriam, frowning. She wore a brilliant blue dress and strings of pearls that stood out nicely against her creamy neck. Once, in Spain, Miriam had watched the movie *Star Wars,* the only Western movie she'd ever seen. When the villain, Darth Vader, appeared on screen cloaked in black, she'd gasped aloud. Saudi women looked like Western movie villains!

Haya had applied a touch of makeup, something she did only when Salman came. "He'll be down in a few minutes," Haya said. "I don't want you around."

"Don't worry, I have no intention of being around."

Haya looked at her with a blank stare. The phone rang.

Miriam crossed to the door, eager to find Samir on the grounds or in the garage. She slipped into her black abaaya, pulled on her veil, and stepped outside. The garage stood detached, twenty meters from the entrance.

Like all males outside the family, Samir was prohibited from seeing her face, and indeed he hadn't...except on three occasions. The first of those times skipped through Miriam's mind as she walked to the garage.

It was three years ago, in the late afternoon, just after she turned seventeen. She'd been on the back lawn walking with her sister, Sara, when Samir ran out to tell them that their mother was waiting for them in the car. His shout startled a goose, which leaped from the pond and rushed at Miriam. Panicked by the honking bird's aggression, she spun to flee.

In spinning she tripped on her sister's foot. Samir rushed to chase the goose away, which he did easily enough. But in her fall, Miriam's veil flew off. She was on her feet and staring at a stunned Samir before she realized her face was bare.

For long seconds, neither moved. Samir gazed at her face as if he'd arrived in heaven and was seeing his first angel. Something in Miriam's soul changed with that look. In his eyes, she was a person. Not because of her beauty, but because in that moment she had become more than a black sack among a million other black sacks.

Samir had fallen in love. She could not resist loving him in return. So began a forbidden romance that took them, on two separate occasions, to Spain, where they slipped away from the family and spent hours staring into each other's eyes and talking about love. On the second occasion he had vowed to love her forever and marry her, no matter the consequence.

"Miriam."

His voice jerked her from her memories. "Samir."

He stood in the shadows of the garage, and her heart swelled. He wore the traditional white cotton thawb, but in her mind she pictured the strength of his arms and chest under the garment. His dark hair swept over milky brown eyes. Miriam glanced back at the villa and walked into the shadows, her heart pounding as much from the impropriety of it as from her love.

"No one saw you?" he asked.

"No. And how is my love?"

"Please, keep your voice—"

"Don't be a mouse. No one can hear." She was bold, wasn't she? Perhaps Sita's wedding had emboldened her.

He grinned. "If you think I'm a mouse, then you don't know what a lion is."

"A lion? I will turn you into a lamb. I miss you, Samir. When can we go away again?"

She still wore her veil, and in a way it gave her courage to know that not even he could guess her expression.

"I'm setting it up," he said. "Next month. To Spain again. Maybe this time we will stay."

"Stay? Don't tempt me if you can't also make a promise."

"I promise that nothing can keep this love I have from stealing you away forever."

She wanted to lift her veil, to see his eyes widen at seeing her mouth and eyes. The thought made her hands tremble.

"I am crazy for you," he said.

"Crazy? Where did you hear such a silly saying?" She rather liked it.

"An American movie. Do you like it?"

"It is expressive, isn't it? Crazy. And I am crazy for you, my lion."

He stared at her for a moment before allowing a shadow to cross his face. "I've been ordered by your father to take you to a meeting today. At eleven."

"Is that so? With whom?"

He turned away. "Abu Ali al-Asamm. The sheik."

Miriam felt her mouth part. "Al-Asamm?" How was that possible? He was one of the most influential Shia sheiks in the country, but not a Sunni, certainly not a Wahhabi. "What on earth for?"

"I don't know."

"I was supposed to meet Sultana at ten in the market."

"Then I will tell her that you'll be there later."

She hesitated. "What does he want?"

"You'll have to ask your father. I'm just the driver. For now."

As if on cue, a black Mercedes nosed up the driveway. Miriam stepped back, mind still engrossed by the notion of her meeting the sheik. Why such a powerful man in no way connected to the House of Saud would request a meeting with her alone was beyond her comprehension.

The car parked on the apron in front of the garage. "I'll meet you here in two hours."

The door behind the driver opened and a man wearing dark sunglasses beneath a white ghutra stood. She didn't recognize him, but judging by his business suit he meant just that—business.

"You're Miriam, the daughter of Salman?"

"Yes."

"Get in," he said, his voice silk.

Miriam glanced at Samir, who was watching the man.

The man in sunglasses stepped back and motioned to the back of the car. "Please, get in. Sita, the wife of Hatam, has demanded to see you. Please, get in."

"It's okay," Samir said under his breath. "Go."

Miriam broke from her stance and hurried for the large black Mercedes. She opened the rear left door and slid in next to the man, who'd seated himself without turning toward her.

"What's wrong?"

The man slammed his door. "Silence."

Sita had called for her. Good news, then. Her husband would never allow his new bride to call for her friends if she was in trouble.

They passed a large white mosque, and she watched the men walking through its gates. Islam was supported by five pillars, simple and beautiful, and, contrary to the more restrictive sharia laws, they did nothing to shackle women. Five pillars: The Creed: "There is no god but God and Muhammad is the messenger of God." Daily prayers: upon rising, at noon, in midafternoon, after sunset, and before retiring. The annual Ramadan fast. The hajj pilgrimage to Mecca. Almsgiving to the poor.

And a sixth to some, the jihad, as the situation warranted, to "spread Islam or defend against infidels." This last pillar was no pillar at all to most Muslims, including Miriam, but it clearly motivated those few radical fundamentalists who'd taken up the sword in the name of God. Not unlike the Jews, who'd entered their so-called promised land by virtue of the sword.

Only when the car pulled into a driveway did Miriam know their destination. The Mercedes pulled up to an expansive villa covered in bougainvillea. They were at Sita's childhood home, which surprised her. Sita did not live here any longer.

A dread seeped into her bones.

The man faced her for the first time. She could see the reflection of her veil in his mirrored glasses. "Did you know that Sita's new husband, Hatam, is a loyal member of the Nizari sect?"

Nizari? She didn't know the extreme Islamic sect still existed. Rumors of their activity made the Taliban of Afghanistan look reasonable by comparison.

"As is Sita's father," the man said. "It's why they do so much business together. Remember what you see today. Consider it a message from Omar bin Khalid. Get out."

What the man meant, Miriam had no clue, but his words made her mouth dry.

Who was Omar bin Khalid?

She followed him, surrounded by silence, through an archway that opened to the green grounds she and Sita had walked so many times. An old swing set built of oak sat unused beneath several tall trees to their right. Palms swayed in a light morning breeze. Still no sound. If anyone from the family was here, there was no sign.

The man led her around the side of the house instead of to the front door. They walked around the corner, toward the pool.

Miriam saw them then. Four people standing on the pool's deck. Sita, her father, and her veiled mother. And another man.

Sita, too, was veiled in black, standing with her arms at her sides. What could this possibly—

Miriam stopped, frozen to the concrete. The person standing next to Sita's father was no relation to Sita, she saw that now. The tall thin man wore the white tunic of the religious police of Saudi Arabia, the mutawa, but a red cloth encircled his ghutra.

From the Nizari sect as well, perhaps?

Images of public beatings and humiliations recounted from days not so old flashed through Miriam's mind. The sharia was a difficult law, but the ways of the extremist sects like the Nizari made even the most devout fundamentalists blanch.

In that instant, Miriam knew her friend had kept her

vow. Sita had refused her husband and would now pay a price.

Oh, dear Sita! For a fleeting moment Miriam thought about running to her friend, taking her hand, and fleeing toward the fence. But Sita's father, Musa, was a good man. Surely he was reasonable as well. The punishment would be his decision, not the mutawa's, Nizari or not. Surely it would be merciful.

Miriam forced her feet forward. Those gathered watched her in silence. Although Miriam couldn't see Sita's eyes, she could feel Sita's gaze like razors on her skin. They came to the edge of the pool, across the span of water from Sita and her father, and stopped.

For a moment no one spoke. Miriam looked at Musa. Deep lines carved the stone of his hard face. It wasn't yet hot, but sweat glistened on his brow. The religious man shifted on his feet, and his sandals scraped the concrete.

"These are all the witnesses?" he asked quietly. Miriam wanted to scream at his bony and dark face, wake him from his terrifying apathy. But she stood still next to the suited man, who nodded once.

A soft whimper floated across the pool. Sita or her mother, Miriam could not tell. She ached to say something, to beg for leniency on behalf of her friend. It will be all right. If they beat her, her wounds will heal. If they cut off her hand for refusing to touch her husband, she will still live free of him. Surely the man had divorced her already. He would never live with this stain on his name.

Neither would Sita's father.

"There is no god but God," the religious man said, "and Muhammad is the Prophet of God. No man shall escape his wrath. It is for our love of God and his Prophet and all that is written that we have gathered, lest we become a people who defile God."

Sita stood motionless, unlike the fiery girl Miriam knew. Nausea spread through her stomach. She had heard that those who administered severe punishment drugged the accused on occasion, to prevent a struggle. If they were going to beat her...

"Let it be known that this woman has defied her husband's rights and injured him bodily in a manner no different from murder. She has made a mockery of God and of Islam and must be punished in accordance with the laws of the Nizari, servants of God. So be it."

Musa's upper lip trembled. Still no one moved. Miriam had seen a beating once, a horrid occasion. But it was filled with anger and yelling, not this silence.

The whimper came again—Sita's mother—and this time it lingered, then grew to a soft, quivering wail.

The religious man lifted his chin and muttered something Miriam couldn't understand. He closed his eyes. "You have heard from God. Do what you must do."

Eyes still fixed directly ahead, Musa took his daughter's arm. The wail turned guttural and shredded the air. Sita's mother grabbed her daughter's other arm.

"No!" she moaned. "She is my daughter!" Terror ripped through Miriam's chest, electrifying her heart.

Sita's mother pulled at her daughter and dropped to her knees. Sita looked like a rag doll about to be pulled apart. Her head lolled on her shoulders.

"Take me, I beg—"

The religious man's hand cracked against her face, stilling the cry and sending her reeling backward. Miriam cried out involuntarily. She took a step to the side, but the man beside her gripped her elbow and squeezed it like a vise.

"Sita!" Miriam cried.

"Shut up!" Miriam's guardian jerked her arm. She felt pain spread down to her elbow.

Sita turned her head toward Miriam.

*Oh, dear Sita! What are they doing to you!*

Sita's father was trembling from head to foot now. The religious man gave him a nudge toward the steps. Musa blinked, then stiffly led his daughter to the steps and into the water. Sita followed like a lamb, veiled and submissive, waiting for her fatal baptism. The clear blue water soaked Sita's abaaya pitch black.

It occurred to Miriam that she had stopped breathing. The unearthly silence returned, punctuated only by the blood pounding through her ears. Long fingers of horror snaked over her nose and mouth, smothering her. What happened next unfolded without fanfare, like a dream, distant and disconnected from reason.

Musa placed his large hand on the docile child's head and shoved her under the water.

Miriam flinched and her guardian's grip tightened. No, no, no, no! Miriam was screaming, but the screams refused to reach past her throat.

Sita's abaaya floated around her like a black cloud. Musa's face trembled red. His eyes, still fixed on some unseen horizon, swam in tears. Miriam's mind tilted. What she was seeing wasn't real. This father was not holding his fifteen-year-old daughter under the water in this pool she'd splashed in as a small child. This was just a horrible vision from hell that would end at—

Sita began to struggle.

Her legs kicked from her white underdress. Her arms flailed and her hands broke the surface, splashing like fish stranded in the tide. Her veil floated up, and for the first time since her friend's wedding, Miriam saw Sita's face. Brown eyes, wide and round. Straining mouth, covered by a wide band of silver tape.

Musa's eyes bulged; his arm trembled. His mouth parted and he began to scream.

But he held his daughter down.

Musa had chosen the drowning.

Miriam's tilting mind fell and crashed. She spun to her right, breaking free of the man's grip. She had to save Sita. She had to get help! She had to dive in and pull her to safety!

Her cheek exploded under the guardian's fist, and the pool tipped to one side. A groan, low and unearthly, broke from her throat. She began to fall. She hit the concrete hard, inches from the water.

Under the surface, Sita stopped struggling.

Her father still screamed, long, terrifying wails past twisted lips. The religious man's emotionless face betrayed the truth: It was not the first time he'd overseen a father drowning a wayward daughter; it would not be the last.

Sita's lifeless eyes stared up through shimmering water. Miriam's world went black.

# 4

KHALID BIN MISHAL bin Abd al-Aziz. That was his name—Khalid, son of Mishal, who was son of the first king, Abdul Aziz. Prophetic, Khalid had always thought, a name that begged him to make his bid for the throne. Technically he was a royal nephew; his father's brother had been King Fahd before the reigning king, Abdullah, took the throne. Although the first king, Abdul Aziz, had sired forty-two sons, the kingdom required only so many kings. Four to be precise, all of them Abdul Aziz's sons. That left thirty-eight less fortunate.

Time was not merciful; the king's sons now grew too old for a crack at the throne—Khalid's father was seventy-eight to his fifty-eight. Those who weren't too old were undeniably far too liberal. It was time for Saudi Arabia to be returned to her great calling as the world's protector of Islam.

It was time for a new king, Khalid thought. He'd planned for this day long ago.

Khalid sat on red pillows with his son, Omar bin Khalid, and Ahmed, the director of transportation. Like the others, Khalid wore the traditional ghutra headdress but topped it with a red circular igaal. The three reclined in a room that looked like a Bedouin tent but was actually a room in Khalid's palace.

Omar picked up a glass of scotch and sipped the amber liquor. Alcohol was illegal in Saudi Arabia, of course, but most of the royal homes were well stocked. Khalid himself did not touch the stuff, but every man was entitled to his vices. Omar had more than his share. Women, for one. Not even Khalid approved of Omar's lack of respect for the young women. He'd bailed his son out of more than one situation involving dead females. One day the gender would be his downfall.

But today he would use Omar to attain his own ends.

Both father and son embraced the teachings of the Nizari, a fact that very few knew. As such, they were uniquely qualified to overthrow the current monarchy and restore the days of glory, as God willed.

"It takes great discipline to be a great leader," Khalid said. "The country is floundering."

"There's a difference between talking privately about changing things and doing so," Ahmed said. "Look at Al-Massari. He was exiled to England with his band of dissidents. Osama bin Laden and his Reformation Committee—we all know what happened to him. The government won't just welcome change for the sake of—"

"I'm not asking them to change," Khalid said. "If there is a cancer, you don't persuade the cancer to change. You cut it out. That was both Al-Massari's and Bin Laden's problem. Neither had the resources to cut it out. I do."

Omar spoke for the first time. "We do."

Ahmed stared at him. Khalid had waited until now to bring the director into full confidence.

"What do you mean, you have it?" Ahmed asked.

Khalid smiled. "Let me ask you a question. If a man in my position was to have the full support of the ulema and twenty of the top-ranking princes, and the undeterred ambition to overthrow the king, could he do it?"

Ahmed glanced at the door. They all knew that talk like this could earn death. He studied Khalid's face. "No," he said. "Even with the princes and religious scholars, it's not enough for a lasting success."

"You're honest. I'll remember that when this is over."

Omar chuckled from his perch on the pillow and threw back the last of the scotch in his glass.

"You're right," Khalid said. "Overthrowing a government isn't the same as installing a new one. But what if a man in my position also had the full support of the Shia minority in the eastern provinces?"

"That would not be possible. We are Sunni."

"Anything is possible when such great power is at stake. You should know that. Indulge me for a moment."

Ahmed hesitated. "Then, yes." His eyes shifted with his thoughts. "It could be done." Eyes back on Khalid. "How would such support be gained?"

Khalid stood and walked to a bowl of fruit. He picked up a piece of nangka, a sweet yellow fruit imported from Indonesia. "Through the sheik, of course." He pushed the fruit into his mouth. If there was a leader among the four million Shia living in the eastern parts of Saudi Arabia, it was Al-Asamm, and to call him the sheik was enough.

"Al-Asamm hasn't flexed his muscles in ten years.

And he's not a friend to the House of Saud. What do you hope—"

"Actually, he hasn't flexed his muscles in nearly twenty years. Have you thought about that? He offers a token demonstration now and then, but not like he was once known to."

"That doesn't make him a friend."

"The Shia are a passionate people. Look at Iran—they know how to overthrow. We wouldn't give them too much power, of course, but they do constitute 15 percent of Saudi citizens. We will give them a voice."

"And how in the name of God do you propose to approach Sheik Al-Asamm?" Ahmed waved his hand. "It'll never work."

"Yes, it will," Khalid's son said.

They both looked at Omar.

"Yes, it will," Khalid agreed. "Tell him why it will work, Omar."


OMAR REGARDED HIS father and Ahmed, trying to keep his contempt for both hidden. He'd sat through numerous meetings like this one, plotting and gathering support for his father's plan. Now, less than a week away from the actual coup attempt, it was becoming his plan. Not because he had conceived it, but because without him, the plan would fail. Then he would become king himself, after Father was killed. The reign of the kingdom would be built on blood, he thought. Blood and marriage. Both at his hand.

"It will work because I will marry his daughter," Omar said.

His father faced Ahmed. "You see? It will work because my son will marry Sheik Al-Asamm's daughter." He grinned.

"What daughter? And how will that help?"

Omar picked up a fig and rubbed its skin, eyes on Ahmed. "The reason Sheik Al-Asamm has remained quiet these past twenty years is because my father bought the sheik's allegiance," he said. "My father convinced Salman bin Fahd to adopt Al-Asamm's daughter in exchange for the sheik's loyalty. Her name is Miriam. When she marries me and bears a son, we will create an inseparable bond between Sunni royalty and the Shia. The sheik insisted that she not be married until she reached twenty-one. Evidently he wasn't in a rush to weaken the bloodline. She is now a week from that birthday."

Ahmed stood. "Salman's daughter Miriam is really the daughter of the Shia sheik? Abu Ali al-Asamm? They are Shia; we are Sunni."

"Thus the secrecy," Omar said. "When she marries into the royal family and has a son, Sheik Al-Asamm will be linked to the throne by blood."

Ahmed looked too stunned for words.

"Miriam will marry Omar in a secret ceremony," Khalid said. "In exchange, Al-Asamm will support our coup. I will give him governorship of the eastern province. This was planned twenty years ago, when Omar was just a boy."

They had no assurance Ahmed would support this plan, but they'd disclosed the same with two dozen ministers, and all but the minister of education understood the stakes. The man died within the hour—a tragic accident.

Omar stood and picked up an apple. He bit deeply into

its crisp flesh. "We need your support, Ahmed. Your position is critical to our plans. We need the airports."

The minister of transportation lowered his voice to a whisper. "This talk is treasonous. You're plotting your own death."

"Today what we've said is treason; in one week your speaking to my father in such a way will be treason," Omar said.

Ahmed glanced at Khalid and then back. "You have Sheik Al-Asamm's full commitment?"

"Would we be talking to you if we did not? I will take his daughter Miriam as my wife in four days."

"And then?"

"Two of our generals have Shia blood," Khalid said. "If we have Al-Asamm, we have them. We will unseat Abdullah the day after the wedding. I will be king in one week. We will be a fundamentalist state within the month."

Ahmed's lips curved into a faint, sweating smile. "Then you have my support." He paused, studying Khalid's face as the prospect sank in. "You have my full support." He dipped his head. "There is no god but God."

Omar took another bite. Just like that, the man had switched his loyalties from the reigning king to Khalid. Of course, if he refused, he would pay dearly.

A bell rang near the tent door. "Come," Khalid commanded.

A thin man dressed in a business suit entered and dipped his head. Omar felt his pulse quicken. His servant approached the table and looked at them without speaking.

"Well?"

"It is done."

The corner of Omar's mouth twitched. "The girl is dead?" he asked.

"She was drowned an hour ago, as you insisted."

They stared at the servant in silence. Stonings were a slow, drawn-out nuisance. Better to drown and be done with it.

"And the girl?" Omar asked.

"As you said."

"Thank you. You may leave."

The man lowered his head and left.

"What was that?" Ahmed asked, face white.

"That was the judgment of God," Omar said. "And a message to my dear bride."

# 5

SETH CROSSED THE North Field and angled for Berkeley's Department of Philosophy. His corduroys bunched slightly over worn sandals as he stepped through the grass. To his right, a dance squad performed flips in short skirts. The Faculty Club building stood beyond them, bordered by a manicured glade. He'd been inside on four occasions, each time for an event that required his attendance. Receptions in honor of his awards, mostly.

Like the one scheduled for Thursday evening. The American Physical Society and the American Institute of Physics had named him something or other of the year, and, like it or not, the graduate dean was obligated to acknowledge the award. Thinking about it now, Seth wondered what would happen if he didn't show. He wasn't feeling too social after yesterday's fiasco with Baaron. He envisioned two hundred faculty dressed to the nines with champagne glasses raised and no one to toast.

"Seth!"

He turned to see Phil—a third-year undergraduate and the epitome of a nerd with glasses, pocket protector, and pimples—run up behind him. Phil was among half a dozen down-and-outers that Seth felt truly at home with.

"Hey, Phil." He slipped his hand into his pocket and rolled the Super Ball between his fingers.

Phil slapped an open crossword magazine in his hand. "You ready?"

"Sure," Seth said. "Let me see it."

Phil held the page up, displaying a four-inch-square crossword puzzle. Seth made quick mental notes of the puzzle's pattern—black squares, white squares, numbers. Category: GOOD MARKS.

"Okay."

Phil withdrew the puzzle and glanced ahead. "So where you going?"

"Meeting with Dr. Harland. You?"

"To the cafeteria. Okay, ready? Seventeen across, ten letters, clue—expropriate."

"Commandeer," Seth said.

Phil flipped a page, checked the answer, and continued. "Good. Twenty-four across, seven letters, clue—horse back in the pack."

Seth considered the clue for a second. "That would be also-ran, Phil," he said in his best game-show voice.

"Never heard of it," the younger student said. "Three down, five letters, clue—subdues."

"Three down? Tames."

"Final answer?"

"Tames, Phil. It has to be tames."

"How do you do that without looking?"

"I did look, remember? The M intersects with commandeer and the S intersects with also-ran," Seth said.

Phil slapped the magazine closed. "I heard you told Baaron a few things."

"You heard that?"

"Yeah. True?"

"True."

Seth saw that Phil was watching the dancers now. Seth decided long ago that women had an inexplicable effect on his mind, minimizing its ability to process thought in logical constructs. Without fail, females turned Seth into someone he really didn't think he was, someone lost for clear thoughts and words.

Phil, however, would kill to sit alone on a bench with a girl. Any girl. He aggressively denied the desire, of course.

Phil saw Seth had noticed and ducked his head. "See ya."

"See ya."

He headed off, hands deep in his pockets, head lowered.

They had named the philosophy building Moses—ironic but appropriate considering its current occupant. Seth had always thought that the chair of philosophy, Samuel Harland, PhD, was the spitting image of Charlton Heston with his dirty blond hair and soft blue eyes. He was the only man in the place worthy of the building's name.

He knocked on the department head's office door, heard a muffled "Enter," and stepped in.

"Good day."

"Have a seat," the professor said.

Seth sat. "That bad, huh?"

"Unfortunately, yes. Baaron is seething."

Seth paused. If there was one person in his life he could confide in, it was this man. "You wouldn't expect the academic dean of an esteemed institution such as this to let a little folly get under his skin."

"You wouldn't," Harland said. "But for whatever reason, you most definitely do get under his skin."

"I engaged him with famous quotations—"

"I know what you did. You could have been a little more selective, don't you think?" Harland couldn't hide the glint of humor in his eyes.

Seth shook his head. "I don't know how I get myself in these crazy situations."

"I think you do. You're a blatant challenge to his theories of order."

"For what it's worth, I did speak the truth," Seth said. "Isn't that what you've always told me? To doggedly pursue the truth?"

"Pursuing the truth and presenting it are two different disciplines. How do you suppose I would fare around here if I walked around blasting my peers into the next county? This is becoming a habit for you."

Seth rubbed his hands together and placed them on his knees. "You're right."

Baaron was brilliant, deserving of his lofty status at the university. But put him in a room with Seth, and half his chips seemed to go on the blink. He was an easy target, one that Seth couldn't resist shooting at now and then. It didn't help that Baaron reminded Seth of his father.

The tension had set in a year earlier, when Seth wrote a paper on the Strong Force that questioned prevailing thought. The paper was picked up by several scientific journals and published to some acclaim. It was hardly

Seth's fault that the prevailing theory, which Seth trashed, was authored by none other than Gregory Baaron, PhD. The world of physics was a small one.

"You're going to have to learn more tact, yes? You have to learn how to blend in a little."

Seth's trust in Harland was in large part due to the man's humble form of brilliance. If Seth's formal education had taught him anything, it was that celebrated intelligence had nothing to do with intellectual honesty, with being genuine. People who appreciated both brilliance and frank honesty were in short supply. The system preferred the kind of brilliance that lined up with the flavor of the day.

Samuel Harland was anything but the flavor of the day. He had no interest in sucking up to the elitists so he could smoke his pipe in the Faculty Club. He simply and methodically pursued every thought to its logical conclusion and put his faith there, in what he saw at the end of the trail.

The smile faded from Seth's face. "Well, you'll have to forgive me, but I'm not built for a system like this one. I can't seem to fit in."

Harland nodded. "Baaron's got some of the faculty on his side. They're talking about official reprimands."

Seth looked out the window. "I'm thinking about dumping the program. Heading back down to San Diego."

"You've said that before."

"Maybe I should have done it before. I talked to my mom last night. She lost her job."

Harland hesitated. "The best thing you can do for your mother is finish your doctorate. What are you going to do for a living—pump gas?"

"We both know of a dozen corporations that would

offer me decent money right now." Seth stared at the window and sighed. "Did you hear about the calculation I drew on the board?"

"I heard something about the Lagrangian field equation."

"That was part of it. But I came up with an equation that limits possible futures to one." Seth smiled. "That should be music to your ears."

"How so?"

"It supports the existence of an all-knowing higher being."

"Ah, yes, the higher-being theory. You've decided to swing that way, is that it?"

"No. I'll remain comfortably blank on the subject for now, despite my proof to the contrary."

Harland chuckled. "You've actually proven God's existence now?"

"I wouldn't go that far, but it does have a ring to it, don't you think?" Seth leaned forward and took a sheet of paper from Harland's desk. "May I?"

"Be my guest. You're going to show me the equation?"

"No. I'm going to translate it into a hypothetical syllogism of sorts." He spoke his argument as he wrote it out in longhand.

(A) If an all-knowing being exists (God) then he knows precisely what THE future is. (He knows whether I'm going to cough in ten seconds.)

(B) If God knows what THE future is, then that future WILL occur, unless God is mistaken. (I WILL cough in ten seconds.)

(C) Because an all-knowing being cannot be mistaken, there is NO possibility that any other future, other than the one future that God knows, will happen. (There's NO possibility I won't cough in ten seconds.)

(D)  THEREFORE, if God exists, there is only ONE future, which is THE future he knows. (I cough in ten seconds.)

Seth set the pencil down. "Basically, if God exists, the probability of there being more than one possible future is zero. And vice versa. To believe God exists also requires you to believe that the future is unalterable. By definition. There can only be one future, and no amount of willing can change it."

"And the ramifications of this theory?"

"Religion has no purpose."

"Knowledge of fact doesn't necessarily prove singularity of future."

"You're only splitting hairs between knowledge of fact and probabilities."

Harland nodded slowly. They'd argued the subject on several occasions, and he didn't seem eager to dive in again.

Seth looked out the window. "You should reconsider deism—"

A pigeon slammed into the window with a loud thunk.

Seth blinked. "Ouch. You'd think that would break the window."

"What would?"

Seth looked at him. "The force of the bird slamming into the window."

Harland looked at the window. "What bird?"

"What do you mean, what bird? You didn't just see that?"

"No."

Seth looked at the window. "You didn't hear a loud thunk just now?"

"No. I didn't hear—"

A pigeon slammed into the window with a loud thunk. It fell away in a flurry of feathers.

"Like that?" Harland asked.

Seth stared at the clear pane of glass. Yes, exactly like that.

"Huh. I could've sworn I just saw that ten seconds ago. Like a déjà vu." He shook his head.

"You okay?"

"Yeah." Odd. Very odd.

"Another year here and you'll be out," Harland said. "Stay with it."

Seth sat back. "Now you're sounding like Clive Masters."

"Anyone with half a brain would say you should finish."

"So you're saying . . . ?"

"Play ball at the reception Thursday. Smile, be nice. Try to keep your foot out of your mouth. Maybe even offer some kind of apology to Baaron—"

"Suck up."

"In the vernacular."

"Be reasonable and do what's best for everybody."

"Yes."

Seth stood and walked to the window. His fingers slipped into his pocket and toyed with the Super Ball. The pigeon was hobbling along the grass, dazed.

"I wouldn't dream of anything else, Professor."

# 6

THE BRUISE ON her face was hidden from Samir, but he had to know something terrible had happened by the tremble in her voice. The tragedy was too large in her mind to discuss at first—they rode in silence.

Miriam had awakened in the car and wept for her friend. At home, her father, Salman, refused to hear anything of it, insisting that if it had happened as she said, the matter was beyond his influence. She went to her room and fell asleep on a pillow soaked with tears. She'd heard of stonings and even drownings before, of course, but only in stories of mad men in remote desert regions. Never could she have imagined seeing her best friend drowned by Musa. Wicked, wicked Musa.

The Nizari sect lived and they were an insane lot!

Haya awakened her before noon. Samir was waiting to take her to her appointment, she said. Miriam had almost forgotten. The sheik Al-Asamm wanted to see her.

Why? Did he have a son for her to marry? Then he would
approach Salman, not her.

She didn't care. Sita was all she could think of. She
washed away her tears and readied herself.

Samir drove her through the streets of Riyadh, seem-
ing to understand her need for silence, past new structures
designed by Western architects. Nearly a quarter of Saudi
Arabia's population was expatriate, imported labor and
expertise to build the city and serve the House of Saud.
The foreigners were effectively cut off from the lives of
most Saudis, sequestered in communities designed for
them, but their touch could be seen everywhere. To many
fundamental Muslims, the slow Westernization of this,
Islam's birthplace, was a blasphemous tragedy.

Today, for the first time, Miriam thought it symbolized
the hope of freedom.

They wound through the suburbs, sandstone brick-
and-mortar construction. Square. Everything square. And
then they were in the desert, which stretched endlessly to
Dhahran on the Persian Gulf. The Americans had used
Dhahran as a base during the Gulf War.

"Sita was drowned by her father this morning for defy-
ing Hatam," she said.

"Wha—No!"

"Yes." She lifted her hand to her mouth, afraid she
might begin crying again. The tires droned under them.

"The savage!" Samir said. "He is a pig!"

Miriam swallowed the lump rising in her throat.

"How is that possible?"

"Her father is Nizari."

He gripped the wheel and shook his head, clearly surprised. "The Nizari hardly exist. Not among the respectable."

He seemed to be at a loss for words. "I'm so very sorry, Miriam. Some men can be beasts to their women." He looked out his window, jaws flexing. "I could understand a beating, but drowning? It's not—"

"A beating?" she cried. "No man should have a right to beat a woman! What gives a man that right? It's inhumane to drown your daughter, and it's inhumane to beat your wife!"

They were the strongest words she had ever spoken in Samir's hearing. He mumbled his agreement, but her words obviously stung his ears. She sat next to him, as she frequently did when they were alone, for the rest of the trip. But today she sat dazed and numb.

Fifteen minutes after they left the city, Samir turned onto a small sandy road that led to a solitary Bedouin tent. Two Mercedes rather than camels formed a kind of gate in front of the main canvas flap.

Samir stopped the car. Dust drifted by.

"He's waiting inside."

Miriam stepped out. A Bedouin woman dressed in a traditional black abaaya, but without the full-face veil, exited the tent and watched her. Bedouin veils rode on the bridge of the nose, allowing the world free access to the eyes.

Miriam reached the tent and gazed into the smiling eyes of the strange woman.

"You may remove your veil in here," the woman said.

Perhaps the sheik was not so concerned with tradition. Not wanting to be rude, Miriam removed her veil and entered.

Abu Ali al-Asamm, a white-bearded holy man, sat on a large silk pillow and talked in hushed tones to a woman on his right. A maroon carpet with gold weaving covered most of the floor, and on this carpet was a single low table. Otherwise there was only a stand for tea and a large bowl of fruit—hardly the furnishings of a typical tent. Apparently, they had come on short notice with only what would fit into the cars outside.

Talk stilled as the tent flap fell behind her. The sheik was on the heavy side, and getting to his feet was not an easy task. He stood and stared at her with eyes that betrayed as much wonder as curiosity.

"Miriam."

She dipped her head, feeling exposed. He knew her name, obviously, but he spoke it as if some mystery were contained between the syllables. What was this all about? Did he know about Sita's drowning?

The sheik walked toward her, eyes beaming. "It is such a pleasure to finally meet you." He took her hands and kissed them. "Such a beauty, just like your mother, may God give her rest."

"I don't know what you mean," she said. "You know my mother?"

"But of course. She was my wife; I would think I knew her quite well."

Desert silence smothered Miriam.

"Forgive me, but you're mistaken. I've never met you. Or your wife. She isn't my mother."

"No, Miriam. I'm afraid you're mistaken. Salman adopted you, yes?"

"What?"

"You were never told?"

"That's ridiculous!"

He stared at her, then turned away. "Come...come sit."

She hadn't heard right! "I don't understand."

The sheik turned back, saw the fear in her eyes, and placed a hand on her shoulder. "Forgive me. It's a shock. How insensitive of me. I've been watching you for all of these years and you're learning for the first time that I'm your real father."

She could hardly imagine it. In fact, she couldn't. Why hadn't she been told? There was no resemblance, no logic, nothing to tie her to this man.

"You're a perfect reflection of your mother, Jawahara, who died giving you birth." The sheik motioned to a beautiful woman who was pouring tea. "This is Nadia, my second wife."

Nadia set the teapot down and hurried over, kissed Miriam's hand. "My house is yours."

Miriam didn't want this house. It had been a mistake to come! But looking at them both, she knew that they spoke the truth. Such a powerful man would never fabricate such a preposterous story unless it was entirely true.

Abu Ali al-Asamm was her father. God help her.

"It changes nothing," the sheik said. "You are who you are. A beautiful woman. Privileged in every way. Royalty. Please, come and sit."

They sat. Nadia offered her fruit, and she took an apple. Miriam bit into it absently, trying to think through the ramifications of this news.

"So how is the House of Salman treating you these days?" the sheik asked. Wrinkles spread from his eyes, crow's-feet formed by a perpetual smile. Miriam felt a knot rise in her throat. Could she trust this man the way she'd always wanted to trust Salman? Could such a strange man be a real father to her?

"Well," she said. It was not the precise truth, but it was the correct answer.

The sheik began to speak about his life. None of it really mattered to her, but she listened politely and asked a few questions to show interest.

What she really wanted to know was why. Why had the sheik given her up for adoption to Salman? What advantage had it gained him?

He talked for ten minutes of the eastern province and Dhahran. Of the Shia and the American involvement in the region. About Miriam's mother and how she had always wanted a daughter. Miriam was her only child, but Jawahara had died happy. Yet the sheik had not brought her here to talk about her mother.

The talk stalled. "Are you feeling well?"

"Yes."

Al-Asamm studied her face. "Your eyes betray you, my dear."

She shifted her eyes. "I have—had—a very good friend named Sita. She was fifteen and forced to marry an old man. She refused him, and this morning her father drowned her for shaming them. I . . . I was forced to watch."

"Oh, dear, dear, dear." The sheik clucked his tongue and shook his head. "It is an abomination. There are far more appropriate punishments than death. I am sorry, child. I am very sorry."

The sheik sighed. "The world is changing, Miriam." He glanced at her carefully. "Perhaps after fifty years in opposition to this government, my day has come. I'm sure you're wondering why I asked Salman to adopt you."

So here it was then. "I am."

"I did it for the good of Saudi Arabia. For the sake of

returning the country to the true teaching of Islam, and for the sake of bringing my people, the Shia, into their rightful place within society." He paused. "King Abdullah has ruled long enough."

His words stung her ears. Treason!

"Strong words, I know," he said. "As your natural father I've retained the right to give you in marriage. When you marry into the House of Saud and bear a son, my grandson will be filled with royal blood."

"But my father—"

"Salman? He agreed to the general plan from the beginning, though it was not for him to say whom you would marry."

Then the sheik told her the details of the planned coup in a quick, low voice, as if he'd rehearsed the words a thousand times. And he probably had, having hatched the plan twenty years ago!

Her biological father had forged an alliance with her adoptive family. She was just a pawn.

"You will be married in four days' time," Al-Asamm said.

"Four days!" She jumped to her feet.

"It's imperative."

Panic pressed her chest, flushed her neck. "To whom? I have made no preparations!"

"To Khalid's son. To Omar bin Khalid."

"Omar bin Khalid? I don't even know him!"

The sheik stood. "And now you expect to know the one you marry?"

"I can't marry Omar," she snapped. "I love Samir!"

Silence, except for her ragged breathing. He stared, mouth agape.

"Samir?" he finally said. "The driver?"

She had made a terrible mistake. For Samir's sake she had to recover. She could not reveal the true depth of her love for him.

"No, you're right. I do not. But what if I did love someone? You would still force me to marry a man I don't love? I don't know a single person who speaks well of Khalid bin Mishal's family. They are animals!"

"How dare you speak such things!" The sheik's nostrils flared. His anger snatched her back from the brink of foolishness. In her mind, she heard a door slam, saw the bolt slide through. Several years ago, a friend who'd argued about marrying was locked up until the day of the wedding.

"I'm sorry. But please, I beg you, don't do this to me!"

"Fathers have always given their daughters in marriage. Now you are telling me that you know better than I who is a good husband?"

She bit her tongue.

"A country is at stake!" he boomed. "We have in our hands the power to save Islam from corruption, and you think only of your fantasies?"

Nadia stood near the corner, facing away. Her posture told Miriam that the sheik's outburst was not a common thing. He had traded her once for peace, and he would do it again, this time for power.

She had to buy herself some time. Four days! She shivered and found her tongue.

"Forgive me. I was thinking irrationally. In one day my best friend has been killed and I learn that I have a wedding in four days. I'm losing myself." She lowered her eyes. "Of course you are right. This must be done."

He stared at her, composing himself. "Yes," he finally said. "I'm sorry."

"Forgive me."

He nodded, exhaled loudly. "This will be a historic day for Islam." Sheik Abu Ali al-Asamm reached out and put a hand on her arm in a gesture of comfort.

"The wedding will be held in secrecy. Samir will bring you to us tomorrow, and you will be pampered like a queen. And when we are successful in taking the throne, your wedding will be celebrated in the open." He paused. "The groom has requested that the ceremonies of marriage be properly followed, including halawa," he said, speaking of the traditional removal of all body hair below the neck. The practice had been instituted by Muhammad in the seventh century, when bathing was not common.

Miriam nodded, suppressing an urge to vomit.

"Now go." He smiled. "Before you are missed."

She dipped her head, replaced her veil, and left the tent without another word.

SAMIR DROPPED MIRIAM off at the souk and agreed to pick her up in one hour. He'd tried to find out what was bothering her and didn't have a clue about the wedding. To tell him would only crush him. She couldn't bring herself to do it, not yet.

The market bustled with merchants peddling their wares. Women, floating around in black, inspected products through their veils. She found Sultana at their favorite stall for fresh fruit.

"The pigs!" Her voice trembled. "How could any sane man drown his daughter?"

So Sultana knew. But the dread of Miriam's own troubles had blunted the horror of Sita's drowning.

"I am being given in marriage," Miriam said.

Sultana took Miriam by the arm. The fruit vendor was staring their way. She grabbed Miriam's arm and pulled her to the end of the row. She kept her voice low. "What are you talking about?"

"I met with my father this morning. He has given me in marriage."

"No!"

"No. My real father. Sheik Abu al-Asamm." Her voice trembled.

Sultana looked at her as if she were mad. "The Shia sheik? What are you talking about?"

"He is my blood father, Sultana. I was adopted into King Abdullah's family in exchange for loyalty."

Sultana appeared dead on her feet.

"Sultana, did you hear me? I am to be married—"

"To whom?"

"To the son of Khalid bin Mishal. Omar. The wedding is in four days."

"Omar bin Khalid!"

Miriam glanced around, self-conscious. "I'm scared, Sultana."

"Oh dear! Oh dear, oh dear, this is terrible." Sultana hurried toward the brick wall that surrounded the market, stopped after four paces, and urgently swept her arm for Miriam to follow.

"Sultana? Sultana, please." Sultana's anxiety heightened her own. "What should I do?"

Safe from bent ears, Sultana spun to her. "Do you know who Omar is? He's my first cousin! I could tell you things about this man that would make you vomit." Sultana was shaking with fury. "I have spoken with Sita's mother. Do you know who pressured her father to drown her? I'll tell you. It was Omar bin Khalid."

"Omar? But how . . ."

The words of the man who'd dragged her to the drowning crashed over her. He said that the drowning was a message. From Omar!

"You can't marry him!" Sultana cried. "I once saw him kick my niece in the head when she was three years old. For taking a toy from one of his nephews! She was in the hospital for a week!"

Miriam swam in fear. "I have to do what the sheik says! Look at Sita!"

"And look who killed Sita!"

"And if I don't obey, then Omar will kill me too; is that what you want?"

"Stop it!" Sultana said. "Just stop for a minute."

They stood under the shade of a palm, breathing steadily in the afternoon heat.

"We're not thinking clearly," Sultana said. "Why does the sheik want to marry you to Omar bin Khalid?"

Miriam told her. She included Omar's message as well.

"Knowing of this is enough to get us both killed. We're still not thinking clearly. Omar is a beast who orchestrated Sita's drowning, don't you see?"

She was right. Dear God, have mercy on them both, Sultana was right.

Miriam looked back at the shops. A woman draped in black faced them. "You're right." She faced Sultana. "You're right."

"There's only one thing you can do," her friend said.

"What?"

"Run."

The possibility stunned Miriam into a momentary silence.

"You can't be serious."

"Yes, I am! You have to run. If you stay, you will either be beaten into submission or end up dead like Sita."

"Run?" Miriam's heart began to pound. A long silence stretched between them. Two years earlier, on a girlish whim, they had drawn up a detailed plan to run away to the United States and convinced each other the idea would work. Not that they ever intended to use it. "Those were childish plans. They would never work."

"Does Salman still keep the same safe?"

"Yes. I think so. What if I get caught?"

"Then they'll force you to marry Omar anyway. That's why this is the right time to run. They need you, don't you see? They can't just kill you."

Her friend had a point. "They may not kill me, but I'd pay a high price."

"The price of not trying could be higher."

Miriam could not decide. Most women she knew had a hard enough time getting out of the house, much less getting out of the country. Who was she to think she could run?

"What about Samir? I can't just leave him."

"Leave him? You will leave him no matter what you choose. You think Omar will allow you to keep this secret love of yours?"

Sita floated to the top of Miriam's mind. She faced the wall. "How will I ever make it? When I went to America to study, I was under guard the whole time. I had servants. Now you expect me to just fly there and strike up a life on my own? This isn't like deciding to go on a shopping trip."

"No, of course it's not. But a shopping trip can't buy you freedom. Freedom, Miriam!"

"What if they come after me?"

"If? They will. But America's a big country. I'm telling you, Miriam, you have to run. Tomorrow."

Miriam closed her eyes. The prospect of marrying Omar wasn't unlike swallowing acid. Samir...dear Samir!

"I'm not sure I can leave Samir."

Sultana grunted her frustration.

They had planned their escapade down to the last detail: the permission to travel required of all women, the passport, the money, the destination—everything. Actually doing it would be like jumping off a cliff, but Miriam was in a free fall already. Yes, marrying Omar might be worse than death.

"Could you get me to Jidda on one of your husband's Lear jets?"

"Of course. I travel there regularly—the pilot wouldn't suspect a thing. But why to Jidda? I thought—"

"Being collected for a marriage wasn't part of our plan. The sheik will come for me tomorrow, but if I convinced Samir that I have to go to Jidda for an urgent shopping trip, they would be forced to wait until my return. It will buy us time. And send them in the wrong direction."

"Samir knows about the wedding?" They were talking quickly, in hushed tones now.

"No."

The wedding—it sounded strange. Horrible. "I would double back to Riyadh for a flight to Paris and then go on. If I'm doing this, I have to do it right."

Miriam saw the faint outlines of a smile through Sultana's veil. "That's the Miriam I know."

They talked for another twenty minutes, reviewing the plan with care. Sultana finally took her arm and steered her back toward the shops. "We have to be careful. Is Salman due back tomorrow?"

"Not for three days."

"Then bring all the documents with the money and meet me at the airport tomorrow morning at nine o'clock. I'll tell Samir I am expecting you."

They entered the market and walked silently for a few minutes.

"Can you get a flight schedule for Paris?" Miriam asked.

"Of course. If you have any problem, call me tonight. I'll do the same."

Miriam took a deep breath. She was going on the run.

# 7

SETH FOUND THE dance squad in Hearst Field, next to the gym. Some called them cheerleaders, but these girls were hardly the kind Seth had seen in high school. They were the kind who competed on ESPN2 at the national-championship level and eventually went on to dance on cruise ships or, in some cases, Broadway.

The squad leader was a blonde named Marisa, a bright physics undergraduate who'd approached Seth for help on several papers. He never quite figured out what she needed help with, but he spent an hour in the park with her once, discussing the distinctions between nuclear physics and high-energy physics.

Marisa was a walking oxymoron—an intelligent student who seemed determined to hide behind a Hollywood persona. She'd smiled and asked him why he didn't have a girlfriend. And when he blushed, she drew her finger down his arm and suggested they get to know each other.

Two evenings later, Seth found himself on his first date

in three years. Everything progressed well at first. She, the perfect twenty-one-year-old babe with enough beauty to boil the blood of most men, and he, the wonder boy with enough brains to send most women into the deep freeze.

They went to the Crab Shack for dinner, and with each crab leg, her flaws increasingly annoyed him. Her blind acceptance of a news anchor's point of view, as if being housed in a television made one a god; her wisecracks about Dr. Harland. By the time they got to the main dish, even her white teeth looked plastic to him. How could such a bright student be so easily swept along with this pap?

He became so distracted, in fact, that he took a sip of the hot butter, mistaking it for his iced tea. She laughed, of course, a high-pitched young laugh. Now her youth glared at him. She was a mere pup, flashing her plastic teeth and raving on about a world she saw through naive lenses.

To Seth's amazement, she asked him out the next day. He politely declined. It was the last time they'd talked.

Seth headed toward the squad. He didn't recognize Marisa until she noticed him. He nodded and smiled. She must have mistaken the gesture as encouragement, because she whispered something to the others and then broke into a punchy cheer that made as much use of her hips as it did her mouth.

Seth covered his embarrassment by clapping and saying, "All right, way to go," or something similar. He wasn't positive, because the better part of his mind was shouting him down with objections.

All six faced him, wearing slight grins. He wondered what Marisa had told them.

"Hello, girls."

"Hi, Seth."

He stopped and shoved his hands into his pockets. "What are you guys doing?"

Practicing their dance, you idiot. He grabbed the Super Ball.

"Working on our backflips," Marisa said.

"Cool."

Silence.

"I heard about your run-in with Professor Baaron yesterday," Marisa said.

"You did? Yeah, that was pretty bad."

"For him maybe. I heard you came out pretty good."

"That depends on how you look at it."

"I think the student body understands exactly what happened."

Seth wasn't sure what she meant. "The irony is that Baaron's holding a reception in my honor tomorrow night at the Faculty Club."

A redhead with hands on hips blew a round pink bubble and then popped it loudly. "What kind of reception?" she asked.

Seth felt inordinately awkward. "Well, there's this award called the Dannie Heinemann Prize. Mathematical physics. It's a pretty big deal to the faculty."

"Who'll be there?" asked a brunette who looked like she'd borrowed her legs from a horse.

"The faculty and guests," Seth said. "Two hundred or so."

She blinked. "Two hundred? Who are you, the president?"

Seth's embarrassment resulted in a smile. "Like I said, it's pretty important to some people. I was thinking maybe you could attend."

Marisa glanced at the others. "Me?"

"All of you."

She stared at him for a moment before understanding dawned. Her mouth curved into a seductive grin. "You want us to spice things up a bit."

"What do you mean?" the redhead asked.

"We could dance."

"Oh, please!" The horse-legged brunette crossed her arms.

Marisa turned to her. "Why not, Maggie? What's wrong with a little routine to liven up the party?"

"Not exactly the kind of party—"

"Exactly! It's not Seth's kind of party, so we add a little flavor."

"Will Brad Baxter be there?" the redhead asked. Brad was the director of physical education.

"Could be," Seth said. "Do you want him to be there?"

"You can do that?"

"Sure," Seth said.

The rest of the squad members were looking at each other, not objecting. Except for Maggie. "What do you want us to do?" she asked. "I'm not sure I like this."

"It's harmless," Marisa said.

"I don't think he's talking about backflips off Baaron's table," Maggie said, looking at Seth.

He nodded. "Actually, I had something else in mind. Something more MTV than ESPN."

"Do we look like strippers to you?" Maggie demanded.

"No." Seth felt his face go red. "That's not—"

"Give it a rest, Maggie!" Marisa snapped. She turned to Seth. "So we come in and do a sexy dance, maybe heat Baaron up a little. I don't see the harm in that. This isn't exactly a parochial school, right? How do you want to work this?"

Seth wasn't sure whether the idea was hers or his, but she was a smooth operator, he'd give her that much. He could see her running for Congress one day.

"Well. When I stand up to give my speech—they always want the guest of honor to tell them how indebted they are to Berkeley—when I get to a certain point, you could come in and do your...routine."

The others were beaming now. The idea had taken root. "So that's it?"

"Maybe table dances would be a good idea. All the department heads and a grand finale with Baaron." What was he thinking?

"I don't know," Maggie said.

"I love it!" Marisa said. "When was the last time the faculty gave us our due? Just think about that, Maggie. This will loosen them up a bit. Talk about making a splash."

"If we have to take the fall—"

"Please, it's only a dance. We're not going in there with picket signs and beating them over their heads. This is Berkeley!"

"If there is any heat, I'm sure it'll come down on me," Seth said. "I seem to have a propensity for heat."

Red flag, Seth.

Marisa looked at the others for a quick approval. An echo of "I'm in" and a halfhearted shrug from Maggie settled the issue.

She turned back. "Okay, we're on. Any other surprises?"

"Only one." Seth faced a petite blonde whom he'd seen Phil ogling on occasion. "I have a friend who needs a date. His name is Phil. Handsome guy with a pocket protector. Trust me, he's quite charming once you get to know him."

"You . . . you want me to go out with some guy named Phil?"

Seth nodded. "Just ask him out to dinner. Maybe a movie."

"No problem," Marisa said. "Right, Suzi? He's charming."

"Okay."

"You'll do it?" Seth asked.

"Sure."

Seth nodded. "Okay. Good."

Maggie crossed her arms and turned to leave. Her foot caught on Marisa's shoe and she tripped. Tried to catch herself, failed to do so, and sprawled on the ground.

Seth jumped forward to help her up.

But suddenly Maggie was standing, not lying on the grass.

Seth jerked back and blinked.

Maggie crossed her arms and turned to leave.

He'd seen this!

Her foot caught on Marisa's shoe . . .

He'd seen exactly this, just one second ago!

. . . and she tripped.

This time Seth leaped forward just as Maggie began to fall. He caught her on the elbow and kept her upright.

"Whoa!" she exclaimed. "Watch your feet, Marisa."

Marisa eyed him. "Pretty quick."

Seth stared at the ground, stunned.

"You okay?"

"Huh? Yeah." He took a step back, looked up at them, and started to turn.

"I'll call you for details?"

"Sure. Call me."

# 8

SAMIR DROVE MIRIAM from the market where they'd left Sultana. Miriam watched suburban Riyadh drift by like a dream of mud and brick, her stomach tied in knots. Her voice came out tight and strained, but she managed to blame it on Sita's death.

Of course, she couldn't let Samir know the truth. God forgive her. She didn't dare tell him. Not only because he had a direct line to her newfound father, the sheik, and by association to Omar, but because telling Samir would put Samir himself in terrible danger. When Omar discovered her missing, he would naturally suspect Samir's involvement and question him thoroughly. The less he knew, the better.

In the morning she would betray the man she loved. This truth made her ill. She repeatedly swallowed the lumps that choked her throat. She couldn't even tell him good-bye! She slipped her hand over his and squeezed. He blushed. One way or another, she knew they would end up together. She would leave a letter for him with Sultana, telling him of her undying love and begging him to come for her. A tear slipped from her eye.

Miriam told him about Sultana's insistence that they make a private shopping trip to Jidda the following day. It was a private getaway, only for part of the day, she explained, so she asked for his discretion. Samir agreed with a knowing smile.

She left Samir in the garage, hurried into the house, and walked straight for her room without removing her veil. Nothing must appear out of the ordinary. The last thing she needed was for Haya to see her tearstained face. Fortunately, her young mother wasn't around.

Miriam locked the door to her room, walked to the bed, and sat slowly. Alone for the first time, she slipped off the veil, lowered her head into her hands, and wept.

An hour slipped by before she wiped her eyes and stood. A full-length mirror showed her standing, still dressed in her black abaaya. The princess.

She walked up to the mirror and studied her face. Her eyes were red and swollen, but the dark tones of her skin hid most of the signs of her crying well. She sniffed and ran her hands through her shiny black hair. A very small black freckle spotted her right cheek. When she was thirteen, she'd wanted it removed. But as she looked through a copy of *Cosmopolitan* magazine that Sultana had given her, she saw a stunning model with a similar mark on her cheek. She agreed with Sultana that men must be attracted to it, or the magazine editors would have covered it up.

She turned from the mirror, set her jaw, and pulled off her abaaya. It was time to get on with it. She sifted through her possessions, deciding what she could take that would fit in a single carry-on bag and a vanity case. In the end, she settled for what Sultana and she first conceived of long ago: two changes of Western clothes—jeans and blouses that would allow her to blend in with the people of California; basic toiletries; the Koran; one jewelry box filled with her most expensive jewels, well over a million dollars' worth; and an iPod. The rest of the space would be occupied by the money. With money she could buy whatever she needed in the United States.

She had talked scandalously with Sita and Sultana about one day embracing Western ways, and now that day was here. Jeans might not be acceptable in Saudi Arabia, but Miriam could hardly wait to don them at the earliest possible opportunity. She would distance herself from the abaaya and arranged marriages and smother herself in the symbols of freedom. In the United States she would be anything but Saudi. She would eat and walk and talk like an American. She'd done it before for a summer in California, and she would do it again—this time permanently. Her accent might not be English, but her heart would be American.

The evening crept by like a slug making its way across a pincushion. Her brother, Faisal, came home, his normal obnoxious self. The meal was inconsequential and she excused herself early.

"I'm going to bed. After my shopping trip today, I've decided the merchants of Riyadh are too conservative for my tastes. Sultana is taking me to Jidda in the morning. Just for the day. And if Jidda doesn't have what I want, I'll just have to go to Spain, won't I?"

Haya smiled. "Maybe I should come with you."

"Wonderful idea. Although I'm not sure Salman would approve without his permission."

Haya's smile softened.

"You won't tell him that I've gone, will you? We're fly-ing in one of her husband's jets in the morning and will be back late afternoon."

"Go ahead, spend my husband's money. Someone has to."

Miriam hurried off, heart firmly planted in her throat.

It was one a.m. before Miriam slipped through the darkened villa and entered Salman's office carrying her small suitcase. His forbidding oak desk flown in from Spain cast shadows under the moonlight. It had taken her nearly a month to find the combination to the floor safe hidden beneath it. Haya knew the combination, of course. Someone besides Salman had to know how to access the valuables. He had entrusted his young bride with the code, knowing she would never abuse his trust. And in her youth, Haya certainly did not suspect that she was violating that trust by bragging about the combination to Miriam late one night. Coaxing the numbers from Haya had not been an easy task, but when Miriam slipped into the office later that same night and opened the safe, she did not mind the trouble.

Except for her own breathing, the house was silent. She walked across the thick carpet, pushed aside his chair, and knelt, trying to still her heart. Using a flashlight, she dialed the numbers in the order she'd burned into her mind. But her fingers trembled and she overshot on the first try. The second produced a soft click, and she pulled the door open.

She played the flashlight's beam over the contents, positioned exactly as they had been two years earlier: the passports and traveling certificates on a small shelf and wads of cash on the safe floor. Like many Saudi men in his position, Salman kept a healthy stash of money in the event that a political emergency might force him to flee. There were several stacks—euros, francs, and American dollars. Miriam was interested only in the dollars.

She paused long enough to satisfy herself that the house was still asleep. Working quickly, she shuffled through the documents and withdrew her own passport and a blank traveling document. She would have time to execute the document with Salman's forged signature, giving herself permission to travel to the United States. Miriam only hoped her attempt would stand up to scrutiny.

She pulled out twenty bundles of one-hundred-dollar bills, each an inch thick, and placed them in the suitcase. She guessed it was roughly $500,000. A small amount of cash in royal Saudi terms, but enough for a start in America, surely. If not, she could always fall back on the jewels.

Miriam closed the safe, spun the dial, and left the room with a new tremor in her fingers. She had just committed a serious crime and had no doubt Salman would insist on punishment if she was caught. In light of today's drowning, perhaps he would order her arm amputated!

It took her an hour to pack and repack the case, hiding the money beneath the clothes. The airport authorities rarely checked the bags of royalty, but there was always the possibility. Unless they rummaged through her clothes, they would find nothing. Of course, if they did open the suitcase, they would rummage, wouldn't they?

She finally locked the case and forced herself to bed again.

The morning came slowly and without a wink of sleep. Each minute of the two hours leading up to her departure with Samir seemed to slow down. Miriam walked downstairs at eight thirty and saw with no small relief that the house was still quiet. She donned her veil and walked to the garage, carrying the suitcase in one hand and her vanity case in the other.

Samir helped her with the bags. If he noticed the weight, he didn't say anything. Once again she was thankful for the abaaya that hid her skin—the adrenaline racing through her blood had surely flushed it red. Or drained it white.

What if Salman needed something withdrawn from his safe before Miriam got to the airport? What if Samir dropped the suitcase, spilling its contents on the ground? What if... There were too many what-ifs! This is a mistake, Miriam! You should run back to the house. You could tell Samir that your cycle came early and you cannot make this trip.

They pulled away from the villa. Traffic bustled with expatriates headed to work and Saudis headed to oversee them.

"What do you suppose the weather in Jidda will be like today?" Miriam asked.

"Beautiful," Samir said. He cast her a glance. "As beautiful as you."

The veil spared her from having to force a smile to cover her grief. "And how do you know that I haven't grown warts under this sheet?"

"Warts or no warts, I would love you, as God is my witness."

"Before you saw me unveiled, I was just a walking sheet. And then you saw me and I became your undying love. What if I'd been ugly?" They teased each other often in the car's privacy, but now the jokes failed to lift her heart.

"True. I'm a man. And like most men, the beauty of a woman does strange things to my mind." He gave her a coy smile. "Your beauty nearly stops my heart. I don't know what I would do, seeing you walk around my house unveiled. It might kill me."

They passed Riyadh's water tower, a structure that made Miriam think of a champagne glass.

"At least you would die a married man." She turned to him. "We can't pretend forever, Samir. You know that I will be married within the royal family. I have to produce a son of royal blood, remember?"

Samir cleared his throat and stared ahead.

"As long as we're in this country, we'll never be allowed to marry," she said.

"Then we'll have to leave this country," he said.

It was the first time he'd said it. Miriam's heart filled with hope. But no, she couldn't say anything now.

"We will?"

He looked at her and then returned his gaze to the road. "I've thought of nothing else for the last year. We have only two options: Either we never love each other as a man and woman are meant to love, or we leave the country. Leaving would be dangerous. But I think ... I really think I would die without you." He took a long breath. "I am a good Muslim, and I will always be a good Muslim. I love this country. But if it makes no difference to God, I think I will take you as my wife."

Miriam felt her heart swell. She wanted to tell him why she was really going to Jidda.

She rested her hand on his arm. "Samir, I would

leave Saudi Arabia to be with you even if all the king's guards were after me." A tear broke from her eye and she paused to rein in her emotions. "I want you to make me a promise."

"I would promise you my life," he said.

"Then promise me that you will marry me. No matter what happens, you will marry me."

"As there is no god but God, I swear it," he said.

She wanted to lift her veil and kiss him. She glanced around, saw that the closest car was nearly fifty meters back, and did just that. She leaned over and kissed him quickly on the cheek. Her lips flamed at the touch.

He blushed and glanced in the rearview mirror. His eyes grew misty and he swallowed. "If I had been born a prince," he said, "then I wouldn't bring any danger—"

"You are a prince! You will always be a prince. The only real danger I face is being separated from you," she said.

They drove toward the airport in a heavy silence of mutual desire, and Miriam thought her heart would burst with love.

# 9

SULTANA WAS WAITING by her husband's black Mercedes. A white Learjet waited on the tarmac, door open and engines running. Princes typically owned several jets—Sultana's husband owned six. The pilot, an American with whom Miriam had flown before, walked out to greet them, grinning wide. Then they were aboard and the door shut and Samir was gone.

Ten minutes later they were airborne.

Less than an hour later they landed at Jidda's international airport on the coast of the Red Sea. Separated from the pilot, they had talked freely and completed the paperwork that gave Salman's permission for Miriam to travel alone and out of the country. Sultana's confidence fed Miriam's, which grew with each step.

The main terminal teemed with people in white and black clothing, more men in white than women in black. The ticket counters for Saudi Arabian Airlines stood to Miriam's right. She waited with Sultana in this sea of wandering men, cloaked in her abaaya, and a wave of doubt swept over her.

"What if Hillary doesn't remember me?" she asked. "Just because she taught Middle Eastern studies doesn't mean she'll be friendly—"

"Stop it before you talk your way out of this. There's a plane leaving in forty minutes. If you hurry, you can catch it."

Miriam looked around again. Sultana's hand rested on her arm.

"Go with God. And tell them in America."

"Tell them what?"

Sultana looked out the window at a rolling jet. "That only a few are like that pig Hatam, drowning his wife." Her voice shook. "That we despise beasts like Omar."

Sultana's crusade.

"What if my father has already discovered me missing—"

"If you don't go right now, I'm going to start screaming. Do you want that? Every policeman in the terminal will come running."

Miriam forced an anemic grin. "Okay, I'm going."

"Take care of yourself."

Miriam took uncertain steps toward the counter, the small bag in her right hand and the vanity case in her left. She stood in line and yet again was grateful for the veil.

"May I help you?"

"Yes, one ticket to Riyadh, please."

The man eyed her curiously. "Papers."

She handed over the forged documents, which explained the emergency nature of her trip, expressly authorized by Salman bin Fahd. A cousin had taken ill in Paris, and there was no male companion available for

Miriam. Whatever the man behind the counter thought, he was in no position to question the son of the king.

Miriam declared no luggage, took her ticket, waited to board, then entered the plane. An hour later the plane landed in Riyadh, and Miriam thought again about aborting. She could still call Samir to pick her up, hurry back to the villa, and replace the cash. Or she could catch another flight back to Jidda and return with Sultana.

And then what?

Then she would be forced to marry Omar.

Her feet carried her out to the main terminal. The ticket counters ran along the far wall, and for a moment she wasn't sure if they were the gates to heaven or to hell. She walked toward them. You've gone too far to go back. If they refuse to sell you a ticket to Paris, you will fly back to Jidda.

But they didn't refuse to sell her a ticket.

Once again she climbed on board, muscles strung taut like zither wires. The large DC-10 lifted off and slowly turned to the northwest. Every time a steward walked down the cabin, she half expected him to approach her with the news: "I'm sorry, ma'am, but your foolish plan to run from your marriage to Omar has been found out. We are under orders to turn the plane around and return you to Riyadh, where a group of a hundred mutawa are waiting at the airport to beat you."

But again her fears failed to materialize. The plane landed. The passengers deplaned.

Miriam walked cautiously down the Jetway, eyes open for armed authorities. She paused ten feet from the terminal entrance, struggling to still her breathing. A young man stepped around her, staring. In her fear, she'd almost forgotten that she was wearing the abaaya.

She reached up, pulled off her veil, stuffed it up her sleeve, and forced herself into the terminal.

Hundreds of colorfully dressed people strutted or milled about, and she was sure that most of them were looking in her direction.

Miriam scanned the crowd quickly. No religious police! Or were they hiding to avoid a scene? She located a bathroom sign up the hall and struck out for it with a new urgency, avoiding any eye contact with curious onlookers.

Is that Darth Vader, Mommy?

She had to shed this black cloak. A wedge of black caught her attention and she glanced up to see another woman dressed in an abaaya, fifty meters ahead. She still wore her veil and trailed her husband by several meters.

The sight emboldened her. Miriam barged into the bathroom and entered the handicapped stall. She threw off her abaaya, set the suitcase on the toilet, unlocked the latch, and flipped it open. One of the hundred-dollar stacks fell to the floor in her haste to pull out her jeans. She stared at it, horrified.

The restroom door opened and someone entered. Miriam bent for the money, shoved it back under her clothes, and quietly closed the case. But she was afraid to engage the latch for the noise it would make.

No one was going to bust in here and grab her because they'd heard two latches clicking closed. What was she thinking?

The door opened and closed again. She was alone again.

She dressed as quickly as her trembling hands would allow. She'd thought to discard her abaaya in the waste bin by the sinks, but now she wondered if it might be better to flush it down the toilet.

Of all the ideas . . . ! The toilet would only flood!

Miriam scooped up the garment, grabbed her bags, and left the stall. She crossed to a large waste bin, set her cases down, and summarily shoved her abaaya through the opening. She faced the mirror.

Her image stared back, face ashen, arms and neck bare. What was she doing?

She lifted her hand to the collar of her canary blouse. It froze there. She was practically naked! What did she think she was doing? She couldn't walk out there like this, baring her skin to the world! She should at least keep the abaaya as a backup.

She reached into the trash, closed her hand around the robe, and pulled it out. Now she stood facing the mirror with a wadded black garment in her left hand, looking like a fool.

Miriam grunted and pushed the cloak back into the bin. She covered her face with her hands. Calm down, Miriam!

The door opened. Her eyes sprang open. Light seeped through her fingers, but she did not remove her hands.

A woman walked past her and then stopped. "You okay?" she asked in French.

Miriam lowered her arms. "Yes," she said. "Oui."

The woman smiled and stepped into a stall.

Miriam turned back to the mirror. That was it. Just "You okay?" and "Yes." The woman was only concerned, not suspicious. And Miriam had responded. All was well. You're okay? Yes!

Yes, yes! I am okay.

It was then, standing in front of the mirror, that Miriam realized her plan was going to work. She was going to escape Omar.

Miriam picked up her two bags and walked out. People filled the busy terminal, but no one was focused on her. No one at all.

MIRIAM CLEARED IMMIGRATION in ten minutes and immediately purchased a ticket to Chicago. Her destination was San Francisco, but as planned, she bought her tickets with cash and in single legs to slow any pursuit.

She spent an hour walking the terminal, browsing the shops, feeling more alive than she could ever remember. She changed a few dollars for francs and bought a mug with Paris etched in gold. She wanted a memento of her first truly free day.

The transatlantic flight to Chicago on United Airlines was a joy. She flew first class, because the royal family always flew first class, and an escapee deserved nothing less. She watched an in-flight movie titled *The Lord of the Rings,* full of magic and strange creatures that made her laugh. A bit scary in parts, but magical. Several passengers kept looking her way, and she finally apologized for her outbursts, unable to hide her grin. She wanted to tell them more. That she was escaping from a terrible man named Omar, and they should be glad that she was sitting here laughing at trolls and goblins instead of marrying one. She wanted to say that, but she didn't.

She wasn't sure if it was the relief or the wine or the growing contentment, but she finally fell asleep.

A friend of Sultana's who lived in Spain had modified Miriam's student visa two years ago, insisting that it was good for four more years. For a few horrible minutes in the immigration line at O'Hare, Miriam began to have her doubts. But then she was smiling politely at an officer and walking through, stamped passport in hand.

She was in the United States. Wearing jeans and a canary blouse. Free to go where she liked. Carrying $500,000 in her bag. She nearly screamed out her thanks to God right then, fifty feet beyond the immigration line, but she settled for a subdued prayer of gratitude.

By now, the wheels would be turning in Saudi Arabia. Sultana would be sticking to her denials; Samir would be vowing ignorance and dying of worry. Dear Samir. Salman would be pacing in rage, and the sheik would be wringing his hands. And Omar...

Omar would be considering that perhaps women could do more than make babies and cook and please their masters.

A group of young men whom she recognized from the flight passed her. On the plane the four talking heads had laughed loudly and sworn regularly. Now she saw they wore baggy jeans that threatened to fall around their ankles. She'd never seen the like! The sight made her feel vulnerable and alone in this sea of humanity. She had been set free, yes, but into what kind of ocean?

Miriam purchased a ticket to San Francisco and spent two anxious hours waiting for the plane's departure, vacillating between the thrill of her accomplishment and worry that she had escaped only to be eventually dragged back to Saudi Arabia. What if Omar had beaten the truth out of Sultana and was even now waiting for her in San Francisco?

No. Sultana's husband would not allow Omar to touch his wife.

Her flight landed in San Francisco at three o'clock in the afternoon, and Omar wasn't there. Then she truly was free, wasn't she? Jidda, Riyadh, Paris, Chicago, and now San Francisco. She had really done it.

Miriam hailed a taxi at three thirty.

"Where to?" The driver looked Indian or Pakistani. She wondered if he was Muslim or Hindu.

"Do you know where Berkeley is?" she asked.

"University of California at Berkeley? Yes, of course." His accent was British Indian and she loved it.

"There is a house on a street near the university. Could you take me there?"

"To where? Do you have the address?"

"No."

"Then I can't take you there, can I?"

"But you can take me to the university. I think I will remember from there, although last time I had a driver who knew where to take me."

"But I've never been there, have I? So how can I take you where I've never been?"

He looked her over, smiled politely, then pulled into traffic. His name was Stan, he informed her, although she doubted it. He should be American if he wanted to be, however. She was doing the same. Stan drove her north on the 101 and then traversed the Oakland Bay Bridge—a bridge he clearly resented, judging by the "fool drivers" who hindered his progress.

She laughed at this, which got him laughing too, and by the time they exited University Avenue for a small university street she recognized, Stan was very friendly. Practically in love with her. She knew because his eyes said so. They were watching her and speaking in the same way Samir's eyes spoke to her the few times she hadn't worn her veil.

Ten minutes later they found Hillary's house, only three blocks from University Avenue, as it turned out. Miriam paid Stan his fee and gave him an extra hundred dollars for his kindness. For affirming her.

Professor of Middle Eastern Studies Hillary Brackenshire was a tall, skinny woman with skin that looked three times her age and gray, wiry hair that she hardly bothered to brush. She reminded Miriam of a walking thistle. The professor had been fascinated by Miriam during Miriam's summer months at Berkeley—a natural reaction, considering Hillary's field of study and her infatuation with Islam.

Miriam hoped the woman would be glad to see her. If not, she would go to plan B, which was hardly more than starting out in a hotel. She set her cases down, glanced around nervously, and knocked on the door.

Within ten seconds the knob rattled, and then the door swung inward. Hillary stood there, dressed in a house robe despite it being only five in the afternoon, looking as much the wrinkled porcupine as Miriam remembered.

"Yes? May I help you?"

Miriam hesitated. "Do you remember me?" Obviously not. "Miriam. I studied at Berkeley two summers ago."

Hillary's eyes widened. "Miriam? The princess?"

Miriam smiled. "Yes, although I'm not sure that I'm a princess any longer."

"Come in! Come in." Hillary waved her in with a flapping hand. "My dear, it isn't every day a princess comes to my door." She saw the suitcases and glanced up at Miriam, then past her to the street. "Where's your ride?"

"I came in a taxi."

"Let me help you."

"Thank you."

Miriam entered and looked around at the rather humble setting. An ungainly papier-mâché bell sat on the mantel. Dried leaves glued together to form picture frames hung over a brown threadbare couch. The lampshades looked like they were made of pillowcases—the same yellow ones Miriam remembered from her last visit. Hillary, a self-proclaimed naturalist, did no better with her living room than she did with her hair, Miriam thought.

"What do you mean, you might not be a princess anymore?" Hillary asked, turning in the center of the room.

Miriam set her vanity case on the floor. "I mean that I've run from the House of Saud."

Hillary blinked. "You've... you've run? You can't run from the House of Saud. You are the House of Saud."

Miriam laughed lightly. "Yes, I suppose I am. But actually"—she looked around, strangely intoxicated by Hillary's mess—"actually, I've fled. Imagine that. I left Saudi Arabia and I've come to the United States. And I was wondering if you might help me for a few days."

She wanted Hillary to hug her, delighted with her courage. Instead, the professor just stared, unbelieving.

"That's impossible," Hillary finally said.

"But I've done it!" Miriam felt her face broaden into a smile.

"No, I mean you can't run from who you are. You shouldn't have."

It occurred to Miriam that Hillary really did not understand, professor of Middle Eastern studies or not. She should have been discouraged, but the joy of her success prevented it.

"May I stay with you for a day or two?"

"Well...sure. It's a far cry from the Hilton, though. Last time you had the whole top floor, and now you want to stay with me?"

"Yes."

"Why on earth—"

"Last time I was a princess. Now I'm just a woman." She smoothed her yellow blouse. "See, a woman. I'll be out of your way tomorrow. The next day at the latest."

"Does the embassy know you're here?"

"I told you, I'm running."

"So you're a fugitive?"

Hillary's tone pushed Miriam down onto the sofa. "Yes. Do you have a problem with that?"

Hillary sputtered. "No. No, of course not. You're welcome to stay as long as you like. As long as you promise to tell me all about it."

"I will."

"Good. Now, a princess must have tea. I have a wonderful herbal blend. China Moon. Yes?"

"Yes."

"Be right back." Hillary slid into the kitchen.

Miriam breathed deeply. She kicked her shoes off, lifted both arms to the ceiling. She hardly knew she was going to yelp before she did so—a full-blooded Arabian yelp with an ululating tongue.

From the kitchen, porcelain rattled and then crashed. Hillary had dropped the teacups. But Miriam didn't care. She flung herself back into the soft sofa cushions, laughing.

Omar could steam all he liked. She was free from him.

# 10

OMAR BIN KHALID studied the great white hall through the study's cracked door. Greek columns supported an elegant carved ceiling forty feet above the glassy marble floor. His father had paid a famous artist two million dollars to paint huge portraits of each Saudi king, six including the one he now planned to kill, Abdullah. The canvases peered from the far wall like sentinels craning for a view of history's next chapter.

Clacking feet echoed through the chamber, but he couldn't see to whom they belonged. He'd called his father from a high-level meeting with the news less than five minutes ago.

The dog had fled.

His father turned the corner and swept into view, his arms swinging with each long step, his thawb swirling around his ankles. Omar eased the door closed, crossed the office suite, sat on the black leather sofa, and crossed his legs casually. The office was a study in the trappings of immense wealth. Not a single item, from the immense gold-layered desk to the quill pens in the drawers, could be bought on the open market. Every item was custommade. Even the thick white carpet had been woven of camel's hair for this room and this room alone.

The door slammed open and his father walked in. "What is the meaning of this?"

Omar folded his hands to still his quaking fingers. "She left the country yesterday for Paris."

Khalid walked to the center of the room, face drawn. "She left with whom?"

The woman had denied him. Miriam's denial was no less offensive than that young feline's refusal of her husband. Omar had known Sita would be a problem for Hatam, predicted that her reaction to him would constitute grounds for her death.

So. His bride was too stupid to get the message.

"She presented the airport authorities with forged travel documents," Omar said. "She slipped away on a trip to Jidda, took a flight to Riyadh, and then on to Paris. On her own."

His father drilled him with a stare. "She's in Paris now?"

"No. She's in the United States. California, where she attended school for a summer."

"And her father? Salman?"

"Furious. But still blind to our intentions."

"If our sources know this much, so will King Abdullah," Khalid said, turning. "He'll want to know why."

"That's hardly the point," Omar said. "Why is irrelevant. I have just been spit upon by a woman."

"Do not get distracted from the true crisis. She was your means to the throne and nothing more. Without her,

Sheik Al-Asamm will withdraw his support. Without her, there is no throne." He took a seat behind the monstrous desk. "Where is the sheik?"

"In the desert. He vows to withdraw if we don't retrieve her."

His father cursed. "Living with the Shia will be like sleeping with the devil. We should kill the lot of them."

"I agree."

But they both knew that without the sheik's support, the coup would fail.

"The woman has fled." Khalid shook his head and closed his eyes. "Of all the insolent…" His eyes opened, blazing. "Everything! We thought of every possibility. But this? What kind of daughter has Salman raised? You see, this is why we must overthrow the throne! A royal daughter is asked one thing—to marry a prince—and she runs like a coward! Don't women know their place any longer?"

"Obviously not," Omar said.

"And if the king learns of our plan?"

"He would never have the proof."

"If he even suspected?"

Omar paused. "If I were him, I might kill the woman, prevent the marriage."

Khalid leaned back in his chair. "If the king killed the sheik's daughter, the sheik might be furious enough to align himself with me without a marriage."

"Then kill the woman and blame it on the king," Omar said, thinking the end would be fitting.

"It might come to that. But the king would deny it as quickly as we would. And we have no guarantees that the sheik would side with me. I can't very well ask him, can I?"

Khalid pushed his chair back and walked to a window that overlooked a pond spotted with a dozen geese. "Bring her back."

Omar stood, turned from his father, and ground his molars to squelch a surge of rage. "I will." He strode toward the door. "I will."

He would bring her back. He would drag her back by her hair, bleeding and screaming. Assir and Sa'id were already on a flight to America, two hungry jackals waiting for directions.

"Alive," his father said. "We need her alive."

Shut up, Father.

"Of course."

But he wasn't sure he could restrain himself.

HILAL'S SHARP BONES pressed against his skin in a way that would have earned him the nickname Knife or Edge had he grown up in New York City. He was the head of King Abdullah's personal security and arguably as deadly as he looked.

Hilal sat to the right of King Abdullah, and Salman faced them both, feeling insignificant despite the fact that he was royalty and Hilal was not. He resented the fact.

He'd been summoned because of Miriam's flight. Why the king was so interested in the disappearance of one adopted daughter was beyond him. Unless they knew more than he'd told them, which was simply that she fled after witnessing the drowning of her friend Sita.

Hilal lifted thin fingers to his beard and ran them gently through the black strands. The king looked at him with a raised brow. "Yes?"

"It's the question of why that bothers me, Your Highness. Why did she run?"

The king looked at Salman without speaking.

"You're accusing me?" Salman said.

"If you have done anything I disapprove of, I would know about it. I'm not blind."

The revelation gave Salman pause. He wondered which of his servants was spying for the king. "I've told you why I believe she fled."

Hilal cleared his throat. "She took great risks in leaving. According to the Berkeley professor who contacted the State Department, Miriam is persuaded that she was somehow being subjected to a scheme that jeopardizes the House of Saud, although she refused to explain herself."

"I cannot imagine what she means." He was sweating under his thawb.

"Either way, I don't like it," Hilal said. "I would request to collect her myself, Your Highness. We must find out why she fled."

"She's only a woman chasing her fantasies," Salman said. "You're overreacting."

"Am I? You should stick your head out of your palace now and then, my friend. Our kingdom isn't as stable as it once was."

"And what does this have to do with my daughter? Please." Salman felt small in the cutthroat's presence. Why did the king allow Hilal to speak like this to a prince? "I cannot underestimate her spirit of rebellion," Salman said. "It took some thinking to break into my safe, and it took even more courage to steal the money. If you ask me, Samir was involved in her escape. I always thought she had him bewitched."

Hilal looked up sharply. "Samir? We questioned him thoroughly. He knew nothing. What do you mean, bewitched?"

Salman hesitated, remembering the occasional glances he'd seen the driver give Miriam. "I mean that they spent time together. Alone. In the car, of course, but if you hadn't insisted I keep him, I would have let him go years ago."

"He's Sheik Al-Asamm's man, you idiot!"

Salman felt an icy blade cut through his nerves. Hilal either knew more than he was saying or was bluffing. If the former, Salman was being set up. He had no choice but to cover his tracks. Give them something now that would later point to his ignorance of any coup plot.

Salman stood. "The sheik's man? You've allowed a Shia into my house? What if Sheik Al-Asamm has something up his sleeve? Have you thought about that? What if Miriam is part of his schemes?"

"Then she will die," Hilal said. "But you yourself swore under oath that she was the daughter of Khalid's servant, spawned by an illicit affair his family hoped to keep confidential."

"Samir, my driver, is Shia?" He flung his arms wide. "For all I know the sky is about to rain fire on my head." They looked at each other.

"We must proceed assuming the worst," Hilal said. "As always."

"Which is?" the king asked.

"That this woman fled more than a drowning. More likely a marriage."

Salman's eyes went wide.

"That she is a pawn in a plot to undermine the monarchy. I'll contact the Americans and leave immediately."

"The Americans will help you?" Salman asked.

"We don't need them; we know where she is. But if we do need them, they would help us. They know what would happen to the Middle East if the balance of power were to shift in Saudi Arabia. They want to keep the House of Saud in power. The fate of one woman is nothing in the large picture."

Salman disagreed without a word. The fate of one woman was everything.

# 11

THE FACULTY CLUB may have been one of Berkeley's oldest buildings, but it was also one of its most stately. A good enough reason for the faculty to claim it, Seth thought. Tonight they had come out in droves, paying homage to last year's recipient of the same award, Dr. Galvastan from Harvard, and the popular caterer. If Seth had not come he might not have been missed. Black gowns and jackets filled the hall, and Seth had decided to conform. He passed on a tuxedo, choosing instead a tailored black suit, and combed his hair back. On a night such as this, it felt good to blend in a little.

Problem was, as soon as any of the faculty recognized him, they seemed compelled to say something. Anything, no matter how inane.

"Seth! There you are. Lovely to see you." Grin. "Here's the official schedule for this evening."

"Well done, Mr. Border. You've made Berkeley proud."

"Congratulations, young man. We're so proud of you."

"You'll make a good professor yet. Good job, man."

These were invariably followed by a look at his attire and a pointed smile that betrayed self-righteous satisfaction. About time, boy. It took him fifteen minutes to work his way past enough of them to find breathing space in the Great Hall.

He paused at the entrance to the Kerr Dining Room, poked his head in, and scanned the hall. Round tables covered in white linens dotted the floor, each one candlelit and set with antique silverware. The room simmered with a gentle hubbub, two hundred heads of hot air expanding the significance of their small worlds. It was a wonder there was any oxygen left in the place.

Seth slipped in through the side entrance and headed for the long table set up at one end for the guest of honor and other notables.

"Seth."

He turned to the low voice. It was Dr. Harland, holding a drink.

"Glad you could make it," Harland said with a twinkle in his eyes.

"Evening, Professor."

"They've come in force for you, haven't they? You okay?"

"Never better," Seth said.

A faculty member he didn't recognize walked by, stuck out her hand, and offered her congratulations. Seth took the hand and nodded.

Harland took a sip from his glass. "I see you dressed the part."

"I'm here to play ball, right?"

Someone slid behind him, and he turned to see a woman with hair going every which way but down.

Professor of Middle Eastern Studies Hillary Bracken-shire. He knew her because of his interest in the region and the single class he'd suffered through under her instruction. She turned to see whom she'd brushed, and her face reddened.

"Seth! Congratulations. You must be very proud!"

"Hello, Dr. Brackenshire. Thank you."

She opened her mouth as if to say more, but then thought better of it and just smiled. It wasn't until she turned to leave that Seth saw the young woman standing several feet to her right. Her round, haunting eyes peered into his for a moment, and then she turned with Hillary and walked away. She wore a white dress fitted to her slender frame. Her hair hung below her shoulders, jet black and shiny. Arabic, if he were to guess. Middle Eastern at least.

"I haven't seen her before," Harland said, following Seth's gaze.

"I haven't seen half these people before."

Harland nodded and sipped his drink. "Please tell me you've given some thought to our little discussion."

"You know me, Professor. I always give whatever you say a little thought. In this case, much thought."

"And?"

"And"—he nodded at a passing professor—"I think you're right. I should finish my formal education."

"They've brought the big guns in tonight; tread carefully."

Seth had thought about telling Marisa to can the dance—had actually picked up the phone an hour ago to put an end to it.

But he hadn't.

"Remember the pigeon that hit your office window?" he asked.

"What about it?"

"I thought I saw it before it hit."

A waiter passed by and Harland set his empty glass on the tray. "The mind's a curious thing," he said.

"It happened again."

"You saw another pigeon hit my window?"

"No. I saw a girl fall before she fell."

"Interesting. It happens."

"Yeah. Well, it happened all right. In living color."

"Hmm." Harland obviously thought nothing of it. He was right, it did happen. People would swear they'd seen a certain thing before, despite knowing they hadn't.

They walked toward the podium. Baaron was up there already, and his glance met Seth's.

"Just in case things do go badly tonight, I want you to know something," Seth said. "When I think of a man I would like to call my father, your face comes to mind. I owe you my gratitude."

"I would gladly accept the position were it not filled."

"It isn't filled. I once knew a man, a sperm donor who brought me into this world and then made sure I regretted it. I don't know anyone I would call a father."

"Then as your newly adopted father, let me reiterate my advice. Be nice tonight, Seth."

Seth stopped by the head table. Baaron was dinging his fork against a crystal wineglass by the podium. The heads began to turn his way.

Seth stepped up on the platform. A spontaneous clap spattered and then swelled across the dining room. Seth gave them a quick bow and walked for his seat. The guests took their seats and Baaron began his spiel.

Dr. Galvastan stood from his chair next to Seth's and

spoke quietly. "Well done, Mr. Border. Well done. It's genuinely an honor to meet you. I've heard your name floating around Harvard for a couple years now."

Seth took his hand. "Thank you. Probably the source of all those UFO reports in the region." He winked. "Floating names are often mistaken for alien ships."

"Yes. Yes, of course." Galvastan chuckled.

Seth took his seat and waited while Baaron droned on. They looked like a convention of penguins, seated in nice round circles and dressed in black and white. Maybe he was too hard on them. The two hundred or so minds gathered here represented more academic achievement than some entire countries could claim. Who was he to say that his mind really saw things any more clearly than theirs? Sure, he saw things involuntarily that most of them were incapable of seeing at all. The relationship between simple facts, for example. How numbers worked and how logical constructs were formed on the most fundamental levels. But did that make him better than these penguins smiling up at him?

It occurred to him that what he was about to do represented its own kind of narrowness. A cold sweat broke out on his neck and he took a sip of water. Maybe he should call off Marisa after all. It wasn't too late—he could skip their entrance cue.

"So, without further boring you with the details of our institution's educational prowess, I present to you the man we've all gathered to honor." Baaron turned his way. "Seth Border."

Applause filled the room and Seth stood. Here we go. The applause died, and complete silence settled for the first time.

The girls were to come out when he said Baaron. It would be in the middle of his speech, he told Marisa, and he would say it with great hoopla. Like a Johnny Carson introduction.

Seth stepped behind the podium and looked out at the eager faces. The Middle Eastern studies professor stood near the back and slipped into the hall with the Arabic woman. Odd time for a bathroom break, he thought.

The words of his speech sat in his mind like crows on a telephone line. "Thank you for those kind—"

A door banged open to his right.

"Give me a B!"

Seth jerked, honestly startled. Marisa stood with one fist over her head, scantily clad in black. She looked at him and winked.

"B!" a chorus of voices rang from his left. He turned. Five girls swirled from three doorways, dressed as a cross between cheerleaders and burlesque dancers. Seth had suggested racy; they were indeed racy. A few nervous chuckles rolled through the auditorium. A few stunned gasps.

"Give me an A!"

"A!"

They swung their hips and flashed coy smiles and homed in on the table to Seth's right where Baaron sat, tomato-red.

The chant continued, but Seth shut it out. For the first time in a long while, he was at a total loss. He should do something—encourage them, discourage them, swing his hips with them, stop them in outrage. Anything. But he couldn't. He looked over at Samuel Harland's table and saw the man shaking his head. The girls had formed a line in front of Baaron and were definitely looking more Las Vegas than Lawrence Welk. The place fell silent except for the girls' chant.

He should do something.

He should definitely do something.

His mind went blank.

The image hit him then, like the pigeon at Harland's office hit the window.

A gun. A brown hand with white knuckles. A face twisted in rage. Another face screaming in pain, with viselike fingers squeezing its cheeks together.

Seth gasped.

He was aware that some of the faculty were staring at him, but what was happening here, in this room, felt distant to him.

His field of vision broadened, and he saw that the face belonged to a woman. To the Arabic woman he'd seen with Hillary. She was in the women's bathroom—he knew that because of the stick figure on the door. She was in the women's bathroom, and a man clenched her face with one hand and waved a gun at her with the other.

And then the image was gone.

A dancer was climbing onto Baaron's table in a way that might have turned Seth himself red a few seconds ago, but the sideshow played in his peripheral vision. His heart was hammering, but from the images that had just played through his mind, not the brunette's sultry moves.

For one lost moment Seth stood dumb. Was it possible that the Arabic woman really was in the bathroom with a man who held a gun? Was it possible that the other two incidents hadn't been strange tricks played by his mind but actual precognition?

The images crashed through his mind again. This time the man's hand hit the woman's face.

Seth whirled from the podium, took two long steps to his right, vaulted the head table, and ran for the hall, leaving the penguins gawking. He sprinted for the women's bathroom, slid to a stop in front of the door with the skirted stick figure, paused for one last moment, and then slammed through.

"Hey!"

His voice echoed back at him. A long mirror showed a man dressed in black and white with slick blond hair, hands spread like a gunslinger. That would be him. He glanced around. No urinals—stalls only. The bathroom was empty. The swinging door hissed shut behind him.

"May I help you?"

Seth's head snapped to his right. The Arabic woman stood in the doorway of the last stall, eyes wide.

Seth just stared at her, confused.

"This is the ladies' toilet," the woman said.

He looked to his left and slowly relaxed.

"Hillary?" the woman yelled. She was calling for the professor.

Seth looked at her again. "No one's out there."

The woman stepped out of the stall tentatively. "Hillary!"

"I told you, she's gone."

"Where is Hillary? What have you done?"

"Nothing." Something was gnawing at the back of Seth's mind. "I...I thought something was wrong, that's all." He looked around one last time. "I guess I was wrong."

"Hillary was just here."

He heard the light sound of feet, and it occurred to him

that Hillary's absence might be a problem. He spun around and pulled the bathroom door open a crack.

He saw two things at once. The first was Hillary, disappearing around the corner at the far end of the hall. The second was a dark-skinned man walking in Seth's direction, head down, now just twenty feet away.

This man was going to beat the snot out of the woman behind him. That's what he'd seen.

Seth didn't have time to analyze what had happened.

He moved with an instinct bred through a decade of beatings at home.

He released the door, leaped for the woman, grabbed her arm, and pulled her toward one of the stalls. It never occurred to him that she might not understand the urgency.

She screamed, and he ducked, startled. He recovered, though, and threw his free hand over her mouth. "Please! I'm helping you here! Shut up or you'll get us both hurt!"

Not exactly the most comforting words in the middle of a mugging. She tried to scream again, through his fingers, but he managed to muffle her voice. Time was running out. He tried to drag her, but she was having none of it.

"Stop it!" he whispered. "Someone's coming for you!" He glanced at the door. A brief question skipped through her eyes. Seth lifted her from her feet and crashed through the stall door. The toilet lid was open. He hefted the woman onto the toilet bowl and let her go—all but her mouth.

She teetered, unbalanced on the narrow ceramic ring.

He snatched a finger to his lips. "Sh! Please, you have to trust me," he whispered. "There's someone coming..."

The door to the bathroom opened.

It occurred to Seth that he'd accomplished nothing by dragging her in here. They were sitting ducks, for heaven's sake! One look under the doors and the gunman would see his feet!

Breathing hard, Seth let her mouth go, grabbed the toilet-paper holder for balance, and eased up onto the seat, pushing her toward the wall. Now they both stood on the toilet with a bowl of blue water between their feet. She kept her mouth shut.

Still, only a deaf person could have missed the thumping that had come from the fourth booth. This fact was not lost on Seth.

He pressed against the woman, mind scrambling. Solving mind-boggling mathematical equations was one thing; being stuck with a pretty female on a toilet seat was another.

Her hair was in his mouth. The booth smelled like perfume. She was breathing hard and her breath was hitting his neck. These abstract distractions skipped through his mind in the space of a heartbeat. He had to get her out of here.

Seth's back was to the door. He shifted his feet to turn around. The woman tilted. Her left hand thumped loudly on the stall. A loud plop sounded in the toilet water.

Seth looked down. A white shoe bobbed in the blue water. Her white shoe. He'd knocked her foot off its perch, and her shoe had fallen into the water.

But it was the sound, not the shoe, that raced through his head. He looked into her eyes, wide and white. Somewhere between horror and fury.

That was it. They had to get out of this deathtrap now.

Seth turned and jumped to the floor. He slammed into the stall door, and the whole structure shook. The woman landed behind him, but as he straightened, she fell backward, the toilet at her knees. She instinctively grabbed his waist and together they toppled onto the bowl. Into the bowl.

It was time to abandon secrecy. "Let go!" Seth said.

"Get off me! What are you doing?"

"I'm trying to..."

He shoved himself up and was rewarded with a grunt from her. "Sorry."

He pulled her up. The shoe floated in the blue water like a sailboat. Without thinking, he snatched it up. Clutching the dripping sandal, he jerked the stall door open and stumbled out.

They spilled into the bathroom three feet from an Arabic man, who took a step backward at the sight of Seth. Seth knew beyond a doubt now—this was the man he'd seen in his mind. And if this man was indeed real, then his intention to hurt the girl must also be real. Make no mistake about it, Seth. This is one bad dude.

The woman cried out. The man's attention shifted to her, and Seth saw his eyes darken.

Seth moved. He tossed the toilet-watered shoe at the man, grabbed the woman's hand, and ran for the door. The man cursed in Arabic when the shoe hit his face.

Seth shoved the door open. It thudded into flesh and bone, and someone yelped. Seth yanked the girl through the door and sprinted down the hall toward the back exit. At the corner he glanced back and saw another Arabic man climbing to his feet.

"Hurry!" Seth said, the woman's hand held tightly in

his own. Back around the corner the sound of running feet pounded on the carpet.

Seth leaned into the exit bar. Then they were out the back, breathing hard and facing the cool night.

"This way," he said, cutting to his right. She seemed eager enough to follow now. She pulled him to a stop, reached for her foot, and yanked off the remaining shoe.

He released her hand and they ran full tilt, past Wurster, past the Hearst Museum, across Bancroft Way, and onto College Avenue.

"Stop!"

It was the woman, doubled over just behind him. He slowed to a side skip and then to a halt. She was heaving, hands on knees. Seth looked past her to the street they'd crossed. Nothing.

"Where are you taking me?" she panted.

Good question. The sounds of a commotion drifted from the direction of the Faculty Club. More likely Marisa and company than the two Arabic intruders. Either way, he felt exposed out here on the street.

"We have to get off the street. My car's over here."

She stood and wobbled toward him. Her white dress was torn along one thigh. Now that he thought about it, he had heard the sound of ripping cloth on their exit.

"Your car?" She glanced back. "Please, I have a friend. I have to find her. We have to—"

"Hillary? Trust me, Hillary isn't your friend."

The woman faced him, eyes round in the streetlight. "Why?"

"I think she led those men to you."

"How do you know this?"

"Well, they weren't planning on dancing with you." He

looked past her again. Still nothing. "We got lucky, but if they find us debating here in the street, I doubt it will go so smoothly."

"And I suppose you think dragging me through a bathroom is smooth?"

He glanced over her shoulder. Still clear. "Please, let's get off the street." He started for the parking lot and she followed, glancing back.

They cut across the parking lot and came to a brown '83 Cougar, rust conveniently hidden by the shadows. His hands shook as he twisted the key for his door. He looked at the parking lot entrance one last time. Still no sign of pursuit. He opened the door and slid in.

What are you doing, Seth? He gripped the wheel and shook his head. The passenger door wasn't opening. He looked out the windshield and saw the woman standing by the hood, arms crossed, chewing on a nail. He cranked his window down and stuck his head out.

"Get in."

He pulled his head back in and rolled the window up.

She wasn't moving.

Please, lady, I'm not your enemy here.

This time he climbed out. "Look, I'm just trying to help. You think I understand this?"

"No, I don't think you understand this. And you'll forgive me if it gives me some concern. A man who has shoved me into the toilet and then dragged me down the street is now asking me into his car. How do you know about Hillary?"

"You're from Saudi Arabia?"

She hesitated. "How did you know?"

"Lucky guess."

She closed her eyes and breathed deeply through her nose.

"You're on the run," he said. "You've fled Saudi Arabia and now someone in your country wants you back." Her eyes flashed. "Which means you're someone important. But since no woman is important in Saudi Arabia, you must be royalty. A princess on the run. I'm surprised you made it out of the country."

"How could you know so much about Saudi Arabia?"

He shrugged. "Those guys didn't fly halfway around the world to give up. You're in a world of hurt."

"A world of hurt? If you would speak proper English, it would be better for me."

Her demand took him off guard. "Sorry. It's slang, and it means your world must hurt. Or something similar. Not exactly your world—"

"I'm not an imbecile," she said. "I get the picture."

"Get the picture?" he said with a grin. "Where did you learn that?"

"You think I've never been to America?"

"So. A Saudi princess who has fled her country, speaks perfect English, understands a few colloquialisms, and is in a world of hurt."

She looked at him for a moment. "Yes. I am a princess and I have fled my country. My name is Miriam."

"Miriam." Seth liked her right away. "Will you please get in the car, Miriam?" He looked around. The lot was empty.

"What is your name?"

"Seth. I'm sorry—"

Seth's horizon blurred. He could still see the parking lot, but his mind clouded on the edges. And then he saw two Mercedes driving down two parallel streets. And he saw that the two streets covered the only two exits of this parking lot.

He blinked and his vision returned to normal.

Seth resisted a relapse into panic. He jerked his head to the right exit and then the left. Nothing. He took two steps around the hood for Miriam, but he immediately turned back for his own door. What was he going to do, set her in his car like he'd set her on the toilet?

"Get in the car! Quick, get in the car!"

She still didn't move. If he couldn't get her to move now...

He slammed his fists on the hood and yelled each word distinctly. "Get—in—the—car!"

She scrambled for the door and tugged. It was locked.

Seth dived in, unlocked her door, and twisted the ignition key. The motor growled. Their doors pounded shut.

"What is it? Why are you yelling at me?"

"They're coming! I'm sorry, I didn't mean to yell, but they're just—" He craned for a view of the exit and saw that the coast was clear. Okay, baby, just sneak on out. Maybe this time you're wrong. Intuition can only be so good, right?

He grabbed the stick shift with a cautious hand and nudged it into drive. The car eased out into the lane, lights still off.

"How do you know all this?" she asked. "Where are we going?"

"Sh. Please."

Come on, baby...

The tires crunched over the asphalt, loud in the night. His hands pressed into the wheel, white in the knuckles.

How do you know all this, Seth? The Cougar rolled toward the exit.

Yeah, baby. Yeah, we got it. We—

Lights glared in the mirror. He glanced up. Twin lamps blazed toward them from the back entrance. Seth slammed the pedal to the floor. The Cougar surged, roared past the last three cars in the lot, and shot out into the street.

Another set of lights, the ones from the second Mercedes he'd seen in his mind's eye, penetrated Miriam's window on a collision course. They would have collided too—broadside at thirty miles an hour—if Seth had kept his cool and yanked the wheel around to escape. The change in direction would have slowed the Cougar enough for the onrushing car to end things right there. But Seth didn't turn—he froze like a crash-test dummy behind the wheel, unable to move as he should have.

The Cougar flew across the street in a fly of sparks, missed a parked car on the passenger's side by inches, pounded over the curb with enough force to bend both rims, and roared over the lawn of the UC Berkeley Art Museum.

"Turn! Turn, turn!" Miriam yelled.

They were zeroing in on a thick maple. Seth regained control of the beast and spun the wheel. The Cougar laid a broad swipe of the lawn bare and shot onto Durant Avenue, where Seth managed to swing the car into the right lane.

But now the Mercedes was on Durant as well, back on his tail.

"Hold on, baby! Ha!"

Seth floored the Cougar, and the 454 accelerated with

enough power to force their heads back into the seats. He was terrified; the cold sweat on his neck said so clearly enough. But he was also alive, wasn't he? Really alive. Like being airborne in a twenty-foot wave with foam roaring two feet overhead. He'd almost forgotten why he loved surfing. Danger. Clive Masters might have been onto something after all.

Miriam whimpered. She twisted in her seat, saw the pursuit.

"Faster!"

"We have a red light—"

"Drive faster! Faster."

"Faster," he repeated and nailed the throttle. They split the intersection of Durant and Bowditch at a good sixty miles an hour. The Mercedes slowed for the light and then crept through.

"Fast enough?"

She didn't respond.

By the time they reached Shattuck, the Mercedes' lights were weaving in and out of view. By the time they hit Interstate 80, the lights were gone.

They headed south, and Seth had no idea where they were going. They just headed south.

"They're gone," Seth said.

She looked back. "Yes."

"Now what?"

She looked over at him, face white. "Maybe they will come again."

"Maybe you should tell me why they want you," he said.

"Maybe you should tell me how you know they want me," she said.

How he knew? He didn't have the faintest idea. But that didn't matter. What did matter was that he had known. He couldn't shake the thought that he was meant to be here, riding down the freeway with a woman named Miriam from Saudi Arabia.

And even if he wasn't necessarily meant to be here, in some strange way he wanted to be. Because she needed him; because he had just felt his blood flowing, really flowing, for the first time in years; because his mind had pulled a couple of very cool tricks back there for the third time in three days.

And then there was the fiasco that awaited him at the Faculty Club.

Yes, he belonged here. At least for the moment.

"You first," he said.

# 12

HILAL STARED OUT the floor-to-ceiling windows of the Hyatt Regency's twenty-third floor, overlooking the millions of lights along the San Francisco Bay. A strange blend of emotions crowded his chest—the same as every time he visited the United States—a mixture of excitement and sadness that left him empty. Somehow Europe and Asia were different. He'd seen plenty of large cities full of excess, beginning with Riyadh, which in many ways bled more exorbitance than the rest put together. If the princes were known for anything, it was spending money. No, it wasn't the wealth boasted by San Francisco's coastline that bothered Hilal.

It was the unlimited freedom of every citizen to bask in this wealth that bothered him. Nowhere else in the world did as many individuals have as much as in America. In most countries the wealthy paid the price of personal freedom with rules.

But here, the people enjoyed both immense wealth and unparalleled freedom. The combination made America unique among nations. The mutawa might accuse him of straying from the edicts of the Prophet and acquiescing to the infidels for such a statement, and in some ways they would be right.

Unfortunately, only a few truly understood that Saudi Arabia faced political extinction if she did not adapt to the changing world. Fortunately, King Abdullah was one of those.

Hilal turned from the window and poured himself a scotch. It felt good to be in a country where he didn't have to break the law to do what he did normally. He threw the drink back and swallowed.

A black nine-millimeter Browning Hi-Power lay beside the briefcase on the bed. His contact had delivered the weapon to him an hour earlier with a few other items he'd requested. Another benefit of freedom.

Six hours earlier he'd arrived and learned that the sheik's daughter had fled Berkeley. Sorting out the details of what transpired at the university had not been easy. Evidently, two Arabic men had passed themselves off as Hilal and an embassy associate and attempted to take her. This meant that someone else valued the woman as much as the king did and knew Hilal was on his way to collect her.

To his way of thinking, there was only one reason any Saudi assassin would go to such lengths to intercept Miriam. They needed her for their own gain. There was only one way to gain from a woman, and that was through marriage. The mixing of bloodlines.

Someone sought Sheik Abu al-Asamm's allegiance. Which meant that someone wanted power over the king.

But who? Who would know of his trip and the woman's whereabouts?

Wouldn't it be ironic if the kingdom's fate was decided by a woman rather than a man? Of course, a single bullet to her head would decide everything.

The shrill sound of the hotel phone interrupted his thoughts, and he picked it up. "Yes."

"Good evening, Hilal."

"General Mustafa. It would be best for me to call you on your cell phone. I've taken care of security. Every six hours, as requested by the king."

"Of course."

Hilal paused. His first call to Saudi Arabia had been directly to the king, but he couldn't interrupt Abdullah every six hours to update him on this mess. General Mustafa was a blood brother to the king and the head of intelligence. If they couldn't trust him, they could trust no one.

"She escaped with an American—Seth Border, a student," Hilal said.

"So, the authorities are cooperating."

"Locally, yes. I'm scheduled to meet with the State Department tomorrow afternoon in Los Angeles. Meanwhile, the local police have begun a search for the car. We believe she's headed south. Several complaints were called in from other motorists. Evidently the man thinks he's in a race car."

"Don't all Americans?" The general chuckled.

Hilal found no humor in the statement. "The police say they will have the car by morning. With any luck I will be on a plane back to Riyadh tomorrow night."

"Good. Then this should be a simple matter."

"Perhaps. She managed to escape the two men who tried to intercept her."

There was a pause. "Will you track them?"

"I have a car; I have a police scanner. Freedom has its advantages, General. I'll call back in six hours."

Hilal hung up the phone, picked up his briefcase, checked the room by habit, and left for the garage.


KHALID SPOKE SOFTLY into the secure phone line. "Those idiots were your men. And now an American helps her?"

Omar leaned back in his chair and said nothing.

"The fact that Hilal himself has gone means the king suspects something."

"The king always suspects something. His days are numbered and he knows it."

Silence.

"Who is this American?" Khalid asked.

"Seth Border," Omar said, shifting the receiver to his opposite ear. "A student. That's all my men were able to learn before they left the scene. Evidently the police showed up in some force."

"That would be Hilal's doing. By now he's working with the authorities."

Omar sighed inaudibly. In the end, men like his father always depended on men like him, didn't they? On killers and enforcers of the law. True strength was always wielded by the sword. Even the Prophet had known that.

Khalid took a deep breath. "You will need to marry her in America if you can," he said. "With Hilal involved, bringing her back could be a problem. And if she does not cooperate, then she must be silenced."

"Killed."

"We can't have her telling the world stories. General

Mustafa called ten minutes ago," Khalid said. "Hilal called him. They've already identified the American's car and expect to take Miriam into custody by morning. She's headed south."

"There's no question about Mustafa's loyalty?"

"No."

"How often will Hilal call him?"

"Every six hours. We will know what he knows before the king does."

"I'll call from New York; if there's any change, I'll make necessary adjustments." Omar paused. "In the meantime you should prepare the sheik for the worst. We need his loyalty even if his daughter is killed."

Khalid snorted. "You are telling me how to arrange my business now?"

Omar ended the call.

# 13

MIRIAM SAT IN the speeding Cougar and watched the endless string of oncoming headlights. They'd spent an hour speculating who was after her and what course would be best for them.

They'd made their way south on Interstate 5 toward Los Angeles. Although they saw no indication that authorities were in pursuit, Seth insisted that the farther they traveled from Berkeley, the safer they would be. Judging by the labyrinth of freeways and endless lines of cars, Miriam didn't believe anyone had a hope of finding them.

After a flurry of discussion, Seth settled into an introspective state, drifting between deep thought and filling her in on America, as it really was, he said.

They stopped once for petrol. He gave her a short tour of the gas station, explaining what the different candies were and why he preferred the red licorice strips over the black ones and why mixing a fruit drink with candy for health reasons made no sense because the candy was bad enough on its own. So were most of the nuts.

They came out with two tall bottles of cold Dr Pepper, two bags of red licorice, and two bags of beef jerky, which he assured her was just as hard on the body as the other "junk" they had purchased. Consistency seemed important to him.

She assured him that she knew most of this—not only had she spent a summer in California while attending Berkeley, she had made several trips to European cities and read a thousand magazines published in the West. Still, he did have a unique perspective.

Seth took advantage of the stop to change out of his suit and into a pair of black corduroys and a faded orange T-shirt, which seemed to loosen him up considerably. She had no such option. The white dress was holding up well enough, but the disparity in their dress made her an inappropriate companion for this bold man.

Miriam finally decided that Seth should know the whole truth of her predicament. It took another hour to tell him of the events that led up to her leaving Saudi Arabia—all of them, including Sita's drowning.

"So you were forced to watch?" Seth asked, horrified. "Omar was making a point? How can anyone..." His voice faded and he closed his eyes for a moment, furious.

"Now you see why I fled?"

He faced her, and for a second she thought he was going to challenge her. But then his face softened. "I'm sorry. That's a terrible thing to have to see." He shook his head. "I can't imagine what the girl's mother must be going through."

"They must be part of the Nizari sect. But she is still

a mother who lost a fifteen-year-old daughter at her husband's own hand. Her devotion is beyond me."

Seth stared at the road and swallowed. Her savior had his soft side. Or were such displays patently American?

"Americans have easy lives," she said, looking away.

"You think so? Not all Americans. Have you ever been slapped around by your father?"

"I've received my share of beatings."

"Not a week went by that I wasn't beaten by my father when I was a child."

"You?" She felt surprisingly appalled by his admission. She'd never imagined mistreatment in America.

"I didn't mean to fish for pity. Never mind."

"I tell you about Sita and you tell me never mind?" she asked.

He considered that for a moment. "My father was an alcoholic, and despite his frequent repentance, he habitually abused my mother and me. My childhood was pretty ugly."

"I'm sorry. Please forgive me."

"It's okay. I can't complain." He forced a grin. "I may not be the most well-adjusted human being you'll meet, but I know how to count my blessings. Not being born in Saudi Arabia, for starters."

"Ha! I don't think you understand. You would do well in my country."

"That's right, I forgot. I'm a man, right?"

"You forgot your gender? Perhaps you're really a woman in disguise."

He smiled, breaking the tension for the moment. Silence filled the car, and they traveled south for a while without feeling the need to break it.

It occurred to Miriam that for the first time, she was traveling America the American way, with an American. Despite the danger in their wake, the adventure of racing down the highway with a true-blooded American was thrilling. At the same time, the fact that the American was indeed a man triggered conflicting emotions. She had never been alone with a male stranger, much less stuck in a car with him for many hours.

The dash lights highlighted Seth's profile—a smooth jaw and blond hair that was decidedly messier now than when she first met him. His ragged features appealed to her on some fundamental, earthy level. He possessed the kind of air she'd expect of a free-willed spirit: handsome, yet purposefully detached from his own charm, an intelligent enigma. Despite his graceless moves back in the restroom, this man had a quick mind.

Miriam removed her stare and smiled, thinking of their narrow escape from the university.

"What?" he asked.

"Nothing," she said.

"That's not a nothing smile. That's a boy, isn't he a strange one smile."

"You think you know women so well that you understand their thoughts with a glance?"

"Maybe."

"Maybe I should slip a veil on. I feel naked here with you reading my mind."

That gave him pause. How many men had seen her face well enough to judge her thoughts? Very few.

"A princess with an exceptional wit," Seth said.

"When you look at my face, do you like what you see?" Miriam asked.

He cleared his throat. "What do you mean?"

"Not so many men have seen my face. It seems to have made enough of an impact on you to influence your assessment of my thoughts. I'm just asking if you see anything else in it." She took no small pleasure in throwing a man of such intellect off guard.

"Yes." He avoided her eyes and glanced in the side mirror although there were no cars behind them at the moment. "You're a woman. A princess. Remember?"

"I've seen more than one princess who would only look appealing next to a toad. On a good day." She looked at the road. "You'll forgive me, but in my country an unmarried woman doesn't hear that she is beautiful. I think a woman is born with a desire to hear that she is beautiful, don't you?"

"Yes. Well... yes. I think so. Sure. Makes sense. Innate desire for the sake of the perpetuation of the species."

She glanced at him. "I never thought of it in such... scientific terms," she said.

"No. Sorry, that's not what I meant. It seems reasonable."

"Perhaps it's more a matter of love than reason," she said. "Have you ever been in love?"

"Love? Love as in what kind of love?"

"Evidently not. Love, as in I would give anything to be in Samir's arms right now, hearing him whisper my name and telling me how beautiful I am. Love."

"Samir?"

"Yes. Samir. The driver I told you about."

"You're in love with him?" He grinned a little. "So while people in high places are plotting your marriage, you're secretly in love with another man. A forbidden man."

"Yes. Desperately," she said.

"Desperately in love with a forbidden man. A princess with enough backbone to defy tradition."

She laughed, delighted at his assessment. He possessed an uncanny sense of her country, as if he'd lived there himself, even though he insisted his understanding came only from books.

Seth cleared his throat again. "Where I come from, a man in love with a woman in danger would rescue her. So where is Samir?"

Miriam's joy disintegrated. "What do you mean? He can't come after me! They'd kill him!"

"That wouldn't stop a man in love."

"And you know this?" she mocked. "He doesn't even know where I've gone. When it's safe, he will come out for me; I can promise you that. In the end, nothing will separate us."

She faced her side window and thought about the way Samir had looked at her when he made his promise. What if he had left Saudi Arabia in search of her? What if at this moment he was in San Francisco, wanting to protect her? What was she doing running with this wild man? Six hours earlier he'd barged into the lavatory and kidnapped her because of some strange vision that he refused to explain. And now she was trapped in a roaring car with him. What if Seth was actually an American agent working with Omar?

"Sorry. I was just asking."

She closed her eyes. Slow down, Miriam. Seth is your protector. He's as innocent as you. Without him, you would be at their mercy.

Her mind filled with a flurry of images. Omar, Salman,

the sheik, Samir, Sultana. Dear Sultana. Where are you, Samir? What had she started? It had taken her enemies exactly two days to catch up to her in Berkeley.

"What are we going to do?" she asked.

He didn't answer.

"Please, Seth, perhaps we should go back to San Francisco. What if Samir is there? I've never been anywhere outside of San Francisco. What are you going to do, just drop me off at a bus stop in Los Angeles and expect that I will find my way back?"

"Don't worry, I'm not going to drop you off at a bus stop."

"Then what?"

"I'm not sure."

She spread her hands, palms up, then let them fall to her lap. "You're driving me to nowhere without a plan? Maybe you should let me out of the car."

"At the next bus stop?"

He had a point.

"Look, I didn't exactly plan on rescuing a princess today. Forgive me if I don't have my handy-dandy Ten Most Efficient Strategies to Deliver a Distressed Princess to Safety handbook in my back pocket. Maybe if you'd given me some notice."

She stared at him, her mind sorting through his jargon. She understood the higher meaning if not the literal one: He was as lost as she and covered his insecurity with this wit of his.

"That doesn't mean I don't have any ideas," he said. "I'm sure there are people who handle this sort of thing for a living at the State Department. I'm assuming their offices are closed at the moment. I'll call them as soon as the sun breaks the horizon. In the meantime, going back toward San Francisco would not be smart; there are people back there who don't like you, remember? And before you forget, I'm as much a hostage to this situation as you are. These people are after you, not me."

She couldn't disagree with his thinking. In some ways his ironclad logic reminded her of Sultana. Sultana should consider leaving the kingdom to marry this man. They would make a deserving pair.

"You're right. I'm sorry. I've been through more than I'd planned in the last few days."

"No, really, it's okay."

"You're really here because of the vision you had?" she said. "If not for the vision, you would be home?"

"I didn't say it was a vision."

"You refuse to call it anything. So I'm calling it a vision. You saw a man coming for me in the bathroom. Where I come from, we would call that a vision from God."

"Of course. Muhammad was famous for his visions."

"You're insulting the Prophet? This is the broad American mind?"

He paused. "I'm sorry. Really, I'm not trying to be disrespectful."

She humphed. "You should examine something more closely before speaking so flippantly."

"I've read the Koran."

"When?"

"Most recently? Two, two and a half years ago. I even memorized most of it, sura for sura, by age twenty-one. Certain things tend to lock themselves in my mind, poetic abstractions being chief among them. As you know, the Koran is very poetic."

He'd memorized the Koran? "You can't possibly understand Islam, living here in America."

"Actually, I know this may sound arrogant, and I apologize in advance, but I think I understand both Christianity and Islam quite well. They have a surprising amount in common."

"They are like black and white!"

"Both claim that there is one God, an all-knowing Creator, which is where I part company. Both believe that Jesus was born of a virgin and was sinless. Both believe that the writings of Moses, David, the prophets, and the Gospels were divinely inspired."

"And perhaps you've read a bad translation of the Koran. A twisted English version."

"Actually, I read and understand Arabic. Language is like mathematics—both come easy to me."

He understood Arabic? She spoke a sentence in Arabic.

He answered in English. "Yes, most Westerners do have difficulty with Arabic. And really, forgive me for taking Islam to task, but to question is the nature of man, right? Every religion has its place. Christianity has its place; Islam has its place. They hold societies together and answer man's unanswered questions and such. But I reject both on philosophical grounds. I'm not ready to attribute my so-called 'visions' to religion."

"So then. Why are you here, Seth Border?"

He hesitated. "I'm here because I saw the future."

"But you won't call it a vision. What is the difference?"

"I'm not sure. I just wanted to make the distinction. Just because we don't understand how something works doesn't mean we have to credit some deity. The world was once flat because religious people said it was flat, remember? Have you ever considered the possibility that time is the same way? It's a dimension that we don't understand, so when someone sees now what happens later, he's stepping beyond that dimension. It may be as simple as that."

"Simple? Oh, I see. How silly of me. Then at least tell me what stepping beyond a dimension feels like. Indulge me."

Seth's tone turned self-conscious, she thought. "I'm not saying that's necessarily what happened. I'm just telling you that it might have been what happened. It's possible."

"Then tell me."

He ran his fingers through his curly blond locks. "You ever been in a dream that feels real?"

"Yes."

"It felt like that. But so fast that it didn't interrupt anything I was seeing in the present." He paused. "Make sense?"

"Sounds like a vision," she said.

"But different," he said.

They drove in silence for a long time after that. Miriam lost herself in comforting thoughts of Saudi Arabia—the best of her beloved homeland. The beaches of Jidda, the sands of the desert, the palaces shimmering with wealth. In some ways it wasn't so bad to be a woman with the run of a palace, was it, veil or no veil? Sultana would slap her for even thinking it.

For the first time since her whirlwind escape, Miriam felt lonely. For Haya and for Sita and for Sultana. For Samir.

Dear God, what had she done?

Seth exited the interstate and pulled into an empty parking lot at two a.m., suggesting they get some rest. Sleep came almost before she closed her eyes.

. . .

WARM SUN ON her face awoke Miriam. She sat up groggily, searching her memory for where she might be. A car door slammed and she looked right. A large man was walking from a white Jeep. He glanced her way as he headed toward a building to the far left of where they—

Seth! He was gone.

No. He was walking toward the car, hands in his pockets, hair in his eyes. The wild man who had memorized the Koran and stepped beyond dimensions of time.

He opened his door and plopped into the seat. "Morning, Miriam. Sleep well?"

"Well enough. You don't look like you slept at all."

"Never could sleep in a car." He shrugged. "I got some."

"Where are we?"

"Two hours this side of Los Angeles. Twenty minutes outside of Santa Clarita."

She just looked at him, lost.

"I called a friend of mine back at the campus," he said. "Dr. Harland. The closest thing I have to a real father." Seth grinned and shook his head. "Boy, did we cause a ruckus. He said the place was crawling with cops within half an hour."

"Did your friend help you?"

"Yes. It seems the police know about you. He told them he thought I might call. They suggested that we go to the State Department in Los Angeles. Someone will be there to take you into protective custody. An old acquaintance of mine from the NSA—Clive Masters. Small world. But I'm pretty sure we can trust Clive. I guess we're supposed to be there at eleven o'clock."

She furrowed her brow. "Why should we trust anyone?"

"This isn't Saudi Arabia, Miriam. This is the place where people like you escape from oppressive governments."

"And what if the police turn me over to authorities from my country? You can imagine what they'll do to me. Think of Sita."

"Why would they turn you over if you tell them what you've told me? Besides, we're not going to the police; we're going to the State Department. The whole point is that you're seeking asylum."

She just looked at him.

Seth averted his eyes. "Harland and Clive won't lie to us. If they do, I'll get you out."

"How?"

"I can always use the bathroom trick."

He grinned and she smiled despite her anxiousness. His demeanor had changed, she thought. His eyes didn't hold hers with as much confidence as they had last night. He looked at her several times, but then glanced away.

"I think you'll be safe, Miriam. Besides, unless you've got some other brilliant plan, I can't think of any better alternative. We can't just take off across the country like Bonnie and Clyde."

She cast him a questioning glance.

"Bonnie and Clyde? Two famous . . . lovers, fugitives?" He looked away again. "Old story. You said you had some money on you. You mind me asking how much?"

"Five," she said.

"And I've got ten. I was thinking you could use a change of clothes, but I guess we'll have to make do."

"Clothing! That's a wonderful idea. There's a store nearby?"

"Santa Clarita. But fifteen dollars isn't going to buy us food and clothes."

"Fifteen dollars? I said that I have five thousand."

He looked at her sideways. "Five *thousand*?"

"Yes. I didn't want to leave Hillary's house without some change."

"Okay. Change is good. Well then, we'll just have to go shopping, won't we?"

"Yes, that would be good."

Miriam ran her fingers through her hair and then twisted the rearview mirror to look at her face.

"The bathroom's in there," he said, nodding at the building. "To the left of the entrance."

"Thank you." She opened the door.

"Hurry back."

"I will."

Five minutes later they pulled back onto the freeway and headed south. She asked Seth if she could listen to the radio, and he obliged her with a tour of the airwaves. He did seem to know music. Watching him enthusiastically expound on why Frank Sinatra and a band called Metallica were really cut from the same cloth, she was once again struck by his strange appeal. A kind of appeal that brought to mind his reference to that Bonnie and Clyde.

The mall in Santa Clarita was still closed when they arrived, but Seth insisted the twenty-four-hour Wal-Mart across the street would work just fine. Same basic clothes, but with different labels for different folks, he said. Most of the threads probably came out of the same factories.

He parked in a near-empty lot and walked her through the doors of the huge store.

"Ladies' clothes up twenty-three paces and to the right five paces, across from photography and this side of lingerie," he said. "All Wal-Marts follow one of several basic footprints, and this one I know. I'm going to the left, where I hope to find a couple of toothbrushes and some paste for whitening the teeth and refreshing the breath."

She looked at him. It wasn't that she didn't understand; it was that his choice of words took her an extra second to process.

"Is that okay?" he asked.

She glanced up the aisles. "You're going to leave me alone? What if I get lost?"

"You won't. If you do, ask someone in a blue vest where the checkout counters are. Trust me, you'll be fine."

She hesitated. It wasn't like she'd never shopped before. "Okay."

He walked several paces before turning back. "And for the record, I'd go with the blue jeans and the white top any day over a dress. Considering our situation, that is."

She stared at him, taken aback. "How did you know I was considering blue jeans or a dress?"

"You were considering that?"

"Exactly that. Nothing more."

"Hmm."

"Now you're seeing into my closet? What else can you see?"

"I'm not seeing into your closet. I'm not really sure what I saw."

"But you did see something?"

He hesitated, as if just coming to the realization himself. "Yeah, I guess I did."

Seth turned and ambled toward the pharmacy. They walked out together twenty minutes later, Seth holding a bag of toiletries and another bottle of Dr Pepper, and Miriam dressed in blue jeans and a white blouse.

# 14

HILAL DROVE SOUTH in the Hertz Mercedes, tuned to the scanner, thoughts drifting while the police tightened their net.

They failed to locate the Cougar, but the American, Seth, had used his Texaco gas card at a station near Kettleman City. He was indeed headed south. They had passed Santa Clarita and were headed into the maze of freeways that covered the Los Angeles basin like a spiderweb.

He reached up and tested the scanner, which had remained silent for a few minutes. Static sounded, indicating a clear signal. A new Kenworth tractor-trailer rumbled past on his left, hauling three large Caterpillar generators to some destination where they would no doubt provide power to some free individual. Personal freedom. America had been built on the notion that the individual's rights were supreme, despite the slow erosion of those rights in recent years.

Perhaps America and Saudi Arabia would one day hold a limited variety of personal freedom in common.

Although King Abdullah wasn't ready to open up his palaces to the average citizen, he understood the power of freedom more than most in Saudi Arabia. The militant extremists, on the other hand, would negate personal freedom in the name of the Prophet and use a sword to enforce their beliefs. A terrible shame.

The world had changed. In his humble opinion, unless Saudi Arabia changed with it, she would be washed into the seas of history. He hoped to protect the kingdom from just that. And if doing so required the death of one woman named Miriam, so be it. Not that he had any intention of killing her at this point. She was, after all, royalty.

Hilal sighed. It was a complicated world.

The scanner burped to life. "Units near 5 and Balboa respond to a possible sighting of a vehicle matching the description of a brown Cougar on the bulletin. Sky reported vehicle exiting the freeway, westbound on Balboa."

Balboa. The exit was directly ahead.

Hilal glanced in his mirror and eased the Mercedes into the right lane. His pulse quickened. So his gamble had paid off.

The scanner squawked again. "Copy 512. Will take that. We're ten miles south on 5. There's not much out there past the truck stop."

A short silence. Hilal sped under a sign that told him the Balboa exit was one mile off.

"Confirm. Looks like the truck stop. Sky's headed south and will be out of visual shortly. What's your ETA?"

"Give me fifteen minutes."

"Fifteen minutes, over."

Hilal instinctively felt for the bulge in his jacket and touched the gun's cold steel. He had fifteen minutes.

THE ISOLATED TRUCK stop sat on the north side of Balboa, roughly three hundred yards from the highway in the center of a dusty dirt parking lot. The dry, vacant setting did not match any notion she had of what balmy California was supposed to be.

"You haven't experienced America until you've sat in a smoky truck-stop diner and choked down their greasy hash browns," Seth said.

"How long will it take to reach the State Department?" Miriam asked. It was now eight o'clock.

"Two hours. We have an hour to burn." They climbed from the car. "Let's eat some grease," he said, winking.

They walked to the dining room through a dim hall lined with video games and pinball machines. The gentle odor of grilled bacon and eggs filled the place. A woman wearing a red-checkered apron smacked some chewing gum as she approached.

"Two?" she said.

"Two," Seth replied.

The woman seated them in a booth that faced the parking lot. Seth's brown Cougar sat next to a dilapidated Toyota Corona, body rusted by the salty ocean air of the coast. Otherwise, the lot was empty. Miriam scanned the menu. The loneliness she'd felt last night had fled. Their new plan and the promise of a hot meal reestablished her good mood. Only a few days ago she'd been standing in the souk with Sultana, hiding behind a veil, plotting her unlikely escape. Now she sat across from an American named Seth, trying to choose between the greasy hash browns and the banana splits on the back cover. If Samir would come to America, she was sure they could build a good life together in this country.

She looked up and saw that Seth was watching her.

"So. What do you want?" he asked.

"The hash browns are potatoes?"

"Shredded and fried."

"You recommend them?"

"I do."

She smiled at him. "Then I want hash browns."

"Me too." He set aside his menu.

"You are very fortunate, Seth Border."

"Why's that?"

"To live in such a beautiful, clean country."

"Don't let the trees fool you, my dear. I hear there are goblins in the forest." He grinned, as if embarrassed. His colorful way was only part of America's charm, she thought.

"And by this you mean what?"

"Well, actually, I was just making an offhand comment that behind the plastic smiles you see everywhere, I promise you'll find greasy mugs that will make the hash browns you are about to eat seem dry by comparison. The ugly side of human nature is not exclusive to the third world."

"So are most Americans criminal?"

"No. But in the plastics department, I'm sure we have the edge."

"Plastic. As in fake," she said. "You are a cynical man; has anyone told you that?" Seth shrugged. "Excuse me," she said, sliding out. "I would like to freshen up."

"Back in the hall next to the pinball machines," he said, pointing behind her.

SETH WATCHED HER walk toward the hall, dressed in her new carpenter's jeans and white shirt, and could not deny the strange feelings that had overtaken him during their drive south. He was attracted to her, but beyond her obvious beauty, why? In an uncommon way they were the same, Miriam and he. They were both misfits in their own worlds, rebels with their causes. In other ways they were different—from separate planets altogether. He had no business feeling anything toward her beyond what a good Samaritan might feel.

Yet here he sat, his belly light and his pulse on edge. He couldn't remember ever feeling so taken by any woman in his entire life.

She disappeared into the hall and Seth picked up his coffee cup. The notion that she was a princess on the run from some sinister characters seemed like something he might read in a book. Rapunzel, Rapunzel, let down your hair. But the events of last evening were nothing out of a book. He would deliver her to safety in a few hours and then . . .

And then he didn't quite know what.

He took another sip of coffee and looked out into the parking lot. A black Mercedes had parked at the far end of the building. He yawned. The lack of sleep was starting to catch up to him. Before he did anything, he would have to sleep. Deliver Miriam to safety and then—

A man with black hair was shooting Miriam in the bathroom. The image struck Seth and he jerked upright.

It deposited itself in his mind, like a foregone conclusion, without reasoning.

The scenario immobilized Seth. Had this just happened? Or was he seeing into the future again?

A second scene popped into his mind next to the first one. Now there was a man in the bathroom standing over two bodies. One of the bodies was Miriam's and one was his. Both were dead. The twin realities lodged in his mind, static. He saw the waitress approach in his peripheral image, slow motion. She was saying something.

A third image. He was in the bathroom standing next to Miriam, facing the Arab. A policeman stood in the doorway. He blinked.

In the first scene he wasn't present and Miriam was dead. In the second he was present but the police officer wasn't, and they were both dead.

In the third...

Seth scrambled from the table and tore for the hall. The waitress backpedaled to avoid a collision. He had to get into the bathroom. What he'd just seen wasn't the future, but three possible futures! He couldn't explain it any other way. And the only future in which Miriam lived was the one in which he was in the bathroom with the officer.

Of course, the only future in which he ended up dead was the one in which he was in the bathroom. If he didn't enter the bathroom, he would live. He knew that like he knew the theory of relativity.

He was seeing possible futures. More than one. Three different outcomes, depending on who entered that bathroom. Could he influence which future became the real future? Or was that power in the hands of others?

For the second time in less than a day, Seth slammed

his way into the ladies' room. He pulled up, panting and sweating. Miriam stood to his left, her face white and stricken. A skinny Arab with sharp features stood opposite her, gun in hand.

For a brief moment, neither of them moved. Seth couldn't go after the Arab, of course. The man had a gun. Without seeing it move, Seth found the gun pointed in his face.

"Lock the door," the man said.

Seth wasn't sure he could turn to lock the door. His muscles had frozen.

"Lock it!"

The crack of the man's voice jerked Seth back to reality. He turned, twisted the dead bolt, and faced them again.

The Arab shifted the gun back to Miriam and spoke in Arabic. "Tell me whom you were to marry? If you think I won't kill you because this man has stumbled in here, you're as big a fool as he. Tell me."

"You're the head of security. Hilal. I recognize—"

"Tell me!" the man screamed.

Hilal's nose was sharp enough to pass for an ax, and his cheekbones pressed against his skin like knives.

"You are frightened, Miriam? I can understand. You are a Saudi Arabian citizen, and your actions in this plot threaten the life of our king. For that you will die. You cannot run from me. You've been gone for only three days and already I've found you."

Miriam wilted against the stalls, no longer the self-assured woman Seth had come to know during their flight from the Bay. She believed this man.

"If you tell me who is behind this, the king might find it in his heart to overlook your flight."

"I'm running from the marriage. Not from the king."

"Then you have nothing to fear. Tell me who's plotting with Sheik Al-Asamm."

Hilal would kill them both. Seth had already seen that much, and the knowledge turned his muscles to lead. The only future he'd seen in which they both survived was the one with the policeman in the doorway. But what control did he have over the police arriving?

And then another future dropped into his mind like a piece of the sky, falling: A police cruiser. An officer slumped over the wheel of his cruiser, dead. Miriam toppled in the rear seat, dead. "What?" he stammered. Both Miriam and Hilal looked at him.

It was an involuntary note of surprise, not a question, but he continued because it seemed that they expected him to. He spoke in English.

"If there's no Miriam, there is no marriage, regardless of who's behind it. As long as she has information you want, she's more valuable alive than dead. So she won't tell you who's plotting with the sheik, right?"

The man stared at him. "He speaks Arabic?" he asked Miriam, still speaking Arabic.

She didn't respond.

Hilal switched to English. "So you are as intelligent as they say you are. And quite perceptive. But like so many Americans, too brave for your own good. What do you suppose I'm going to do with you now? Hmm? Do you know who is behind this marriage?"

A small idea came to Seth. A very small one, like the light seeping past the hinges of a locked door.

"You're planning to kill me," he said. "I know too much. And I would be a witness to your murder of Miriam. But you have three problems. The first is that Miriam's death will come back to haunt you. There's more to this story than you know. If she dies, Sheik Abu Ali al-Asamm will be freed from his bond with the monarchy. That may not seem like an insurmountable problem in your mind, but it will be, I can promise you that."

He let that drop and watched the man's blank stare. There was no truth to his words, but they had their intended effect of confusing the man. Seth continued before he had the time to lose his nerve.

"The second problem you have is that the police are on the way. Even if you pulled the trigger now, I'm not sure you'd have the time to get your big black Mercedes down the road before they cut you off. And your third problem is that neither Miriam nor I am in a hurry to die. In fact, you have us pretty much terrified here. See? So we're going to use every trick you've ever thought of and a few you haven't to throw you off. You're already having difficulty deciding what is a trick and what is not a trick. Am I right?"

The man still had not moved.

"You're—"

"Mostly you are a trick." The man reached into his breast pocket and pulled out a small black cylinder. A silencer. He began to screw it onto the barrel of his pistol. "There are many things you clearly don't know, or you wouldn't waste your breath with empty threats. I have diplomatic immunity, and I'm dealing with a fugitive subject to our justice system. The police are powerless to arrest me, you fool."

True. This guy could kill Miriam and walk out untouched. Seth had to stall the man. He'd seen a future in which both he and Miriam survived, at least up until the point the police showed up. He had to assume that the futures were possible futures and that he could influence which one actually happened.

"I can see the future, Hilal," Seth said.

The man tightened the silencer. "Very good." He faced Miriam. "I'll give you one last chance to tell me. If it's true that you have no argument against our king, then you will reveal his enemies. Your silence only proves your guilt."

"Please, stop being an idiot and put that thing down," Seth said. What on earth was he saying? "I've seen the future and you don't kill us here. You're not that stupid. You may be able to walk into restrooms with a bazooka and blow people away at will in your country, but this is the United States, my friend. Now lay the iron down and let's negotiate terms of surrender here. How much money will you give me?"

"I'm offering you your life, not money, you imbecile!"

"Exactly. But as I said, neither of us is eager to die. Maybe for some dough we would be willing to spill the beans. All we really want is to live together happily ever after. Miriam came to the land of the free to find herself a real man, and God has smiled on her. Let us go with a million dollars each, and I personally will tell you exactly who's plotting against your king and how he plans to do it."

The gun wavered in the killer's hand. Hilal's right eye twitched and Seth knew he was going to pull the trigger. The exchange had bought them a few minutes, but Seth had made one true remark: This man with the sharp nose was far from stupid.

Seth's body felt as though it were on fire. He was trapped somewhere between full-fledged panic and a dead faint. But he had to move, and he had to move now. So he forced himself to do the only thing that came to mind in that moment.

He walked up to Hilal and slapped his face with an open palm.

"Stop this!" Seth said. "Don't be a fool!"

Hilal's eyes widened.

It occurred to Seth, sweating before the killer, that he had just signed his own death warrant. Hilal's gun was still trained on Miriam, but at any moment it would swing his way and a slug would smash through his chest.

"I can give you what you want," Seth said, "but you have to stop pretending to be Rambo here."

The color flooded back into Hilal's face, which twisted into fury. He swung his gun around.

"Police!"

Someone pounded on the door.

"Police, open up!"

With a practiced flip of his wrist, Hilal spun off the silencer and slipped both it and the gun into his breast pockets. "You will be sorry for this," he said.

Then, as if this were an everyday event, he stepped behind Seth, twisted the lock, and opened the door. "Thank God, you are here," he said. "I kept them as long as I could."

A state trooper stood with one hand on the butt of his gun, taking visual inventory. "Is everything okay here?"

The fear that had gripped Seth only moments before turned to terror. He'd seen the trooper before. In his mind's eye. Dead. With Miriam dead behind him.

"You're Miriam and you're Seth?" the trooper asked.

"Yes," Miriam said.

"You're going to have to come with me. There's a warrant out for your arrests." The trooper looked at Hilal. "Who are you?"

Hilal pulled out a small wallet and flipped it open. "I'm the legal guardian of this woman, on assignment from King Abdullah of Saudi Arabia. I would be grateful if you would take her into custody immediately. We've wasted enough time."

"I don't care how much time you think you've wasted. I wasn't told a thing about meeting you here..."

The trooper kept talking, but Seth heard nothing else. Another outcome to this scenario had dropped into his mind. Another possible future. Then two futures. Then six, all at once, like a string of posters, each one different.

Then a hundred possible outcomes, a barrage of the unseen, seen now by him.

Miriam survived the next ten minutes in only one of them.

Hilal was talking to the cop now, smooth and cooperative.

Seth shoved a shaking hand into his pocket, wrapped his fingers around the Super Ball he carried by habit, and stepped forward.

"Where do you think you're going?" the cop asked as Seth barged toward him.

"I'm coming to be arrested," Seth said.

He stepped through the doorway and spun around to present his arms behind his back. Halfway through the spin he removed the ball from his pocket and released it. He wasn't sure how he knew precisely when to release it;

he only knew that if he did, it would roll just so toward the diner.

And it did.

Seth now faced Miriam, whose wide eyes questioned Seth. Hilal smiled softly, just inside the door to his right.

"Just walk to the car peacefully," the cop said. "I'm not gonna use cuffs. Ma'am, if you'll please come with—"

A scream ripped through the air, followed by a hollow thud and the horrendous crash of shattering plates.

"Call an ambulance!" someone cried from the diner. "Hurry!"

The cop took a single step in the direction of the diner before stopping himself. But Seth was already on the move. Without warning he stepped into Hilal and gave him a hard shove. The Arab backpedaled and slammed into a stall door, which sprang open, accepting his flailing body.

Before Hilal hit the toilet, Seth had Miriam's hand in his. "Run!"

She let him lead her through the bathroom door, right past the cop, who was palming his gun.

"Stop!" the officer yelled.

"Run! He won't shoot us," Seth said.

They crashed through the exit doors and sprinted for the Cougar. Thank goodness it wasn't valuable enough to lock. Seth threw Miriam's door open and managed to climb across the passenger seat before the cop made an appearance at the door, weapon trained on the Cougar.

"Stop!" he yelled again. He snatched up his radio, calling for backup. Seth knew he wouldn't shoot, not at a Saudi princess and a student whose only real crime was running out of a bathroom. Besides, the place was loaded with gas pumps.

"Go! Hurry, go!" Miriam shouted.

"I'm going!"

The Cougar's tires kicked up a cloud of dust.

"Believe me, I'm going."

"Did you hurt anyone?" she asked.

"No. The waitress will have a few bruises, but she'll live."

"How do you know?"

They peeled onto Balboa and roared for the freeway.

"I just do."

# 15

YOU SAW THE future," Miriam said. "You really saw the future again?"

Seth veered down an exit. "I'm cutting across to the 210. We have to get to the State Department. The police know what the car looks like; if we don't change things up a bit, they'll pull us over before we get downtown. I'm not sure I'm ready for a full-on chase."

"I don't understand." Miriam pulled one knee up on the seat and sat sideways to look through the back window. "We're going to the State Department; why don't we just let the police take us?"

"Because"—he paused and glanced at his mirrors—"because, in every outcome I saw with the cop, you ended up dead."

She stared at him. "I...what do you mean, dead?"

"I mean slumped over in the backseat of his car with a hole in your head. Hilal's obviously not the timid type."

"You said outcomes. You saw more than one future?"

"Yes."

"How many?"

"Many. A hundred."

She tried to understand this. To see into the future was possible. Many mystics and prophets had seen visions. But this idea that a person could see more than one future—she'd never heard of such a thing.

"Why did you throw the ball?"

"Because the future in which I threw the ball was the only future in which you survived."

She turned from him and stared ahead. How could she believe such a claim? He drove on, somber.

"I don't understand it any more than you do," he said. "I only know that prior to a few days ago, I'd never experienced anything remotely similar to clairvoyance. Then my mind short-circuited or something, and I began to see glimpses. Now I'm seeing what I know are possible futures and I'm seeing more than one at a time. I was sitting at the table and I saw Hilal in the bathroom with you. How else would I know to bust in like that?"

"And you saw me dead? You saw many possible outcomes of the situation, including the arrival of the police, and the only one in which I wasn't killed was when you threw the ball?"

"Yes."

"But..." It still made no sense to her. "What if the ball had bounced somewhere else? Then the waitress wouldn't have fallen."

"Right. Which means that I'm seeing what actually will happen given certain conditions, not what might happen. Small distinction maybe, but pretty mind-blowing. I didn't make a future to save us; I chose the one that saved us."

"And what if none of the futures provided an escape? You couldn't do something to change it?"

He shook his head. "I don't know. Maybe not."

She sighed and put her face in her hands. Twice now he had saved her. She couldn't be sure about the intentions of the man at Berkeley, but the look in Hilal's eyes was unmistakable. The realization weakened her. She removed her hands and looked at him.

"You haven't...seen anything else?"

"No. No, I don't have a clue what's next. I just see in spurts. We're going to the State Department."

His face was pale. A bead of sweat ran past his temple. The agnostic in him was shaken, she thought. She gazed out the window. Her fleeing was in vain. Maybe Samir was on the way at this very moment. She breathed a prayer for her safety.

"This is crazy," he said.

She couldn't disagree.

"This'll make the propeller heads go ballistic. Do you have any idea what this means?"

"It means that God is speaking to you," she said.

"Umm...No. Actually, this means that God can't exist."

"Don't be absurd," she said.

"By definition, an omniscient God must know the future. If God knows the future—if he has seen into the future and knows what will in fact happen—then the probability of there being another future, other than the one God knows, is zero. By definition there can only be one future. Follow?"

She thought about it. "No."

"If God knows that I'm going to cough in exactly ten seconds, then I'm going to cough in ten seconds, right?"

"Unless he changes his mind."

"And he would know that he's going to change his mind. He would still know the end result, regardless of what caused it. Right?"

"Okay."

"That's the future an all-knowing being would know, the one that will ultimately happen. That's what it means to be God."

"That's what you just said."

Seth paused. "But that means any other future has a probability of zero, that there's only one possible future, the future God knows."

"I think you're repeating yourself."

"But I've just seen more than one actual future. I didn't just see one. I saw many, and I know for a fact that they were all possible. Therefore, there can't be a God who knows only one. Yet God, by definition, would know the one." Seth looked at the horizon. "Unless there is no God. I do believe I've just proven atheism."

"This makes no sense," Miriam said. "I understand your logic, but it all falls apart when you bring more than logic to bear. Have you considered the fact that you only seem to see these futures when you're with me?"

He stared at her. Obviously not.

"Not true," he said. "It happened before I met you." He looked at her and smiled. "Then again, you do make my mind...I don't know...crazy."

"Perhaps it's women. They do that to you."

"Women?"

"Yes. Your exceptional understanding of women and love, remember? It's evolved to the point where when you're with one, you can actually know what they're going to wear and say before they do. You're nothing less than the supreme male."

He blushed. As he would say, she'd scored, but she hardly felt satisfied by it. The fact was, despite his spiritual misguidance, she felt safe with him. He was true to the bone. Genuine.

"The woman has a brain after all," she said, smirking in spite of herself.

"Not bad, princess. Not bad at all."

"And this woman with this brain thinks your logic, though arguably sound, is still somehow flawed."

"An oxymoron," he said.

"Nevertheless, my heart tells me that what I'm saying is true. Do you trust my heart?"

He had not expected that, she thought. They were sparring—he with his mind, she with her heart. No, not with her heart, because her heart belonged to Samir. Both with their minds, then.

"I'll have to think about it," Seth said.

"Then think with your heart," she said.


THEY DROVE FOR over an hour, switching freeways several times, slowly closing in on their destination. Although Saudi Arabia covered as much territory as the western United States, her population was no larger than this one city. Los Angeles. Seth made passing remarks about the massive metropolis, but for the most part they were cynical and hard to grasp. Miriam felt alien in this crowded land. Lonely again.

Samir, Samir, my dearest Samir. Where are you, my love? A knot rose into her throat. She could have planned to flee with Samir, but they had no time. Perhaps once the Americans gave her safe harbor, she could contact Samir.

She had left most of her money at Hillary's house. Maybe Sheik Al-Asamm would send money with Samir. But what would the sheik do? He was in his own bid for power. He'd sold her into the king's house for power in the first place. He wanted her to marry Omar! How could she ever trust him? No, she would have to make contact directly with Samir. Maybe through Sultana.

"Okay. Here we are," Seth said. "That gray building across the street. See it?"

"Yes."

Seth pulled into a parking spot, muttering that the vacancy was a miracle. She was tempted to ask him how miracles could exist without a God, but she knew he'd used the word only as a figure of speech. He turned the engine off and sat staring at the building.

"What if they aren't friendly?" Miriam asked.

"I don't see any reason why they wouldn't be. You're seeking political asylum—they can't just pull out their guns and shoot you."

"You could choose better words."

"Sorry."

"I'm not worried about being shot. But being sent back to Saudi Arabia and that pig Omar would be worse than being shot."

"I won't let that happen," he said. "At least if you go back, Omar's behavior will be exposed."

"And why should I trust you?"

He looked at her, dumbstruck. "Because I've saved you twice already. Or maybe because I actually care about what happens to you."

"Do you?"

Apparently he hadn't expected the comeback.

"Yes."

She looked at the doors across the street. "Then I'll trust you, Seth Border." She opened her door and stepped out.

They walked in, an inconspicuous couple, she thought. Seth was just another American citizen, dressed in his corduroys, black canvas shoes, and orange T-shirt. His slightly disheveled hair was not so uncommon, she'd noticed, at least in California. She felt at ease in the blue jeans and white blouse, not because she was accustomed to wearing them, but because they made her feel like a woman. A woman free of that beast, Omar, walking into a public building with an unmarried man.

They stopped inside the swinging doors and gazed across a large lobby crowded with people of all races. Seth took her arm and guided her toward a desk under a large sign that read Information.

She was aware of his warm hand on her elbow, only the second man ever to touch her skin. She wondered what he thought of her bare arms. You're being silly, Miriam. You've been tied up in the black sack so long that you don't know what it means to be touched innocently by a man.

A woman with black-framed glasses who wore her hair in a bun eyed them from the information counter. Three security guards stood behind her, legs spread and arms folded, at ease.

Her mind returned to Seth's hand. Here she was, about to entrust herself to the Americans, and her mind was distracted by the touch of a man. Juvenile, but true.

The first time Samir had touched her was in Madrid, in a park—she couldn't remember the name. His fingers lightly brushed her right cheek, and a gentle wave of warmth spread down her spine. She threw her arms around him and wept.

They sat trembling in each other's arms for an hour. She learned then that love was like a drug. Although they didn't find another opportunity to be alone on that trip, the intoxication of that one hour melted the two remaining days into a dizzying, forbidden pool from which she thought she would never emerge.

Feeling Seth's fingers on her elbow now was like putting her toes back in that pool.

What has gotten into you, Miriam! You may be a woman on the outside, but you're a foolish girl—

Seth's grip on her elbow tightened.

"What is it?" she asked.

His eyes were wide, fixed on the guards. They blinked.

"What? Seth?"

He turned toward her and forced her around. "Just walk out. Don't look back, just walk."

The urgency in his voice said enough. She walked. Stride for stride with him, tense from head to toe now.

"What—"

"Don't speak."

She swallowed.

At the door, a guard she hadn't noticed lifted his radio and spoke into it. His eyes met hers. The guard walked toward the door to cut them off.

Seth stopped. His hand released her elbow.

"You're frightening me," she said. "There's a problem?"

"We have to get out of here!"

"I thought—"

"Don't move! Don't speak, don't breathe."

"Please—"

"I'll be right back. Please, Miriam, don't move. If you want to live out the day, do not move."

Seth left her side, stepping toward one side of the atrium. The guard saw him and stopped. Miriam's heart beat steadily. She glanced back—two of the guards from behind the counter walked toward her. Don't move? She should be running!

She turned back to him. "Seth?"

Seth had reached the wall. She saw the red box on the wall and knew it was a fire alarm before he pulled it.

A shrill bell clanged to life. For a long moment the bustle of the room seemed to freeze. Seth spun around and yelled above the bell. "There's a bomb in the building set to go off in thirty seconds. Please exit immediately in an orderly fashion!"

Contradicting his own advice, Seth ran. "Out! Everyone out!"

Bedlam broke out. Seth raced for her, and a broken dam of people rushed for the door, set in motion by Seth's sprint. Screams joined the bell and Miriam fought the impulse to join them.

Seth reached her. "Hurry. Follow me!"

They ran for a side door with Fire stamped on its surface. The guards cut across the room, hampered by the flood of running bodies. Seth and Miriam reached the side door well ahead of the closest guard.

A gunshot sounded over their heads. "Freeze! Stop where you are!" Whether the guard addressed the entire mob or her, Miriam didn't know. Whatever the case, the action refreshed the crowd's panic. New screams broke out, and the rush for the door became a stampede.

Seth and Miriam crashed through the fire door. Seth took five long steps toward the front of the building and slid to a stop. The street filled with people.

"Run!" Miriam panted.

He grabbed her hand. "This way!" They sprinted to an alley and then behind the building, where a couple dozen cars sat parked. Seth pulled up just around the corner, panting.

"What about your car?" Miriam asked.

He released her hand and bolted from car to car, grabbing at door handles and muttering through clenched teeth. "Come on! Come on!"

A male voice yelled around the corner, and Miriam stole a quick glance. A guard had exited the building and was running toward the alley.

"They're coming!"

"Try the cars! Find an unlocked car!"

This was his plan? "An unlocked car?"

"Unlocked!"

He ran to another car and yanked on the latch. Locked. He ran to another. "Come on. Help me!"

Miriam ran for a blue Mercury Sable and pulled on the handle. The door sprang open. She turned to tell him, but he was already racing for her.

"Get in!" He was whispering now. "On the floor."

She clambered in and flattened herself on the front seat. She didn't know how he expected her to get on the floor—the steering wheel was in the way and...

A knee or a hand pushed into her back and she grunted.

"Sh!"

He was climbing over her. His full weight crushed her and she nearly yelled at him. But she quickly decided that he would never climb over her unless it was his only option. She gasped for air.

He eased the door closed. Silence smothered her. She pushed up on her elbows to give her lungs room to breathe. His body was dead weight.

"Don't move!" he whispered.

"You're crushing me!"

He was silent for a moment, as if considering this information.

"The guard's in the parking lot," he whispered. "He'll see me if I get up."

"You're...suffocating me."

Another silence. Imagine: She wouldn't die by drowning at the hands of the mutawa, but by suffocating under the body of an American.

"Should I move?" he asked.

"Y-yes. Off my back."

"What if he sees me?"

If he didn't move, she would die for sure. She swung her elbow back in self-defense. It landed in his ribs and he grunted.

Now he moved. His weight shifted from her back to her legs and she nearly cried out from the pain. At least she could breathe. His knees found the seat between her legs, and then his weight eased.

They remained motionless for a long minute, breathing hard. Then his body began to tremble, and it occurred to her that the poor man must be supporting himself in a strenuous position.

"Should I look?" he asked.

"Yes."

He eased himself up.

"I think we're clear," he finally said. He reached forward, shoved the passenger door open, and scrambled out over her, all elbows and knees again, apologizing with her every grunt.

He spilled out onto the gravel, sprang to his feet, and gave her a half smile as she struggled to sit. He scanned the lot and then ran back around to the driver's side. He climbed in and shut the door.

"Sorry. You okay?"

"No."

He grinned sheepishly. "But you're alive."

"Barely. There's no key."

"Who needs keys?"

Evidently not Seth. It took him less than a minute to pull out three wires and press two together to start the car. Thirty seconds later they eased out of the alley and pulled onto the street. Behind them, lights from a number of fire trucks and police cars flashed. The Cougar was blocked in by two cars.

Seth sped down the street, smirking, leaving the chaos behind.

"Boy, that was close," he said.

"Thanks to you."

They drove a block in silence, Seth checking the mirrors every two seconds.

"Are you going to tell me why we ran?"

"They were going to turn you over to Hilal."

"You're sure?"

"Pretty sure. Yes, I'm sure."

"You saw that in the building, but you saw no way of escape once we got to the alley. So your gift has its limits."

"It's sporadic. But I think it's gaining strength. I'm seeing more and I'm seeing longer."

They turned onto a side street and then onto another. Still no sign of pursuit. Miriam began to relax.

"Now what?" she asked.

He looked at her for what seemed like an inordinate amount of time and then faced forward, took a deep breath, and let it out slowly.

"Now we run, princess. Now we really run."

# 16

HILAL EYED THE diplomats around the conference table, thinking that debating protocol while the woman and the American fled was a waste of time. The State Department's cooperation was critical now, but not at the expense of Miriam's disappearance. The fact that she had escaped him once infuriated him enough.

He closed his eyes. Seth Border had handed him an insult. The man's words ran circles through his head still. Stupid, flippant words that he should ignore. But he couldn't. Dealing with Seth Border was in some ways as important to him now as dealing with the sheik's daughter.

"...if it makes any difference to you, Mr. Sahban."

Hilal looked at the man who addressed him. Peter Smaley, deputy to the secretary of state, was fortunately available, having been in Los Angeles with Iona Bergren on unrelated business. Bob Lord, the undersecretary for State Department affairs, sat beside them, waiting for his response. The only other person in the small conference room was Clive Masters, from their National Security Agency. Within a minute of the meeting's commencement, Hilal had judged them accurately. Smaley was here to administer the meeting and ensure that Saudi-American relations were not threatened by this event. Lord was here to play the antagonist—the individual-rights activist who would rather see a hundred Arabs die than one American. Iona, the woman, was the most knowledgeable of the Middle East's sensitivities, despite her gender. And Clive Masters was the killer here. Of them all, he was the only one who gave Hilal some pause.

"Forgive me, my mind was elsewhere," he said. "Could you restate the question?"

"Bob has suggested that we withdraw and let them surface under a false sense of security," Smaley said.

"I'm afraid this matter is too urgent for such tactics," Hilal said. "I'm not sure you appreciate the difficulty this evasion puts my government in. You do not sit back and let a coup surface."

Iona cleared her throat and leaned forward. She looked to be of Mediterranean descent, pretty, with olive skin and a rather large nose. He wouldn't mind making her acquaintance.

"You are saying that the princess confessed to being an integral component of a planned coup? Why would she confess this?"

"I believe she thought it would dissuade me from taking her home."

"And you believe her?"

"I have no doubt."

"Seems rather assuming," Bob Lord said. "But if you know about the coup, I can't see why you need her to deal

with it. Arrest the parties involved. We certainly don't need
to bring in gunslingers to hunt down a couple of people
who've done nothing more than run for their lives."

"She has broken our laws, Mr. Lord. And your assumption that we can simply arrest the suspected parties in
Saudi Arabia shows your ignorance of our society. Even if
we did know who was behind the coup—"

"You said Sheik Abu Ali al-Asamm was behind it."

"He is surely an accessory. But the coup would not
come from him," Hilal explained. "If arresting the sheik
made any political sense, we would have done it twenty
years ago. He's too powerful to arrest. We need his allegiance, not his head. We must expose the man among our
own, and I am convinced the woman knows his identity."

They were silent for a moment.

"You'll take the princess back and torture her for this
information," Lord said.

"Our government is at stake, Mr. Lord. We will do
what we must. And if she can't be returned, then she must
be... dealt with here."

Lord just stared at him.

"I'm sorry, I don't understand how anything beyond
her apprehension's in our interest," Smaley said.

"It's in our interest because it effectively squashes this
coup attempt," Iona interjected, "even if it doesn't expose
the parties involved."

Hilal gave her a soft smile. "Precisely. It also gives my
government leverage with Sheik Abu Ali al-Asamm."

At the far end of the table, the NSA operative chuckled. He stared at Hilal with pale blue eyes and nodded.
Clive Masters was no idiot. His hair was a sandy red
and his skin was unusually fair—a strange sight with his

gray-blue eyes. Disturbing, even. He would have to watch this man.

"Please explain," Smaley said.

Hilal turned from Clive Masters. "The sheik will be distressed to learn that his daughter has been killed. Naturally, so will Prince Salman, her adopted father. We will approach the sheik and explain our suspicions that she was killed by the man whose marriage she fled. It may be in the sheik's interest to reveal that man's identity and look for favor with King Abdullah, which we will be pleased to extend."

"So the woman's death renews an alliance with the sheik," Lord said.

"Precisely."

"You assume that the United States is interested in keeping your king in power at the price of an innocent woman's life."

Iona turned to the deputy secretary. "The question is more accurately a matter of regional stability. I'm confident that the secretary would agree. Where Saudi Arabia goes, the Middle East goes. The United States can't afford a coup in Saudi Arabia. Period."

"I wasn't aware that you were so partial to the House of Saud," Lord said.

"Please," Hilal said. "The next king of Saudi Arabia may not be as progressive in his thinking as King Abdullah. In fact, the reason we are here today is likely because some extremist considers the king too progressive to remain in power. Miriam is a pawn of those extreme elements. Dealing with her is not so different from dealing with a terrorist."

"Terrorist?" Lord objected. "She's no Bin Laden. She's

a refugee seeking political asylum. We have laws here too, Mr. Sahban."

Iona still studied Hilal. "I am partial to the House of Saud only to the extent that the alternatives are less appealing," she said. "I think that's the administration's policy as well. Moving Saudi Arabia into the twenty-first century is a tedious task, but as long as the movement's forward rather than backward, I support it. If a militant seized control of Saudi Arabia, a dozen neighbors would swing his way. So in some ways the minister makes a good point."

She looked at Lord. "However unfair it may seem, the fate of your innocent princess may have more bearing on the fate of the region than you would guess. I'm not sure I'm ready to gamble the stability of the Middle East on the survival of one woman."

Lord's face darkened a shade. "What are you suggesting? That we assassinate this woman?"

"I'm suggesting that we avoid a bloodbath in the Middle East, Bob. You may think of her as a refugee; I see her as a fugitive. We have an obligation to help our ally bring her to justice."

"Justice in this country doesn't come at the end of a gun."

"I don't recall mentioning a gun. I'm simply laying all of our cards on the table."

Hilal couldn't have made a more convincing argument. As far as he was concerned, the discussion here was over. It was time to go after the couple. Regardless of what the Americans did or did not do, he would hunt them down. He could use the Americans' intelligence, of course. For that alone, perhaps this meeting was worth the time after all. But either way, he could not allow Miriam to remain a free woman.

"And what about the American? Who is Seth?" Smaley asked.

"He's a student from Berkeley," Iona said. "Mr. Masters?"


CLIVE MASTERS FACED the group, amused by the banter. Smaley and company weren't necessarily slouches, but the Saudi diplomat had them hog-tied and properly disciplined. Diplomat was the wrong word for the man. He was a killer, pure and simple. And judging by his hard eyes, a good one.

"Seth Border," Clive said, shifting in his chair. "The man you're after just happens to have an IQ that makes Einstein's look average."

"I wasn't aware we were after a man," Lord said.

"Well, if you're after the woman, you're after the man. I don't know how the brightest mind in the country happened to team up with our princess, but I can tell he's the one causing your trouble. You find him, you find her. I'm just curious, sir," he said, looking into the Saudi's dark eyes, "but how exactly did Seth manage to stall you at that truck stop?"

If the Saudi registered the slightest surprise, he didn't show it.

"If I were in your shoes, I would have killed her then," Clive continued. "But Seth pulled some trick, didn't he?"

Smaley cleared his throat. "I'm not sure what you're suggesting, Clive, but this isn't a run-and-shoot operation. We're dealing with complications that require a measure of caution. You're here because of your past association with Seth, but that doesn't mean you get to go after them with a bazooka."

"A bazooka? Not exactly the weapon of my choice. I was merely pointing out, Peter..." He paused for the simple reason that the deputy's facade annoyed him. Before they'd gone their separate ways, they attended the FBI's Quantico school together. Small world. They'd each exceeded the highest academic scores the bureau had given before or since.

But not all bright minds see eye-to-eye. Some are cut out for the grind and gore of detective work, and others make better politicians. Clive had gone on to receive a doctorate in psychology and put in five years as an FBI profiler before moving on to the NSA. Peter had pursued a career with the State Department. Now, twenty years later, they found themselves on opposite sides of the same coin. The perfect diplomat and the perfect detective.

Clive resumed his thought. "I'm saying, Peter, that if our friend here had killed the woman in that bathroom, as he probably intended, we wouldn't be trying to keep the Middle East from blowing up. And we all know that if the House of Saud is overthrown by militants, sooner or later the Middle East will blow up. But he didn't kill her, did he? And frankly, I'm just a tiny bit curious how our fugitive managed to pull one over on an accomplished...diplomat's head."

"Try to control yourself, Clive," Smaley said. "Whatever you might think, not everyone's a gunslinger."

"Perhaps if I had been in my own country I would have taken care of the problem," Hilal said, staring Clive down with those black eyes of his. He dipped his head slightly. "But I am not. Now it will be your job. And by the sound of it, you are well qualified."

The man was either sucking up or insulting him, and Clive wasn't ready to decide.

"Can you bring them in?" Iona asked.

"Do you want her dead, or do you want her brought in?" Clive asked.

"Brought in," Smaley said. "Preferably."

A faint smile curved Hilal's lips.

"They're headed east in a blue Mercury Sable reported stolen from the alley behind this building," Clive said. "They have a two-hour head start, and, according to the clerk at the Wal-Mart they stopped at, they're loaded with cash. We'll put out a new APB, cast a broad net, and try to anticipate his next move. Run-of-the-mill. But Seth Border's not exactly run-of-the-mill. If he hadn't given the slip to three different parties, you might guess that he's better suited for breaking the light barrier than for leading a chase. But you'd be wrong."

"A simple yes or no would do," Smaley said.

"I'm not sure it would, Peter. As I've explained, in a case like this, the best way to get to the girl is to get to the man. But I'm not sure it's in our best interest to end Seth Border's life. He's not exactly an easy human being to replace. We can't kill him."

Smaley smiled. "I didn't know you were so softhearted. Your friend may be a genius, but I doubt he's worth the stability of a region. I'm sure you can figure out a way to outwit him. Live up to that reputation of yours."

His old rival hadn't lost his touch. Clive gave him a polite nod. Give credit where credit is due, but owe no man anything.

"In the meantime, we will keep you informed," Smaley

said to the Saudi. "You may tell your government that you have our full cooperation."

"Then I'm sure you wouldn't mind allowing me to follow the investigation on a real-time basis," Hilal said. "I would like to be updated on the hour."

The snake was going after Miriam on his own, Clive thought.

"Of course. Now if you'll excuse me, I have a plane to catch." The deputy secretary stood. "Please keep me informed." He cast a glance at Clive and left with Iona.

Hilal stared at Clive in the brief silence that followed. Clive stood. "You'll excuse me as well, gentlemen, but I have a fugitive to catch."

"He's very quick," Hilal said, holding his stare.

"How so?"

"With his mind."

So, the Saudi had been outwitted after all. Lord watched them with a raised brow.

"And if you were Seth? Where would you go?"

"I don't know your city. But I would get out of the city."

Smart man. "You wouldn't go underground?"

"It would be difficult to go underground with a Saudi princess. Yes?"

"Yes." Clive walked for the door.

"I believe that he may also be unusually...intuitive," the Saudi said. "Perhaps clairvoyant."

Clive turned back. Clairvoyant? Hilal was a Muslim. Evidently a mystic. Clive could see how facing the man *Scientific American* had called the next Einstein might feel like going up against Elijah himself. Though Clive doubted Seth was clairvoyant, Hilal was right: He would be an elusive prey.

Clive, however, had built his reputation on tracking elusive prey. Not one had yet evaded him. Granted, Pascal Penelope had taken seven years and Al Cooper three, but both were now behind bars alongside another twenty-three fugitives he'd collared.

"Thanks," Clive said. "I'll keep it in mind."

He left, knowing he'd see Hilal again.

# 17

THEY ARE IN a blue Mercury Sable, believed to be headed east out of the city. The police have issued an order to stop the car when it is located."

Omar stared down through the smoked-glass window ten stories above Century Boulevard without acknowledging Assir. Sa'id stood to Omar's right, hands held at his waist. These two had failed once, but they would not fail again.

An orange-and-yellow plane floated by the window on its final approach to LAX. Southwest Airlines, the tail read. It looked like a lizard.

He'd left his thawb in London Heathrow Airport in favor of a dark-gray silk suit. With his trimmed beard, he looked more Mediterranean than Arabic—his intention. He'd been in the United States a dozen times and learned early that Saudi Arabians tended to draw attention, especially if they placed the title of prince before their names. There was a time for attention, of course, particularly in nightclubs frequented by women.

But this time he was after only one woman. She was a Shia Muslim, she was rightfully his property, and he would have her or she would die, either option in accordance with the law.

He remembered watching his first stoning as a boy of seven. The Nizari sect had pulled the woman out of a wagon and pushed her roughly to the ground. The wagon was piled high with stones the size of a man's fist. After a short pronouncement of guilt, ten men started throwing the stones. He learned later that she was seventeen and her crime was flirting with a man. The punishment was a harrowing sight at first, seeing the stones bounce off her body as she waddled around on her knees. She wore her abaaya and veil, which only made the stoning mysterious. He tried to picture what was happening under those garments and then picked up a rock himself and lobbed it. Amazingly, it landed on her head and bounced off. The black cloth darkened with blood. His father laughed and handed him another stone. The woman passed out four times and was reawakened after each instance before she finally died.

The flight over the Atlantic had given him time to stew over the matter of his bride, and with each passing hour his anger swelled. This chase wasn't simply about his right to claim what belonged to him; it was about the future of Saudi Arabia. The future of a sacred culture in which man was ordained to rule and thereby ensure the worship of God. The future of Islam itself was at stake. Not the Islam followed by most Arabs, but the true Islam of the Nizari, a tiny minority now. In power, it would expand.

Someone had once compared the Nizari to the Americans' KKK, a small Christian minority. In truth, when he looked at America, all he saw was the KKK, and he hated them all.

Omar turned from the window. "This is from General Mustafa or from the scanners?"

"Both. The lead investigator on the case is making his way toward San Bernardino."

Mustafa had filled them in on Hilal's meeting with the State Department. The fact that the Americans expected the NSA to track down his wife both pleased and angered Omar. They could be instrumental in leading him to her. The agent on the case reported to Hilal on the hour, and whatever Hilal learned, Mustafa learned. This was good.

No one had a right to the woman but him, however. Hilal's pursuit was not as large a concern as the American agent's involvement. Whoever found Miriam first would have to be killed, but the prospect of killing the king's man was like child's play next to killing the NSA agent. Even so, Omar wouldn't allow the Americans to take her into their custody and coddle her. They would return her to the king. His marriage to her would be lost.

Omar decided on a straightforward approach. "Then we go to San Bernardino," he said, moving toward the door. This Clive would lead him to Miriam, and he would be the jackal, would close in after she'd been found. He would steal the prey, would make the prey his wife, and then extract payment for her insult to Allah. To Islam.

To him.

SAMIR STOOD AT the gates to the great mosque in Mecca, dressed in a traditional white seamless ihram. He stared at the three-story cloth-covered cube known as the casbah, which sat in the sun sixty meters off, black and oddly plain considering its reputation as the most holy place on earth. Allah gave it to Adam after expelling him from the Garden of Eden and then later led Abraham to it. Through the ages, many idolatrous people had bowed at its base to any one of a hundred gods worshipped in Mecca before the prophet Muhammad claimed it.

The pagans came here to worship before dawn, stripped of their clothing, wailing. The mystery that lay behind that black cloth felt to Samir like a physical force that squeezed his chest every time he came to the holy mosque.

The courtyard boiled over with several thousand Muslims on pilgrimage. Mumbled prayers rose to the sky, a steady groan to God. But Samir wasn't concerned with their prayers; he sought guidance for his own dilemma. Only now, eyes fixed on this most holy of holies, did he finally know the will of God.

There could be no greater love than the love he felt for Miriam. Nothing mattered now except her.

Not once did the suras in the Koran call God a God of love. But he agreed with the teachers—this was because God's love was self-evident. One didn't need to say that the casbah is black if everyone already knew its color. Muhammad had no need to expound on the love of God, because love was at the very heart of Islam. So then, Samir's own life would have to be a life led by love.

Samir left the mosque and hastened toward the limousine that waited on the main street. His love for Miriam was as essential to life as the beating of his own heart. He'd never exposed himself to any other human being as he had to Miriam. The memories of their innocent touches in Madrid haunted him still.

In Saudi Arabia, where flesh was so deliberately covered, one tended to take note of the flesh one saw. Miriam had seen his bare chest and upper arms only three times, once by mistake when he was changing shirts in the garage, and twice when she'd pulled his thawb aside in curiosity. He'd never exposed himself beyond this, of course. That would wait for marriage.

But she'd seen more of him than any woman had. Tracing his chest with her index finger, she'd wondered aloud how a driver came to have such strong muscles. He made a joke about lifting all her heavy bags in and out of the car, and they laughed as only lovers can laugh at the slightest hint of humor.

What Miriam didn't know about him would shock her, if she didn't suspect his true identity already. Miriam's intelligence had first attracted Samir to her, before he even saw her face. Surely she would know that her true father, the most powerful sheik among the Shia, would not entrust his daughter to a common man. But he doubted Miriam knew that the man she'd fallen in love with was well-known in small circles as a warrior. An exceptional one, worthy of the task given him.

The sheik had spared no expense in training him to be Miriam's protector. Now, for the first time, he would put that training to good use.

He opened the rear door and slid into the limousine. The sheik sat against the opposite door.

"Drive," the sheik said.

The driver pulled into the street.

"So. What has God told you?" Al-Asamm asked.

"God has told me that he is a God of love."

The sheik looked at him. "You will go?"

"Yes. I will go. For love."

The sheik nodded. "They're already ahead of you. Hilal, Omar, and now the Americans."

"Good. They will only make my job easier. You're receiving the information still?"

"Yes. You'll know what they know. But we're running out of time. They can't be allowed to reach her before you do, Samir. Hilal, at least, will kill her. And there's no telling what Omar will do out from under my eyes. He won't kill her, but he may maim her."

"I won't let that happen. You trained me to protect her. I will do just that. And I have the advantage—your daughter knows me. As soon as I'm in a safe position, she'll come to me."

Samir looked out the side window at the faithful streaming to the mosque and breathed a prayer for her safety until he arrived.

# 18

MIRIAM SAT BESIDE Seth, aware that something special was happening to them. In the few days since she'd learned of her betrothal to Omar, her life had been turned both upside down and inside out, as Seth said.

This unlikely character sitting beside her was the living antithesis of everything she knew, from his haphazard dress, to his whimsical outlook on life, to this madness about seeing into the future. She found him fascinating, which was just as inside out as anything else she had experienced. He should repel her, not attract her. Not that she was truly attracted, at least not in any romantic sense of the word. No, definitely not!

The entire matter both frustrated her to the bone and thrilled her in a confusing way. If only she could get word to Samir, he would come; she knew he would. He would come for love.

The car veered into an alley to the right, sending her leaning hard to the left. She threw a hand out to avoid falling into his lap, shoving Seth into his door. His head knocked against his window.

"Ouch!"

She righted herself. "You're driving like a madman!" she said.

He glanced in the mirror and slowed, sweat beading his forehead. His mind was on the chase. She doubted he even heard her.

"Are you listening?"

"They know that we're in a blue Sable," he said.

"They do? How do you know?"

"Because a dozen police cars within a mile of us are looking for a blue Mercury Sable as we speak. There was one coming our way back there, which is why I turned when I did."

She looked at the approaching cross street. His knowledge of what was about to occur—these possible futures, as he put it—flew in the face of her worldview, but she could hardly deny that he saw things.

"How do you know we won't encounter any police on this street?"

"I don't. I can only see what happens in the next few minutes or so. But I'm pretty sure that if I take a left up here, I can get on 10 headed east without being spotted. It's a future in which we don't get stopped. At least for a few minutes."

"Why can't you just see what we need to do to escape all this nonsense?"

"That's not the way—"

His eyes widened for a brief moment, and he slammed the brake pedal to the floor. The car jerked to a stop, and she crashed into the glove box.

"Ouch!"

He stared ahead. "See, that's what I'm talking about."

"You're going to kill us!"

He raised an open hand, motioning her into silence. She looked through the windshield, saw nothing but cars crossing and a teenager with yellow hair walking across the alley mouth, staring at them.

"What?" she whispered.

"A police cruiser must have turned onto that street ahead," he said in a low voice. "Onto Atlantic."

"I thought this street was safe," she said.

"So did I."

Miriam wasn't sure what to think of these antics. One minute he knew what was happening—or might be happening—the next he didn't.

He faced her. "I can only see what happens to us in different futures, depending on what we do now. And depending on what other people do now."

His eyes shifted past her, lost in bright blue astonishment. "It's fluid. Whatever happens in this moment changes the next. But…" He looked forward. Their breathing muted the rush of the cars crossing the street fifty meters ahead. Miriam stared at Seth, struck by the thought that she was looking at a miracle. Under his tossed blond curls, behind his clear blue eyes, Seth's mind was encountering the future. Like a prophet. Like Muhammad.

He spoke as if to himself. "What I saw a few minutes ago has already changed by what other people have decided to do since. I can stay ahead of them, but only for as far as I see. A few minutes ago I didn't see the police car spotting us on Atlantic. But two minutes have passed and now I do. He must have just decided to turn onto

Atlantic, which changed the future. So then I saw a future in which we'd be seen if we proceeded onto Atlantic. But now that we've stopped, the future has changed again. The officer will only stay on Atlantic long enough to look up the street, see nothing, and then turn up another street. So now we should be okay." He looked at her, a smile twisting his mouth. "Incredible."

It didn't make sense, not really. Seth eased the car forward.

"You saw all that in the last few seconds?" she asked.

He nodded. "Crazy, huh?"

"But you can't see past a few minutes, so really we could be seen once you turn onto the street anyway?"

"Yes. But, if I'm right, I think I can stay ahead of them. If I could see out even, say, half an hour, they wouldn't stand a chance! Assuming I could keep all those futures in my mind. Incredible."

He started the car forward, turned onto Atlantic, and headed north toward the freeway that Miriam could see arching over the street about half a mile ahead.

"Like right now, we'll hit the freeway in less than three minutes. I can see out that far." He looked out the windshield, lost in his own explanation. "And I can see that when we do, we'll be okay. But every second that passes now opens another second of sight for me. Just because I don't see any problems in the next three minutes doesn't mean there isn't a problem waiting four minutes out, created by a decision someone is making now. A chopper pilot might decide to fly over the freeway . . ." He trailed off.

Miriam lifted both hands and rubbed her temples. Her heart thumped, unrelenting. Yes, this was indeed inside out. Seth wasn't seeing the future as a prophet might, in snapshots of events far to come. He was seeing a steady stream of events as they might occur, depending on what everyone did. How many possibilities could he see? She was afraid to ask.

"You're seeing more than one future; that's hard enough to believe. And you're seeing them only a few minutes out. I'm really supposed to believe this?"

"Come on, Miriam," he said with a side glance. "You're smarter than that. This is actually happening. Was I wrong about Hilal?"

"I don't know. We ran off."

"Ouch. That hurts."

"You're hurt?"

"No, your doubting me hurts."

"I'm sorry, I didn't mean to offend you. But have you ever heard of seeing a few minutes into the future? Many futures?"

Seth turned to the west one block before they reached the freeway.

"I thought we were safe until we entered the freeway," she said.

"We were. We are. But now I see that a mile down the freeway, a cruiser is headed west. I couldn't see that until just now—it was too far out. We need to delay our entry onto the freeway for a minute."

Even with Seth's extraordinary gift, they were vulnerable. If he made a misjudgment in one minute, they could be caught in the next. And what would happen when he fell asleep? He hadn't slept in nearly two days.

"Do me a favor," Seth said. "I put the Advil in the glove box. Could you dig out a couple? Thinking like this is giving me a headache."

She gave him two and he swallowed them without water.

"Thank you."

They entered the freeway at the next intersection and made their way east, out of the city, where there were fewer prying eyes, Seth said. The fact that this unusual ability had latched itself onto him persuaded him that he should be her guide. He said that much, but she suspected he was beginning to enjoy himself. And if not himself, then perhaps her company.

Three times he pulled off the freeway to avoid detection, twice by regular police and once by an unmarked detective's car. So he said, and she believed him. Each time, he seemed pleased with himself for having avoided trouble. Like a man who'd just discovered he could sit down at a piano and play whatever he wished without practice, the power of his gift intoxicated him.

They turned north on the 15 and then north again on a smaller state highway, leaving the crowded roads behind. They settled into an introspective state, Seth undoubtedly mulling over the next few minutes, Miriam considering what she would do if they escaped.

Where was she running to now? She could no longer say "America," and, as Seth pointed out, every police officer this side of Las Vegas was on the lookout for them.

Her mind drifted back to Saudi Arabia. Riding in the car, next to Samir. His gentle eyes smiling at her veiled face, knowing what lay beneath. By fleeing her country she had fled him. What was she thinking? He might have come with her. What if she had lost Samir forever? What if by seeking freedom she had consigned herself to a life without Samir?

She cleared her throat. "What will we do next, Seth?" She looked at him. "I mean, if we do escape."

"I don't know. I've been wondering the same thing."

"We need to get word to Samir. I would not be here with you if not for Samir. It was my love for him that convinced me to leave Saudi Arabia. The thought of marrying another man made me run. Now I've been delivered from Omar in a way I could never have asked for. It can only mean, that I am meant to be with Samir."

"I wouldn't say that you're delivered just yet." He paused, scowling. "Why didn't you just run off to Spain with Samir in the first place?"

"I've told you, I couldn't tell him what I was doing. It was far too dangerous. Both sides would kill him if they learned he was involved."

Seth said nothing. With a quick glance in his mirror, he pulled off at the next exit, headed for a Texaco station a hundred yards off the road, pulled behind the building, stopped the car for a few seconds, and then drove back onto the highway. This time she didn't ask him whom they had avoided.

"I just think you could have gone about it differently if your objective was to be reunited with Samir," he finally said.

"Maybe. I'm not exactly an experienced fugitive. Now that I'm here, I realize I have to find Samir again. This whole exercise will be meaningless without him. So, unless you can think of a better objective—"

"Our objective should be to get you to safety. You can worry about Samir later. Right now we have people with guns on our tail—it's not the best time to be getting homesick."

"Don't be silly! You have no idea where we're going. You're just running away, from one minute to the next. I'm only saying that while we are running, we need to make contact with Samir. I think this should make sense to a mind as perceptive as yours."

He scowled. She wasn't sure if he was irritated or just thinking.

"Can Samir leave Saudi Arabia?" he asked.

"Of course."

"Then why didn't he? With you, I mean?"

"How many times do I have to say he had no knowledge of my plans? If I didn't know better, I would say you were jealous!"

"Please, no. That's...that's not what I meant." But his face had turned a shade lighter, and it struck her that he might indeed be jealous!

She faced the road. Goodness! Was it possible? No, she had to be mistaken. He would know that such a thing was inappropriate. Were Americans so quick to find attraction? Had she sent him even one signal that she wanted his affection? No!

Miriam let out a short, impulsive humph.

Seth glanced at her. "Okay," he said, swallowing. "You're right. We should make contact with Samir. I'm sorry, I just..." He stopped talking.

"Yes?" she said.

For a long time neither spoke. The silence turned awkward.

"We need to get you out of this country," Seth said. "The State Department obviously wants you as badly as your own government does. They're more interested in keeping peace with Saudi Arabia than in protecting you."

"Where would you suggest?"

"England, where you should have gone in the first place. They have a history of protecting dissidents."

"I didn't realize I was a dissident."

"You are. You're dissenting from your country's prevailing view of its women."

"Okay, then I'm a dissident."

"Miriam, the lovely dissident." He smiled, and the tension in the car eased. "Bottom line is, we need to get you to England, from where it will be much easier to make contact with Samir. Assuming he wants contact."

"Of course he will."

"Okay, we'll assume that. The hardest part will be getting you out of the United States. I imagine your passport is at Brackenshire's place?" She nodded. "Not that it would help you anyway, now that the State Department is on alert. We'll have to get you out another way, which will probably take more than five thousand dollars. A lot more."

She bit her lip. She'd been a fool to leave all that money at Hillary's house. "How much?"

He shrugged. "Air travel isn't as easy as it once was. We'll have to find a charter and leave illegally. A couple hundred thousand maybe."

"We?"

"Someone has to keep you out of trouble until Samir arrives." Seth glanced at her with a twinkle in his eyes. "I'll think of something. What's a few hundred thousand dollars to a man who can see into the future?"

THEY TRAVELED NORTH, and with each passing minute, Seth seemed to regain his good nature. Perhaps she had misjudged his motives. He was wired and wide-eyed, despite the dark circles forming under his eyes. In thirty miles he didn't change course once—the threat fell behind them for the time being. Instead he spent the time explaining what he was seeing in their futures and how he was trying to manipulate those futures. He could see out six or seven minutes now, and he could only see futures directly related to either of them, but even those amounted to hundreds if not thousands.

He couldn't say what was happening anywhere else or what would happen beyond seven minutes, but he could see with stunning accuracy what might happen to them. If he saw two possible futures—one in which she took a drink from the water bottle and one in which she asked for a drink of his soda instead—he would attempt to manipulate her choice without being obvious, and then he would tell her what he'd done, grinning wide.

"Can you read my mind?" she asked.

"No. I can only see events. But I'm pretty sure I can tell what you're going to say. Speech is an event."

"You can't be serious!"

"As a heart attack. Believe me, this thing is absolutely incredible."

She had no clue what he meant by the heart attack, but she was too taken by his claim to ask. "Then what will I say now?"

"That depends on what I say, and on what I do, and on a bunch of other variables. But I know what you will say in each case. Including what you'll say now that I've told you. Isn't that wild?"

She hesitated. He was saying that he knew exactly what she would say next. How? Because he had seen her saying it. And what if she changed her mind and said something different? It didn't matter; he knew what she would say, not why.

"That's—"

"Very clever," he finished with her, grinning.

She stared at him. This was disconcerting. "I do not believe you can influence what I say!"

"I'm afraid there's some truth to it." He was still grinning.

"I don't see the humor," she said.

"Sorry. It's a nervous smile."

"If you can influence what I'm going to say, then make me say something," she said, defiant.

He paused. "I think you're very beautiful."

She hadn't expected that. He was manipulating her, of course. Somehow in his mind he saw that if he told her she was beautiful, he could draw a particular response from her. Probably a thank-you, or something like that. She decided to throw him. Something he could not possibly expect.

"Your eyes are like the…" She waited for him to finish.

"Blue waters of the Al-Hasa oasis," he said.

It was precisely what she was going to say.

"And thank you," he said. "But they can't be as beautiful as yours."

"You know the Al-Hasa?"

"Never heard of it. Is it a nice place?"

"Of course. You have beautiful eyes. But then you already know I was going to say that. That's unfair."

"I wasn't aware that we were playing a game. Besides, I'm your savior. How can I be unfair to you?"

She sat back and frowned. "If you can't read my mind,

then maybe I should say things deliberately off base, so that you'll have no idea what I'm thinking."

"You're right, you could say all kinds of things that don't match what you're actually thinking and I wouldn't be the wiser. I don't mind at all."

"I've gone from having my face unveiled to my mind unveiled in a few short days. I feel positively naked."

"I can't read your mind—"

"But you can trick me into saying things. You might as well know my mind."

"No, I can only say or do things that will make you say one of the things you were going to say anyway."

She shook her head. "Either way, it's positively maddening."

"I meant what I said. You should know that."

"You've said many things."

"One of them was that you are very beautiful. I meant that."

She looked away. So then she hadn't misread him. How could he be so bold? "And I meant what I said," she replied. "I'm in love with another man."

"That's not what I meant."

"But it is what I meant." Was she really so beautiful?

Her comment seemed to have no impact on him. He changed the subject and talked to her about Saudi Arabia, a subject he seemed to know nearly as well as she, despite never having been there. She considered apologizing, but withheld after realizing that if she was going to say anything, he would have seen it already. Better to keep him guessing. God knew she needed some advantage.

They rolled into Johannesburg as dusk settled on the small town. Seth checked them into separate rooms at a small U-shaped Super 8 Motel off a side street and parked the car in the rear lot. Miriam found her room decorated in orange, like a pumpkin. But the sink functioned well enough, and she was grateful for the chance to freshen up after a day and a half on the road. They would need to buy more clothes at the earliest possible opportunity, she decided. If she'd known they would be on the road overnight, she would have purchased several changes at the Wal-Mart.

She'd just finished brushing her teeth when Seth knocked on her door and suggested they get some dinner at the Denny's down the street.

"You're exhausted! Look at you, you can hardly walk straight."

"My mind's too full to sleep," he said.

She glanced down the empty street. "You're not concerned about being discovered here?"

"The last time we were spotted, we were in Los Angeles. We're way off the beaten path. Actually, sleep may be more dangerous than going down to the Denny's. Somehow I doubt I'll be able to see when I sleep."

Miriam looked at his tired eyes. If the police were still on the prowl and Seth was fast asleep, they would be powerless to avoid any search. Maybe it would be best to keep him awake a few more hours.

"Can we go shopping?" she asked.

"Shopping?"

"You expect me to wear this shirt all the way to England? And why do you need to ask? Don't you know my response already?"

"I can't know a response unless there is one. And there can't be a response unless there's a question."

She was beginning to understand.

"There's a large truck stop on the corner. It should have a few overpriced items of clothing. I could use some too."

"Promise no tricks?"

"I wouldn't dream of it."

She stepped past him. "Why do I find no comfort in that?"

# 19

THIS BUSINESS ABOUT reporting every hour was about as sensible as hiring a chaperone for your twenty-fifth wedding anniversary, Clive thought, especially considering that chatter about the vanishing blue Sable had crossed every secure police channel in Southern California. But he dutifully kept the State Department updated. No need to get the Saudis all whacked out of shape. He understood as well as anyone that, despite the House of Saud's poor record on human rights, the alternatives to its leadership in the region could prove disastrous. A successful coup led by fundamentalists would be a nightmare. Hilal might be a snake, but he was a snake in the service of a government the United States knew how to handle.

Clive thought the man was probably after Miriam for personal reasons and was lucky enough to have information from the State Department to close in. Well, there was nothing to close in on now, was there? Seth had vanished.

Clive angled the Lincoln Continental into a Diamond

Shamrock truck stop on the outskirts of San Bernardino and parked behind a row of purring rigs. A band of teen-agers crossed the graveled lot, headed for the store. Gang-bangers. Probably headed to some joint to fry their brains. The collective mind of America was headed down the toilet. At some point during the last twenty years, some-one decided that intelligence wasn't such a hot commod-ity after all, and the rest of the country licked up that nonsense as though it were a melting vanilla cone on a hot summer day.

The mind he was after, though—there was an excep-tion if ever one existed. He'd met with Seth four times over the past two years, and each time he walked away knowing that he couldn't give up his pursuit of this one. Seth possessed all the qualities for greatness in the world of intelligence. Brains were one thing, but genius plus a thirst for danger was exceedingly uncommon. He'd never imagined that his pursuit of Seth would take on a physical nature.

Without looking, Clive retrieved the round walnut from his coin tray. Over a period of years, he had rubbed the nutshell smooth by turning it slowly in his hand, as he did now. The mind was like this walnut, he often thought, smooth on the outside and wrinkled on the inside. His task was to figure out what was happening on the inside, where wrinkles made the task more difficult.

His arrangement with the NSA was unusual, but he had come to them with an unusual list of accomplish-ments that granted him unique negotiating power. He was a throwback to the old days, when trackers sniffed out criminals with keen noses rather than with fast-flying fingers on a keyboard. More like a bounty hunter in the

Wild West than the agents churned out of today's high-
tech schools. Not that he had any dislike for his peers who
preferred the road of high science; they were an exceptional lot in their own right. He just preferred the hunt
one-on-one, hand-to-hand, mind against mind. May the
best man win, and may the loser hang until dead. Figura-
tively speaking.

Clive depressed the toggle on his radio. "Five into one,
you have any new information?"

A short hiss and then the voice of Sergeant Lawhead,
the clearing-house for all the uniforms on this one, crackled. "Several blue Sables, but not the right one."

Clive picked up a map he'd folded to frame the Los
Angeles basin. He'd highlighted in yellow the five primary
exits out of the region. Checkpoints stood along each one,
far enough out that Seth couldn't have slipped by before
they were set up. If the couple had passed through, they
weren't driving a blue Sable.

He scanned the street to his right. A Ford Taurus drove
by, followed by another, blue instead of yellow. Would
Seth have traded cars?

Minds like his didn't overlook details; in fact, they
tended to consume vast quantities of minutiae. One of
those particulars was that in this computer age, the police
could track down a car purchase in a matter of minutes. If
Seth bought a used car in some remote lot under his own
driver's license, he would trip the wire. And Seth hadn't
come into this chase with a fake ID. For all Clive could
ascertain, he'd stumbled into it without a clue.

Short of buying a car, Seth would have to steal if he
wanted to swap vehicles. He'd done it once and he could
do it again, and in fact twelve cars had been reported

stolen in the last six hours. But none of them was Seth—
too far out of the zone.

He looked at the map again. Of the five exits out of the
city, one headed south to San Diego—out. Seth wouldn't
head home for the simple reason that all stupid criminals headed home. He would suspect a ring of cruisers
around his house already. Two exits headed north, the
Pacific Coast Highway and I-5—both out. You don't head
back into the pursuit unless you know exactly what you're
doing, which Seth didn't. He was no seasoned criminal.

That left two exits east. One toward Palm Springs
and one toward Las Vegas. Both passed through San
Bernardino. Clive toggled the radio. "Any word from the
Nevada authorities?"

"Checkpoints on all the state crossings, but nothing
yet." A pause. "How about south across the border?"

"No. Border's too tight. He's headed east—Arizona or
Nevada."

The radio remained silent. Clive set the receiver down
and studied the map. *Where are you, my friend? Hmm?
Where have you gone?*

He ran his right index finger over the routes slowly,
caressing the paper, tracing every road and judging for the
hundredth time its viability as an escape route.

*Which road does a twenty-six-year-old surfer-turned-
Einstein in the company of a Muslim woman take?*

Hilal's assessment came back to him. *Clairvoyant?*
Now that would be a challenge, staying on the trail of a
man who could see the future. To have escaped Hilal,
Seth must be crafty enough, but clairvoyant?

Clive took out his pencil and shaded a red line on the
map, highlighting a road that headed straight north off 15.

Two miles this side of the observation post. It ran all the way north through Johannesburg and dumped into Death Valley. No cover. That would be almost as dumb as heading home. Unless . . .

Clive shifted his attention from the small highway and returned to alternative routes southeast, toward Twenty-nine Palms and Parker. Maybe. He lifted the walnut and absently drew it across the skin under his nose, and then over his right cheek. What are you thinking, Seth Border? Tell me your secrets.

To have a mind like Seth's would be like playing God among the mortals, leading a lonely existence in which only you have the unique view of reality.

Well, I've got a secret of my own, Seth boy. I have a unique view of reality too. Maybe I don't see what you see, but I know enough to follow your lead.

Clive lifted the mike. "Sergeant, I want some heat on 395 headed north through Johannesburg. What do you have up there?"

It took a moment for Lawhead to answer. "Small local force. I could send a couple of cars up."

"Couple won't do. I want a roadblock north of Johannesburg, and I want every parking lot this side of Ridgecrest methodically searched."

Static. "That'll take some doing. You want to ease some assets from other observations?"

"Move your people up from 5 if you have to. He's not headed south."

"You know something we don't, sir?"

"Nope. Let me know when you have the roadblock up."

He set the mike down and took up the walnut again. You may tell the world how to travel faster than light one day, my man. But for now you'll have to settle for trying to outrun me.

OMAR SLOUCHED IN the back of the BMW, watching the black American landscape drift by, invisible. A luminescent clock on the dash read 2:24 a.m. The police had taken their search north of San Bernardino; no doubt Hilal had followed them. As far as he could tell from the radio traffic, there was no particular reason why the authorities believed that the fugitives were here, to the north, and they could just as easily be driving away from Miriam as toward her. The thought clawed at Omar's mind like a demon. Still, he had no other leads to follow.

He closed his eyes. Once they found Miriam, he would take matters into his own hands. The suitcase in the trunk contained enough firepower to assure that much.

He replayed his right of revenge, loitering with each detail. She would not die quickly. If possible, she would not die at all. First he would take her to a safe place. Alone. A hotel room. An expensive hotel room with proper insulation in the walls—he didn't intend to gag her.

She was beautiful; that was all he knew about her appearance. His mind had already sculpted her face a hundred times. He saw her as fair skinned, with high cheekbones and pouting lips. Her eyes were a light brown, like sand, and her eyebrows arched in velvet black. Her nose was small and her nostrils would flare with each breath, as much from desire as from fear. Women with spirit walked a fine line between fear and desire. In his arms she would discover both. If she was any less beautiful than the image now firmly in his mind, he might have to fix that.

And the American? The more he thought about it, the more he realized that Seth Border would have to die. The man had defiled his wife. He had taken a woman betrothed to another. Seth had earned his sentence as a matter of principle and morality.

The scanner hissed to life. "One-oh-two to one. We've got a blue Sable with a matching license plate."

Omar's eyes snapped open.

"Come again. You have the Sable in question?"

"That's affirmative. We're in Johannesburg, behind the Super 8 on Main. Unlit parking lot."

"Copy. Stand by."

Omar sat up. "How far is Johannesburg?"

Assir was already studying the map. "Ninety miles."

"Go."

The scanner burped. "One-oh-two, could you give me that tag number?"

The officer read the plate number.

"No sign of activity?"

"The place is dark. We haven't spoken to the manager yet." There was a pause.

"Okay. We're sending three more units your way. Clive Masters from the NSA will give you your orders on the ground. He's an hour out—wait for him. And don't let the car out of your sight."

"Roger that."

"Move!" Omar screamed.

# 20

SLEEP HAD EVADED Seth for two days, and when it finally came at 2:08 a.m., it swallowed him whole, a welcome reprieve from the onslaught of impressions that made up his strange new sight.

They'd retired at ten after buying the clothes in the truck stop down the street. He'd discovered with surprise and relief that the moment he entered his room, all future possibilities related to Miriam faded.

The enigma had swelled like a tide through the day, flooding his mind with more images each passing minute than the minute before. His understanding of the future had begun with glimpses of major events, like the threat to Miriam's life at Berkeley. But the precognition had steadily broadened in scope. Now he could see hundreds, if not thousands, of possibilities extending farther into the future with each passing hour, simple possibilities that had no bearing on anything of substance.

Entering Denny's for dinner, he'd seen that the hostess

might have seated them at any one of eleven tables—it was a slow night. Which table she would select depended on dozens of other possibilities held in the balance. How they responded to her questions; which direction she was facing when they approached her; whether she decided to turn to her right to scratch an itch on her hip; whether the busboy with the overloaded tray took the first exit to the kitchen or the second; whether the man seated in the first booth coughed into the aisle, prompting her to avoid his spew, or whether he coughed into his hands, diffusing his germs over his own table. These possibilities, among a couple dozen others, flashed through his mind in the space of half a step.

But with them came several hundred other possibilities yet to be realized in the ten minutes that followed. Possibilities of what they might eat, or what they might say, or what the waitress might suggest to them—all dependent on what preceded the moment. He was a prophet on steroids. The labyrinths of the future had been opened up to him; the gauze that kept man from seeing beyond time had been ripped from his eyes.

Seth's eyes opened. He really was thirsty. Amazing how that worked. He should get up and—

The images crashed in on his mind then, like a full load of bricks dropped off the end of a dump truck. He jerked up in bed, heart thumping against the walls of his chest. They'd found the car!

A hundred futures streamed through his mind, and in all of them his door broke down under the kick of a boot within the next five minutes.

He twisted to the clock radio—2:51 a.m.

Seth threw the covers back, rolled out of bed, and

grabbed his pants. He had no clue what was happening to Miriam. As far as he knew, they already had her. He cursed himself under his breath and pulled on his cords, arms trembling. Think. Think!

He ran to the window and was about to pull back the shade for a peek when it occurred to him that he would be seen by an officer in the lot. He'd seen that. He was still seeing the future.

Seth stepped back, breathing hard. Control yourself, Seth. Find a future in which you get out before they kick the doors in.

His mind flashed through dozens of scenarios.

He paused on a single scenario—one in which the door was kicked into an empty room. Hope flooded his veins. He had to find the thread of possibilities that led to that scenario! He had to get out of the room. Focus! Start at the beginning.

Still shaking, he took a deep breath and closed his eyes. Focus. Swirling in a frothing sea of futures, an action popped to the surface. It was the only one he could find in which he got out of the room unseen.

It occurred in precisely ten seconds, when all the officers in the courtyard below had their eyes averted for a span of three seconds, allowing him just enough time to slip out and into the shadows beside the door.

Seven seconds now . . .

Beyond that . . .

Six seconds.

Seth ran for the door, shirtless and shoeless. He slipped back the chain, unlocked the door, and counted. Three, two, one . . .

He twisted the knob, eased out onto the second-floor

concrete walkway, closed the door, and sidestepped into the shadows beside an ice machine. He pressed himself against the wall and held his breath.

Silence hovered over the cool morning. No sign of the threat below. What if he was wrong? He exhaled slowly through his nose and squinted.

Three black-and-whites cordoned off the motel lot. A group of officers gathered around a fourth car parked kitty-corner behind them. Seth scanned the walkway on which he stood. A cop stood at the top of each stairwell, awaiting orders. Streetlights cast pale light on the door next to his—Miriam's door. No room for shadow tricks there.

Panic tickled Seth's spine. He may have gotten out of the room, but escaping was an impossibility. Something else flashed through his mind—a full-fledged firefight with the officers below. But he didn't have a gun.

One step at a time. He closed his eyes. Just concentrate.

He still couldn't see any of Miriam's futures. He had to get to her. He saw a myriad of attempts to do so that ended in the same two words: "Stop! Police!" In another scenario he managed to reach her back window from the roof. A muzzle flash momentarily lit the back lot. A bullet took him in the head.

And he saw one future in which he dropped into her room from the return vent above her bed.

But how? He started to sweat again. He was concentrating on events too far down the road—several minutes out. He had to find a way to get out of this nook unseen first.

He saw it immediately.

Miriam's door was to his right. There was a linen closet

to his left, on the other side of the ice machine. Attic access was through the closet's ceiling. From the ceiling he could wrench free a portion of the two-foot-square ducting, slide through, and drop into Miriam's room.

Because he saw futures in which he did that, there had to be at least one in which he got into the closet unseen. He saw it. A faint groan of relief cleared his throat.

Blink.

Seth caught his breath. Something had just changed. Everything had just changed! The images of his entry into Miriam's room vanished. Someone had heard him. One groan had changed his future. He'd drawn attention that cut off the possibility of his unseen entry into the closet. Someone who wouldn't have been watching the ice machine now scanned its shadows.

But couldn't he change that?

He searched his mind for another thread—another future.

Cough. Yes, cough.

If he turned his head just so and coughed, he could get into the closet. Because the cough would sound as if it had come from the far corner, momentarily distracting them while he slipped around the ice machine.

The rest of the thread popped back into his mind. It had probably been there all along, hidden among a hundred others, but he'd been too focused on the other option to see this one.

Time was running out. Seth faced the far corner, took one last breath in a futile attempt to soothe his twitching muscles, and coughed softly.

Without waiting, he slipped out into the open, expecting a cry of alarm. Trust yourself, Seth. Walk.

He walked around the ice machine, opened the closet door, and slipped inside. In the darkness, he shuddered. He could see the faint outline of the attic access above. In less than a minute he climbed over the boxes of toilet paper, pulled himself into the attic, and found the duct. He couldn't see a blasted thing up here, but in his mind's eye he saw all he needed a fraction of a second into the future, like a movie playing in his mind. The hardest part was trusting this new sense of his, trusting that if he put his hand right here, he would find the loose piece of duct tape that he could tear free because he'd seen it as part of the future just a heartbeat ago.

He made a ruckus banging through the duct—unavoidable. It only encouraged him to move faster, which made even more noise. If they could hear him, they might think an elephant was stampeding through the place. He dropped onto the grate above Miriam's bed without giving full thought to how his entrance might affect her. With a screech, the grate tore loose, and, together, he and the grate crashed down on the sleeping woman.

His world exploded in a flash of new futures.

Miriam's futures.


MIRIAM DREAMED THAT the roof had collapsed on her, but she knew it wasn't a dream. She grunted and tried to sit up, but a heavy mass pressed her into the mattress.

A moving mass. Breathing hard.

An animal!

She shrieked and tried to get away. The animal flailed, startled by her sudden movement. Miriam swung her elbows and the covers flew. The animal hadn't managed to bite her yet, but it was still there, on her calves, waiting to pounce. She twisted to her back, jerked her legs from under the beast, and kicked furiously, groaning in horror.

It tumbled off the end of the bed, hissing. She snatched her pillow and hurled it at the mass. The door! I have to get to the door!

It bounded to its feet, tall like a ghost, draped in the blanket.

"Stop it! It's me!"

She froze. The thing was speaking!

The figure tore the blanket from its head. It stood there in the dim light, a bare-chested man with disheveled hair, panting.

Seth!

What was he doing in her bedroom? She wore only an oversized T-shirt with an eagle soaring over a shimmering ocean which she'd purchased at the truck stop.

"Are you mad?" she demanded.

He shoved a hand out to silence her, then gestured toward the drawn curtains.

"What?" Half of her mind was on his inexplicable entry, the other half on her exposure. He was gesticulating and whispering urgently, but she couldn't understand a word of it.

"I can't understand a word—"

"They're outside!" he said, aloud this time.

"Outside . . ." Suddenly she understood it all.

Seth jumped up on the bed. "Hurry! We have to get back up into the vent."

"I'm nearly naked!" she said.

He towered over her on the end of the bed. "Where are your pants?"

If the authorities were outside, they had very little time. She glanced at the chair where her jeans were draped. A bag on the floor held the rest of the clothes she'd purchased.

Before she could move for them, Seth bounded off the bed, grabbed the jeans from the chair, and ran back. He didn't see the tennis shoes in the middle of the floor and tripped on them. He crashed into the bed, face planting into the mattress beside her leg, holding the jeans outstretched to her like a warrior who'd just barely managed to return with the magic elixir.

Miriam snatched up her pants and quickly pulled them on.

"These too," he whispered, shoving the shoes toward her.

She yanked them on without bothering to tie them. "My bag."

"Too slow. Where's the money?"

"In my pocket." She grabbed at her jeans and felt the lump. Seth jumped back up next to her, panting from his efforts. He looked up and she followed his gaze. The vent opening looked like a black hole.

"I'll shove you up first," he said.

"Are you crazy? We can't go through that!"

"I just did. Trust me! I know what happens here." He put his hands on her waist and she smacked them away.

"Stop it! I can't fit—"

"We don't have time for this!" he snapped.

"I don't care—"

His lips were on hers, smothering her words.

Seth pulled back, leaving her in shock.

"Sorry, I had to. I'll explain later."

He grabbed her waist and shoved her up before she

knew he was doing it. Limited on options and horrified by his kiss, she grabbed the duct's lip and pulled herself in. Utter blackness paralyzed her, legs still dangling out of the duct. Below he was pushing at her legs, whispering urgently. She scrambled forward.

Behind her, the tin crashed with the sound of his hands, slapping for purchase. He slipped and fell out, and then tried again. He'd never get up! She'd come to America to climb through air vents in the dead of night, pushed by a maniac who had kissed her and...

"Miriam. Back up! I need your legs!"

She scooted back so that her feet touched the lip. His hands grabbed her ankles and he hauled himself up. Smart man.

Her right tennis shoe came off in his hand. With a mighty crash that she could only guess was his head on the tin, he fell back to the bed.

Miriam was left with the echoes of her breathing.

Thud, bang. Here he came again. This time he made it by grabbing her jeans, although he nearly pulled them off in the process.

"Go, go!"

She went. Scrambling into the darkness. She stopped.

"Where?"

"To the end! Hurry!"


OMAR CROUCHED ON the hotel roof, eyeing the police through the rifle's scope. They had reached the hotel at breakneck speed, but not before the others took up their positions in front of the Super 8. Cursing under his breath, he left Sa'id and Assir in the rental car behind a grove of trees, withdrew the AK-47 from the trunk, and quickly scouted the perimeter. With so many police, his chances of taking Miriam here were minimal.

The authorities had abandoned the rear of the motel for the exits in the front. In doing so, they left the roof access unguarded. He climbed the two stories and eased into position here, behind a large air-conditioning unit near the crown of the roof.

Omar had never killed in the United States. Tonight that would change. If he did this right, they would conclude that Seth was the shooter.

Omar steadied the scope on an officer bent over the hood of his squad car, pistol trained on the front of the hotel. "In my country you do not interfere in another man's business, my friend. She is mine."

He squeezed the trigger.

The night exploded. Omar shifted the rifle before the man hit the ground. He took down two more officers standing to the rear of the cars before they could find cover, one through the head, the other in the shoulder, judging by the way he spun.

Omar pulled back and slid down the roof to the ladder.

"Shots on the roof!" a voice yelled from the front. "He's on the roof!"

Omar shouldered the weapon and scrambled down the ladder. He ran for the grove of trees behind the hotel. The car door opened for him and he slid in, weapon first.

Assir fired the engine.

"Shut it off!" Omar said.

The car died.

"Are you begging for their attention?" He turned to see the motel through the trees.

"We're sitting—"

"Shut up. We don't move until I say we move."

MIRIAM AND SETH had just dropped into what appeared to be a closet when the muffled explosions sounded.

"What was that?"

"Shots," Seth said. "An Arab is shooting from the roof."

She faced him, two inches from his face in the cramped quarters. "Shooting at whom?"

"The police." His voice sounded strained. "I think one of them is dead."

She was too stunned to respond.

"I...I didn't see any way to stop it." He turned from her and gripped his skull. "They think we did it. I. They think I did it."

It had to be Hilal. Who else could possibly be shooting at the police? But why would Hilal...

Miriam gasped.

Seth spun back. "What?"

"Who is the Arab?"

"I don't know, but not your bathroom friends. I see events, and that includes faces sometimes, but not names, and it's hard to tell—"

"Omar!" she said.

He said nothing.

"Or Omar's people. At the very least someone who doesn't want the Americans to turn me over to Hilal."

"Your father?" Seth asked.

"No. No, he would never send this kind of man!"

Seth turned from her and leaned his forehead against the wall. Voices yelled outside. Boots thumped on the cement walkway. Wood splintered and doors crashed. Miriam swallowed at a dry throat.

A man's muffled voice reached them from the walkway, only feet away. "Rooms are empty. They're gone, sir. A vent cover is torn loose; looks like they escaped to the roof."

"Copy that," a walkie-talkie rasped. "Clear the vent."

The officer's muffled voice carried from the room. "Okay, clear the vent, Danny. And watch for fire. This guy's armed."

"What now?" Miriam whispered.

"Now we wait. We have a window in a minute. Then we run to the side alley and down the back stairs. We can't take the Sable."

"So you're still seeing all this. This is madness. Why did you ... kiss me?"

"Because. I'm sorry about that. Look, a police officer was just killed out there and you're worried about a kiss? It was the only future I saw in which you moved quickly, and we needed to move quickly."

The vents creaked above them.

"I'm saving your life," Seth said. "Time to go. Follow me. Ready?"

"I suppose."

He gripped the knob.

"They won't see us?" she asked.

"Trust me. Three, two, one."

He opened the door and ran to his left. She followed him, glancing at the open courtyard to their right. An ambulance had arrived, lights flashing. Several men were scurrying around the cars. She and Seth ran unnoticed.

They flew down a flight of concrete steps and spilled into an alley separating the hotel from an abandoned garage. Seth led her across the alley around the rear corner of the garage, glancing each way for danger, although she suspected he knew the route was safe.

"Wait here," he said, turning. "Don't move until I tell you to."

"You're leaving me here?"

"I won't be out of sight. But I've got to do this. Trust me."

To her surprise, she trusted him implicitly. She wrapped her arms around herself and backed into the dark shadow.

Seth walked into the alley and gazed out at the street, thirty meters off. A siren burped from the far side of the hotel. Several more sounded from far away. More police. Shouts carried on the air. Surely Seth realized that the place would be crawling with...

A figure stepped into the alley, at the far end, backlit by the glow of streetlights. Miriam caught her breath and pulled back.

Seth spread his arms. "Good evening, Officer."

The man stopped.

"Hello, Clive. As you can see, I'm unarmed."

The man lifted a gun with both hands. He scanned the alley. "What did you do with the gun, Seth?" the man said coolly.

"I never had a gun. But I think you know that, don't you?"

The man approached Seth, ten meters off. A shaft of soft light fell across his pale face. The redhead looked more amused than concerned.

"Where's Miriam?"

"Safe," Seth said. "I have to be leaving in just a second, but I knew you would be coming and I wanted to tell you something."

"Just like that, huh? You just happened to know it would be me? And you knew I would check this alley? I don't think so. I think I caught you with your shorts down. Or should I say with your shirt off? This is no way to win the Nobel, Seth."

"I saw you coming just like I can see now exactly how I'm going to leave you in this alley. Like a lost puppy."

The man's face twisted to a grin and he waved his gun at Seth. "You may be smart, but I think you're confusing intelligence with science fiction. I'm gonna have to take you in, son."

"You ever hear of precognition? Well, it seems that I've been graced with it as of late. I see the future, my friend, and I see it in all of its possibilities. Or at least in bunches of them. Only a ways out, I'm afraid, but I see every possible outcome ahead of me. That makes me pretty hard to stop. That's why I'm outrunning a thousand cops. Not because I'm a crook. Make sense, Clive?"

Clive quit smiling. "Okay, Seth. You're going off the deep end here. You're not even armed."

"I don't need a gun to leave you panting, Clive. I have precognition. And you should know that gunning down a police officer isn't only stupid, it's not my style. That wasn't me on the roof. You make sure they know that."

"I'm sorry, but I don't believe in precognition—"

"You will. I'm not the gambling kind unless I know the lay of the cards, if you know what I mean. Unfortunately, I don't have the time to discuss it with you. We've got fifty seconds before a uniformed officer comes running around that corner. I have to leave before he does. There are hundreds of things I could do in an attempt to escape you, and I've seen them all. All of them but two fail miserably. I could shout at you; I could walk up and punch you; I could run to the right, to the left, or straight past you. But I've seen all those possibilities among a hundred others, and I know exactly what you would do in each case. Unfortunately for you, I'm going to pick one of the two in which you make the wrong move. You can't stop me."

"You're rambling. The girl's a fugitive. You're taking me to her. End of story."

"You take her and I'm pretty sure she'll end up in the wrong hands. The world isn't ready for that. And frankly neither is she. Gotta go, Clive."

The man's face twitched. "Lift your hands slowly—"

"Step out, Miriam," Seth said.

Step out? Miriam hesitated.

"Now, Miriam!"

She stepped out. Clive's eyes jerked to her, and Seth sidestepped to Miriam. Clive swung his gun to cover her.

"You won't shoot her, Clive, at least not in the next few minutes. I've already seen that it's not one of the possible futures."

He grabbed Miriam by the waist and pulled her behind the wall. No shot was fired.

Another man's voice echoed up the alley. "Sir?" The officer Seth had predicted.

"Hurry!" Seth whispered. "Run for the end of the building!" She ran.

She could hear Clive's feet running in the alley. A thump. She spun to see that Seth had run into a barrel. He sprinted after her.

"Run!"

She ran, then heard a hollow crash, followed by a grunt and a curse. A shot went off, booming around her ears.

Miriam tore around the far corner of the abandoned building. Seth ran past, grabbing her elbow. "Follow me!"

He chose the most unlikely path, she thought—right under a blazing streetlight, out into the middle of the street. To their left, colored lights turned lazily in the night. Six or seven vehicles flashed red and blue. She couldn't bear to look. They would be seen!

But they wouldn't, would they? Seth knew.

Seth vaulted a hedge and disappeared. She leaped blindly after him.

Miriam dropped to her knees and slammed into him.

"Sh! They're coming!" He didn't move.

Clive roared around the corner of the garage across the street and pulled up. She could hear him panting.

"Over here!" Clive yelled. "You head up the street. I'm cutting back."

The sound of running shoes followed. Then silence.

Seth pulled at her arm. "Come on."

They ran around a house, passed through a back gate, and wove through the neighborhood, away from the hotel.

# 21

THE SUN CAST a glow over the eastern sky, waking the sleeping valley to another day. Two patrol cars remained at the hotel, one in the front with a forensics team just now finishing up their work in the parking lot, and one in the back next to the abandoned Sable. A tow truck waited with amber lights flashing, preparing to impound the evidence.

Clive leaned against the door of the Sable, studying the hotel roof. He rolled the walnut between his fingers and squeezed it tight. The crime scene read like a book. Seth and Miriam had slept in different rooms—the manager and the couple's abandoned belongings vouched for that. At some point in the night, presumably after the police arrived, Seth had somehow managed to get into the linen closet, work his way up to the ducts, tear loose a piece of duct tape—a move that could have been made only from the outside of the duct—wiggle into Miriam's room, and return with her. They exited via the closet and made the alley unnoticed.

Signs of an unplanned journey littered the car: Dr Pepper bottles, empty chip bags, and half a dozen fashion magazines and cheap corner-store paperbacks. Toiletries. Crest. Johnson & Johnson dental floss. What kind of man picked up dental floss on the run? A man with a woman.

Clive had reviewed the sequence of events in the alley a hundred times, retracing each step by aggravating step. They scoured the streets and alleys surrounding the motel. Nothing. The search extended to the limits of Johannesburg. Still nothing. Seth and Miriam had simply vanished.

Clive had perfected the art of chasing down criminals by adhering to a simple principle: Follow the path of least resistance. Almost without exception, criminals took this path. They were not the most brilliant lot. If common sense dictated that they should duck behind a building instead of running out into the open with flailing hands, ninety-nine times out of a hundred, that's where they could be found: behind the building.

Standing in the middle of the alley, waiting for the adversary as Seth had done, was not a move brimming with common sense. It was, in fact, downright idiotic. But Seth wasn't an idiot.

"AK-47," a voice said.

Whitlow, the LAPD detective in charge of the physical search, approached from Clive's left. The officer held a small, clear evidence bag containing one of the shell casings from the roof between his thumb and forefinger.

The detective was a city chump used to back-alley chops and drug deals. Not a bad man, just a bit far from home in Clive's judgment. Whitlow removed a Dodgers baseball cap and scratched his head. "Common enough rifle around here. No telling where he got it."

"He wasn't the shooter," Clive said. "We have another interested party."

Whitlow forced a grin, replaced his cap, and put his hands on his hips. "So says the detective from the NSA."

"So says common sense," Clive said. "You find a weapon? No. And he didn't have one. Someone else took that weapon."

Whitlow studied him for a moment. He looked at the roof. "How exactly did this guy get away from you? He was unarmed—or so you say—and with a girl." He glanced at Clive without turning his head. "Seems kinda odd."

Odd? Clive hardly believed it himself. Only one explanation made any sense at all: Seth's explanation. He knew what was going to happen before it happened. He knew exactly which course of events would allow him to escape, exactly when to tip the barrel, exactly where to run to avoid detection.

"Let's just say that our man is pretty clever, Detective. You know who he is?"

"Seth Border. Some student from Berkeley."

Clive smiled. "A student from Berkeley with an IQ of 193."

Whitlow whistled.

"The man we're after just happens to be one of the most intelligent human beings on this planet, my friend."

Whitlow nodded, smirking slightly. "He's still flesh and blood, right? As long as he bleeds, we'll get him."

Clive considered the man's statement. They had managed to approach the hotel with Seth inside, hadn't they? While Seth slept. Every man had his weakness, and if Seth had by some strange act of God been doused with precognition, then sleep might very well be his Achilles' heel. He couldn't know the future while he slept. Even if he could, he couldn't run.

They had to exhaust Seth. A man couldn't stay awake much longer than two days, maybe three, without help from doctors. According to the hotel office, Seth's light hadn't gone off until after two. He might be wide awake now, pushed by adrenaline, but what goes up must come down.

"And how would you get him?" Clive asked Whitlow.

"They can't be far. We're setting up a perimeter now—there aren't a heck of a lot of choices out here. The highway south is sealed off. That leaves twelve possible roads out. Shouldn't be impossible to find a yellow Ford Pinto on one of twelve roads." Whitlow grinned at Clive's surprise. "The car was reported stolen a few minutes ago. Like I said, we'll get him."

Clive knew it all except for the report of the stolen Pinto. He'd ordered the checkpoint plan himself. A yellow Pinto. Like renting a neon sign that read Come and Get Me. Didn't make sense. Nothing made sense.

"If someone else doesn't get him first," Clive said. He shoved the walnut into his pocket and straightened to leave. "I want the entire grid blanketed, not just the roads. He may try to hole up, and we can't let him do that. Any sign of them and I want to be informed. We go in quiet. You got that? I want this guy smothered."

"You got it. Where you going?"

"To talk to our Saudi friends." Clive stepped away. "Don't forget about the other shooter."

"WE LOOK LIKE a giant lemon," Miriam said. "They'll spot us from Saudi Arabia."

"Hold on."

The Pinto's tires ground over a dirt road ten miles north of the hotel. Seth turned into a deserted driveway, rumbled over a knoll, and angled for a rickety barn that looked as if it had been abandoned for a century. Two large doors hung cockeyed off rusted hinges and baling wire. He threw the car into park, managed to pull open the left door, and plopping down behind the wheel again, drove the car into the barn. He turned off the ignition.

"We had to get off the road," he said. "They're clamping down pretty hard."

She looked around at the dim interior. Dilapidated bales of hay leaned against what had once been a stall. An old tractor sat rusting, cocooned in cobwebs. Smells of mildew and oil laced the air.

Seth's door banged, and she turned to see that he'd gone to close the barn. She climbed out. It wasn't so different from a stable at home, she thought, at least in the smell, which was enough to momentarily pull her mind back to Saudi Arabia. Straw covered the floor. At one time someone had kept animals in this place. Horses and cows. No camels.

She turned to Seth, who sagged by the car. "So we're safe here?"

"For a while." He walked over to the stall and wiped his hand along the rotting wood.

"How far are you seeing?"

"I'm not sure. Longer. Half hour maybe."

They'd stolen through the sleeping town, cutting this way and that, sometimes hiding in the shadows for a few minutes before darting across streets. The yellow car came from a house on the edge of town, and Seth had taken it for the simple reason that it was unlocked with keys in the ignition. Rust had nearly consumed the right rear fender, and the tailpipe hung precariously low, but none of this seemed to bother him.

They'd passed the first hour doubling back and driving virtual circles in the deathtrap. She'd seen a new side of Seth, a brooding brought on by the death of the police officers. It was tragic to be sure, but she'd seen much worse. He evidently had not. Americans were not as accustomed to death, she thought. This was a good thing—one of the reasons she had come here.

With the dawning of the sun, exhaustion overtook Seth's brooding. He'd slept less than an hour, he'd said. This was not good.

She had no idea where they were now, and she doubted he knew either. He was simply playing cat and mouse, driving where he knew they wouldn't be.

A shaft of light cut through two loose planks on the wall, illuminating a fog of floating dust particles. Seth looked at her with his pretty green eyes, now darkened with sadness and fatigue, and for a moment she felt sorry for him. She had led him into this. Apart from the next half hour's myriad futures, he was as lost as she. An enigma, to be sure. A stunning creature with that mind of his—American to the bone and yet so different from any man she'd ever met. The only man other than Samir who had kissed her. She was no longer sure if she wanted to slap him or thank him.

Seth lifted his eyes to the rafters, but she kept her gaze on him. He was still shirtless. She let herself look at his chest and belly. He was as strong as Samir, she thought. Taller and perhaps broader in the shoulders.

Samir, my love, where are you?

"I think they're using their manpower to cut off the roads," he said. "They'll get around to searching this place, but for now they'll assume we're on the run. We have some time."

"You think they're cutting off the roads? You can't see it?"

"Well, things are a bit fuzzy right now. I'm not exactly at my best." He sighed and squatted by some hay bales. "My mind's wasted."

"And you can only see half an hour out. That's not exactly comforting."

He looked up at her and caught her stare. "But I'm seeing all the possible futures of the next half hour. At least to the extent I can wrap my mind around them. I'd say we have a definite advantage."

Miriam sat next to him. To their right, the old tractor sat, discolored by the gray cobwebs. To their left, the Pinto sat, pale like a ghost. The silence hollowed out her chest.

"Thank you," she said.

"For what?"

"For saving my life. Four times now. I'm indebted to you."

"You're not indebted to me," Seth said. "I'm here because I need to be here. I want to be here."

"I'm scared, Seth." She was. The last few days had flown by with such speed, filled with so many new sights and mysteries, that adrenaline overrode her fear. Now, the adventure of it all was giving way to terror. An army of American police had them surrounded, and now that one of their own had been killed... How would Seth and she ever escape?

She hadn't prayed in two days.

"You're a long way from home," Seth murmured.

She knew he meant to comfort her, but a lump rose through her throat. If Seth were a Muslim, they could take solace in God together.

Her vision blurred and she looked away. What did they have in common? Funny, she'd always thought of Americans as fundamentalists set out to destroy Muslims. Maybe in the same way that most Americans thought of all Arabs as Islamic extremists committed to burning down their cities.

Seth leaned his head back onto the hay and closed his eyes. "When my father used to beat my mother, she and I would run into this closet we had in the hall. I sat in there and cried with her. There was nothing I could do. I was too small. But a week after I turned thirteen I hit him hard enough to break his jaw. That's when he left."

He lifted his head and looked at her.

"In some ways I feel like that boy again. I know what you mean? I feel lost too. Powerless."

It occurred to her that he was seeing into her heart. He couldn't read her mind, but he could see what she might say in the next half hour. It was enough to lift her burden.

She swallowed. "You aren't powerless," she said. "You might be the most powerful man alive right now."

He nodded slowly.

"You've been a gift to me," she said.

"But I'm as powerless to heal your wounds as I was my mother's."

When had this mad scramble become more than an effort to deliver her to safety? When had the bond begun to develop between their hearts? It was unlike the bond between Samir and her, another kind, but in its own way as strong. A friendship. And yet he was a man.

The thought of friendship flooded her with warmth and worry at once. Something had been pulled from her eyes—a veil that once distorted her vision. And what she saw unnerved her.

"You're a special man, Seth. I would be desperate without you."

They looked into each other's eyes and she felt the unreasonable impulse to embrace him. Not in a romantic way, but as a friend.

His arm reached around her shoulders and he pulled her to him and kissed her hair. "I'll take care of you," he said. "I promise. No woman deserves the life you've been dealt. Don't ask me how, but one way or another we're going to fix this."

His eyes glimmered with a subtle light that she couldn't mistake for anything other than true attraction. The kind that mere friends did not share.

"Thank you. I owe you my life. And I can promise you that Samir will be as indebted."

He nodded, lowered his arm, and sighed.

"I have to get some sleep while I can," he said. "You think you can stay awake?"

"Won't that put us in danger?"

"I've got to sleep at some point or I'll be no good at all, and I know I have at least thirty minutes now. I might as well take advantage of it." He shifted his weight and settled back. "Wake me in thirty minutes."

Miriam stood and walked for the tractor. She could use the time to pray, she thought. Maybe she could find some old clothes around this barn.

"Sleep," she said.

. . .

"AN OLD BARN," the pilot's voice crackled. "There are marks on the grass that I can swear were not there twenty minutes ago when I made my last pass."

Clive's Lincoln ground to a stop on the graveled shoulder. "Do not, I repeat, do not approach. Are you close enough for any occupant to hear you?"

Static. "Ash . . . negative, sir. I don't think so."

"How far north?"

"Ten miles, give or take."

A barn was just the kind of place Clive himself would choose to hole up in for a couple hours of sleep. He hadn't expected a break this soon—for that matter, this might not be a break at all. But in the absence of any other affirmative ID, the chopper pilot's claim would do. If Seth was there, he would be asleep. Otherwise his precognition would have alerted him already.

"Okay, we go in quick and we go in quiet. I want ten cars on the main road ASAP. Stay high and out of their sight. I'll be there in fifteen minutes."

"Copy that."

Clive dropped the mike and pulled the car through a U-turn. "Sleep on, my friend. Sleep like a baby."

# 22

KHALID BIN MISHAL sat in the elaborate Bedouin tent, studying his host. A silver teapot steamed between them, spreading a pleasant herbal aroma.

Sheik Abu Ali al-Asamm nodded. "We walk a fine line, my friend. If the king doesn't already know of my involvement, he at least suspects it. There is a reason Abdullah has survived so long, and it has nothing to do with good fortune."

"We assume he suspects your involvement. You've made no secret about your leanings."

"There's a significant difference between 'leanings' and a coup attempt."

Khalid took a sip of the hot tea and felt the liquid hit his stomach. "Regardless, he knows you represent the sentiments of a large group of people. The streets would erupt if he detained you."

"Don't you mean kill me?" the sheik said, lifting one corner of his mouth.

"My identity," Khalid said, "is the king's more pressing question. If he discovers I am behind a plot to dethrone him, I will receive my death sentence."

"And he would learn this from whom? He would need proof to move against a prince of your stature."

"Miriam. She's demonstrated her evil nature plainly enough."

The sheik flashed a stern glare. "Don't mistake a strong will for an evil nature. You are talking about my blood."

"I mean no insult. I would say the same about my own son. We all have our weaknesses." They were cut from the same cloth, father and daughter. Today, Miriam was the problem; tomorrow, this man could be the problem. Khalid would keep that in mind when he became king. "The point is, Miriam has become a problem. I would like to propose that we continue without her," Khalid said.

"No," the sheik said. Then he seemed to remember the need for diplomacy. "I may be a pliable man when the time calls for it, but I can't change a hundred years of history and tradition in a single stroke. Without the bond of marriage, my people won't join me in support of you. You need the support of several million Shia."

Khalid knew as much. The desert was built as much on tradition as sand. "And we will have our marriage. But let's be reasonable. The time to strike is now, before the king expects it. We will claim that your daughter has married my son in the United States. We both know that your daughter will return wed." Or dead, but that went without saying.

"If my people discover I have deceived them, even I will lose their trust," the sheik said. "No."

Khalid sighed. "Very well. But your decision places us in a dangerous position." He paused and delivered his final thrust. "I'm afraid that the king's men will attempt to kill Miriam."

"And risk losing my loyalty? I don't think so."

"Unless he was to blame it on me."

The sheik lowered his teacup, unprepared for this thought.

"If the king wouldn't do it, then Hilal would," Khalid said.

"Then you will have to find her before Hilal does." The sheik stood and walked toward a bowl of fruit at the side of the tent. "What is the latest word from your son?"

"If not for the Americans' interference, he would have her already."

"Will he succeed?"

Khalid hesitated. His son was a ruthless warrior, even a wise one. His quick decision to shoot the policeman was a brilliant stroke. He had forced Hilal to make an accounting of himself, freeing Omar to close in undetected. But the man who'd abducted Miriam was proving to be a challenge for everyone. Local authorities had brought dozens of officers into the search, which lessened the likelihood that Omar would bring the woman out alive. If he could not take Miriam into custody, neither could Hilal.

"Yes, I believe he will." Khalid smiled. "Your daughter is proving to be quite smart for a woman. She has your blood."

The sheik turned around. "Of course she does. I wasn't aware that gender was a factor when it came to intelligence."

These desert dwellers, they were thickheaded!

"Of course not," he said and took another sip. The cool tea suggested it was time to leave.

"You must know something, my friend," the sheik said. "We may make our plans, but in the end the will of God will prevail. His ways are sometimes...mysterious. I will bring the full weight of my influence to bear on my daughter, but she does have a mind of her own. I won't resort to barbarian extremes."

Khalid blinked. What was he saying?

"I trust that your son will win the love of my daughter, but even if he does not, I will not allow her to be maimed or killed." He waved a dismissing hand. "But I'm sure you assumed nothing less."

"I assure you that she's in good hands. If there's one thing Omar excels at beyond the sword, it is courting a woman." He managed a graceful composure. "He has the blood of his grandfather, Abdul Aziz, in his veins."

"That's what I'm afraid of."

They looked at each other until Khalid dropped his eyes.

"No matter," the sheik said, breaking the moment. "She will love whomever God wills her to love." He reached for his cup of tea and raised it.


OMAR LAY IN the grass, scoping the barn below the sloping hill, poised for a shot. A line of police cars waited down by the road, out of the barn's line of sight. No fewer than twenty policemen crept over the meadow toward the peeling red building. If Seth and Miriam were in there, they would not escape. So, Clive Masters was proving to be an efficient tracker.

This was not good. Once the Americans had Miriam, his job would become significantly more difficult.

He had two options. He could begin shooting now and send the police scurrying for cover, which would give Seth a chance to escape. Perhaps the safer option.

Or he could affix the silencer, wait until the police were closer to the building, and then shoot one in a way that made it appear as if the shot had come from the barn. Risky. He might miss and Seth might not escape. The police, however, would reconsider the possibility that Seth was armed and dangerous. They might also think the shot had come from Hilal.

Omar lifted the scope and scanned the surrounding hills. The snake was out there; Omar could almost smell him. He would have heard the report and would be waiting. Another reason to use the silencer.

His scope caught a pinprick of light and Omar adjusted his sight. The profile of a rifle materialized through the grass, five hundred yards off.

Hilal!

Omar put his crosshairs on the form in the grass and tightened his trigger finger.

The silencer! He rolled to his back, pulled the tube from his breast pocket, screwed it on, and then rolled back into position. The police were no more than thirty yards from the barn now.

He swung the rifle toward Hilal, acquired the target, and squeezed the trigger. His rifle coughed quietly. The rifle across the meadow jerked from view. He would not kill Hilal yet—he needed the information the king's man passed back to Mustafa. But he wouldn't allow Hilal to kill Miriam either.

Omar spun his sights to the lead officer in uniform and dropped him with a long shot through the chest.

For a moment his colleagues stopped, stunned. Perhaps they thought the officer had fallen for cover.

Omar was about to put another round in the man's fallen body when the officer rolled over. His moan floated through the valley.

"Man down! Man down!"

Pandemonium swept through the men strung out along the field. Several retreated in a quick sprint; the rest dropped for cover. Omar hugged the earth and slowly pulled back.

The rest he would monitor by radio.


SETH WAS SNORING. Miriam dusted off the old boots she'd found and watched him rest, his mouth half-open, chest rising with each breath. She'd discovered the leather shoes along with a blue plaid farmer's shirt in the toolbox behind the tractor. The shirt was missing its top four buttons and the shoes were splitting at the toes, but she had no doubt that Seth would be pleased with them.

She heard a moan. The wind, most likely.

Miriam smiled, set the boots and shirt on the Pinto's trunk, and walked toward Seth. Time to . . .

Seth jerked up, eyes wide. "Huh?"

"Man down! Man down!"

Miriam spun toward the door.

Seth was on his feet already. "In the car!"

Miriam grabbed the clothing from the trunk and piled through the passenger door.

"How long did I sleep?" he demanded.

"Less than thirty minutes!"

Seth paused, hands on the steering wheel, staring intently ahead. "That's not good. I should've seen them."

Miriam twisted around, expecting police to storm the old barn at any moment. Seth sat still, jaws flexed. "What are you doing?"

"Thinking. Don't worry, I can see now. He's not dead."

"Who's not dead?"

"The policeman who was shot outside." Seth's face looked strained. "Crap, this is gonna be like threading a needle by candlelight."

He fired the car and stomped on the accelerator. The Pinto roared for the far wall. Miriam threw her arms over her head and ducked. With a mighty crash the car slammed through the brittle wood, sending splinters flying.

Seth fixed his eyes dead ahead. They flew over the grass, picking up surprising speed. Miriam turned and saw that they'd left at least a dozen policemen by the barn.

The Pinto screamed. They skirted a pond and then slammed through a picket fence. Still, Seth did not ease their speed. She looked at him and wondered if he was going too far this time.

"It's amazing how easy it is to elude the mortals when you see clearly," Seth said above the engine's roar. "They don't have a chance!"

But she knew he was wrong. Seth had his weakness and it had almost betrayed them back there. If the police were this good, their troubles weren't over. Not even close.

Seth took the car into a wooded area and slowed. For five minutes he threaded his way amid thickening foliage. "Helicopter," he said.

He stopped by a large oak and they climbed out.

"There's a house a mile to the south. They have our car."

She lifted an eyebrow. "Our car? Here." She tossed the boots and shirt to him.

"Where'd you get these?"

"In the barn, while you were snoring."

He grinned. "Now you're talking." He pulled the boots and shirt on. "Come on!"

They ran south. A helicopter beat the air above them and then turned north. Sirens wailed to the west, from the barn. Seth jogged south, unconcerned.

"How did they find us?" she asked.

"I don't know."

"How did you not know?"

He didn't respond right away. She knew, of course. His mind needed rest. If he didn't find rest soon, they would be caught. But there was no time for rest.

"I need rest," he said.

"The next time we might not be so lucky," she said.

This time he didn't respond at all.


CLIVE PICKED UP a piece of straw and absently sniffed at it. Wasn't so different from the scent of his walnut. He tossed the straw and fingered the walnut. Lights spinning atop three police cars parked outside the doors lit the barn's interior in hues of red and blue. Two spotlights lit up the red tractor like a dusty prize tomato. They scoured the grounds, but he knew evidence wasn't what they needed. This was a new game, of a kind he'd never played before.

The hay on which Seth had slept was still warm. He had slept here; Clive was sure of it. The officer's yell must have awakened him. The helicopter would complete its search and the men would sweep the grove of trees, but Seth would be long gone.

And yet Clive now knew not only one of Seth's

weaknesses, but two. The two Achilles' heels. The first was obvious: sleep. The lack of sleep would eventually catch up to Seth and leave him unguarded.

The second was the future itself. If a particular event wasn't part of the future, then Seth could not know it. There had to be a way to bring darkness to Seth's world of futures. A way to blind him, by removing futures.

The idea gnawed at Clive, faint and unformed, but just there, under the surface, begging to be uncovered.

"He's here, sir."

Clive sniffed at the walnut. Where are you hiding now, Seth? He crossed the bright lights and walked up to the Mercedes that had pulled up. Hilal was sitting against its hood.

"Good morning," Clive said.

"It could be better," Hilal returned. For a man who'd spent the last hour defending himself under a barrage of questions, the Saudi showed no sign of humility. He'd persuaded them that he had nothing to do with either shooting, not that Clive had ever suspected him. Hilal had no reason to open fire on the police. If Hilal wanted to kill, he would be aiming at the girl.

"Let's get one thing straight," Clive said. "The State Department may insist we give you some rope, but that doesn't mean you get to run around the countryside, shooting up the night."

"Please, don't insult me."

"You've been warned. Tell me, what really happened in that bathroom?"

Hilal flashed a coy smile. "So. Now you're interested. The man told me precisely what was going to happen. I think he actually knew. He threw the ball."

"Which ball?"

"The one the waitress fell on. It came from his pocket."

That hadn't been in the report. "You saw it?"

"As plain as day, as you would say. He let it roll and then ran, as if he knew precisely what would happen. Tell me what happened in the alley."

If Seth could do this trick of his at will and actually manipulate events . . . God help them.

"I'm sure you know what happened." Hilal probably knew more than most of them. He struck Clive as the kind who would listen in on more than his share.

"This man has a gift," Hilal said. "He's escaped certain capture five times now. Miriam is still alive. I would say that you have a problem."

"Really? I thought it was your problem. And I wasn't aware that killing Miriam was our primary concern."

"You have a dead police officer."

"Yes. Quite convenient for you."

"Please. We both know that I had nothing to do with the shootings. As I've said, I am not the only Saudi who wants this woman."

"Someone who vanishes as quickly as Seth?"

"Someone whose identity is a mystery to both of us. Someone who has been trained in my country as an assassin. Someone who would shoot at me."

"You? And where were you when you were shot at?"

"Watching."

"Uh-huh."

Hilal stood and crossed his arms, looking back toward the barn. He was right about the shooter, of course, but Clive had no doubt that he would kill an American officer as quickly as the presumed assassin had.

"So. How do you plan to deal with this problem?" Hilal asked.

"How would you catch a clairvoyant who knows every step you're going to make before you make it?"

Hilal paused. "I would anticipate him."

"Very good. It always comes down to a battle of wits, doesn't it?"

"In which direction is he headed?" Hilal asked.

"You're listening in on our conversations—why don't you tell me?"

Hilal shoved his hands deep into his pockets and turned away to face the night. "We are both looking for the same party. I suggest we work together, my friend."

"I work alone," Clive said.

Hilal faced him. "And so do I."

He'd had enough of the Saudi. And he had a phone call to make. "He's headed north. We've issued a nationwide bulletin. This whole valley is sealed, but that hasn't stopped him so far. My guess is he'll try to take her out of the country. Most fugitives wouldn't, of course, but as you've so eloquently pointed out, he's no ordinary fugitive. I doubt he's still on foot. You figure it out. And remember, he's an American citizen. You touch him and you'll deal with me."

Clive turned and walked for his car.

"Mr. Masters," Hilal called.

He stopped. Looked back.

"This other shooter, I would not underestimate him. The next bullet might be intended for you."

Clive nodded. He walked to his car, slid in, and closed the door. The Continental's dash lights glowed a soft green. What was it like to know that if you tossed a ball just so, a waitress would fall just so and create just the right kind of distraction to allow for your escape? It would be like knowing that if you tipped over a barrel at just the right time, the man behind you would trip over it.

A solitary thought had drifted in and out of his mind since his first encounter with Seth in the alley. Now it had taken up permanent residence. Like a tumor.

He picked up his phone, dialed the number, and massaged the walnut.

"State Department."

"Peter Smaley."

"I'm sorry, but Mr. Smaley—"

"It's Clive Masters with the National Security Agency. He'll take the call. And if he doesn't, I'll go over his head."

The woman hesitated. "Hold, please."

It took them three minutes to track down Peter Smaley at whatever meeting he was attending.

"I'm in the middle of a meeting, so make it quick."

"We've bitten off more than we anticipated."

"Come on, now. Don't tell me you're actually getting a run for your money—"

"He's clairvoyant, Peter."

A beat.

"This isn't a good time—"

"He's not only clairvoyant, but he sees a number of possible outcomes and he knows what to do to make any of them actually happen."

"Clive. You're talking nonsense."

"I'm telling you this only because I want my bases covered, Peter. My next call is to the secretary of state."

That got his attention. "Hold on." The deputy secretary's voice carried through the covered phone. "Excuse me, gentlemen, I'll be right back." A door closed.

"For God's sake, Clive. This isn't exactly the kind of call I would expect from you."

Clive rubbed the walnut and glanced back at the flashing lights. "I want you to imagine something. Imagine that you're in a battle. You're a general, directing the battle. But you have an advantage. You already know exactly what your enemy will do, to the last bullet. And you know exactly what to do to stop him anywhere you want to. You know because you've seen every possibility, every move and every countermove, and you have the luxury of mapping out the course of battle precisely as you choose. What would you say about such a general?"

There was a short pause. "I would say that he is unstoppable. And I would say that I feel a bit silly talking to you about it. It would be an embarrassment to both of us if anyone overheard this."

"Imagine something else with me, Peter. Imagine an assassin sent in to kill the president. A unique assassin who could see a thousand possible approaches to the White House and know with absolute certainty which one would succeed. What would you say about such an assassin?"

"This isn't amusing, Clive. There's no way you're telling me that this fugitive could walk up to the White House—"

"No, I'm not. But in my estimation, he's exactly what I've described." Hearing himself say it, Clive wondered if he'd just thrown away his career.

"You're actually suggesting that I pass this on?" Smaley guffawed.

"We're courting a man who may be either the greatest asset or the greatest liability the United States has ever seen. I know it, and now you know it. So do the Saudis. Yes, I suggest you pass it on. Today."

Smaley's voice softened. "God help me, Clive. If this is some kind of . . ." He stewed for a moment. "Has anything like this ever been documented?"

"Clairvoyance? Not exactly an unknown phenomenon. But actually, no, I've never heard of anything quite like this."

Smaley was trying to get his mind around the idea. That was a start.

"I hope you don't mind my saying that I sincerely hope you're all wet on this, Masters."

"Wouldn't be the first time you harbored such sentiments."

"I'll call you as soon as I have a reaction. You have any idea where he is now?"

"No. But I'm pretty sure I know where he's headed."

"Then for God's sake, do your job. Bring him in or whatever you have to do. This is getting ridiculous."

"Have you heard anything I just said? This isn't like tracking your common terrorist."

"And you're no common tracker. You're telling me you don't know how to catch this guy?"

Clive closed his eyes. "I have a pretty good idea. You just do your job. I'll expect a call later today."

He disconnected and dropped the phone on the seat.

# 23

THEY DROVE THE Volkswagen Bug Seth had lifted from the farmhouse for less than an hour before ditching it by a deserted shack. They would have to go on foot, Seth said. It was the only way past the roadblocks.

They walked slowly. Dragged was more like it. Not only did Seth lack the energy, but there was no hurry. They had to wait for darkness.

His precognition continued to expand to one hour, then two. More futures, generations of futures that added up to millions. He couldn't see them all, of course, only those he intentionally isolated. But the constant bombardment daunted him and, more worrisome, tired him and generated a bad headache.

If he were able to see only what would happen instead of what could happen, the matter would have been simpler. He explained it to Miriam this way: "How many different words do you think I could say right now?"

"As many as you know, I suppose," she'd responded.

"Say a thousand, for an easy number. I could say any one of a thousand words right now, and for each one, you might respond with any one of your own thousand choices. If I focused hard enough, I think I could see each word and each of your responses. That's a million possibilities in one generation. Extend that out a few minutes and you get the idea. That's just the possible futures of our talk."

They skirted the first roadblock at ten o'clock, a half mile off Route 190. In fact, they could have walked within two hundred yards of the police and not been noticed, Seth informed her with a tired smile.

He led her due north, through a field and over a fence, where they would find another unlocked car, he said. If they took certain back roads, they would be safe for at least as far as he could see.

It was then, walking in the dead of night beside Seth, that Miriam finally understood the full weight of his gift. They were virtually invincible, weren't they? As long as Seth was awake and thinking—as long as there was at least one possible avenue of escape among the thousands of possibilities—they could simply choose it and walk on, unharmed.

In this moment, she would rather be here, walking with him, than anywhere else in the world. Except in Samir's arms, of course. A warmth rose through her chest.

She looked at Seth in his oversized shirt, hair loose, jaw firm in the moonlight, and she smiled. He smelled musty, a blend of straw and sweat—but to her it was the scent of a man, and it only reinforced her sense of security.

He looked at her, his eyes sagging. "What?"

"Nothing."

She slipped her arm through his, as content as she could remember feeling. She could feel his skin on hers, along their arms, and that was good, because here in America you didn't have to be a fifteen-year-old bride to be touched by a man. An image of Sita floating underwater flashed through her mind and she felt a momentary stab of pain.

You are a woman and he is a man, Miriam. What would Samir say to this display of affection, however platonic? And you know that Seth is falling for you. No, she did not know that. It was her fantasy. Miriam pulled her arm away. She was losing her mind with him.

Seth seemed too exhausted to react.

They found the car exactly as he'd predicted. An old white Cadillac with a shredded vinyl roof. It was unlocked.

"The owners are probably in the basement right now, praying someone will come along and swipe this beast," Seth said. He looked at her. "Ready for a ride?"

"I was born ready." It was a phrase he'd used earlier and she liked it.

He grinned wide. "Born ready, huh? I didn't see that one coming. Let's go."

He was too busy considering the future of their escape to dwell on what she might say. That was a good thing. It also meant he was making mistakes. They had to rest.

They drove north to the outskirts of a town called Ridgecrest, where Seth pulled the beast, as he'd taken to calling the car, into a graveled parking lot adjacent to a large steepled building. A church. He eased the car around the back and parked behind an old shed. He simply could not go on.

"We're past the roadblocks, and it's dark. We should be okay. If I don't get some rest, my body's going to start shutting down on its own."

"What if you don't wake up?" she asked.

"Nothing's happening in the next three hours. Three hours past that and the sun comes up. The sun comes up, I awake. Always been that way; always will be that way. Relax, princess. It's time for sleep."

He leaned against his door, and the heavy breathing of sleep took him within minutes. The window felt like a stone against her head, and Seth kept grunting in his sleep, as if fighting unseen demons. In a groggy fit of frustration she leaned toward Seth and rested her head on his arm.

She finally slept.

The heat woke her. A suffocating blanket that smelled of oil. Light streamed in through the window, hot on her thigh like a magnifying glass...

Miriam jerked up. It was day! The Cadillac was surrounded by a sea of cars. They'd been found!

Seth leaned against the window, mouth hanging open in a snore, dead to the world.

She hit his thigh. "Seth!" she whispered.

He didn't budge.

She pulled her fist back and slammed it into his arm. "Seth!"

"Huh!" He jerked up, eyes wide. A trail of saliva hung from his gaping mouth. He clamped his mouth closed and wiped his mouth with the back of his hand. "What?"

"Look!"

He gazed around, blinking. "Cars."

"Who...who are they?"

A lopsided grin split his face. "It's Sunday."

Sunday. Christians went to their churches on Sundays. They were in a church parking lot, swallowed up by the cars of worshippers.

"Do you see anything?"

"I see that in twenty minutes, a cruiser's going to roll into this parking lot."

"Twenty minutes? We would still be sleeping if I hadn't awakened."

Seth had fixed his eyes on the church.

"Seth?"

"Religion is so screwed up, don't you think? Christianity is such a sham. So is Islam, frankly. The religious institutions, that is."

"We don't have time for this," she said.

"So full of contradictions. "

"We should go."

"Who was the greatest prophet?" he asked. "According to Islam."

A melody reached faintly through the walls. Children were laughing somewhere. "Muhammad," she said.

"That's not what your sheiks teach. Muhammad was the final prophet, but he never claimed to be perfect. According to him, Jesus was the only perfect man and as such the greater prophet. This is the teaching of Islam."

Put as such, it was true. But she didn't understand his point.

"And?"

"The greatest prophet was also the prophet of love."

"Love?" What was he saying?

He faced her. "Love your neighbor as yourself, wasn't

that his best known teaching? The Rabbi Akiva called it the great principle of the Torah. And yet all three religions ignore it."

"You've read the Torah too?"

"And the Talmud." He winked. "Time to jet."

# 24

SAMIR EXITED THE Los Angeles International Airport terminal Sunday morning, carrying only a single, medium-sized bag. He'd been in the United States once before, on a five-day visit to New York for Sheik Al-Asamm. It was two years after he began working as a driver for Miriam, while she was still twelve and he only twenty. The sheer volume of new sights and ideas had sent him virtually running back to Saudi Arabia, begging the sheik never to be sent again.

Since that time, he'd been to Paris and Madrid on a number of occasions, but they hadn't affected him like New York, whether because he was older or because those two cities were more reserved he did not know. He'd also been to Cairo. Many Saudi men went to the more liberal capital of Egypt for their pleasures, though that was not Samir's reason for going. Samir never understood the blatant disregard for Islam's moral code, which was almost always associated with such trips. He despised it.

He always confined his pleasure to what was permissible according to the Koran, and always restricted his pleasure to the company of one person whom he loved more than any other man, woman, or child in the universe.

Miriam.

He hailed a taxi and was soon riding down Century Boulevard, headed for the car-rental agency. His plan was simple. He would allow Miriam to find him, and then he would take her away from this nightmare. He needed nothing but his own love and the will of Allah. And a little help from the others, of course. But they were already helping, far more than they could possibly realize.

In the last hour alone they had told him where to find her.

Whatever information the Americans turned up on the ground, they passed on to Hilal, who in turn told General Mustafa, who informed not only the king, but Khalid and the sheik. Hilal knew a third party was after Miriam, but he didn't know it was Omar. In fact, because Samir knew about Omar, he knew more than the American Clive Masters. Omar knew everything that Hilal knew, but he was not aware of Samir's involvement.

Only Samir and the sheik knew the full picture. And it was appropriate, Samir thought, because he was here for love.

The taxi driver swerved and cursed at a passing bus. By his accent the man was from Pakistan. Likely a Muslim.

"You have lived long in America?" Samir asked.

"Three years. I'll be lucky to survive another three with these crazy drivers."

"That's a comforting thought for your passenger."

The man laughed. "You get used to it. This is your first time to the States?"

"Second. I've been to New York."

The man nodded.

"You are a Muslim?" Samir asked.

"Yes. There are many Muslims here."

"And you are a good Muslim?"

The man glanced in the rearview mirror. "A good Muslim, yes. I try my best. It's not easy to be a good Muslim in America."

"Then you should go home to Pakistan."

The man nodded, but the wind was out of his sails. "Perhaps."

They drove on in silence.

Samir looked to the east. Somewhere out there in this vast landscape of lost souls, Miriam was running for her life. Afraid, abandoned, and desperate. He took a deep breath and begged God for her safety. One more day. Give me one more day.

THEY HAD MISSED Seth and Miriam by five minutes, and Clive knew it might just as well have been a week. Ten units had searched the streets of Ridgecrest for the next hour and turned up exactly what he expected them to: nothing.

Clive drove out of the church parking lot. With any luck, none of this would matter soon. He was putting the final touches on a plan to upstage Seth. The only way to deal with Seth was to put him in the dark; Clive knew that like he knew the walnut in his pocket was round. And if he was right, he was closing in on a way to do just that.

The first step was to track Seth's movements and establish, with as much confidence as possible, his destination.

For that he needed more manpower. If he could determine the destination, Clive thought he had a pretty good chance of getting there without being seen in Seth's futures.

Peter Smaley had called an hour earlier and initiated a conference call with Secretary Paul Gray and NSA Director Susan Wheatly. Clive had talked to Susan before. The straight shooter took a personal interest in his unique position with the agency. It was his first time, however, to speak with the secretary of state, who was upset about having to tolerate Saudi diplomats running amuck in "this crazy manhunt down there." The secretary understood the sensitive nature of the country's relationship with Saudi Arabia better than anybody, but it didn't mean he had to like it.

Clive patiently retraced the events of the last three days and then gave his estimation of the situation.

"You're saying that Seth rather than Miriam presents the bigger problem to us," Susan had observed. "Not because he's assisting the princess, but because of this... this ability of his."

"Yes. And I'm suggesting we make bringing him in the top priority."

"You have over a hundred members of various law enforcement agencies directly involved now. And the rest of the country on full alert for this guy," the secretary said. "Sounds like top priority to me."

"I want more. He may try to take her from the country. I want all ports closed to private flights unless they've been thoroughly searched. I want to bring in Homeland Security and I want to set up interstate roadblocks. I'm suggesting we view Seth as a terrorist on the loose with an atomic weapon. And then I want you to give me authority over all resources. Nobody moves or talks without my saying so. That's top priority."

The phone went silent for a few seconds.

"You really think a college student from Berkeley is that dangerous?" Susan said.

"I think he's the most dangerous man on the planet at this moment."

Now, an hour later, Clive waited for their response. His patience was a formality. He already knew what the answer would be.

He slid into the car, fired it up. Hilal hadn't shown himself since their talk last night. He was probably headed for Nevada already. Clive now thought of him as an enemy of sorts. He had the will and the means to take both Seth and Miriam out. Clive wanted them alive. At the very least, he wanted Seth alive. No man could do what Seth was capable of doing. Killing him would be a mistake of the worst kind.

His phone rang.

"Yes."

"You have it, Clive," Smaley said. Amazing how his attitude had changed since Clive interrupted his meeting the previous day.

"Okay. I call the shots?"

"You run the show in-country. The border is being handled."

"Good enough."

Smaley breathed into the phone. "I have to say, I'm pretty skeptical about this...theory of yours."

"Okay."

"So. If you had to call it now, where would you say he's headed?"

"Las Vegas," Clive said.

. . .

"LAS VEGAS," OMAR said, dropping the phone on the seat. "Drive."

"How do they know?" Assir asked.

"They don't. But neither do we. The agency man believes they're headed for Las Vegas, and Hilal believes him. So we go to Las Vegas. We stay with our plan. Sooner or later the student will make a mistake."

After two days of cat-and-mouse games, it felt good to have a destination. He'd watched the meeting between Hilal and Clive Masters through binoculars at nearly a thousand yards and received the pertinent points of their conversation an hour later, when Hilal reported his suspicions to Saudi Arabia.

Now Seth and Miriam's entourage was headed for Las Vegas, and he would beat them there as well.

Omar laid his head back on the leather seat and closed his eyes. If the hunters were right about Seth's gift, then there was only one way to trap the student, and the agency man would be the one to do it. But no matter how the scene played itself out, Omar would witness the end. He would be the vulture. And Miriam would be his prey.

His wife would be his prey.

# 25

SETH CALLED THEM the "eyes from the sky." Helicopters. They were unquestionably the most annoying and most threatening factors in the route through Death Valley. Given the Cadillac's white paint, finding cover in the endless brown landscape was like trying to hide a mosque in the middle of the Rub' al-Khali desert. If not for Seth's three-hour sight into the future, they would have been apprehended long ago. He'd pulled the car into hiding no fewer than six times since their departure from the church yesterday morning.

The other annoying element was the heat. Particularly after the Cadillac's ancient air-conditioning unit quit functioning.

They decided Sunday afternoon that traveling at night might be a better idea. The darkness would provide cooler temperatures and hamper the helicopter's search. They freshened themselves up at a gas station manned by an old codger, purchased enough junk to fill the backseat, and went looking for a place to wait out the afternoon.

Seth's "old codger" was really just an older man who didn't care what was happening beyond his driveway, and the "junk," as he called it, consisted of necessities like toiletries, food, water, and clothes. The food was arguably unhealthy, and the clothes didn't fit Miriam as she would have liked. But after washing and changing into a fresh shirt in the station's restroom, Miriam felt nearly giddy.

They found an outcropping of bleached rock off the road, parked the car under it, and did their best to sleep in the stifling heat. Seth certainly needed the sleep. Despite his insistence that all was "peachy," she knew differently.

"You may say you're crisp as a fruit, but you can't hide your tired eyes," she'd said. "You're taking the Advil as if it were candy, and your eyes are puffy."

"Don't be silly." He looked in the mirror and then sat back without comment.

"It's wearing you down."

He looked past her with glazed eyes. "I'm sure that's what Clive is thinking. He's trying to push us to exhaustion and then close in. But as long as I don't sleep longer than three hours, we're okay."

He picked up a battery-operated alarm clock they'd purchased with their other supplies. What if it didn't work? Or worse, didn't wake him? She decided not to worry aloud. He needed sleep, not her concerns.

The issue turned out to be moot. Seth couldn't sleep. They resumed their journey after dark, and Seth seemed his energized self again. They talked about fashion in terms Miriam didn't know were part of the fashion world's lexicon. His was a unique view of the world, to be sure. And then they talked about surfing.

She'd been to the beach in Jidda, of course. But always draped from head to foot in the black abaaya and veil. The notion of diving into the ocean wearing nothing but shorts and a T-shirt had never struck her as such an intoxicating idea until now, hearing Seth talk. For that matter, what would it be like to swim in the waves naked? What a lovely idea!

Constant detours forced on them by the pursuit made their progress slow. They must have avoided a dozen police cars in one four-hour stretch. By eleven o'clock that night, Seth could barely keep his eyes open. He gave up in defeat and rolled the car into a ravine well off the road. Clive and his group would not likely discover them before daybreak. They both fell asleep within the hour.

The alarm chirped three hours later. Miriam pulled herself out of sleep's haze long enough to turn it off. She was asleep within seconds.


MIRIAM WAS THE first to awaken Monday morning. She pushed herself up in the rear seat. Seth was gone. She peered over the front seat. Nothing.

"Seth?"

The car moved under her and she realized that she was sitting on him. Alarmed, she clambered for the door, planting her elbows in his back and on his head in the process. That woke him. He rose groggy and grumbling, but none the wiser.

"We're safe?" she asked.

He looked around, waking. "Safe. What happened to the alarm clock?"

Only then did she remember. "I...I think I might have turned it off."

He rolled his eyes. "That was smart."

"Forgive me. I was depending on your infallible rising with the sun."

He smiled and winked. "Touché."

"Touché."

They devoured three large bags of Doritos, pulled back onto Highway 178, and headed east. Today they would reach Las Vegas.

Seth had explained his plan the night before, and it sounded like something actors might try in a movie rather than a reasonable course for two international fugitives. Nonetheless, she couldn't deny that this city of sin had a certain appeal. Riding here next to Seth in the desert, she felt perfectly scandalous.

A voice within kept telling her she was throwing herself to the winds of iniquity even thinking such thoughts. She should have her head buried in the Koran, begging God for his grace.

Seth had said nothing more to suggest his affection for her. She thought he was only being courteous, because his eyes spoke clearly enough. Although she appreciated his discretion, she was surprised to discover that a part of her regretted his silence. She was indeed a woman, and he was a compassionate, strong, and handsome man.

Was she actually falling for Seth? She looked out the side window and forced her thoughts in a new direction.

The Mojave Desert was not like the great deserts of Saudi Arabia. Sand dunes rose in the distance, but mostly the land comprised rocky ground shifting in hues of red and white. Seth drove past a sight called Artists' Point, where the rock was green in parts. The Americans called Death Valley—over three million acres of this rugged ground—a "park."

In a strange way, driving through the desert toward the mysterious city of Las Vegas with Seth at her side felt like a metaphysical passing from death to freedom. There he was again. Seth.

They'd driven for some time without encountering a single vehicle when a sly grin split Seth's face.

"I have an idea," he said.

She looked at him. "This is new?"

He slowed and veered off the road. Gravel crunched under their tires. The desert was flat on either side of the highway here. Rough outcroppings of rock rose from the ground two hundred meters to their right.

"What are you doing?"

"We have some time. I've decided you need to really experience freedom."

"Oh? I thought I was free already. Here with you."

He put the car into park and looked at her. "You haven't even begun to experience true freedom until you have wheels, princess. In America, wheels are synonymous with freedom. Everyone knows this. Come on."

He opened his door and climbed out.

"What do you mean?"

"Trust me. Get out."

Miriam climbed out. She stood by her door and looked at him over the Cadillac's shredded vinyl roof. "What?"

"Over here."

She walked around the hood, grinning with him, clueless to his intentions. "What are we doing?"

He held the door and invited her to the driver's seat. He wanted her to drive?

"I can't drive!"

"Exactly. That's why I need to teach you."

"Why?" The idea terrified her.

"We may need you to drive. We don't know what waits beyond three hours. It just makes sense."

"Now? Out here? We don't have time for this!"

"But we do have time, princess. I should know. And I also know that you will give this a try. I've seen that as well, so you might as well hop behind the wheel and give it a go." He grinned deliberately.

Miriam looked around. "Have you seen me running into anything?"

"What's there to run into?"

"You're not answering my question."

"Okay. Actually there are a few scenarios in which you have a few mishaps, but we'll do our best to avoid those. Come on, don't tell me a princess who risked her life by crossing oceans is afraid of a little joyride in the desert."

"What kind of mishaps?"

He shrugged. "Nothing noteworthy really. Driving off a cliff. Hitting a truck head-on. Please, I insist."

She looked at the steering wheel. Women were not permitted to drive in Saudi Arabia. Perhaps that was reason enough to try it. She felt a grin pull at her lips.

"You promise me it will be safe?"

"There's always risk in life's most rewarding pursuits, isn't there?"

She slid in behind the wheel.

Seth bounded over the hood and climbed in, ecstatic.

It took him three minutes to explain the basics, not that she didn't know them, but because she felt comforted by his repeated explanations. This is the brake, used to stop the car; this is the accelerator, used to speed the car up; this is the steering wheel, used to keep the car on the road; this is the radio, used to keep you awake so you don't drive off a cliff.

She turned off the radio and demanded he stay serious. She also insisted he show her how all the turn signals and lights worked. If she was going to learn to drive, she might as well do it right.

He told her to drive out toward the rock outcroppings. The ground was hard enough here to resist tire tracks, and he'd seen what would happen if they took to the road. It wasn't pretty. Miriam put the gearshift into drive and gripped the wheel with both hands, knuckles white.

"Let's roll," he said. He was already trying hard not to laugh, and she wondered what he was seeing.

"Let's roll," she said and pushed the pedal on the floor. The Cadillac jerked forward. She immediately shoved her foot down to stop. Instead of stopping, the car shot out into the desert like a bullet from a gun.

Miriam screamed. Beside her, Seth was laughing. Cackling uncontrollably, in fact.

"Seth! Stop..."

Her limbs froze, fixed by terror. The car raced forward, headed directly for the rocks.

"Seth!"

"Turn!" he shouted.

He grabbed the wheel and tried to turn the car, but rigor mortis had seized her arms and she held fast.

"The brakes!" Seth yelled. "Stop the car!" He swung his leg toward the pedals and stabbed at the floor, shoving her against her door in the process. "Push the brakes!"

One thought rose above the panic that had immobilized her. Seth was scared. He hadn't seen this as a real possibility. He needed her to stop this car because he was powerless to do it without her.

Her limbs came free. She swung her elbow into his rib cage with enough force to take the wind from him. He grunted and released his grip. She spun the wheel to her right, just as the windshield wiper made its first pass on the glass, clearing her view. The rocks loomed twenty meters ahead.

The car slid sideways. It occurred to her that her foot was on the accelerator rather than the brake. But she decided that it should stay there. She should use the power of the car to take them out of harm's way. Ride it out, as Seth had said once.

The back of the car swept around in a great half-circle, wheels spewing debris back toward the rocks. They came to a near stop, engine still roaring, and then shot back out into the desert, away from the outcropping.

Miriam blinked. Exhilaration flooded her veins like a rush of cold water. She eased off the accelerator. "Whooo-haaa!" she shouted. "Let it ride, baby!"

Seth laughed tentatively.

Miriam steered the car right and then left. She pressed the accelerator and sped up again.

"Easy..."

"I have it under control, dear. You just sit back and relax."

Listen to her. She was sounding like him. She grinned,

pulled the car through another wide turn, and sped back out into the desert.

"Now you're talking," Seth said. His confidence was back. "Take it behind the rocks and out into the desert a bit. We need to get out of sight. Someone's coming down the highway."

His revelation alarmed her only because he seemed comfortable in depending on her to take them from danger. She guided the car around the boulders, weaving more than she would have liked. Perhaps her confidence was a little premature. But she did manage, and she had saved them from crashing into the boulders.


SHE DROVE FOR twenty minutes while he continued to give her pointers. They headed farther out into the desert, weaving around boulders and sandy patches. By the time she parked the car behind a large rock formation, they were a good distance from the road. The traffic on the highway was hopeless for the next hour anyway, Seth said. In fact, he had yet to figure out how they were going to make it across the California-Nevada border. At the moment, law enforcement officers seemed to have the upper hand in all possible futures there.

They sat on a rounded rock next to each other and shared another bag of chips with a bottle of water, and Miriam wasn't sure she had ever been so thrilled in all her life.

She looked at Seth as he tilted the bottled water to his lips and drank. His neck was strong and bronzed by the sun. His hair was loose, not unlike the Greek sculptures that graced her uncle's villa in Riyadh. Allah had sent her a Greek god to take her through the desert in a Cadillac.

She looked away from him. Listen to you, Miriam. You're being taken by him. She reached into the bag of chips and ate one.

Yes, of course, because the Greek god called Seth was a master at the art of love, equipped as he was with this foreknowledge of his. He had an unfair advantage.

"Are you manipulating me?"

He turned his head, eyebrows arched. "What do you mean?"

"I mean, are you taking advantage of me?"

"Do I act like I'm taking advantage of you?"

"Of my mind."

"What are you talking about? I can't take advantage of your mind."

She looked at the tall western peaks. He seemed genuinely surprised by her questions. How, if he had already seen the possibility of her asking it? Maybe he was losing his touch. He had missed the possibility of her driving into the rock earlier.

She stood and dropped the bag of chips in his lap. "Please don't play with me. I know very well that you know what I'm going to say before I say it. I know you can simply choose the right words to evoke the right response from me. And now that you're pretending to be confused by my question, I can't help but think that you are manipulating me."

"Fine, I might have seen the possibility that you would pursue this line of questioning, but you have to understand, it's only one possibility out of thousands wandering around in my mind. I never took it seriously."

"You still possess this crazy ability to make people do things. I can't believe that you don't do that with me all the time. I think you're manipulating my feelings."

He hesitated. "Nonsense. I would never do such a thing. And just so we're clear, this crazy ability, as you so affectionately refer to it, is saving your life."

"So you don't deny that you can make me feel things?"

"Of course I can't!"

"How do you expect me to handle this show of affection you've thrown at me?" *You're saying too much, Miriam.* "First you tell me that you have feelings for me, and then I begin to think that I may have feelings that—" She caught herself.

"What feelings?" he asked.

Miriam pushed past the embarrassment that flushed her face. "Do you deny that you can at least make me *do* things?"

"Yes, I do deny it," he said. "I can't make you do things."

"But out of all the things that I might do, you can make me do those things you want me to do."

He hesitated. "No, not necessarily."

"Ha! I don't believe you."

"I can't make you do anything you don't want to do."

"Is that right? Please, let's not mind the technicalities. I think you can see an almost unlimited number of my responses to what you say or do, and then you can do whichever results in the response you want."

"It's not exactly like that."

"Then show me what it *is* like. The least you can do is be forthright with me. Let me test you. See if you can make me do something."

"Please, Miriam. We shouldn't do this." He was afraid,

wasn't he? She felt a twinge of empathy for him. And then she wondered if he hadn't manipulated her empathy by the phrasing of his words.

"I insist." She paused. "Make me do something. Make me kiss you."

His pallor reddened. "You're assuming that's something I want you to do?"

"Okay then, let's pretend that you want me to kiss you. Deep inside, you probably wouldn't mind. That's close enough, isn't it? So then make me kiss you, Mr. California."

He chuckled nervously.

"I'm waiting."

"Don't be ridiculous. I can't make you kiss me."

"Do you want me to kiss you?"

"Right now?"

The way he said it betrayed him. Surprisingly, she was pleased by the fact. And then conflicted.

"Sure, why not," she said. "The desire has obviously crossed your mind. Just pretend it's resurfaced here, in this hot desert so far from the nearest living soul." She couldn't suppress a small grin.

For his part, Seth was now thoroughly embarrassed. He looked off in the direction of the road and shook his head.

"You're saying that at this moment, you see no possible futures in which I kiss you in the next few minutes?" she asked.

"That's not fair," he said.

"You don't want to be forthcoming with me? You want to hide the truth from me? You have a gift, use it!"

"Stop it!" His tone caught her off guard. She had pushed him, as much to see him squirm as to know the truth. And what if he actually made her kiss him? She would never do it! This was the power of a woman.

"Then tell me," she said.

"Okay...There's one future in which you kiss me."

"That's impossible!"

"So I tell you the truth but really you don't want to hear the truth after all," he said. "I'm sorry, princess, but it is indeed true."

Miriam stared at him, shocked by his claim. He was avoiding her eyes.

"Then make me do it," she challenged.

"I can't."

"Do it! Don't you dare tell me that I will kiss you without giving me the opportunity to prove you wrong."

"Okay. Roses are red, violets are blue; I'll kiss a toad, but I won't kiss you."

She blinked at him. "What is that supposed to mean? This is your way of enticing a woman?"

"You're right." A sly smile spread across his mouth. "Roses are red, violets are blue; you are without doubt the most beautiful woman I have ever seen."

She paused. "That's better but it doesn't rhyme. And as you see, my lips are still not on yours. I don't feel the slightest impulse to kiss you. You can do better."

Perhaps a very small part of her did want to kiss him.

"Okay, how's this?" He jumped to his feet, ripped open his shirt, and put one hand behind his head and the other on his waist, cocking his hips in a pose, so that his stomach muscles rippled. "Hey, baby, you like what you see?" he said, winking.

She stared at him, astounded at his gall. A giggle rose from her belly. He grinned and relaxed his pose. "No?"

She swallowed her laughter but could do nothing about the grin on her face. "I still haven't run into your arms."

He shrugged his shirt closed. "That's because I can't make you do anything. And I never would, even if the thought of kissing you did cross my mind in a mad moment of brutal honesty, as you put it. And for the record, the future in which I saw you kissing me involved a kiss on the forehead. Just so you know."

*In another life, I'm not sure I wouldn't have kissed you, Seth Border.* She walked up to him, put her hands on his shoulders, and kissed him on the forehead. "There you go. Now I've fulfilled your prophecy," she said, satisfied by his blush. She picked up the bag of chips and walked away.

"WOULD YOU LIKE to test the truth in your heart?" Seth said behind her.

She turned. "I thought we just did."

"I was thinking about you being a Muslim. God and all that," he said. "We don't see eye-to-eye on the issue, my not being religious and such. But it's occurred to me that I may have a way to test your God. A tangible test, no arguments."

"Isn't it okay that we disagree?"

"Actually, there is a problem. According to your faith, I'm an infidel. Your godsend—that would be me—is headed for eternal torment. How can you be okay with that? We need to...reconcile, so to speak. Get on the same page."

Miriam tucked a strand of hair behind her ear. "Fine, reconcile us."

"Okay. Christian Nazis killed the Jews. The Crusaders killed Muslims. Islamic extremists killed Christians in the World Trade Center. Right? All guilty of breaking the greatest commandment."

"Very few Arabs are extremists."

"Of course not. Neither are most Christians Hitler's. Point is, they all broke the cardinal rule."

"Love your neighbor as yourself," Miriam said.

"Correct."

"And what does this have to do with the existence of God?"

"It has more to do with proving that I am not an infidel. Let me prove God doesn't exist."

"You can't test God."

"Maybe I can."

Seth bounded over to a group of small boulders and scooped up an armful of medium-sized rocks. He ran to a bare patch of ground and set them in a circle. Miriam watched him curiously, afraid to ask.

He returned to the pile and grabbed up more stones. "Ever hear of Elijah and Mount Carmel?" he asked.

"No," she said.

"God supposedly descended in fire."

He seemed enthusiastic about his idea, but Miriam was still unclear about his intentions. "You want God to descend in fire?" she said. "This won't prove a thing."

"No, not fire. But if I ask God to do something— anything in the immediate future—I will be able to see if even the possibilities of the immediate future change."

"And if he doesn't want to do it, you will say he doesn't exist?" It was unorthodox to be sure, perhaps foolish even, but she didn't see the harm. This was her eccentric

Seth at work. At least there were no mutawa around to see his mockery.

"Don't you get it?" he said. "Even a refusal will affect what I see. It's like having a giant stethoscope up to the heavens. If there's a God, and if that God responds in any way, I'll know it. For all we know, this is the first time in history such a thing has even been possible."

"But I won't know that anything has changed," she said.

"True. You'll have to take my word for it." He looked at the altar. "It's been a while since I said a prayer. Maybe you should do the honors."

"I'll have no part in this."

"Fair enough. But I'm not sure I really know how to speak to God. You do. Better chance of getting through, don't you think?"

"This is absurd."

"Still, worth a shot, right?"

She said nothing.

He fidgeted with his hands for a moment, considering how to proceed. Then he closed his eyes.

Miriam shook her head, embarrassed for him. Her Greek god was determined to prove something she didn't care about in the first place. Her confidence was a matter of faith, not proof. Whatever he did or didn't see wouldn't change that.

Seth looked at her and smiled.

"Well?" she asked.

"I do think I just talked at God. Whatever that is."

"And?"

"Nothing."

"What did you expect, the clouds to roll back?"

"I expected nothing. The futures are flying by and I see

no change." He stepped toward her. "Absolutely nothing, nada, zip. I rest my case."

"It proves nothing."

"Exactly."

"It was a foolish exercise."

"Absurd. I feel like an imbecile. But I did it for you, not for me."

"So kind of you."

"Such a soft heart, I have. We'll have to depend on good old—"

Seth froze midstride, eyes wide.

"What is it?"

He composed himself. "Nothing. Let's roll." He walked past her.

She hurried for her door, evidently on the passenger's side, considering he had his hand on the driver's door already.

"Don't say nothing. I know you saw something. What did you see?"

"I saw that we have to roll. Now!"

# 26

THEY APPROACHED THE Nevada border on Highway 178 and stopped five miles from the crossing. Seth remained quiet about the altar episode. He said he was still trying to figure it out but refused to explain what it was.

But she knew. The future had changed; the fact that they were making a run for the state line was evidence enough. He had tossed a prayer into the sky and the future had changed, and Seth was not at all at ease with the fact.

Slowly Seth came to himself. He stared at the blacktop ahead, hands on the wheel. A mischievous grin grew on his face.

"Okay, the way I see it, we have three ways to do this." He looked at her. "One way would be violent and bloody, one would be crafty and brilliant, and one would be bold and silly. Which is your pleasure?"

She thought through the choices. Violence was unacceptable to both of them. What could he mean by silly?

Either way they would succeed, wouldn't they? Although he had made some errors lately.

"Bold and silly," she said.

"You sure?"

"Maybe not."

"No, I think it's a daring choice," he said. "Let's do it."

"Okay."

Seth slapped the steering wheel. "Excellent!"

He climbed out, ran to the front of the car, yanked off the Cadillac hood ornament, and hurled it into the desert. Miriam got out, amused.

"What is this?"

"This is our disguise, princess." He ran to the trunk, popped it up, and returned with a large knife. Without warning he bent and slashed the right front tire. With a terrible hiss, the air bled out. The sound struck her as maniacal.

"I cannot imagine this is a clever idea," she said.

He ran to the rear wheel and slashed it as well. "You chose bold and silly, remember?"

"Yes, but I didn't choose stupid."

Seth laughed and jumped around to the other side, where he repeated the slashing. All four tires were as flat as millet cakes.

"Let's go," he said.

"You can drive on these tires?"

"For a few miles. That's the point."

They started down the road, and within a hundred meters the thumping began. Within another hundred the racket was so loud that Miriam was sure the wheels would fall off.

"This is ridiculous!"

"Ha! You think this is ridiculous?"

Now she began to worry in earnest. He had never failed them, but this madness was a new thing. Perhaps he had actually lost his gift as the result of the prayer.

A loud bang sounded from the engine and Miriam flinched. Steam began to seep from the hood. Now what? The engine was going to blow up!

"Seth! Shouldn't you stop?"

"No!" He was delighted. "This is it!"

"What on earth are we doing?"

"Mess up your hair and put some of that white sunblock on your face. Could you do that for me?"

"Not until you tell me what we are doing!"

"We're putting on a disguise. Just enough so that he won't recognize you for a few seconds. That's all we need. I thought white sunblock would be better than grease."

"Who is he?"

The smile left his face. "I'm sorry, but we're starting to run out of time. We're committed, and honestly, if I tell you too much, this won't work. I swear I'll make anything you find less than hilarious up to you later, but now you have to make yourself look non-Arabic."

Smoke was streaming out of the hood. A tremendous thump sounded under them.

"We lost a tire," he said, grinning again.

She stared at him for one last moment, and then scrambled for the back where a small bag held their toiletries. "I don't like this," she said, pulling out the tube of white cream. She smeared the paste over her face. "I don't like this at all."

"You look like a ghost."

She grabbed the visor and looked at her image in

the mirror. A streaked white face stared back. The car stopped in a cloud of smoke.

"Perfect," Seth said. "The crossing is just around that corner. Just drive nice and easy and stop before you get to the police cruiser."

She spun to him. "Drive? I can't drive!"

"I told you it would come in handy, didn't I?"


CAPTAIN JOHN ROGERS had just put out his last Lucky Strike and was thinking he'd much rather be back in Shoshone, having a cold brew at Bill's Bar, when he saw the cloud of smoke rolling his way from around the bend.

His first thought was that someone had ignited a smoke bomb, but he discarded the thought when he saw the grille. It was an overheated car, limping as if running on the last cylinder. Banana peckers, that thing was barely crawling. Didn't the fool driver realize he was frying the engine?

He couldn't make out the car because it was crawling under a mask of steam, but by the square grille he pegged it as an old sedan. These here were tourists from New York or Vermont, come to take a picnic in Death Valley without knowing the first thing about the harsh realities of the place. John had seen it a hundred times.

He grunted and leaned back on his hood. "Banana peckers," he said. He didn't know how the fool could see past the windshield. It was wobbling too. In fact, if he wasn't mistaken...

Good night, the thing had burned its wheels off! Was that even possible? The situation had just gone from New Yorker stupid to hardly imaginable imbecile. In his eleven years patrolling these parts, he couldn't remember seeing anything quite like this.

He stood up and put his hands on his hips. "Double banana peckers," he said. "Wait'll the boys get a load of this."

The car sounded like a limo pulling strings of empty cans after a wedding. It clanked to a steaming halt ten yards off.

John rested his right hand on his gun. Never could be too careful. A man stupid enough to drive this deathtrap was stupid enough to do anything.

The engine died. Hissing smoke boiled skyward. All four tires were gone. Now how in the world was that possible?

The door flew open and someone stumbled out, coughing and gagging on the smoke.

"Hold it there!" John yelled. "Just hold it right there!"

The person straightened, frantic. It was a woman and her face was white. Either sunblock or makeup. Her hair flew every which way, and she reminded him of Gene Simmons wearing that Kiss makeup.

She gripped her hair and turned in a slow circle, moaning.

A faint breeze cleared the smoke for a moment. The car was empty. He edged forward and peered through the haze.

"You must help me," the woman moaned.

"You alone, miss?"

She began to jump up and down, screaming at the top of her lungs. "The arks are after me! The arks are after me! Help me, the arks are after me!"

Startled, he followed her terrified look back down the road. "Okay, just go easy, miss. I don't know what you're on, but everything is fine now. There are no arks after you."

"The arks! You don't understand, I have the ring and the arks are after me!"

He eased toward her. The woman was either high and hallucinating, or a plain lunatic. Not a bad thing, actually; she would be his ticket off this post. He held out a reassuring hand.

"Please, miss. I've been here all day and I can assure you, there are no arks in these parts. Now if you'll just calm down."

It dawned on him what she was trying to say. He stopped four feet from her and waved a hand through the smoke. "Do you mean the Orcs are after you? Like the Orcs from *The Lord of the Rings*?"

She stopped jumping, surprised but no longer frantic, as if a light had just gone on in her head.

A door slammed behind him and he spun back. The cruiser!

"Hey!"

A hand slapped at his waist, and he twisted back to see the woman hurl his revolver over the guardrail. He grabbed at her, but she was past him, running for the cruiser. He took a step in the direction she'd thrown the gun and immediately realized he would never retrieve it before they took off. He chased her.

"Stop!" He knew then that these were the two they had been looking for. "Stop!"

The engine fired and the woman piled in. With a squeal of tires his cruiser shot backward, peeled through a U-turn, and then roared off, leaving him straddling the yellow lines on the road.

He glanced down at his waist. No radio. He could get the gun, of course, but…John turned around and looked at the steaming car they'd abandoned. The tireless wheels were mangled. It was going nowhere. The trunk was open. The man had come from the trunk and snuck around, using the smoke for cover while the lady went on about the arks. Orcs.

Banana peckers! This was not good. Not good at all.

# 27

THEY DEPOSITED THE police cruiser in a small town called Pahrump and took a bus into Las Vegas. Miriam made it abundantly clear to Seth that his notion of "bold and silly" was far better characterized as "crazy and ridiculous," and then only in generous terms. Even so, she had done her share of laughing as they sped away from the stranded cop at the state line.

The fact that she had raved on about an ark when she should have said Orc was the worst of it. He insisted he'd said Orc, not ark. And after all, he claimed, she'd seen the movie; she should know. But she finally decided to forgive him. The whole incident seemed to have endeared her to him, even more so than before.

Still, despite his outward pleasure with her performance, he maintained the same introspective nature he'd adopted after his experiment with the prayer. His ability to see forward in time hadn't stretched beyond three hours, but now he seemed to see more futures within that time. His sight was broadening if not lengthening, if she wasn't mistaken, and his headaches had increased, judging by the number of Advil he kept taking.

Las Vegas was a city of true wonder, its lights and colors surpassing her wildest imaginations. Seth referred to the huge casinos as hotels, but in her mind they were nothing less than enclosed cities.

They took adjoining rooms in Caesars Palace, both deluxe rooms in the Forum Towers. Miriam wasn't unaccustomed to luxury, of course, but nothing she'd experienced compared to the magical aura that surrounded them in this magnificent palace.

The rooms were trimmed with gold and mirrors and ancient symbols of Greeks—pillars and horses and, yes, Greek gods like her own.

"It's a waste of resources," Seth said as she swept through the room, delighted. She stopped at the window high above the city and looked out at a dizzying ocean of colors, red and blue and orange and green, moving and flashing with glitter and glamour.

She let the sights go and faced him. "A waste on whom? I'm not worth this?"

He looked at her, blushing, and she knew his mind was scrambling. "No. That's not what I meant. For you, this is hardly acceptable."

For a moment they searched each other's eyes. His were soft and lost, and looking into them, sadness overtook her. *In another time, in another place, I could love you, Seth. But not here. Never.*

Seth cleared his throat and turned to the window. "Hilal is here," he said. "But he's not what I expected."

"And what did you expect?" Miriam asked, disappointed

that he had guessed their destination before they'd had a chance to enjoy it.

"I expected Clive to have the police out in force, searching the hotels and streets. But the Las Vegas police aren't even aware of us. I can see numerous incidents in which we could walk by the authorities without being noticed, much less shipped off to prison. Hilal must be here on his own."

"Are we safe or are we not?"

He paused. "Safe."

"Then let's go shopping," she said.

"Sure."

They wandered through the shops in the forum, engulfed by a sea of people who meandered about in a daze. The prices seemed high by Seth's estimation, but price was one thing Miriam had learned to ignore. Being a princess did have one or two advantages.

In addition to the costumes they bought for the coming day, Miriam could not resist purchasing suitable clothing. A simple yet elegant emerald dress for her and a pair of black slacks with a beige shirt for Seth. And new shoes for both.

They dined at the Terrazza restaurant on lobster and crayfish, a favorite of Seth's. She insisted and he agreed. It wouldn't have mattered what they ate; Seth was clearly more interested in her than in the food. She decided then, for the first time, not to discourage him. Women were created to be beautiful for a reason. Their faces were not meant to be hidden away by black veils for their husbands alone. And she was in Las Vegas, for heaven's sake! Seth liked her, maybe even loved her. She liked him very much as well. She would make nothing more or less of the matter.

Miriam sat across from Seth and laughed with him, unencumbered by the shackles of her upbringing for the first time. They drank wine and they drank freedom, and Miriam could not have imagined either tasting so delicious.

They retired early and she, at least, slept like a baby, properly pampered and refreshed for the adventure before them. It was ten o'clock in the morning before Seth knocked on the door that separated her suite from his.

"Come."

Seth opened the door, grinning. "The gentleman has arrived."

She stood back and looked at him, stunned by the transformation. His hair was neatly slicked back above his ears. His face was clean shaven and smooth except for a mustache he'd attached to his upper lip. Dressed in the black slacks and beige shirt, he looked every bit the dashing man.

"My, you do clean up, don't you?"

"And you, my princess," he returned, eyeing her, "you are absolutely stunning."

"Yes?" She cocked both hands and touched her wig. "You like it?"

"But of course. I think I would find you beautiful in a gunnysack, but you are quite ravishing in this dress."

"Thank you."

The straight brown wig hung just below the ears, masking her own long black hair. The disguises were Seth's idea, and despite the apparent lack of danger, he had insisted they carry through. They would be at the gambling tables for some time, perfectly framed by a dozen cameras. No need to advertise.

Seth smoothed his shirt and walked in, upright. "Your future awaits us. Are you ready?"

"I'm breathless with anticipation," she said, stretching out her hand for him.

He took it, kissed it lightly, and then spun her around in a dance. She twirled so that her dress rose to a bell.

"Queen of dancers," he said. He bowed, put one hand on her hip, and marched her across the room in a stiff dance. She was positive he was faking. When they reached the window, he spun around and marched her back.

"This is the way we dance in California," he said in a British accent.

One end of his mustache had detached and fluttered over his lip. She couldn't hold back a giggle.

"What?" he demanded, still in proper British character.

"It seems that the gentleman's mustache is objecting."

Seth felt his upper lip. "What? This?" He ripped off the mustache. "Nonsense! This isn't a mustache at all. It's a morsel left over from dinner last evening. I've been saving it for now." He stuffed the strip of hair into his mouth, jerked his head back as if swallowing, and then promptly spit it out.

"Whew! Terribly stale, what."

Miriam put both hands to her face and howled.

His clowning turned to embarrassment. She walked up to him. "You've ruined your disguise. Although I will say, with your hair combed you look quite different."

Someday she would either be forced back to Saudi Arabia or delivered safely to Samir by this man. Her heart surged with gratitude. She would miss his company. Miriam looked into his eyes and placed a hand on his cheek. "I owe you my life, Seth. I want you to know that. There is nothing I can ever do to repay what you've done for me."

She stood on her tiptoes and kissed his cheek.

Seth turned beet-red. She could grow accustomed to the power that a woman held in this country, she thought.

"Well, then. Let's go win us some money," he said. "This should be like taking candy from a baby."

He turned for the door, reached for the knob, then hesitated. He stared at the door. A bolt of fear killed the moment. Now what?

"Seth? What is it?"

He gazed ahead, frozen.

"Seth?"

He blinked once. Twice. Then he swallowed and cleared his throat.

"Nothing. It's nothing," he said.

"I've seen nothing with you, and nothing is always something. What's going on?"

He forced a grin and faced her. "Really, it's nothing. Nothing."

"I won't accept that!"

He stepped forward and kissed her on the forehead. "That's in case I don't see you after today."

"What do you mean?"

"You'll understand later."

He turned around and—just like that—shed the strange trance that had overcome him. "Ready? Let's go."


CLIVE MASTERS WAITED patiently in the Learjet as it taxied to the Las Vegas airport terminal. Now that he'd arrived, he couldn't waste any time. Assuming his gamble worked at all.

He picked up his telephone and dialed the Las Vegas

chief of police's private number. Benson answered on the second ring.

"Send the car."

Benson spoke off the phone and then returned. "It's on the way."

"Good. Now I need you to do me a favor—"

"Listen, Masters, NSA or not, I need to know what you're trying to prove here. I'm not accustomed to working blind. I agreed to the car, but—"

"I'm trying to explain. Forgive me, but I honestly didn't know myself until just a few minutes ago. I need you to launch crash surveillance on the casinos. In particular the larger ones with high-stakes tables. I can't tell you who we're looking for, or what they look like. Just check for anything unusual."

"Do you know who you're looking for?"

Clive hesitated. "Yes. But I can't tell you. This will make sense later. And I don't want any suspicious characters apprehended, just reported. Can you do that?"

The phone was silent for a moment. "I suppose. Why no word until now?"

"You wouldn't believe me if I told you. Just go with me on this. I need eyes. I'll wager my pension you'll find something, and if I'm right, we have only two or three hours."

"Can't you tell me anything?"

"No."

"I'll see what I can do."

"Another thing. I know this goes against every rule you've ever been taught, but law enforcement needs to stay out of this. No police, no nothing. This needs to come strictly from camera operators at the casinos."

"Now you're over my head, Masters. That's not the way we find people in this town."

"It is today. Just do it. I'll explain when I get there."

He hung up and sat back. The terminal building rose to his left.

The whole idea was simple, really. Everyone was in the dark. Clive was little more than a blind fool chasing a man who could see clearly in this world of futures. He could not see into the future himself, so he would blind Seth by taking the futures away. At least those futures that involved a pursuit.

He had barely convinced the teams to pull back from Las Vegas, rather than smother the city with every available law enforcement officer from Los Angeles to Salt Lake City.

If what Seth had told him in the alley was true, then Seth's gift was characterized by two critical elements: One, he was seeing potential futures. Two, he was seeing futures only a brief time out. He was whipping them on the street because he knew their next move before they did to the tune of two or three hours.

So then, they wouldn't give Seth their next move.

The only way not to give Seth their next move was to remove their next move from the universe of his futures. And the only way to remove their next move from any futures in Seth's world was to remove those futures from their own worlds. Confusing, but true. He hoped.

In words that the politicians could understand, it went like this: If Clive didn't know what he was going to do next—if he deliberately removed any plans for chasing Seth from his agenda—then his own future would be removed from any of Seth's futures. Seth would suspect nothing until Clive formed a specific plan to apprehend him. And in fact, Clive had no plan to apprehend Seth. At least to the best of his knowledge. Neither did Benson. Benson was just looking without knowing what for or why.

At least that was the theory. A few mind-boggling possibilities turned Seth into an invincible foe, but Clive refused to accept any of them.

Thinking about it now, the whole plan—or the lack thereof—was a bit shaky. First, Clive had removed from Las Vegas anyone with any notion that there even was a hunt on for Seth. Second, he specifically did not decide to go to Las Vegas. He simply planned to make a decision at some point to fly into the city and set up immediate surveillance. If all went well, he would intercept Seth before any of their futures crossed.

The single greatest variable in this gamble was timing. His "unplanned" decision to go had to correspond with Seth's presence at the casinos. Nailing this was pure guesswork, and he'd guessed that Seth was not only going to Las Vegas, but that he would take two days to arrive.

This chase would be won by the fastest mind rather than the fastest runner, and Clive had most definitely met his match.

It took them fifteen minutes to reach the station. Clive virtually crushed his walnut during the drive. Every second counted; every passing moment created a slew of new possible futures; at any time one of those futures could cross one of Seth's and he would know Clive was in town.

Another five minutes passed before he found himself in Benson's office, and by the time he closed the door he convinced himself he had failed already. This whole plan would never work. They were way too slow.

"Well, well," Benson said, dropping the phone in the cradle, "you wouldn't believe your fortune. That was security at Caesars Palace. They have a man and a woman running hot on the roulette tables as we speak."

Clive's doubt fell away. "Pictures?"

The fax began to hum. "On the way now."

Clive stepped over to the machine and wiped sweat from his eyebrows. Settle down, boy. You're gonna have a heart attack on this man's floor. He was as keyed up as he could remember being. He took a calming breath and ripped the first page from the fax machine.

A fuzzy black-and-white of a man and a woman sitting at a roulette table stared up at him, with a note scrawled along the bottom.

$32,000 in 30 min.

The man wore a mustache, and his hair was slicked back. The woman, short dark hair. Wrong.

"Not them," Clive said. "Keep looking."

Every second's another thousand futures, Clive. One of them is going to tip him off. He grunted, crumpled up the sheet, and tossed it in the waste bin.

"That's a lot of money," the chief said. He picked up the phone and dialed. "Not them, Sam. Keep your eyes peeled."

"Ask him how often someone wins like that," Clive said.

Benson glanced at him. "How often does someone win like that?" he asked. He nodded. "He says never. First time he's seen it."

Clive blinked. He dipped into the wastebasket, pulled the crumpled fax out, and smoothed it flat.

It's a mind game, Clive. Forget the hard evidence; go for the mind.

"How long will it take us to get to the casino?"

"Twenty minutes. To the tables, another ten."

The fact was, Clive had no idea if these people were Seth and Miriam. If he apprehended the wrong couple, he might tip off Seth's world of futures. But the longer he waited, the greater the chance Seth would figure Clive out on his own anyway.

Then again, winning thirty-two thousand dollars in half an hour at the roulette wheel would be like sleeping for a man like Seth.

Clive moved. "We go. Three cars, six men. Now."

"Security can pick them up."

He stopped and turned. "No. There's a chance he doesn't know we're onto him yet. If he's the one, the minute security makes a move, he'll be gone." He paused. "Tell them to seal the exits. Don't say why."

"And he won't be gone if you go?"

"I've got a shot; they don't."

"Oh? And why would that be?"

"Because I'm smarter, Benson."

# 28

BLACK TWENTY-FOUR," SETH said, pointing to the spot on the roulette table. He stared into her eyes and stroked the mustache he'd reapplied in the elevator. "What do you think, honey? Twenty-four feel like a lucky number to you?"

"I don't know. Is twenty-four in any of our birthdays or phone numbers?"

"No. But if you divide 327,115.2 by 13,629.8, you get exactly 24. I say we go for it."

Miriam bit back a smile. The poor dealer had long ago given up his cute comebacks to Seth's ramblings. He stared at them, mute.

"How much?" Miriam asked.

"All of it," Seth said.

"I told you, there's a thousand-dollar limit," the dealer said. He tucked the steel ball under the lip of the wheel and sent it hurling around.

"That's right, junior. I forgot. I'm not especially good with numbers. Ten thousand is a pretty big number." Seth looked at her, eyes sparkling. He had purposefully lost many bets, as planned, but the pile of chips was growing steadily.

Seth raised an eyebrow. "A thousand, then?"

"That means if the ball lands on the black twenty-four we will win how much?" she asked, knowing full well.

"Thirty-five, I think."

"Let's do it." She slid a thousand-dollar chip out on the space and winked at Seth.

A crowd of seven or eight onlookers gathered behind them, peering over their shoulders as the ball slowed to a crawl, dropped into the wheel, bounced around like a pogo stick, and then rattled into the small square. Twenty-four.

Someone gasped.

"We won!" Miriam exclaimed, throwing her hands up. She wrapped her arms around his neck and planted a kiss on his cheek.

"Yes, will you look at that. We did win. I'll be a toad on a stool at the bottom of a pool." He reached out and pulled back a tall stack of black chips, each etched with $1,000 in gold. Seth tossed the dealer one of them. "That's for you, junior. It's our lucky day."

Chips were as good as cash in Vegas. The thin dealer blinked, looked over at the pit boss, and palmed the tip. "Thanks."

Seth dipped his head and smiled coyly. "Which number, honey?"

Miriam had never felt so bold and thrilled in all her life, pretending to be his starry-eyed lover, staring into his bright green eyes. They were sitting under the cameras Seth said were planted in all the black domes above

TED DEKKER

them, winning at their will and doing so without breaking a single rule. They could win millions and millions if they placed the right bets. A man like Seth could never be poor.

This game of roulette was basic. Seth had another plan up his sleeve. Initially he'd calculated that they would need over a million dollars, but he told her in the elevator that they now needed less. Something had changed, but he refused to tell her what. It would be a surprise.

"I don't know," she said with a sigh, feigning reluctance. "Perhaps we should stop while we're ahead."

"We're on a roll," he said. "I say we go again."

"Okay then. Again."

"I say eleven," he said.

"Is eleven part of our birthdays?"

"No. But if you divide 24, which was a pretty lucky number, by 2.18181818 ad infinitum, you get 11."

She paused. His way with numbers was not a part of his ability to see into the future, she knew. He simply had that kind of mind. "Then eleven it should be."

He reached for the chips, and his hand stopped just short of them. It trembled.

Miriam glanced up and saw alarm cross his face. She was growing accustomed to his morphing moods, and this time she took it in stride. "No? Maybe eleven is not the best choice."

"No. I think our luck has just run out."

Seth scooped up the thousand-dollar chips—over fifty of them—and stood. "The rest are yours, junior." He turned to Miriam. "Let's go."

They walked from the table, leaving a stunned group of spectators.

"What is it?" Miriam asked as nonchalantly as possible.

"Clive has arrived."

"Clive?" Her heart bolted. "Then we have to go! You didn't see him coming?"

"No. No, it seems Clive has pulled a fast one." A grin crept onto his face. "Pretty smart."

"Where will we go? We have to get out! I can't be taken into—"

"We can't leave. Not yet. Besides, the exits have been blocked for over ten minutes now."

"But you see a way out."

"Yes and no."

"What is that supposed to mean, yes and no? You are making me nervous. We should leave immediately!"

"We can't. Not yet. What we can do is finish what we started here. It's time to rock and roll."


OMAR TOOK A room in the Tropicana, because that's where Hilal had taken his room. Three doors down the hall, in fact. Like clockwork, Hilal made his calls to the general, growing more frustrated by the hour. He still received updates from Clive, but they were filled with meaningless drivel. Hilal was sure that Clive was with-holding information, and he was just as sure the agent's reticence had to do with this clairvoyance Seth evidently possessed.

Either way, everybody was coming to Las Vegas; Hilal had staked his reputation on it.

Omar knew Hilal's every move, which meant he knew Clive's moves and at least what Clive knew of Seth's moves. The wait in this box high above the strip had been maddening, but that all changed an hour ago when Clive landed.

"I don't like this," Assir said.

Omar leaned back in his chair, one hand on the scanner that sat on the table. They'd been listening to police traffic for two days. The city was a sewer filled with low-lifes and prostitutes. One day, under better circumstances, he would have to return.

Hilal lived because Omar needed his information. But the chase was dragging out; he couldn't risk Hilal's interference any longer. Omar's life would probably be easier if Clive just took the girl into custody. Without Hilal to whisk her back to Saudi Arabia, the State Department would have to make other arrangements. Even a short delay would give Omar all the time he needed. If he had to, he would kill Clive and take her then. Either way, Omar was where he wanted to be.

"Sit down, Assir," he said.

Assir walked into the kitchen.

The radio crackled with endless police jargon. Americans were bent on crime. A few good laws could change that. Islam could change—

"Roger. We have Clive Masters with the"—Omar glanced at the radio—"NSA now. ETA Caesars Palace, fifteen minutes. We got a man and a woman, possible fugitives. I'll call back in twenty. Out."

Assir ran in from the kitchen. "It's them!"

"Yes." Omar stood. "It's them." He grabbed his bag. "Hilal first." Caesars Palace lay only one block to the north, but getting in and out of these monstrous hotels quickly was a challenge.

Assir ran past him and entered the empty hall, silenced pistol cocked in his hand. They walked toward Hilal's room, but the door flew open before they reached it.

Hilal had only just stepped into the hall when Assir's first slug took him in the head and knocked him against the doorpost. He stared wide for a brief moment, then slid slowly to the ground. One less hassle for Omar.

Without speaking, Sa'id and Assir pulled the body back into the hotel room, quickly wiped the blood from the doorframe, and closed the door.

"Caesars Palace," Omar said. "We have to hurry."


THEY PRACTICALLY RAN among the tables, dodging the gamblers as if running an obstacle course. Miriam lost her sense of direction, but Seth seemed to know exactly where he was headed.

They burst into a room where about twenty gamblers, mostly gentlemen, sat or stood around several tables. Two men hovered in the corners, arms folded, overseeing the action. A waitress served drinks to a large man dressed in a tuxedo. These were not your typical gamblers.

Seth scanned the room. To a man, the gamblers turned to face the intrusion.

"I would like a wager," Seth said loudly.

No one responded. The man from the right corner, a bearded man who looked like he might have the power to break Seth's neck with a single swipe, dropped his arms and walked toward them.

"One bet," Seth said. "And then I will leave you to your small games."

The fat man chuckled.

"I'm sorry, sir," the guard said. "This room is reserved for invited guests only. You'll have to leave."

Seth ignored him. "I have fifty thousand dollars in chips." He held up his full hands for all to see. "I'm willing to put these down on any wager that anyone here will make me."

"You'll have to leave now, sir."

A thin man with white hair and large ears spoke. "Hold on, John. Let's not be so hasty." He approached and held out a hand. "Name's Garland."

"Hello, Garland. I would be polite if I had fewer chips."

The man eyed him with a smile and then nodded to one of the dealers, who picked up five golden chips. "Fifty?"

"Count them."

"Oh, I will." This got a few chuckles. The dealer took Seth's fifty chips and gave him the five golden chips. Seth shook Garland's hand.

"What kind of bet do you have in mind?" the fat man said.

"An interesting bet. I now have five chips worth ten thousand dollars each, and I need to walk out of here with fifty of them in under five minutes. I'm afraid that's all the time I have today."

Despite the urgency in Seth's voice, Miriam could not help but smile. The fat man humphed and turned away, dismissing them. Others followed his lead. They weren't taking him seriously.

"Well, now. I've never turned down a donation," Garland said. "Any bet?"

"Any bet that requires me to beat the odds." Seth walked over to a table and set down his chips. "I'll wager these five chips against a pool of fifty from five brave souls, that I can guess any number any of you writes down in five consecutive turns. I can do it blindfolded, and I can tell you the name of every man who writes a number."

The skinny man turned slowly to the others and raised an eyebrow. "Is that so? Any number or all the numbers?"

"All. But we're running out of time."

"That's the stupidest thing I've ever heard," the fat man said. "We're here to gamble, not to watch a magic show."

"Please remain quiet, sir. You're not going to play anyway. I see that. But Garland here is and so are you, you, you, and you." He quickly pointed out five men. "You're going to play because a hundred thousand isn't that much money to you, and no one has ever placed such an absurd bet for so much money in all your life, and you can't just let it pass by without taking him up on it. So let's do this. Who's got the blindfold?"

Garland was enjoying this immensely, judging by the smile on his face. He pulled off his tie and handed it to Seth, who took it, wrapped it around his head, and turned his back to them.

"Each of you put your ten chips on the table and take a card. Write a number on the card. Then put your name on the card and give it to Mr. Garland here. Can I trust you, Garland?"

"I suppose we'll find out, won't we?"

"I'll take that as a yes. Are you writing?"

They each did what he said, although not quickly and not without exchanging cynical glances.

"I have the cards," Garland finally said.

"Good, Tommy." Garland's eyes jerked up. "Now mix them up." He did so.

"Now the rest of you children gather around Tommy

for a look-see. The first card is a jack of spades, and Peter has written the number 890.34 on it. He was trying to be tricky with the decimals, but that's okay."

Three of the gamblers glanced around the room, looking for mirrors. "My God," one of them said. "How did you do that?"

"God may or may not have anything to do with it," Seth said. "I'm undecided on that point. The second card is an ace of diamonds and Don has written a 5 on it."

Seth went down the list, reciting as though reading. He whipped around, pulled off the tie, and grinned at the stunned onlookers around the cards, ten now.

"Thank you, gentlemen. And by the way, the fat man is about to hit a winning streak, although now that I've told you, he will not win as much as he would have. Never turn down a sure thing. Good day."

He swept up the stacks of chips and marched from the room, Miriam smiling at the gentlemen in his wake.

"Now that is what I call sweeping the board."

"We have to hurry." Seth's stage persona fell away. "We only have a few minutes."

"But we will—"

"Samir's here, Miriam."

She stopped. "What?"

"Samir. Your great lover. Remember? He's here and he's looking for you. We have a five-minute window. If we miss it, we miss him."

"Where is he? How?" She knew it! He had come!

"I don't know. But I knew while we were in your room that he'd be here."

The kiss!

"At the moment he's hurrying this way, searching the

casino for you. I can only guess that he knows what Clive knows."

Miriam craned for sight of him. People crowded the floor, blocking her view. "I don't see him."

He sighed. "You will, princess. You will." It struck her that Seth was not thrilled about this development. But, Seth, don't you realize, this is what I want! You are so dear to me, but Samir...Samir is my love!

For a moment she wanted to say that, but she knew as soon as she thought the words that they would only hurt him.

And then another thought filled her mind, the thought that she was about to leave Seth. What would happen to her then? She couldn't leave Seth!

Of course you can. And you must. He is your savior, not your lover! She took a deep, settling breath.

They rounded a tall bank of slot machines and there, not ten feet away, stood Samir, neck stretched, looking the opposite way. She began to cry. This was the man she loved, the man who loved her and had been with her nearly every day of her adult life.

"Samir."

He whirled, saw her, and softened. They stared at each other as if caught in a trance. Moisture flooded his eyes and he smiled.

"Miriam."

She walked up to him and he swept her up in strong arms. Like a tide, relief swallowed her. Seth would be okay. He would take one look at Samir and know she was happy with him. That would please him.

"I knew you would come, Samir! I knew it!" She stepped back, unable to stop the tingles that swept over her skin.

Samir saw Seth and for a moment his face darkened.

"We have to hurry," he said. "The authorities have sealed off the building."

"Actually, you have a couple minutes to spare," Seth said, studying Samir. "Where are you going to take her?"

Samir glanced at Miriam and then back. "And who are you?"

"He is my savior," Miriam said. "Without him I would be dead."

"Then you have my country's gratitude," Samir said.

"Where are you going to take her?" Seth repeated.

Samir searched Seth's face. "There is a hall that leads to the—"

"I mean after you escape."

"To…to Madrid. I'm not sure it's any of your business."

Seth frowned. She'd never seen him so serious. "The hall to the kitchen is a mistake," he said. "There's only one way out. Instead of taking the door to the kitchen, take the next one. It will lead you to a window with a fire escape. Take the ladder down to the back alley and head for your car. You'll be safe for at least the next three hours."

Samir blinked, confused.

"Samir, we must listen to him."

Seth picked up a white bucket and dumped the chips into it. "Here's five hundred thousand dollars. I doubt you'll need it, but it's Miriam's. I would hide out for a while and then return to cash it in. Not all at once."

Miriam saw that he was finding this difficult. She walked over to him and looked into his eyes. Her back was to Samir. "Thank you. So very much."

"Your material needs are my spiritual needs," he said, winking at her. "A Jewish proverb from my grandmother."

"Your grandmother?"

"Jewish. Crazy, huh?"

She raised an eyebrow, then let the insinuation slide.

Samir stepped forward and took her hand. "We must go."

"Good-bye, Seth."

Samir pulled her, and then they were hurrying around the slot machines, running for the exit. They had just reached the door Seth advised them to take when she heard a yell over the cacophony.

"Police, freeze!"

She spun. Others stared at the spot where she'd left Seth, and she knew he'd been caught. He'd allowed them to apprehend him. Why?

Samir tugged on her arm. "Hurry!"

They ran.


OMAR WATCHED WITH five hundred other onlookers as the police handcuffed Seth. He'd arrived half a minute too late and seriously considered shooting the blond American right out from under them. This, after all, was the man who'd taken his wife and surely violated her.

He wasn't foolish enough to risk his mission for the sake of revenge, however. He'd come for Miriam, not Seth. And Miriam was gone. Which meant she was either alone, hidden by Seth, or...

Omar worked his way closer to Clive and Seth, careful to avoid eye contact.

"Where is she?" he heard Clive ask under his breath.

"She's gone." Seth seemed at ease, not in the least bit concerned.

"Is she still in the building?"

"No."

It occurred to Omar that Clive asked such matter-of-fact questions because he knew Seth would answer truthfully.

"Alone?"

Seth looked up into the detective's eyes. "She's gone, Clive. She's in good hands and she's no longer a concern to the State Department. You want me. You have me. Let's go."

Clive wiped his sweaty brow and gestured toward the four policemen who had drawn guns. "Put them away. Let's go."

They led him out under the gaze of the crowd.

She's in good hands and she's no longer a concern to the State Department. It could only mean one thing. Omar smirked. Khalid had said he suspected that the sheik sent his own man. Samir. So. Miriam was with Samir. Headed back to Saudi Arabia with her lover.

My, my, what a surprise she was in for.

Omar turned and walked for the rear exit. It was time to go home.

# 29

FEW KNEW OF the room deep in the bowels of Cheyenne Mountain, down the hall from the command center and the JFT system, one of the only computing rooms in NORAD's massive digital complex that hosted only one desk. On the desk were mounted four active-matrix monitors, two on top of two others. Opposite the desk, a ten-by-ten screen virtually exploded with the contents of the four monitors—strings of numbers and symbols that made Clive's head spin.

Clive peered into the space from an observation room above and behind the desk. Two technicians, Peter Smaley, and four-star general Harold Smites watched with him. But it was Seth Border, the man who sat behind the two keyboards and manipulated those numbers, who held most of Clive's attention.

Seth insisted on working alone, without the distraction of propeller heads leaning over his shoulder. Their breathing bothered him. Three days had passed since

Seth's apprehension. Testing him was Clive's idea; testing him in the war room was Smaley's.

But testing a man's mind required his willing participation, so Clive and Seth reached a simple compromise. The government would drop all of its charges against Seth in exchange for his cooperation. On the way to the Las Vegas airport, Clive explained the consequences of aiding and abetting a known fugitive and then presented their deal. Seth looked out the window, silent, and finally nodded.

Smaley arranged for the tests at NORAD and actually arrived in Colorado Springs before Clive and Seth. The deputy secretary had developed a fascination for the case. It took a day to modify the scenario programs with Seth's help, during which time he remained quiet and introspective.

Clive spent four hours debriefing him on the chase while the geeks set up the computers according to Seth's specifications. Apart from engaging him on a string of fascinating though rather trivial facts, Clive came away with three significant conclusions.

One, Seth might have saved Saudi Arabia from a coup by breaking the law and aiding Miriam.

Two, with or without his clairvoyance, Seth's cognitive powers surpassed Clive's greatest expectations. Destroying a mind like Seth's would indeed have been like killing a young Einstein or Sir Isaac Newton.

And three, Seth's clairvoyance was changing. What had started out as an increasing ability to see possible futures now fluctuated like a swinging pendulum between massive breadths of sight and a complete loss of it. Seth could see beyond himself and clearly beyond Miriam, but only sometimes.

"This is incredible," General Smites said, breaking the silence. He crossed his arms and rocked back on his heels. "If I wasn't watching it with my own eyes, I wouldn't buy it for a second. How many of these simulations has he completed?"

"Sixteen in the last two days," one of the techs, Garton, said.

"And he's won them all?"

Garton nodded. "The first battles were oversimplified sea battles in which he commanded a single destroyer against a slightly superior force. We moved him up to tank battles with odds stacked in the enemy's favor and then on to full-scale invasions."

"So he just sees what's going to happen and counters it?"

"Not exactly," Garton said, tapping his pencil on the window. Seth turned toward the noise, eyes darting. Garton held up his hands in apology, and Seth dived back into the simulation in front of him.

He wasn't unlike an overgrown kid playing the world's most complex video games, battling the likes of IBM's ASCI White, a computer that ran at a speed of 7,226 gigaflops. One gigaflop was equal to a billion mathematical operations per second. Even for a man with Seth's capabilities, the task was daunting, and he hated distractions.

"Strung pretty tight," Smaley said.

"Wouldn't you be?" Clive said. "He's holding countless bits of information in his mind, tracking each from one moment to the next and adjusting for countless variations. I get a headache just thinking about how he does it."

Garton smiled. "And that's only half of it." He looked down the windowpane to the general. "He's not seeing the future, just possible futures. There's a big difference. If he were seeing what's going to happen, that would be easy enough. But evidently the future doesn't work that way. I mean, what's going to happen one minute from now hasn't been decided yet. If a tank is standing on the battlefield facing ten enemy tanks, the future may hold a thousand possible outcomes, depending on decisions the commander makes. Seth has to see them all and choose those in which his tank destroys the other ten tanks and escapes unscathed. That might entail a half-hour battle and a unified string of decisions chosen from a million possible decisions."

He chuckled and faced Seth again. "Now try that with a thousand tanks, each facing ten tanks, and try commanding all thousand tanks at once. If you can imagine that, you have an idea of what he was doing yesterday."

A few moments drifted by. Clive couldn't imagine it, not really; none of them could.

"And what's he doing today?" the general asked.

Garton took a deep breath. "Today he's directing a zero-casualty campaign. It was actually his idea. Took us most of the night to set it up."

"A battle in which he incurs zero casualties?"

"Sort of. That was his initial idea, but we took it further. It's not a battle; it's a war, and he's trying to win it without any casualties on his side."

The general came off his heels and stared at Seth, who hunkered over the desk, hands flying nonstop over the keyboards.

"This boy's invaluable."

"Actually, it's more than just a war," Garton said. "It's a nuclear offensive. Question: How do you win a worldwide nuclear offensive without sustaining a single casualty?"

"That's possible?" It was Smaley this time.

The tech they called J.P. answered. "Winning is possible, yes. This morning, at 0843 our time, Seth saw two different futures in which the United States could launch a full-scale attack, including the use of nukes on China, parts of the former Soviet bloc, several Arab states, and a dozen smaller targets, and walk away pretty much having a lock on world power."

Smaley cackled. "Seth knows how to take over the world?"

"Not necessarily. I'm telling you that he saw two unique futures in which that would have happened if the United States had done specific things beginning at 0843 our time. It's now 1315. Those futures don't exist anymore. The premier of China might have eaten a bad steak for lunch, gotten indigestion, and as a result might now react differently to the news of incoming nukes than he would have if they were launched before he ate the steak. Seth's seeing a ton of stuff, but he can still only see three hours out."

"But you could go down there now and ask him for a scenario in which we could take over the world, so to speak, and you're saying he could give you one?" the general asked.

J.P. frowned and nodded. "If there was a way now. And if he wanted to give it to us."

"That's not the point! The point is he actually has that capability?"

"That's what we're saying, yes. It sounds a bit James-Bondy, but I'm sure he could just as easily tell us how to shift power in the Middle East, say, or neutralize China, at least in the next three hours."

The general was beginning to understand what they had here, Clive thought.

"As I was saying," Garton said, "the two scenarios Seth saw this morning included hundreds of thousands of American casualties. He's trying to figure out how to conduct a similar campaign that returns zero casualties, using mostly conventional weapons. That means he's directing hundreds of battle groups, feeding each one precise orders. It's tantamount to giving every field commander specific directions and then telling every soldier when to duck and when to fire."

Clive knew men like the general well enough to realize that Smites was already thinking about both sides of this equation.

"So basically we're looking at the most powerful man in the world," Smaley said, sober now.

"And the most dangerous," Smites said.

Indeed.

The general shook his head, still staring through the glass at Seth. "This is unbelievable. You're absolutely sure all this is possible?"

"Two days ago I would have said no," Garton said. "But hard data doesn't lie."

"Has anybody ever shown this kind of clairvoyance before?"

"Well... not that we've been able to quantify. I'm quite sure this kind of ability to see into so many futures all at once and to see them only for a short time out has at least never been recorded. This is a first."

"Phenomenal."

Clive decided it was time to throw the wet blanket on their fire.

"There is a slight problem. At least some might consider it a problem. His clairvoyance is...changing. It's become cyclic."

"It comes and goes," J.P. said, as if the others needed the clarification.

"It started four days ago, while he was still with Miriam," Clive said. "His ability to see began to expand beyond their immediate concerns, but it also became intermittent. Every few hours he regresses."

"Meaning what?"

"Meaning when he sees, he sees a whole lot, but his clairvoyance only lasts a few hours. It's almost like his batteries wear out, and he needs a few hours of rest to recharge them. At first the periods of blindness were short. He says he made some mistakes out in the desert. But with each passing day they seem to be lasting longer."

"How long do we have?" Smaley asked.

Clive rubbed his bloodshot eyes. "It's not like we can go to the local library and get a book on how to sustain clairvoyance, Peter. It could last his entire life, or it could be gone tomorrow. Ask him and he'll tell you it's on the way out."

"Then we should proceed as though he will lose the ability at any time," J.P. said.

"You're recording what he's doing?" Smites asked.

"Yes."

"Then we could create models from his work, right? They would at least give us scenarios to study. Like creating histories that we can learn from."

"Yes."

"Or we could actually use Seth now," Smaley said. "Feed him a real scenario without telling him. Feed his directives to the battlefield as he enters them and execute them in real time."

"He would see what we're doing," Clive said. "Now that you've mentioned it, he probably already sees it as a possible future, if only subconsciously."

The general shook his head and grunted. "I have to make some calls, gentlemen. Keep me informed." He walked out, leaving them to watch.

Clive's thoughts returned to a lingering problem. One he wasn't of a mind to speak aloud. The problem was Seth. Seth was no ordinary man, with or without this sight of his. He had a mind of his own, and Clive was sure it was occupied by more than how the United States might take over the world.

# 30

TO SETH, THE barrage of futures far outstripped his capacity to single out any specific one. Still his mind handled it without conscious effort. At least most of his mind.

The other part was consumed by Miriam.

The part playing these games was in an autopilot of sorts, albeit an intense autopilot. He supposed the process was not unlike the mind's control over involuntary bodily functions. His fingers seemed to follow their own will, striking the keyboards with commands that isolated the future he wanted.

The part consumed with Miriam slogged through an abyss of pain. Her face had parked itself in his mind's eye and refused to budge, no matter what tricks he threw its way. He had known long before they reached Las Vegas that he was falling for her, but he assumed that once she was safely out of his life, his good sense would make quick work of her. He was an intelligent man, after all, not given to emotional reasoning. It seemed his heart had betrayed his mind.

Yes, he was in love with her. Not just love, as in it's-springtime-I-think-I'm-in-love love, but Love, as in pass-the-poison-I-must-die-without-you love. This new beast presented a more difficult challenge than any he'd ever encountered.

He had thrown himself at the games because he agreed to, but also because he needed to. They provided a necessary distraction. From her face. From her long black hair, shimmering in the desert heat. From her lips kissing him, and her eyes winking at him across the roulette table, and her throaty laugh as he spun her through an absurd dance in her hotel room. From Miriam, the bronzed princess who had swept into his life on the winds of . . .

A box in the monitor's upper right-hand corner caught his eyes. Casualties sustained = 0.

Seth lifted both hands and rubbed his temples. The seeing had sustained itself for four hours already. Soon it would release him for a reprieve before returning again.

The door opened behind him. "You okay?"

He closed his eyes, then opened them. The casualty box had changed. 3. You see, you lose your concentration for a few seconds and see what happens? You're killing people.

"I'm fine," he lied.

Clive stepped in. The casualty numbers started climbing. 100. 300. 700.

"Take a break," Clive said.

Why not? He'd blown the simulation anyway. Seth nodded.

Clive led him to a break room near the back of the complex.

"Coffee?"

"Advil," Seth said.

Clive tossed him the bottle from the counter and poured himself a cup of coffee.

"I don't know how long I can go like this," Seth said, dropping into a chair. "I'm not sure which hurts more, my mind or my fingers."

"Any changes?"

"Yeah. About three seconds ago. I found my sanity again."

Clive looked at him over the rim of the mug. "So right now you can't see—"

"Right now I'm as blind as a bat. Futuristically speaking, that is. And if I could take a drug that would keep me here, in the land of the blind bats, I would take it intravenously."

Clive sat back and sipped his coffee. "I'm not sure I blame you." He paused. "The Saudis are having a fit about Hilal's death. The State Department told Abdullah your theory that Miriam was supposed to marry Omar as a part of a deal with Sheik Al-Asamm."

Seth glanced at the NSA operative. "They're just hearing that now? That's not a theory—it's Miriam's testimony. Do they know where she is?"

"Evidently not. And in their eyes the testimony of a woman doesn't hold water against the word of a prince." Clive shrugged. "Besides, it's a moot point now. Miriam's been saved by Samir. Remember? Even if there was a planned marriage, it's off now." Clive lifted his eyebrows.

"So why are the Saudis having a fit?"

"They're accusing us. Abdullah's hold on power is tentative enough without rumors of a coup floating around." He coughed. "In honesty, I think they don't know what to believe. But they can't just arrest a prince and kill a sheik based on a woman's word. Doesn't work that way in the House of Saud."

"I'm not sure it is a moot point," Seth said, looking down at his fingers. They were red. He touched the tips. Maybe bruised.

"And why not?" Clive said. "Miriam's gone, right? You turned her over to Samir. No one knows where they are, but wherever it is, it isn't Saudi Arabia. He'd be a fool to take her there. They're probably holed up in Spain under false names about now."

"Seems sensible. But there's only one problem." Seth wasn't sure how to say this. Wasn't even sure he believed it.

"And that would be?"

"That would be…" He frowned. "I can't get her out of my mind."

Clive sat back and sighed. "The curse that follows beautiful women."

"It's messing with my mojo."

Clive picked up a walnut off the table and began polishing it with his thumb. "Really? So she's to blame for your loss of vision?"

"Maybe." Seth walked around the table. "You're pretty sharp, Clive. Don't ask me to explain now, but today I know a few things I didn't know yesterday. I know that everything we do changes the future. I know that something changed my future in the desert and it wasn't me."

"And?"

Seth sat back down. "What I'm trying to say is, there's a whole other dimension out there, and I feel like I'm drowning in it."

Clive set the walnut back on the table. "And yet you're losing that gift."

"But she's still out there. And she can bring it back."

Clive sat still, eyeing him. "Don't let your infatuation with a girl—"

"I'm not. But I think Miriam may still be in trouble. And that, my friend, isn't merely about my love for a woman. It's about the stability of Saudi Arabia and the Middle East. It's about the future of America, far beyond what I can see with this gift of mine."

# 31

MIRIAM SAT IN a beach chair beside the villa's pool, overlooking the beautiful Madrid skyline, drawing delicately on a tall banana daiquiri, feeling as vacant as a dry lake bed.

Samir had brought her here, to this wonderful city in which they first spent time alone. To her surprise, no one interfered with their trip. Although he had false identification for her, she expected his own name to raise questions at the borders. But they cleared customs without the slightest delay.

The reunion was wonderful in so many ways—she was once again with the guardian of her youth, the man who represented freedom and love. That alone was enough.

Samir treated her with a measure of aloofness during the trip—he was, after all, a Saudi citizen traveling in the open with a woman. But she was confident that as soon as they arrived at their final destination, which she assumed to be Madrid, the flowers of love would once again bloom.

They had been in this grand villa for two days now, and Samir was gone, "tending to their future," he'd said. Miriam wondered what that meant.

Seth would know.

A grin drifted across her face. Her mind had flitted to Seth a hundred times since leaving him in the casino. She'd become a different person in his company. He was like a fragrant aroma that had swept into her life and revived her from a living death. Delightful and intoxicating.

Your material needs are my spiritual needs. She believed they were. Had been, anyway.

When she allowed herself to listen to the quiet voices of her heart, they told her that she'd been sick to leave him. Yes, sick—the kind of sickness that comes from having a hole in your heart.

But that was nonsense, because how could she have a hole in her heart while she was with Samir? Who was Seth but a conflicted American who'd stumbled into her life?

And he was Jewish. Or his grandmother had been. Not that it mattered now.

"Would you like another drink, madam?"

She looked up at the servant who'd approached from her right. "No, but thank you." Even her voice sounded vacant, she thought.

The servant dipped his head and walked away. Miriam glanced back at the courtyard for Samir. A friend owned the villa. They were here for her protection. That's all Samir would tell her. Not that it mattered; she was here in his care and she trusted him. He'd been mostly absent since their arrival, returning only for dinner, because he was arranging a secret future for them. Perhaps a journey to an island, or a city in southeast Asia.

There was no sign of Samir now, and she settled back into her chair.

Seth wouldn't have left her alone by the pool, would he? He would have taken her with him to choose their future together. Please, Miriam, you cannot compare Seth and Samir. You're comparing a rose to a Mercedes. They're incomparable.

For most of the trip, she'd successfully buried the images that kept trying to resurrect themselves. But here by the pool with hours to waste, she found herself powerless to resist them. Memories of Seth hauling her onto the toilet, and dropping from the vent over her bed, and praying with arms raised before his hasty altar, and leaning over the roulette wheel, pretending to be a lucky fool. If anyone else had done these things, she would think him a fool. But Seth was her rose in the desert. Her savior.

Perhaps one day, if Samir would agree, they would go to the United States and find him. They both were in his debt. Miriam for her very life and Samir for his bride-to-be.

Miriam rolled to one side, heart aching. Think of the future, Miriam. Think of the freedom before you.

But sadness swept over her instead, and she could not stop the tears that swelled in her eyes. How could these memories bring her so much pain? Why couldn't she just wipe him from her mind and indulge in her new freedom?

Seth, Seth. My dear Seth, what have I done?

"Miriam."

She jerked up. Samir approached, dressed in a blue suit and dark glasses. She dabbed her eyes.

"We have to leave. Your clothes are waiting in your bedroom. Our flight leaves in one hour. Please hurry."

Miriam stood, alarmed. "Our flight? To where?"

He hesitated. "To your father."

"I'm going to see my father? How? I thought—"

"You can't be married without your father's blessing," he said, smiling.

Married? Yes, of course, but would the sheik change his mind and bless this marriage? That couldn't be right! "My father's future depends upon my marriage to Omar! Now he's agreed to our marriage?"

"You think your father is so heartless?"

"But, I thought..." She didn't know what to think.

"Hurry, Miriam. The plane is waiting." Samir walked away.

His blessing! And why not? She watched Samir—the suit looked good on him. He was not himself, she thought. He's about to be married; what do you expect?

Miriam flew to her bathroom, thoughts of Seth vanquished by this turn of events. She showered quickly, strung with nervous energy. It was Egypt to be sure. The sheik had gone ahead to Cairo and made the preparations. She was to be married to Samir in Egypt!

She ran to the bedroom. Married! Her suitcase lay open, already packed. And Samir had laid a black gown over the pillows for her to wear. He was thinking of his bride already. She took two steps toward the bed and froze.

It was an abaaya. And a veil.

The sight of it made her think only of Omar.

Trembling, she pulled on a dress from the suitcase and ran from the room. She found Samir standing at the large picture window, hands in pockets, staring out at the pool.

"Samir! There is—"

"You must wear it, Miriam." He turned and she saw that his jaw was set. It softened. "Please, we are going to meet your father. Surely you know that he must approve. Are you thinking to throw out everything you hold dear and chase the American way? This is what that man has done to you?"

For the first time, she heard anger in his voice, anger directed at her, and it terrified her. He was talking about Seth. Did Samir suspect anything? He was wounded.

"No." She took a step toward him. "No, Samir. But this is not Saudi Arabia."

"But your father is a Saudi. Put it on."

She blinked. Perhaps he was right. One last time, out of respect for her father. It was just a piece of cloth. They faced each other for several long seconds. *He is only trying to do what is best. Because he loves me. This is no easier for him than for me.*

Miriam turned, his chastisement burning in her ears. *Be a good, obedient woman, Miriam. You cannot just throw out all of the past and pretend you are someone you are not.*

She entered the room and stared at the black cloth. How could she possibly put it on? But refusing would only drive a wedge between her and Samir.

Miriam closed her eyes and picked up the abaaya. Working blind with her breath held, she pulled the robe on.

*It is nothing. It is only a piece of cloth.*

She slipped the veil over her head without looking. Ten days had passed since she last wore the veil, and to her it felt like a lifetime.

She opened her eyes. The world was gray.

She would not look down; she would not look in a mirror; she would pretend she wore sunglasses. After all she'd been through, was this so impossible?

Driving to the airport, Samir sat in the limousine's front seat and ignored her entirely. She walked through the airport behind him, her mind buzzing. Rage and despondency formed a bitter pill that she swallowed and allowed to poison her. She saw nothing—refused to see. She stood in the corner, arms crossed, and let Samir make the flight arrangements. He collected her after some time, and she followed him again, toward a private jet ramp.

Just a few hours, Miriam. After you see Father, you will tear this sack off. Many Arabs did not require their women to wear the cloth. Most in fact. Islam was hardly about what you wore.

But she was a Saudi princess of the Wahhabi sect. She—

Miriam stopped. They were entering the Jetway. She'd been so humiliated by the dress that she hadn't paid any attention to her surroundings. Now she saw the pilot, and she was sure she recognized him. She glanced out the window to her left. It was too dark. She lifted the veil and saw the jet. It had Saudi markings!

A man angrily motioned to her to lower her veil. She dropped it and ran to catch Samir.

"Where are we going?"

"I told you—to your father."

"But where? Where is he?"

Samir took her elbow firmly and pulled her forward. "Please, Miriam. Don't make a scene. There are those who will do anything to stop us."

She hurried down the ramp with him. "Then tell me where," she whispered harshly. They entered the jet, which was empty except for a dozen men seated near the rear. They stared at her as one.

"We are going to your father in Riyadh," Samir said. "Sit here." He pointed to a seat in first class.

Miriam's legs went numb. She wasn't sure she was breathing. She sat without realizing that she was doing so. Riyadh! Why? Wasn't that where Khalid and his son Omar were? Wasn't Riyadh the city she'd fled?

Samir sat in the rear of the plane with the other men. Something had gone terribly wrong. She could understand the necessity of everything else that had happened, but not this. Not Samir choosing to sit with men in the back when he had the choice to sit with his bride in first class.

Unless he was only protecting their marriage by being discreet. But why Riyadh?

Miriam hated every minute of the short flight. She spent the time carefully constructing scenarios in which all this made perfect sense. Samir was doing only what must be done for their future. She could not expect to walk into paradise without paying a price. The sheik wanted a Saudi wedding in Saudi Arabia.

They landed, and for a few brief minutes Miriam was thankful to be hidden beneath the veil from prying eyes. Then they were in a limousine once again, speeding for the countryside. Still Samir refused to talk to her. Of course. The driver.

The limousine came to a stop before a tent—the same one she'd met the sheik in less than two weeks ago—but this time a dozen smaller tents stood nearby, and at least a dozen vehicles. In her eagerness, she stepped past Samir and ran into the tent. She pulled off her veil.

"Miriam!"

She spun to the sheik's voice and walked in, confused but hopeful. He kissed her and invited her to the same table she had eaten at before. Two men stood to her left—guards.

She walked forward. "You must know how much danger coming here—"

"Life is full of danger, Miriam."

"But if I am to marry Samir, why couldn't we have the wedding in Cairo, or at the very least in Dhahran?"

"Sit, Miriam." He glanced over her shoulder.

She followed the glance. Samir stood just inside the tent, looking at her with glassy eyes. He was crying? She faced her father, terrified.

"You will marry Omar," the sheik said. "I have given my word for the kingdom and for God. Sit!"

"Omar?" She turned around and stared into Samir's eyes. "Omar?"

"We cannot put our desires ahead of God's will, Miriam," Samir said. "What we do now must be for the love of God. The kingdom is at stake. You have been chosen by God to deliver us. I am only glad to have loved a woman so chosen."

"This is absurd!" she cried. "What kind of God would force me into marriage with a beast? Your love will kill me! Omar will kill me or keep me in a living death! And you will allow this?"

"He won't kill you! Your death would sever ties with your father. Please, Miriam—"

"No!" Rage swept through her. She hated them. She

hated them all! She flew at Samir, screaming, fists flying, beating at his face as he warded off her blows.

"Miriam! Please, I beg you!"

"I hate you!"

Hands grabbed her from behind and pulled her back. Something hit her back.

"Don't bruise her," her father said. "She is to be married tomorrow night. The groom will not want her bruised."

With those words, all of the life Miriam had found with Seth drained from her body. The horror she'd always feared had finally found her.

She, like Sita, would die.

# 32

THE DEEP SLEEP had somehow intensified Seth's clairvoyance. Close as he could figure—in the way one figures things while dead to the world—the new and improved sight hit him while he was still in REM state, spared from the barrage of concerns that had pummeled him during the day. As a result, he could suddenly see with an unprecedented degree of clarity.

He was in the future; he knew that. But it wasn't like the futures he'd seen before, focused on the events that might transpire in his life or in the computer models. He was in a future unbound by time. Perhaps in the very fabric of the future itself.

That's the only way he could think of it. Light roiled around him, like a translucent sea of fireflies. Each pinpoint was a possibility; each was fueled by some unseen force.

He reached out his hand and brushed through the pinpoints of light. A thousand blinked off and another thousand sprang to life. It was how the future changed, in the blink of an eye, fueled by the creative force of the universe itself, yet so easily changed by the movement of his hand.

One of the tiny lights caught his eye and expanded. He was looking at a future the way he had become accustomed to seeing it. He was about to turn away when a detail of this particular future arrested his attention.

Miriam.

Seth jerked up in bed, fully alert and breathing hard. The sheets were soaked in his sweat.

It was the first time he'd seen her in the futures since Las Vegas. Not only Miriam; Miriam and Omar. He knew that because he'd pulled up a picture of the Saudi prince on the Internet two days earlier.

"Oh, God!"

He threw his covers off, tumbled out of bed, and ran down the hall. Clive's room was the second on the right, and he crashed in without knocking. Hit the light switch. An overhead fluorescent flickered and hummed. The agent bolted up in bed and clawed under his pillow. For a gun, maybe, but there was no gun there.

Clive blinked away sleep. "What are you doing?"

"I just saw the future." Seth walked past the bed and then back, grasping for words. "I mean, I saw it like I've never seen it before. I saw Miriam."

The agent hesitated, then swung his feet to the floor.

"You sure it wasn't just a dream?"

"She's marrying Omar. There's going to be a coup."

"You saw that far out?"

"I don't know how far it was. I didn't actually see the coup, but I saw his eyes. Whatever he was after, he's gotten it. If he was after a coup, there's going to be a coup."

"I thought Miriam was with Samir."

"She was!" Why hadn't he seen anything in Samir at the casino? "But she's not now, that's the whole point. I have to go."

Clive tugged on his slacks. "Forget it. You're staying here. We'll turn this over to the State Department..."

"Warn them, yes, but you know I have to go! The State Department can't help her now!"

"You can't go. They'll never let you go. And even if they did, you can't just hop on the next United flight and fly into Riyadh. Saudi Arabia's a closed country."

"So was the Nevada border."

Clive paused. "That was before your clairvoyance became intermittent. Can you see now?"

"No. But I'll see again."

"You can't be sure of that."

"She brings it out in me. I don't know how, but she does. Tweaks my mind."

He had to find a way to make Clive understand. They were locked away in the world's most secure fortress; without Clive's help he was going nowhere.

"Like it or not, you're the single most valuable asset this country has in its possession right now," Clive said. "You're also the most potentially dangerous. If I let you walk—"

"If you don't, she'll die and the United States will face a major political crisis."

Seth slapped his back pocket. Still there. He pulled out a disk and held it up. "This is a scenario I ran on my own while the techs were going over this morning's battle results. It's the only copy."

"And?"

"And it's a look at what will happen if Khalid takes power away from King Abdullah. It isn't pretty."

Clive shook his head. "How can you see what might happen in the Middle East without looking past three hours?"

"By stringing together consecutive three-hour segments."

"How? You did that?"

"On the computer. I went out three months, and trust me, a lot of people will die if Khalid takes control. If I'd known it was important, I would've told you earlier. Now it is important." He tossed the disk to Clive, who caught it.

"And how does this help you?"

"It helps me because I don't think there's any way for the U.S. to stop a coup without my help. You may think that I'm valuable in here, playing your games, but I may just be the only option you have out there, where it really counts."

"There's no guarantee that you could even reach Saudi Arabia, much less stop a coup. The State Department—"

"The State Department will fail," Seth said.

"You know that?"

Seth took a deep breath. "No. But what if I'm right? What if the only way to stop this whole mess is through me?"

"Assuming your clairvoyance returns."

"And I'll gamble my life on that assumption."

Clive stared at him for a few moments. "Do you have any idea what you're asking?"

"Yes."

"Do you even know what you would do?"

"No."

"No. Listen to yourself. You want me to let you walk out of here on a thin hope? Three generals are on their way here for a meeting with the secretary of state tomorrow."

"Show them the disk and tell them that if I'm wrong, I promise I'll come back and let them pry through my mind. Keep me here and I'm dumb. Your dog and pony show tomorrow morning will be an embarrassment. In fact, I may just feed them with miscues. You'll wish you'd never found me."

Clive walked across the room, hands on hips. "Now you're blackmailing me?"

"Call it what you want."

He stared Seth down. "I can't believe I'm considering this."

"You'd be an idiot not to," Seth said.

"This is really about Miriam."

"Maybe. But where Miriam goes, Saudi Arabia goes."

A frown settled on the agent's face. "You win. But if you're going to try this, whatever this is, let me at least help you get the papers you'll need to enter the country. Follow me."

# 33

THE MORNING CAME and went in a vague cloud that barely registered in Miriam's consciousness. She resolved to show no emotion. None at all.

The afternoon crawled by, bustling with activity, but distant—a nightmare to which she had resigned herself.

Because of the secretive nature of the marriage, the usual party of close relatives was absent. Instead, the sheik's wife, Nadia, and her servants made Miriam's preparations. They brought in an elaborate peach-colored silk gown, which Samir had purchased in Cairo, they told her. Miriam stood on numb legs while they pulled it over her head for a hasty fitting. The dress felt loose, and one of the wives ordered a maid to take it in at the waist. Miriam decided that peach was a ghastly color.

She lay obediently for the halawa ceremony, performed by the women. A sweet-smelling mixture of lemon juice, sugar, and rose water that had been boiled to form a glue was spread over her entire body and allowed to dry. When they peeled it away, her body hair came out with it. Under any other circumstances, she might have protested the pain, but it felt like no more than an abstract annoyance. The physical pain was easy to bear.

The women rinsed Miriam's hair with henna to make it shine and painted her nails a rose red—preparing their whore for this ungodly union. Two weeks earlier she had watched Sita endure the same preparations, encouraged her friend to make the best of her new reality. Sita had glared at her with glassy-eyed dread. Her friend had sentenced herself to death, and now the notion grew on Miriam. She could not fathom the idea of Omar touching her. She would die first.

But Omar would not kill her. No, instead he would keep her in a living hell, bound and gagged in a dungeon, maybe. Whipped and bleeding for his own pleasure, perhaps. If she could only find a way to die without killing herself. God would not smile upon suicide.

As night approached and the prayer calls crooned from the minarets, Miriam whispered a helpless, hopeless prayer under her breath.

Unable to maintain her resolve, Miriam began to cry. The gnawing horror that she'd ignored all day rose over her like a black dragon. The stupidity of her leaving Seth showed its true colors now, and it was nothing less than the most sickening kind of foolishness. She had willingly left the one man who truly did love her. Her savior, her love, who would be stealing her away to fields of flowers now instead of turning her over to a slaughter at Omar's hands.

She cried long and hard, alarming the two women who watched over her. She cried for Seth. She didn't care that she distorted her picture of his love into more than it was.

She needed someone to love her now, and now there was only Seth.

A religious sheik came at dusk and asked Miriam's father for his consent to the marriage. They signed documents, and then the sheik left to repeat the process with Omar. Her father's will was sealed. In exchange for his daughter, he would receive the agreed upon bride price, in this case loyalty and power rather than money.

Nadia gave her a pill to swallow—a drug to calm her nerves, she said. Miriam thought of Sita, drugged before the drowning, but she took the pill anyway. They led her into a limousine at dark. She sat in the back with her father. A train of cars followed.

For the first time since accepting her fate, Miriam felt the cords of fear wind around her heart. Her father remained deathly quiet as they rode for Omar's palace. *I am their sacrificial lamb.* She thought of jumping from the moving vehicle. She eased her hand onto the handle. The doors were locked. She could feel the drug start to take hold. Sweat lined her palms.

"Father?"

He turned his head, smiling as she imagined a proud father might smile before giving his daughter to the man she loved. "You are a beautiful bride, Miriam. You will make a wonderful wife."

"I don't want to do this."

He looked away. "Your fear will pass. You can't always think only of yourself. You are a woman now, and you must begin to think of your husband."

"I don't think he will make a good husband."

"Don't worry, he will earn your love over time. I have demanded it of him."

She sank into the seat, begging it to swallow her whole. Nausea swept through her stomach. She closed her eyes, but the swaying of the car made her dizzy, so she opened them again.

They came to a large palace and Miriam was led into a study with Nadia. The sound of drums and laughter reached her from the other side of the walls. She wondered how many guests had been summoned. Whether they knew of the circumstances surrounding her marriage to Omar.

A knock sounded on the door and Nadia stood. She smiled sympathetically. "Be strong, Miriam. For your father's sake, be strong. There is nothing we can do."

She held out her hand and Miriam stood. Nadia lowered Miriam's veil and led her out to a large hall with towering pillars. Several dozen women watched them walk to the front of the assembly. Miriam heard her shoes echoing on the marble floor. There was no sign of Omar.

She was left at the front and stood alone, facing the women. She couldn't bear to look at them, now standing without veils and colorfully dressed, as was customary at weddings. The ceremony intended to show the true woman in all her splendor, but to Miriam it was only a farce, a mockery that made them foolish for believing—

A door opened to her right. Her father stepped out followed by another man she recognized as Khalid bin Mishal. And then another man, dressed in black. Omar.

A tremble shook Miriam's body. It was the first time she'd seen Omar. His hard shoes clacked on the marble floor.

She looked away, terrified to catch his eyes. Their walk seemed to stretch forever. From her left the religious man

who'd met with her father earlier stepped through another
door and approached. The drug she'd taken an hour earlier seemed to slow everything down. Perhaps it really
was just a nightmare after all.

The footsteps stopped. She could hear Omar's breathing. The religious man stepped out in front of them and
began to talk to her father and then to the others. He did
not address her. The transaction was between her father
and Omar.

Then Omar was there, in front of her, lifting her veil. The
bearded face she saw wore a gentle smile but she could see
it only as evil. If not for the effects of the drug, she might
have run. Instead, she began to cry silently. They ignored
her and said a few more words to complete the ceremony.

Omar walked past her and headed for a side door. The
room broke out in the ululating cries of the women, like a
flock of crows warning her.

The religious man stepped forward and told her to
follow Omar. She turned and walked, hardly aware that
she was moving. Omar entered the same study in which
she had waited, held the door for her, and then closed it
behind them. She stood with her back to him, terrified.

His hand touched the top of her veil. He ripped it off
and slowly stepped around her. "You are more beautiful
than I imagined," he said.

She would not look at him. She would never give him
the satisfaction of looking into her eyes.

"Are you afraid of me?"

She didn't answer.

Omar lifted a flask from the desk and poured himself
a drink. The clinking of the glass hurt her ears. He took a
drink and set the glass down.

"I think you are. And I want you to know I prefer that. Fear has a way of transforming a woman into a thing of terrible beauty. Did you know that? There is nothing worse than a submissive woman." He walked around her, drawing his finger over her shoulders. "But you aren't only afraid; you are angry, yes? I'm not sure I've ever had a woman who is both afraid and angry. I think it will be a great pleasure."

"I will never—" Miriam stopped, surprised that she had spoken.

"Yes? Go on."

Her voice was hoarse. "I will never offer you pleasure."

"Yes, I think you actually believe that. That's very nice. There will be consequences, of course, but this, too, could be part of our game."

He squeezed her cheeks with a powerful hand and wrenched her head to face him. "You are my wife now, Miriam. That is what you are. Nothing more, nothing less. You will please me, and you will bear me a son. That is all you will do. Do you understand?"

The room swam through fresh tears. She closed her eyes.

"I have something special planned for you, Miriam. A special chamber. Something so delicious must not be rushed. You will take a night to prepare yourself for me. Let the drugs wear off and let your fear take hold. It will be delightful, you will see."

Then he released her. She swayed on her feet, nauseated again. When she opened her eyes, he no longer stood in front of her. After a moment she looked around cautiously. The room was empty.

Miriam allowed herself to sink to the solid floor and began to weep.

• • •

"YOU HAVE GOT to be kidding me!" Peter Smaley said. "Running from a manhunt in California is one thing. Waltzing into Saudi Arabia on a half-brained rescue attempt isn't remotely similar. What were you thinking?"

"You don't exactly control a guy like Seth," Clive said. "When he's on, he's unstoppable."

"When he's on."

They sat in the same conference room they had planned on using to debrief Seth: the two generals, a colonel, the secretary of state, and the deputy, Smaley. Clive had told them about Seth's ultimatum and departure; he was holding back the disk as his ace.

"Either way, you allowed him to leave," General Smites said. "That's not unlike giving them the keys to this mountain."

"Overstated," Clive said. "It's a mistake to assume that he intends to do anything in Saudi Arabia but help Miriam. His actions will benefit our interests as much as Abdullah's. And like I said, he was going, whether we agreed or not. I couldn't have stopped him."

"You put a guy in a locked cell and he's not going anywhere; I don't care what he can see."

"That's not necessarily true," Clive said. "And he wasn't here as a prisoner." It wasn't altogether true, but it was the best he could come up with at the moment. Honestly he wasn't sure if they would end up giving him a medal or a death sentence.

"I realize how significant a man with Seth's abilities is to the military," Secretary Gray said after a long silence. "But frankly I'm more concerned with the stability of

Saudi Arabia. I don't need to educate you on the pains we've taken to keep militants from seizing power in the Middle East. If what you're saying about this marriage is true, we could have a real problem on our hands."

Clive cleared his throat. "Then you may want to take a look at something Seth left with us." He rolled his chair over to a computer and slid the disk into the drive. "This is the scenario he ran yesterday afternoon while we were occupied. It starts with a future in which Khalid succeeds in toppling Abdullah, then extends out three months."

"How's that possible?" Smaley asked. "I wasn't aware he could extend beyond three hours."

"Neither was I. He found a way to string consecutive episodes together. I showed this to Garton; he checked Seth's algorithms. He's convinced it works."

Clive tapped a few keys. The monitor blinked and then filled with numbers. Streams of text rolled up the frame too fast to read. Several hundred lines passed by in a blur, and then a single page popped up. Key Indicators of the Kingdom of Saudi Arabia and Region—Plus Three Months.

Clive rolled the monitor stand toward them. "Not a pretty sight."

They read Seth's conclusions.

The secretary looked at Clive. "What are the chances that this might be accurate?"

"If Khalid takes control, pretty good. Short of having another scenario contrary to this, we'd better assume that what Seth provided is at least probable."

For a moment no one spoke. Gray pushed his chair back. "Where is Seth now?"

"If he makes all the flights, he'll be in Riyadh"—he glanced at his watch—"in seven hours."

"Do you have any confidence that he might upset this wedding?"

Clive shook his head. "Your guess is as good as mine. When he left, his clairvoyance was cycling, a few hours on, a few hours off. Without it, he's a sitting duck over there. He can read Arabic, maybe even speak a bit, but there's no way he'll pass for an Arab. And there's the distinct possibility that his periods of remission might lengthen. It's a crapshoot at best."

"The king doesn't know?"

"No, sir," Smaley said. "We don't have any corroborating intel—"

"This is good enough for me," the secretary said. "We tell him that we suspect Miriam has been returned to Saudi Arabia and is being given in marriage to Omar bin Khalid in an agreement with Sheik Al-Asamm. We urge him to arrest Khalid bin Mishal immediately."

"He won't have the political will to arrest Khalid without concrete evidence," Smaley said.

"That's his choice." The secretary stood. "I'll make the call myself." He looked at Clive. "No offense, but I pray you're wrong. God help them if you're not."

# 34

KING KHALID INTERNATIONAL Airport sat thirty-five kilometers north of Riyadh, a city covering roughly six hundred square kilometers, occupied by over three million inhabitants. Seth knew without a shred of doubt that negotiating his way through immigration and into the city would be impossible without his clairvoyance.

The travel documents that Clive had drummed up took him to London and then on to Beirut, where he'd caught a four-hour flight into Riyadh. So far so good.

There were only two problems. One, Saudi immigration would reject his visa—he'd seen that in every possible future. His fake ID was no masterpiece. And two, his clairvoyance was about to run out. He couldn't see exactly when—he couldn't ever look into the future and see how his clairvoyance would act.

But he'd been seeing plainly for about two hours now, and by his last calculations, two hours was now his limit.

The duration of his clairvoyance was shrinking steadily. Worse, the blank slate was expanding by nearly an hour between each episode. When his seeing faded this time, it would not return for at least six hours.

Even worse still, he saw less each time the clairvoyance returned. Gone was the expansive sight that reached beyond his immediate circumstances. His clairvoyance was simply fizzling out.

Seth deplaned and walked for immigration, sweating bullets. He was still seeing. The trick was to thread his way past their eyes. He had to go only when and where he would not be seen, effectively walking right past them without their knowing.

Even if he did get past them, he would still be no closer to finding Miriam. Fear sat like lead in his gut.

His mind's eye showed him precisely who would look where and when. At least as a sea of possibilities. He would have to isolate a particular current in which none of the immigration authorities would be looking at a particular spot at a particular time. He would have to be in that spot at that moment, then string together another few dozen unseen spots before he could slip by.

Three lines wound into immigration stations where officers examined and stamped passports before allowing the passengers through. Two stations to his left were unmanned, roped off. He could slide under the red rope easily enough.

Problem was, he couldn't actually see any futures in which he was unnoticed. The likelihood of all the guards averting their attention long enough for him to evade them was very small. Very, very small. He discovered a number of futures in which the left of the hall went unsupervised for a period of several seconds, and a few futures in which the right went unseen for brief moments, but neither for long enough.

He stepped behind a large pillar and did his best to look relaxed. Dripping in sweat and shaking like a leaf wouldn't help his effort. Unless something came to him soon, he would be detected in the next four minutes.

Maybe he should go back to the plane, pretend he'd left something on board. That would buy him time. But no, he had to make his move while the immigration stalls were still busy with other passengers.

They wouldn't kill him, would they? No, he was an American. Unless a coup changed loyalties. The thought did nothing to lessen his anxiety.

A mother cloaked in black, with two daughters clenching fistfuls of her abaaya, passed by. Seth forced a smile and stepped out. The immigration line was just ahead.

An image of Miriam filled his mind. She was sitting across a table, cracking a crab leg with her teeth, smiling over the candlelight at him.

Seth bent to tie his shoe and buy more time. The problem with the future was that it depended on others' decisions as well as his. In this case, the authorities'. He saw that he could actually get up to the gate without being spotted, but there at the gate, a guard who now stood behind the stations would spot him in every future.

Wait…He had to allow time to open up some other potential future. But he couldn't tie his shoe forever. Heart thumping in his ears, Seth slowly stood, and only then, while his eyes were still on the floor, did his mind snag a new thread.

*Walk! Now! Walk!*

Seth wiped his palms on his corduroys, walked forward three steps, and turned to his left. He took two steps, counted to four, and then turned right.

No one yelled. No one shouted out.

*Trust it, Seth. You can't stop now.*

He strode ten paces to the right.

If any of the authorities had seen him, they would have undoubtedly stared in amusement. The American in black corduroys was walking ten paces to the right, stopping, ducking behind another passenger, and then crossing at a slight angle to the other side of the hall. A lunatic marching around the terminal as if he were engaging a dozen other invisible characters.

In reality, he was stepping precisely where their view of him was blocked by a head or an arm, or when this one or that one was looking down. One small boy watched Seth the whole way, for all three minutes it took him to reach the gate. But the boy was clearly too mesmerized to do anything except watch.

The new future that had come to him required that he stand at the gate, face the far wall, and clear his throat. The sound bounced off in such a way as to pull a distant guard's attention away just long enough for Seth to walk by.

And then he was through. Trembling and nauseated with dread, but through. He walked away from the immigration posts on numb legs.

He was still seeing. That would end at any minute, and then he would be blind.

Seth quickly located the bathrooms and hurried for them. An abaaya hung in the ladies' room—he needed that abaaya. Thank goodness he had seen at least that much.

He slipped into the restroom, hands quivering from the exhilaration of his success. If he could just...

The world winked to black and he blinked.

The clairvoyance was gone...

He saw the black abaaya and grabbed it off the hook. Fumbled for an opening. Found one. Top or bottom, he didn't know—he'd never touched an abaaya, much less worn one.

He threw it over his head and pulled it down. This one had no arms as such and he quickly gathered it around him in a fashion that matched the pictures he'd seen. His leather shoes poked out the bottom—that might be a problem. He snatched up the veil and pulled it over his head.

The door opened and another woman entered.

Another?

She looked at him curiously for a moment then stepped over and straightened Seth's head covering, mumbling something in Arabic. He nodded his thanks and walked out.

He stood still for a moment, gathering his senses. Did women in Saudi Arabia ever wear leather tennis shoes? Not too likely. He couldn't very well slip on a pair of pumps, though, could he?

He'd seen enough of the future to know what he should attempt now, but he hadn't seen whether he would succeed. He could get to the city riding a shuttle bus. But the specifics of that future had faded. Not the general future, but the tiny things that made a difference. When to say what, which seat to sit in—those sorts of things.

He struck out for the sign that indicated buses. There was no going back now. This was Miriam's homeland. The thought brought her rushing to his mind. She was here; he had no doubt. Where was another matter entirely.

The bus ride involved little more than suffering through an hour of humiliation. Several men glared at him, focusing first on his hairy hands, which he quickly hid, and then on his shoes, which he could not. Whether their scorn came from his choice of shoes or from traveling alone, he couldn't guess. It took some effort not to slap the one male who evidently saw it as his duty to scowl at him, but otherwise Seth survived his first hour in Saudi Arabia.

He stepped off the bus in downtown Riyadh near midnight. He walked away from the bus as quickly as possible, painfully aware that most Saudi women were not out at this hour.

The city was virtually deserted. If he had his sight, he might be able to begin his search for Miriam now, but he would have to wait for at least another five hours. And hide.

Seth found a deserted alley and settled to his haunches behind a large garbage bin. The night hid him well. He was the night. A black blob in a dark alley in the dead of night.

He hadn't felt so anxious since his father had kicked him out of the house for spilling his Coke on the kitchen table at his fourth birthday party.

THERE WAS SCREAMING and there was hitting and Seth awoke.

"Get up, get up!" someone screamed in Arabic. A stick hit his head, jerking him to full awareness. A man stood over him wielding a stick, one of the religious police, the mutawa, by the way he was dressed.

Seth scrambled to his feet. The mutawa drew back to

strike another blow, and Seth did the only thing that came to his mind. He ran.

Curses rang down the alley after him. The abaaya flapped around his ankles and he pulled it up to his knees for the getaway. Something about the sight silenced the mutawa. Seth's shoes, maybe. Or his long stride.

He couldn't take any chances now. If the man suspected that Seth was something other than a woman, he would investigate. Cross-dressing wasn't exactly encouraged in Saudi Arabia.

Seth cut up another alley. He lurked around the shops in the souk for ten minutes until satisfied the mutawa was no longer a threat. The abaaya disguised him only among other women; at this dawn hour they weren't yet out.

The day's first prayer call warbled through the cool morning air. That would summon some men—those devout enough to rise early—but he would have to wait to start his search until enough women could give him cover. Someone somewhere had to know something about Omar. If he could find Omar, he was sure he would find Miriam.

The absurdity of his situation hit him as he walked through the market, trying to look as if he belonged. But the fact was, he didn't. He imagined Miriam walking this same market before her flight to America. In so many ways, she belonged.

If she were with him, he would belong; without her he was lost. And without his clairvoyance, he might as well be in a tomb. The thoughts brought a lump to his throat.

An air-raid alarm wailed across the city. Then the sound of automatic-weapons fire, like popping corn. The air fell silent. Trouble. But not for him. This was something bigger.

He exited the market and headed toward a large structure that stood against the horizon, half a mile ahead. Looked palatial enough to him. Until his clairvoyance returned, he could only blend in, but he might as well put himself in a place where royals were more likely to be found.

And if the clairvoyance didn't return?

It did return, two hours later. Seven hours after it had left him. And it would be gone in under two.

The futures came out of nowhere as, this time, a voice spoken by someone in a passing car.

"What I'm saying, Faisal, is that we can't just pretend that nothing is happening. The royal palace is under siege!" The voice faded as the car sped past.

The coup was under way. Which could only mean that Miriam had married Omar. He searched his mind for more futures. Nothing.

If militants had the palace under siege, they kept it well concealed—it hadn't upset daily life in any obvious way here at the city's heart. A few police cars screamed by, followed by lumbering army trucks, but otherwise the streets were filling with pedestrians, unconcerned or unaware.

Seth hurried out onto a crosswalk that overlooked a large courtyard of the Al-Faisaliah Center, milling with pedestrians, and stopped at the center. The mall's central structure towered high above the skyline to his right, a narrow pyramid shape, surprisingly contemporary. His task was simple: he would simply imagine asking any and all where he might find Omar and examine their potential answers. Surely someone down there would know.

The futures spun through his mind, fruitless for ten minutes. And then twenty. And then thirty. Still nothing.

A hundred thousand people must have passed in the crowd below and not one of them knew Omar? Actually, eight would have responded in the affirmative to his first question, but as to where Omar lived, they possessed no more information than he. If he could just find one who knew, he could probably trick them out of the answer.

What if the coup had already succeeded? If Miriam was married to Omar, what could he, an American citizen with no diplomatic status, possibly do? Kidnap her? The questions made him weak.

A girl coming across the walk caught his attention. She was hardly more than a child, still unveiled, and he knew immediately that she was the one. She spoke English and his conversation with her would have gone like this:

"Excuse me. Do you know Omar bin Khalid?"

She looked at him, amused. "You are English?"

"Yes."

"Then speak English. Do I look like a fool? And why are you dressed like a woman?"

"I am dressed like a woman because I'm from the theater."

"We don't have theaters."

"There is one and it's a secret. Do you know of Omar bin Khalid?"

"I don't believe you. There are no theaters. Yes, I do know Bin Khalid."

"You do? That's wonderful. And where does he live? I must speak to him about the theater as soon as possible."

She looked at him for a few moments and then smiled. "I still don't believe you. Omar has many villas, but his newest is the Villa Amour, in the wealthy district on the west. It is well-known."

"It is? That's wonderful! And do you know, was there a wedding there recently? In the past few days?"

"I could never tell you that. You are a man," she would have said.

And indeed, she never would tell him. But she just had, hadn't she? The conversation could have become interesting, but he had what he needed.

Seth whirled from the railing. He had to find a way to the Villa Amour. He had less than an hour before the clairvoyance ended. Maybe less.

# 35

KING ABDULLAH STORMED into his office, furious. Incompetence surrounded him. He felt vulnerable without his security chief, who lay dead in a box somewhere on its way back to Saudi Arabia. Hilal would have ended this madness already if he hadn't gotten himself killed. For that Abdullah blamed the Americans.

"How many men do they have?" he asked, sliding behind his desk.

General Mustafa crossed his legs. "The sheik claims to have ten thousand just beyond the city to the west."

Abdullah eyed his brother. This man had persuaded him not to act after receiving the call from the American secretary of state. With the crown prince in Indonesia, Abdullah weighed his general's advice and agreed. Now that Khalid had taken control of the palace perimeter, Abdullah wondered whether General Mustafa was not divided himself.

"Where is the crown prince?"

"His plane has been turned back to Jakarta," Mustafa said. "Khalid has taken control of the airport as well."

"Ahmed is with Khalid?"

"It would seem so."

"How many other ministers?"

"At least twelve. Khalid has planned this for a long time to have such a broad base of support."

Abdullah stared out the window. It wasn't the first time a prince had tried to remove him from power—the threat was constant. But this one seemed to have some momentum. "You are speaking about my death, General. Not a political rally."

"No, Your Highness. They've made no such threats. They've given you twelve hours to evacuate the government. If they planned to storm the palace, they would have done it while they had the advantage of surprise."

"They've given me twelve hours only to appease those who support me. They have no intention of allowing me to walk out of here alive. I've always been a threat to the militants."

The general waited before answering. "Perhaps they have other plans to contain that threat."

"I have no intention of rotting in a cell. How many men does Khalid have outside now?"

"It's not how many, sir. It's where he has them. They control all of the security outside the palace itself. And they control most of the ministries."

"No change in the military?"

"No. Both the air force and the army are standing down. They aren't necessarily with Khalid, but they aren't against him either."

"So in the end, Khalid's real force consists of the sheik's men?"

"Yes. And the sheik has another twenty thousand standing by."

His predecessor, King Fahd, had always prevailed, using both cunning and brute force. Cunning was all Abdullah had. Cunning and the Americans.

"We still have communications?" he asked.

"No telephones," General Mustafa said.

"Then get a message out with a courier. You can do that, can't you, General?"

"Perhaps. Yes, I think so."

"Good. Let the city know what's happening here. We will create as much confusion in the streets as we can. Tell them that the Shia have besieged the palace. That should get a reaction. Sheik Al-Asamm is the key. Perhaps we could do what Khalid has done. Perhaps we could dislodge his loyalty to Khalid."

The general was silent.

"What do you think, General? Can the sheik's allegiance be shaken?"

"I don't know. If it can, Khalid will fail. But Al-Asamm is bound by marriage, and he's a traditional man."

"Yet he broke his bond with me."

"Only because the religious leaders agreed that he could, under the circumstances."

"And what about you, General? Where do your loyalties lie?"

"With the king."

"And if Khalid were king?"

"The king will be whomever Allah has willed. But I believe that he has willed you, Your Highness."

"I see. And is Khalid following God's will?"

The general didn't have an answer. Conviction had

divided the country between fundamentalists and more moderate Muslims. But like many, Mustafa himself was probably torn. Fatalism was indeed convenient at times.

"If I don't hear rioting within the hour, I will assume you haven't spread the word, General. That is all."


"THE COUP IS six hours old from what we can gather, but we have no direct contact with the House of Saud so we can't be sure," Smaley said. "You're still in Colorado Springs?"

So Seth had been right! Clive shifted the cell phone to his right hand. "I'm on my way to the airport now. You're saying that Khalid bin Mishal has actually succeeded?"

"Too soon to call it."

"Then Seth may be our only hope."

"As far as I'm concerned, he's dead in the water. He obviously failed to disrupt the wedding, and we haven't heard a thing from him. You, on the other hand, may be able to help us out." Smaley paused. "Look, you were right on this one, and you have my apologies. Meanwhile, we have a serious situation on our hands. Khalid has sealed off our embassy in Riyadh and both consulates in Dhahran and Jidda. We have no idea how Jordan and his staff are doing; communications are down. It's a mess."

"Miriam's alive?" Clive asked.

"We assume so. Sheik Al-Asamm has gathered a pretty decent force east of the city. Which is why we want you back in the lab with that last scenario Seth ran. Was the sheik a factor in Seth's simulation?"

Clive used his free hand to maneuver the car into a 7-Eleven. "He must have been. In any real scenario the

sheik would have to be dealt with. You want me to analyze the actions of the sheik and Omar in Seth's scenario?
Makes sense." He swung the car around.

"The techs are already doing it, but they don't have
your sense of this thing. We think that our best hope may
rest with the sheik. We need to know his weaknesses, his
responses to real situations. If Seth's scenario was real, it
could give us that, right?"

"Maybe. Maybe not. Do you have contact with the
sheik?"

"Not yet, but we think we can get to his personal line.
Either way, we don't have a lot of time here."

Clive motored back onto the 24 bypass and headed for
Cheyenne Mountain. "I'm on my way. So nothing from
Seth, huh?"

"Not on this end. That may be a good thing. The last
thing we need is for some maniac American to walk in
and kidnap the sheik's daughter. We need Al-Asamm's
cooperation, not his anger."

"You still don't get him, do you, Peter? It's a good
thing he's beyond your reach now. At the very least, don't
go out of your way to stop him."

"For all we know, he's dead," Smaley said. "You
should've never let him go. Forget it, Clive. He's no longer
a factor."

Clive wanted to object, but on the surface, the deputy
secretary made sense. For all he knew, Seth had lost his
gift altogether by now. And if Miriam was married . . .

Still, even without clairvoyance, Seth was no idiot.

"I'll call you if I get anything," Clive said. He turned
the phone off.

# 36

TIME WAS EVERYTHING now. Seth found a taxi driver who knew the location of the Villa Amour. Despite butchering a few words in Arabic while using his best impression of a woman's voice, Seth convinced the driver to take him. But the effort wasted fifteen minutes.

A tall wall ran around the villa, and guards stood at the gates. Didn't matter—he saw no way past the gate anyway. The only way to sneak in was over the wall at the south end. Thank God he was still seeing.

He ran as best he could in the abaaya without looking like a wounded bat. He jumped for the top of the wall, caught it, and hauled himself over.

The villas were called palaces, and he could see why at first glance. Tall Greek pillars framed a fifteen-foot entrance made of wood. But he had no intention of using the front door. It was the servants' housing near the back that interested him.

Not so long ago, he would have been able to stand here

and know precisely what was in the villa by scanning through possible futures. But at the moment he was capturing only glimpses, like at the start of this whole mess, when he'd first seen Miriam about to be attacked in the ladies' room at Berkeley.

Seth ran under cover of bushes and palm trees that lined a huge fountain, spinning through the questions that had plagued him during the long cab ride. Why hadn't he seen Miriam in any future? This was Omar's newest villa; he knew at least that. And he knew that a wedding had been performed here recently. But he still did not know with certainty that Omar had married Miriam here or, if he had, that she was still here.

Seth swallowed hard, aware of how thin his chances were. He placed his hope in the Filipino maid who would engage him in the servants' quarters. He didn't know how cooperative she'd be, but he had seen that she would talk to him. At least he had that.

One step at a time, Seth. Just one step.

He paused at the door and glanced back. He couldn't take his seeing for granted anymore. He put his hand on the knob and turned. The door swung in.

A wood table, window coverings made of sheets, and an old wood stove furnished the dim room. A dark-skinned woman, unveiled and dressed in a dirty tunic, turned from the stove, eyes wide.

Seth stepped in and closed the door. She would talk to him, in English. He knew that, but he also knew that he had to come off as a woman.

"Hello, could you help me, please?"

The servant just stared at him.

"I'm an American," he said. "I beg you for assistance."

"American?" She glanced at the window, obviously nervous. Filipino servants who'd come to the cradle of Islam in search of work were common in Saudi Arabia, but they held very little status.

"I'm willing to pay." Seth slipped his hand under the abaaya, took two hundred dollars from his front pocket, and held them out. "Please."

She looked at the money for a moment, glanced one more time at the window, and then reached for the cash. By the look in her eyes, it was probably more than she'd seen at one time in her whole life.

"I must speak to the woman who is here. Her name is Miriam. She was married here, yes?"

The woman looked up, untrusting.

"Please, she's my friend. You must help me."

"No woman married here," the servant said.

Darkness dumped into Seth's mind. He was blind again!

The woman took a step backward. He was standing in the middle of a guarded palace on the Arabian Peninsula with a coup raging about him, and he was blind.

Dear God…

He cleared the frog from his throat and hitched his voice up an octave. "Please, I didn't mean to startle you. I have a pain in my stomach." That was ridiculous.

"You cannot be here! If I am caught, they will beat!"

"No, they will not catch you. I will leave. But first I must know." He reached into his pocket and removed another hundred. "Here, take it."

She reached forward, but this time he pulled the money back. "Tell me. Where is the woman?"

She eyed him carefully and then looked at the money.

"Yes. There was a wedding," she said.

"When?"

"Last evening."

"Where is she?"

The woman held out her hand. "Give me money."

Seth gave it to her.

"I don't know," she said. "You go now. You go!" She picked up a broom and jabbed it at him. "You go now!"

"Tell me where she is!" he boomed.

The servant snatched the broom higher and swung it at his head. The handle smacked him on his head, but now the woman's cries were more pressing than her attack.

"Okay! Hush! Sh." He warded off a flurry of blows, but she continued beating, unfazed. Seth fled and slammed the door behind him. He ran five paces before thinking he must look like anything but a graceful Saudi woman. He pulled up, heart pounding. But the grounds were still quiet.

Miriam was here. He knew that now. There was only one way to find her.

For a blond-headed, green-eyed, fair-skinned male racing through a Saudi Arabian palace and pulling open doors, an abaaya was a wonderful thing.


MIRIAM SAT ON the couch, suffocated by purple. The subterranean room had no windows, yet its decorator, presumably Omar, had lined the walls with heavy velvet curtains. The red carpet reminded her of blood, and it clashed with the drapes. The silk bedspread was black. The violet candles smelled like licorice. The room was nothing more than a lavish dungeon.

To her it all smelled of Nizari, that dreadful extremist sect, though she'd never smelled Nizari.

They'd brought her here an hour after the wedding and locked the door. Since then she'd seen or heard no one. The hours crept by with mounting dread, and she managed to sleep only for a couple hours, here on the couch.

She'd thought to kill herself rather than face Omar again, but suicide was not her way. She would rather be killed by him, and she intended to provoke him to it. The mutawa who oversaw Sita's drowning said that she had done Hatam bodily harm; Miriam wondered how her friend injured him. Scratched his eyes out, maybe. Or smashed his nose. If Omar tried to kiss her again, she would bite him, and not gently.

She thought of biting down on his lip hard enough to sever it. I'll show you that I'm not your toy. No, she was a woman. But in this man's hands she couldn't be a woman. He didn't even know women existed. To him they were merely flesh, possessions. Something to use up and throw away.

Her vision blurred with tears. What have I done to deserve this?

The phone rang and Miriam jerked.

The white porcelain receiver hung on a brass hook—she'd thought the device was only a decoration, but its shrill ring proved her wrong. She stood. Should she answer it?

Miriam let it ring a dozen times before picking up the receiver and placing it to her ear.

"He is coming," a woman's voice said. "He has asked that his bride be ready."

Miriam shivered.

"Do you hear me?"

"I will never be ready!" Miriam whispered.

"And that is as he wants it. So then, you are ready. If you anger him, he will love you for it. If you submit to him, he will hate you. He has the blood of a king, and you are his queen."

Miriam slammed the receiver down. There was only one way. She had to kill him. She would distract him and bury the candlestick deep into his skull.

A noise sounded at the door. Miriam ran to the dresser and flattened herself in the shadows. The candlestick! She reached out and snatched it off the dresser.

The door opened a crack. Miriam pressed into the darkness and held her breath.

A woman stood in the doorway, clothed in black. Veiled. Was this Omar's sick fantasy? To come dressed as a woman?

Revulsion swept through her gut, threatening to explode in a scream. She could do it. She would take his head off before he—

"Miriam?"

It was a man! Omar had come to her in an abaaya to mock her. If she let him come in and swung at him while he had his back turned, she might succeed.

"Miriam, are you in here?"

The man was speaking in English.

Her mind filled with the voice and only one name surfaced. But...No, it couldn't be Seth. She was now hallucinating.

"Miriam? Are you here?"

It was Seth's voice! It had to be!

The figure turned to leave.

Miriam stepped out of the shadows, wielding the candlestick like a weapon.

"Seth?"

He spun back. "Miriam?"

Take off the veil, she tried to say, but she couldn't. Her throat was swollen shut. He yanked the veil from his head.

It was Seth.

Miriam felt her knees weaken.

He rushed to her and she fell against him, unable to hold back deep sobs. She was saying things to him, telling him everything, but the words all came out like moans. Long earthy groans, echoing around the chamber.

"What have they done to you?" He sank to the couch, embracing her.

Omar was coming at this very moment—she had to warn Seth! But her voice would not cooperate.

"You're safe now. You're safe with me. Do you hear me, Miriam? I'm here now."

"He's coming," she managed.

"Who? Omar?"

She tried to catch her breath. On impulse she grabbed him by the abaaya and kissed his face. "Thank you!" She kissed his hair, repeating herself through more tears. "Thank you, thank you. Thank you, Seth."

"Where is Omar?"

She sat up. "He's coming!"

Seth looked at her, unsure. "Now?"

"Yes, now!" She pushed off him and ran for the door. "We have to leave now! Can you see the futures?"

"No." He jumped to his feet and jerked the abaaya off. "Here, you wear this."

"No!"

Seth stopped at the anger in her voice.

"No," she said. "You wear the abaaya. Give me your clothes. Hurry!"

He understood. It took them only a few seconds, fumbling madly with buttons and zippers, but in the end Seth was still hidden in a cloak of black, and Miriam wore his corduroys and a white shirt twice her size.

"My hair," she said.

He spun her around and tied her hair in a messy knot behind her head. Horrible! She needed a ghutra. Anything to cover her head. She ran for the bed, pulled one of the pillows from its case, and tied the case over her head.

"You make a lousy man," Seth said.

"And you make a terrible woman," she said.

Seth reached for her hand. "Come on!"

They ran from the room and headed for the stairs. "Where's the garage?" he asked.

They had come through the garage yesterday, but she did not make a note of it. "I don't know. The back! Toward the back."

Together they burst onto the main floor. Seth seemed to know better than she where the back was, because he pulled her into a hall and motioned to the end. They walked quickly now. A servant entered the hall and took two steps before turning back to them.

They walked on, a man and a woman: two strangers in the villa, oddly dressed perhaps, but nothing more. She hoped.

"May I help you?" the servant called after them.

"No," Seth said, and his Arabic was good enough, she thought. He said he'd lost his gift, which meant he was on his own. They were on their own.

Dear God, help us.

They found the garage at the back, beyond the study that Miriam had waited in yesterday. A row of cars lined the stalls. Mercedes, all of them. Shouts reached them from the villa. Omar.

"Hurry!" Miriam tore for the first car, blinded by fresh fury. She would never go back. Not alive. Never!

"I can't see a…" Seth ripped the veil from his face, vaulted the railing, and raced for the second car. Both were locked.

They tried all five cars. The one on the end ticked as it cooled. It was unlocked. She knew without a doubt that Omar had just arrived in this car.

Seth piled in on the driver's side and stabbed the garage-door control.

"You can't drive!" Miriam cried. "They'll think you're a woman!" She glanced at the garage door that was rising at Seth's command. "I'll drive."

He hesitated and then scooted over to the passenger side.

Miriam slid behind the wheel and turned the keys. The black Mercedes thundered to life. Movement from the door caught her attention. Omar exited the door that led to the house.

You're too late, you filthy pig.

She set her jaw, jammed the shifter down, and punched the accelerator. They plowed through a half-opened garage door, metal screeching and wrenching, but Miriam hardly noticed. She was breaking down the walls of prison.

"Go!" Seth yelled. "Go, go, go!"

She went. Straight for the front gate. But the gate was closed.

Seth grabbed the door handle. "Ram it!"

"Ram it?"

"Punch it!"

"Punch it?"

"Go! Hard! It's a Mercedes; we'll make it!"

She had learned to trust him in the desert, and she had no reason to doubt him now. She pressed the gas pedal to the floor and they roared for the gates. They both ducked at the last moment. With a tremendous crash and a jolt that threw Miriam into the steering wheel, the car slammed through the gates. They dragged one of the gates for a few meters and then broke free.

Miriam spun the wheel to the right. The car swerved a few times before she straightened it out. Then they were flying through an intersection to the sound of honking cars.

"Slow down!"

She eased off the pedal. "We made it!"

He stared at her, wearing a sly grin. "For the moment. Do you know where we're going now?"

"Out of the city."

"Then where?"

"Then I don't know where. Do you?"

"No."

An army truck blazed past them and careened around a corner toward a mob of men surrounding a petrol station. So, the coup was under way.

Miriam looked at Seth, hardly able to comprehend his presence. "I can't believe this is happening," she said. "You came for me."

"Did you ever doubt me?"

She looked out her window, still dazed. "This is really happening, isn't it? We are free?"

"Not exactly. The palace is under siege," Seth said. "Chaos is spreading. Let's hope we can get out of the city."

She only had to consider the matter briefly to know they would never make it out of Saudi Arabia. But they had escaped from Omar, and that was enough.

"I won't go back, Seth. I will never go back alive."

Seth didn't seem to have heard her. "What's this light?" he asked, tapping a black box beside the steering column.

"Did you hear me, Seth? Promise me that no matter what happens, you will never allow them to take me alive."

He looked into her eyes. He knew what she was asking. He said nothing.

"I would rather you kill me," she said.

"What's this device?" he asked again.

Her father's car had the same—it was common in a country with many rich and many poor. "It's an antitheft device. If the car is stolen, they can track it."

He looked up at her with round, blank eyes.

"They already know our every move. There's no way out of Saudi Arabia, Seth." Tears swelled again. "Promise me, Seth. Not alive. Never alive."

He rested his hand on her shoulder and squeezed it. "Even in dying, you need mazel," he said.

"Mazel?"

"Luck."

"Another Jewish proverb from your grandmother?"

"Yiddish, but yes." He swallowed his fear, but the stress did not leave his voice. "I'm not ready to give up yet." He cleared his throat. "You're free now. That's what matters, right?"

She sniffed. "Yes. And I owe you my life. Again. Thank you. Thank you with all my heart. But I cannot go back. That's all. As long as you understand that."

He looked at her and offered a forced smile.

"Drive, Miriam. Drive fast."

# 37

"WHAT I'M TELLING you is that she's with another man!" Omar shouted into the phone.

His father's voice crackled in the receiver. "Find them! And when you do, kill the man. This woman makes you look like a fool. She escapes you once and now twice?"

Omar closed his eyes and gripped the phone. She was not the smart one; the American was. Who else could have possibly found their way into the palace and then taken her? Who else even knew where he'd kept her? For that matter, he had no idea how even the American could have known.

"You should concern yourself with the rioting," Omar said. "They're tearing the city apart."

"Let them riot. If the coup fails, it'll be because of your woman, not the protests in the streets. We must have the support of the sheik!"

His father was right, of course. Abdullah's supporters needed the opportunity to vent their objection, but in the end they would follow the new king. It was the way of the desert. But if Miriam came to harm, the sheik might become a problem.

Khalid's voice eased. "Omar, we are very close. Everything has progressed exactly as I planned. The borders are sealed; the ministries are sympathetic; the allegiance of the armed forces is split, and they've agreed to stand down. Abdullah has until nightfall, and then we will crush him. But without the sheik, we will falter. He'll turn on us as quickly as he turned on the monarchy if we don't keep our end. Find your wife!"

His father didn't often show desperation. "The car is headed south. It's low on fuel. I will have my wife before you have the city."

He cut the connection.

In his driveway, ten sedans lined the street, waiting. He walked to the first one and slid into the passenger seat. Beside him a simple tracking device showed the location of the stolen Mercedes. Royals routinely used the devices; surely Miriam knew that much. But then, she could do little about it. She could exchange cars possibly, but finding a car to steal in this city would not prove as easy as it had been in America. And for that matter, tracking any car would be quite simple on these sparse roads. He would use the helicopter if he needed it. This time the chase would be short.

"We have twenty men and are well armed," Assir said.

Omar nodded. "Go."

The train of cars moved out, a long black snake of Mercedes slithering through Riyadh's streets and then onto the highway, south toward Jizan.

Smoke from burning tires blackened the eastern sky.

Scattered gunfire popped sporadically. The highway was nearly deserted, an uncommon sight for the noon hour. Change floated in the air. How easily and quickly it could come when all the pieces were in place. For twenty years, a rising tide among fundamental factions had threatened the monarch's power, and now someone would finally succeed. In reality, fundamentalists comprised more than half the country; the coup was merely returning power to the majority. By day's end, the kingdom of Saudi Arabia would have a new face. His father's face, the face of Khalid bin Mishal.

Then one day, his own face.

His mind returned to Miriam. How ironic that a woman was proving to be the final stronghold. The next time he put his hand on her, he would not release her until she understood what it meant to be one of his women.

"Faster, Assir."

THEY TRIED STOPPING for fuel once, but the station was engulfed by a mob. Then they were south of the city. Turning back to find petrol would only increase the likelihood of running into Omar. If Seth could only see the futures . . .

But he couldn't. And if he was right, he wouldn't be seeing anything beyond his own eyes for a long time.

He tried to remove the small security box. He kicked at it in a frenzied attempt to disable it, to no avail. The tiny red light refused to stop blinking.

"We're running out of gas," Seth said. "This isn't good."

Miriam drove with both hands white on the steering

wheel, her mind scrambling for ideas. The desert sands drifted by, strewn with sandstone and small shacks.

Seth lowered his head into his hands and groaned. He was as frightened as she had ever seen him.

"Please, Seth. You're frightening me."

"I'm frightening you? You should be afraid of the fact that we're almost out of gas while a maniac is on our tail."

"You're frightening me! We can only do what we can do. We've made it this far—maybe there is a way. If not—"

"How can you be so nonchalant about this?"

It was true that she did feel a certain peace she'd never felt before. She'd escaped the jaws of a living hell.

"I was dead in there, Seth. At least for now I'm alive."

"Well, I for one would like to keep you alive. I realize our situation looks hopeless, but I can't just give up, not after all we've been through."

He had a point. Still, she was resigned.

"You say you won't see again for at least five hours. Maybe we can survive five hours."

"Maybe," he said, but dread paled his face.

He took a deep breath and let it out slowly. "Okay. We have to find a place to hole up. If we run out of gas on the highway, we're toast. Do any of these side roads lead anywhere?" He indicated a dirt road that ran west.

"They must go somewhere."

He turned and looked out the rear window.

"Any sign?" she asked.

"No. Take the next dirt road. We have to get off the main road."

"If they're close, they will see our dust."

"I'm sure they know where we are anyway."

Miriam slowed at the next exit, turned right, and motored up the packed dirt road. They were a good thirty kilometers south of the city now. Perhaps the riots had slowed Omar's pursuit. Maybe they were out of tracking range.

"What's west of here?" Seth asked.

"The desert. Jizan."

They rode in silence for several minutes.

"Did I tell you that you look ridiculous in that abaaya?" she asked. "You look like a monk."

He faced her. They shared a brief smile, and Seth turned back to his window.

"Did I tell you that I couldn't get you off my mind?" he asked.

"I was on your mind in America?" she asked. He, too, then.

"Like a plague."

"Is that a good thing?"

"Depends on how deadly the plague is," Seth said.

"Now your American jargon is losing me."

"It depends on whether you have the same plague that I have," he said.

She thought about that. He was referring to his feelings for her, and he was asking if she shared them, if she loved him as he did her.

"How could I possibly not love you?" she said softly.

"Right. It's hard not to love your savior."

There was no sign of civilization this far out. They drove over a knoll and dipped into a vacant valley. Dust billowed behind them in clouds of brown. On the dashboard, the fuel indicator rested a millimeter below the E.

"I think we may die together out in this desert, Seth Border. If you could still see the futures, that would be the most likely future, wouldn't it?"

He thought a moment. "Maybe."

"Then before I die I should tell you that you've changed my life. You've made it impossible for me to love any man who is not as gentle and understanding to a woman as you have been."

He smiled. "I'm terribly sorry."

"Don't be." She paused. "I am merely following the commandment of your prophet. If the world did the same, we wouldn't be in this mess."

"Love your neighbor as yourself." That brought a small grin to his lips. "Glad to make your acquaintance, neighbor." Seth took her hand, lifted it to his mouth, and kissed it.

Before she could react, he pointed to a shack nestled at the base of a cliff. "What's that?"

"Looks like an abandoned home. A squatter maybe."

"As good a place as any."

There was no driveway that she could see. The ground was rough and rocky. She swung the car off the road and gunned the motor. They bounced over the dirt.

"Just like Death Valley," Seth said.

She chuckled. Why not?

"Like Bonnie and Clyde," she said.

"Just don't run over the place. Park behind."

"Absolutely."

"Well, okay then." He smiled, but she knew he forced it.

Miriam eased the car to a stop between the rickety old structure and the cliff, then turned off the ignition. Dust drifted past them. A faint ticking sounded from the engine.

The shack was no more than twenty feet by twenty feet, constructed of mud bricks and topped with a tin roof. A single grenade would tear it to pieces.

"Ready?" she asked.

"Now or never."

They climbed out and walked around the hut. A faint dust lingered over the road, but as of yet they could see no pursuit from the direction of the highway.

"You think they missed us?" she asked hopefully.

"Maybe."

"You don't think so."

"We can always hope," he said.

The wooden door hung on a single hinge. Seth pulled it open, stepped through after her, and closed it as best he could.

Light fell across a dirt floor from a boarded window beside the entry. A rustic wooden table stood against the right wall, flanked by two shelves and a couple benches. A small bed made of planks filled the shadowy space opposite the table.

Miriam crossed to the shelves and righted two large candles. Several pots and pans rested on the table next to an old dusty Koran.

"It's a common hut," she said. "Used by travelers on occasion." She picked up a box of matches and struck one. "They even left matches."

The lit candles dispelled the shadows. Miriam replaced the matches and turned around. Seth stood looking between the window's boards. He did look like a monk standing there, craning for a view, she thought. The monk who had been able to see many futures.

She watched his Adam's apple move and her heart

swelled. She looked at his strained face and knew that despite his attempts to pretend otherwise, her monk was a desperate man at the moment. He had come to the end of his world.

Not an hour ago, she'd been as desperate, at her own end. But now she was seeing with different eyes. No ending could compare to the one from which Seth had rescued her.

Seth turned from the window and walked to the bed, one hand on his hip, the other gripping his jaw, deep in thought. He stopped with his back to her, facing the dark corner.

Miriam took a step toward him. "Seth."

His shoulders rose and fell in a deep sigh.

"Seth." She stood behind him. "There is one more thing I must tell you." She put her hand on his shoulder, but he didn't turn.

She pulled him gently and he turned. His eyes swam in tears. One had broken down his cheek, leaving a trail that glistened in the candlelight.

"No, there are two things that I will tell you," she said, wiping the tear from his face. "The first is that you have not failed me. You think you have, but I am happy to die with you today."

He closed his eyes, fighting back more tears. She stepped into him and pulled his head down to her shoulder. She stroked the back of his head, fighting the knot in her own throat.

He lifted his head, wiped his eyes, and sniffed once. "This is ridiculous. I don't know what my problem is." He turned away. "I've always been able to reason my way through this world. I've always been strong, you know."

He walked to the window, glanced out, then turned and leaned back against the wall. "I really don't know what I was thinking, coming to Saudi Arabia."

She took a step toward him. "You came to give my life back to me," she said. "And you've done that."

He looked at her and his eyes misted again. She knew he couldn't understand how freeing her did anything but postpone the end.

"The other thing I must tell you is that I wasn't completely honest with you," she said. "You've done more than change my life. You have stolen from me." She smiled. "Do you know what the punishment for theft is in this country? You're terribly guilty."

He stared at her without understanding.

"You have stolen my soul and my mind," she said. "You have stolen my heart. I can no longer live without you."

The words sat between them, beautiful and elegant and demanding silence.

She touched his face. "I am in love with you, Seth. I think I have been in love with you since we first met. Not as a neighbor."

She leaned forward, rose to her tiptoes, and touched her lips against his. It was the first time she had initiated a kiss, and she felt as though a fire were sweeping over her mouth.

For a moment he did not respond. Then she felt his hands on her waist, and he kissed her in return, soft as a rose petal.

He pulled her to him and kissed her again, on her lips and then on her cheek. He wrapped his arms around her and held her tight. A soft sob broke from his chest and he caught himself.

"It's okay, Seth. We will be okay now," she said.

"I love you, Miriam. I missed you so much."

She was going to die—she knew that. But she felt safe and complete, and if she could arrange it, she would die in his arms. All she needed was mazel.

# 38

CLIVE STUDIED THE printout and drew his finger over the information, nerves taut. Pencil marks covered the margins in a maze of arrows and notes. Three months of Seth's foresight had translated into seventy-three pages. He'd circled each event that mentioned the sheik, fifty at least. Abu Ali al-Asamm figured importantly in a government run by Khalid. The question was, what part of this future yielded any useful information that might be common to all futures, including the one they faced now?

The coup was only nine hours old, and already the world was scurrying. A militant Islamic government in Saudi Arabia would wreak havoc in the Middle East, providing a safe haven for terrorists and dissidents, that very small minority of Muslims bent on the destruction of all who stood in the way of their extremist utopia.

Those who followed the politics of the region knew that the destabilization in Saudi Arabia could easily spread to other Arab countries, as well as to other Muslim countries.

The U.S. military was already developing plans to take out a Saudi kingdom run by Khalid, but Clive held an extrapolation of such plans, and it didn't read as though removing a militant king would be easy. In fact, according to Seth, they would fail, at least in the first three months.

He glanced at the clock. Time was running out. According to information from within Saudi Arabia, Khalid would storm the palace in less than four hours.

"Come on, Seth," he muttered. "What am I looking for?"

An image of Seth bent over the computer, typing away, ran across his mind. What made a mind brilliant?

"You're still out there, aren't you, Seth? This isn't over, is it?"

Clive looked back at the printout. The secretary was right about one thing: A militant government would depend on the cooperation of the sheik and the Shia. A thin thread of an idea tickled his mind. If Seth still had his gift, he would be able to tell Clive whether this mind-bending exercise would yield anything of value in the next few hours.

Forget Seth. Back to the printout.


SHEIK ABU ALI al-Asamm stood at the entrance to his tent, looking over the valley filled with his men. If God wills it, he thought. For twenty years, thirty years, God had not; today he had changed his mind.

Riyadh sat on the horizon, dirtied by a haze of smoke from a hundred tire fires. The afternoon prayer call was just now warbling over the city. Yes, pray, my fellow Muslims. Pray, as I pray.

The House of Saud had grown softer with each passing decade. Abdul Aziz would roll in his grave if he could see Abdullah today. They had abandoned the central teachings of the Prophet for favor with the West. So now those who were faithful were called fundamentalists and regarded with distaste and suspicion. Was religion a thing to change with cultural moods?

Evidently, most thought it was.

One of his most trusted servants, Al-Hakim, approached from behind. "We have received another message, Abu."

The sheik didn't remove his gaze from the city. "From whom?"

"It's the Americans," he said. "They are saying that should the coup succeed, they will not allow fifty years of progress to slip into the sea."

Al-Asamm closed his eyes. Why the Americans insisted on putting their fingers into every jar, he would never understand.

"Go on."

"They say they are drawing up plans for the removal of Khalid already."

Al-Asamm smiled. They were a cunning lot; he would give them that. And it was true that his bloodline would not be fully established in the kingdom until Miriam bore a child. But they underestimated the value of both his mind and his word. Everything was negotiable in the American mind, including their own religion. Not so with the sheik, Abu Ali al-Asamm.

"Tell them I am more interested in the will of God than in the will of men. Then remind them that they are merely men." The sheik paused. "On second thought, don't tell them that last part. It will only send them into a panic.

Just tell them to mind their own business and stay on their own side of the ocean."

Al-Hakim bowed and returned to the room where they kept the telex machine. Al-Asamm crossed his arms and walked to his mat. It was time to pray.

# 39

THEY SAT AT the table, her hands in his, sharing precious minutes. As they talked, Seth periodically stood and crossed to the window before returning.

Their predicament was hardly comprehensible. Miriam was an Arab. A Muslim. She was a Saudi princess, daughter to the Sheik Abu Ali al-Asamm, and now she was married to a Saudi prince. Seth, on the other hand was...well, what was he? A brilliant man, surely destined to change the world by discovering light travel or a longer-lasting light bulb. Seth was a Jew, at least in heritage. An American, not a Saudi.

And they were in love; this was a problem.

He told her briefly about his trip to Saudi Arabia, about how he'd awakened in Cheyenne Mountain after seeing her in his sleep, and about how he passed through Saudi immigration. But he seemed disconnected from these events. He'd had these powerful experiences so recently, but recounted them as if they were only distant dreams.

For Miriam they were not remote abstractions at all. Their implications burrowed through her head. Perhaps the problems of love were only illusions of the mind.

Miriam stood and walked toward the candles. When the light was on in Seth's mind, he could see so clearly, but when it was off, he became blind. Yet the truth was unchanging, waiting to be lit by a candle, wasn't it? And what was that truth?

Seth sat in silence behind her. She lifted her hand and slowly ran it over the flame. So small and yet so hot, so real.

"Do you think it's possible that so many millions of people could be wrong about love?" she asked. She felt her pulse quicken even in speaking the question.

He was quiet.

"That love is the only way?" she said. "The implications are almost too much to bear."

"How so?" He looked at the candle.

"How can you kill your neighbor if you love him?"

Seth nodded. "I suppose you can't."

"Why are we not taught this in our mosques? Why do your churches and synagogues and temples ignore this greatest truth?"

He thought about that for a long moment. "Because politics and power are greater in most eyes."

"They'd do better to think with their hearts."

"That's one way to put it."

"But you now believe?"

"In love?"

"In the God of love, as you put it."

"I saw a new future open when there was none, didn't I?" The candlelight flickered in his eyes. "So then I must.

But I can't say I'm a fan of man's religion. Man screws it all up."

"We're all guilty of that. I have a lot to think about."

He sighed. "I'm not seeing the future any more."

"Because you're depending only on your mind!"

"What do you mean?"

"When you see things in your mind, they're easy to believe. All your life you've depended on this brilliance of yours. But when these things—these futures you see— are no longer in your mind, you lose faith. The whole world puts the mind before the heart. It's killing us all."

He stared at her. She could almost see wheels spinning behind his eyes.

"You saw the futures and you believed, enough to come to Saudi Arabia to save me. But now that you can't see, you lose faith. Have a little faith, Seth."

Miriam stood and went to the window. She crossed her arms and looked out. A small plume of dust rose on the horizon, but it was too far away to tell its source.

"Just like that?"

She turned. "Just like that."

# 40

OMAR HELD UP his hand. "Stop."

Assir brought the Mercedes to a halt. They'd crested a knoll on the dirt road. The desert rolled out before them, unbroken except for this trail that divided north from south. A small shack rested at the base of a cliff, three hundred meters ahead and a hundred meters off the road. According to the tracking device, the car was there, perhaps behind the hut.

"The common hut." He pointed at the cliff. Assir eased the car forward and Omar picked up the radio. "They are in the common hut to our right. Do you see it?"

The radio crackled. "Yes."

"Weapons ready. Form a perimeter around the front. Don't underestimate them." He tossed the radio on the seat, pulled out his nine millimeter, and chambered a round.

The cars split the desert and approached the shack from multiple angles, raising ribbons of dust as they converged on the cliff. Assir followed a pair of fresh tire tracks and brought the car to a stop fifty meters from the shanty. Dust drifted by and then cleared. From here the hut looked abandoned.

The other Mercedes stopped, one by one, in a great semicircle around the shack, pinning it against the sheer rock.

"There's a car at the rear of the hut," Assir said.

Omar nodded. The Mercedes purred. For a full minute he waited, not expecting anything. No one spoke over the radio; they would only follow his lead. He would prolong this menacing sight, this display of power, for Miriam to see from her pitiful hiding place. Ten black cars with tinted windshields, poised for the final kill, at his leisure.

Omar opened his door. The afternoon heat displaced the car's conditioned air, coaxing a sweat from his brow before he stood. He looked down the line of sedans over the roof of his own. One by one their doors opened and twenty men joined him, loitering behind the cover of their doors.

"I will give you to the count of ten to come out unharmed," he called. "Then we will open fire." He lifted his pistol and fired a round into the corner brick.

"One!"

"Don't be stupid," Miriam's voice called out.

The strength of her voice surprised him. This in front of his men. He clenched his jaw.

"If you kill me, your father will take your head off," Miriam called out. "And if he fails, then I promise you my father will not! Put your silly toy away."

A hawk called from over the cliff. He hadn't expected them to buy his threat, but neither had he expected her to dismiss him as a fool.

"And if you think you can come in here and kill Seth before dragging me out, you'd better reconsider," she called out. "Do you really believe that I would allow myself to be taken alive, only to be forced to look at your hideous face for the rest of my life?"

She defied him in front of his men to draw out his anger. He knew it and was powerless to stop the chill that ripped through his bones. He decided then, staring at the shack, that Miriam would live only long enough to bear him a child. A son was all he needed from her.

"I hear the sounds of an animal," he said calmly. "I would like to speak to the American."

"Take a hike, Omar," a male voice called out. "She said she doesn't want to see you. Capisce?"

Perhaps for the first time in his adult life, Omar was speechless.

"Okay, I'm sorry," Seth called out. "I take it back. But I'm afraid that Miriam has fallen hopelessly in love with me. We must allow love to—"

"You are talking about my wife!" Omar shouted. "My *wife*!"

His voice echoed off the cliff.

"Yes, well, that is a problem. But we think we have a solution to this mess. We've decided that it will be okay to share it with you. That is, if you're man enough to come in and join us."

Omar glanced at his watch. In two hours the sheik would storm the palace. It was time to be done with this foolishness.

"Your wife has demanded that I kill her if you come in after her," the American called. "We'll be Romeo and Juliet. We'll both die in the embrace of true love. I'm fresh out of poison, but there's a shard of glass in here that we think will do the trick."

Would he do such a thing? No.

And yet...the American had to know the situation was hopeless for him. And Miriam would probably prefer death over capture. The realization drove a small wedge of agitation into Omar's mind. He glanced down the line of cars. Seth stood to gain nothing by killing him. Twenty others here would storm the shack and take out their fury on him.

"I'm going in," Omar said to Assir.

"Sir—"

"He has nothing to gain by killing me. If anything happens, storm the place."

"And Miriam?"

Omar hesitated. "Keep her alive."

He stepped out from behind the car door. Assir barked an order to the others behind him.

"The gun, Omar," Seth called. "Drop the gun."

He tossed the gun to the sand and walked on. The door came open with a gentle tug. He stepped into the dim room.

"Close the door."

The American stood in the corner, dressed in an abaaya, eyes flashing in the candlelight. He held a shard of glass against Miriam's throat.

"Close the door!" Seth said.

Miriam winced. She was dressed like a man. Omar pulled the door closed and faced them.

"Think I was kidding?" Seth asked. "Empty your pockets."

Omar pulled out some coins. He tossed them onto the table. "You do realize that there is no way out of here. We are surrounded by twenty heavily armed men."

Seth seemed not to have heard. "Pull up your pant legs."

The American was after his knife. How did he know? Omar pulled out a ten-inch bowie knife from the sheath around his calf. He briefly considered rushing Seth then, but dismissed the idea with one look at the pressure of the glass against Miriam's skin. She could not be harmed. Not yet.

He dropped the weapon on the table.

Seth retrieved the knife, walked to the window, and slipped the glass shard through a crack. He waved the knife through the air and held his hand out to the table, inviting Omar to sit.

"Please. Have a seat."

Miriam backed to the corner, giving Omar a wide berth.

"You have nothing to gain by playing these games. You will give me my wife, or I will take her by force. It's that simple."

"Your wife. Yes. Actually, that's what I want to talk to you about. Indulge me. Like you say, you have twenty men outside."

Something about the American engaged Omar. This man with the loose blond hair, clothed in this black dress, possessed one of the highest intellects of any living man, they said. It hardly seemed possible. What could the man be thinking?

"You're in no position to order me around, you fool. This is—"

"Sit!" Seth spun to Miriam and pressed the knife against her neck. "Sit, man! Sit, sit, sit!"

The American was crazed. For a moment their eyes challenged each other. Seth wasn't as confident as he sounded. Omar had learned to recognize fear, and he saw

it now in the American's eyes. Still, Seth had the knife. If
he were in the American's position, he would not hesitate
to use it.

Omar walked to the end of the table and sat.

"Excellent." Seth pulled Miriam over to the opposite
end. Now the table acted as a barrier between them. This
man might not be a warrior, but Omar saw that he'd positioned himself well.

"You say that Miriam is your wife?" Seth asked.

He refused to dignify the question with an answer.

"But I don't think she is," Seth said. "Not really. And
she doesn't think she is either."

"I have a dozen witnesses who say otherwise."

"Shut up. Hear me out."

"Then speak quickly. The city is burning, or hadn't you
noticed?"

"We don't think she's married because she hasn't married you, Omar. She was forced to go through a ceremony,
but that's like saying I'm rich because I walk into a bank.
You have to take possession of the money before you
become rich. Miriam hasn't taken possession of you." He
forced a grin. "But don't worry, we're not going to split
hairs. We know that in both your eyes and her father's
eyes, she is married and, unfortunately, married to you."

"Then get on with it."

"We want you to divorce her."

Omar laughed aloud. The man was not only mad; he
was a brazen fool.

"In your tradition, you can divorce her by simply
telling her in front of a witness that you divorce her. If
you divorce Miriam, everyone's problems are solved.
The coup will fail, because her father will withdraw his

support; you won't have to chase your runaway bride around the world any longer; she will be free to pursue the love she has for me. It's a perfect plan. A happy ending."

The sheer gall of this man was appalling. "If you knew our ways, you would know that neither of you is a legal witness," Omar said. "Even if I wanted to, I couldn't divorce my wife here, you imbecile! You called me into this place with the expectation that I would divorce my wife? Simply because you ask me?"

"No. I'm asking you to divorce your wife because it's what's best for Saudi Arabia and because she loves me. You say you believe in God. Isn't that what he would want you to do?"

"I won't listen to this!"

Seth slammed the flat of his palm on the table. "You will listen!" He tapped his temple with his forefinger. "Think, man! Think!"

Omar squinted, unnerved by this presumptuous show.

"Okay, here's how it works," Seth said. "I evaded you and a couple hundred cops in the States. How? Because I could see into the future, right?"

He didn't respond.

"Right?"

"So you say."

"No, so it was. I could see everything anyone might do, and I knew what to do to facilitate any possibility." Seth and Miriam exchanged a look. "The future can be changed."

"Believe me when I say there's no possibility that I will divorce my wife."

"Ahhh. But we've both come to the conclusion that divorce is a possibility," Seth said. "It's possible that I have this gift to keep the Middle East from spinning out of control. So there must be a way, whether any of us can see how or not."

"Then we will see God's will," Omar said. "And I can assure you that God's will is to sustain the marriage constituted in his name."

"Really? Are you willing to test that?"

"What is there to test? God has given me a wife!" Omar stood, exasperated.

"Sit!" Seth slashed at the air with the blade. The American had the appearance of a man who would kill. Omar sat.

Seth took a deep breath. "We've come to an understanding between us. Now we'll just have to see, won't we?"

"See what?"

"We'll use your own language. You seem so bent on God's will. Everything is as God wills it, isn't that your mantra? Half the whole world excuses their behavior citing God. Okay, fine. Let's put it to a test. See what futures materialize. To see if you're truly following."

"I already know God's will, and this country is waiting for me to fulfill it in a city fifty miles north of here. I am returning Saudi Arabia to God!"

It was all a bluff, of course. A nonsensical ploy to confuse and stall him. Who had ever heard of such an absurd proposition based on this impossible notion of changing futures? The American had lost his mind.

Fires were burning the city, and he was in a hut with his wife and an American infidel. He had to regain control.

Seth still held the knife.

# 41

CLIVE HAD READ and reread the printouts three times when the idea dropped into his mind without warning. It wasn't the most unique thought; frankly, he wondered how he'd missed it earlier. He sighed and reconsidered. If Miriam was killed, the coup would fail, wouldn't it? Yes, everything was based on the bloodline Miriam would give the sheik. And if Seth was in the country...

Clive grabbed the cell phone and hit the last-call button.

"Smaley."

"I think I have something, Peter." Clive took a breath. "On the surface this may not seem like an obvious course of action, but just listen for a second." He paused. Smaley would never buy this.

"Well?"

"Only the mixing of blood would guarantee the sheik a royal. What would happen if we were to cut off the bloodline?"

"I'm not sure I follow."

"If anything were to happen that would prevent Miriam from bearing Omar a child, the sheik might reconsider his allegiance. He would have no guarantee of royalty without a son. Marriage alone doesn't cut it. The sheik needs a son out of this."

"I still don't see how—"

"If something were to happen to Miriam, she couldn't bear a son, could she?"

Smaley was quiet for a moment. "You're suggesting what? That we kill Miriam? We've been over this."

"No. I'm suggesting we tell the sheik that we'll kill his daughter if the coup succeeds. We buy time."

"Buy time for what?"

"For Seth."

Smaley paused. "I thought we settled this. Even if we knew Seth was in play, he's not an assassin. We can't rely on him."

"No, no. He wouldn't kill Miriam anyway; he's in love with her, for heaven's sake. I just want to bluff. Worst case, we buy time for plan B. This may be our last chance."

"You're saying that I tell the sheik we have an assassin in their country, ready to pull the trigger and end Miriam's life. If Seth is in play, we can't put him in that position. And if he isn't, I can't put us in a position of crying wolf. We'll erode our own credibility."

"We have to!" Clive wiped his forehead of sweat. Smaley was right, but Clive's gut was telling him that Seth was still out there and needed time. Time for what, he wasn't sure. Just time.

"I've been after Seth, remember?" Clive said. "They have to catch him to kill him. This buys us more time. This gives him a chance."

"This is crazy. We don't even know that he's in the

country. What if the Saudis decide to take Seth out? Worse, what if they have already? Besides, all the sheik has to do is make one call to verify that his daughter's fine, and the whole ploy falls flat."

"Maybe. But it forces the sheik to make that call. And taking Seth isn't easy. Look, don't ask me why this makes sense. Just do it. Please. The idea that we have a man in place ready to kill his daughter will get the sheik's attention. Guaranteed. Even if she's fine now, he'll realize we could take her out before she bears a child. This will slow him down. He won't be able to rule out an assassin in a matter of minutes. It could take him hours."

"We're down to two hours," Smaley said. "Delaying them one more won't change a thing."

"Unless Seth has actually made some progress. Don't count him out. This guy may still be able to see their moves before they can."

Another long silence. Smaley muffled the receiver to speak to someone else and then returned.

"Okay, Clive. I'll see what I can do. That's all I can promise."


THE SHEIK STORMED into the tent. "How can they have an assassin in place already?"

"His name is Seth," Al-Hakim said. "The one who evaded Hilal and Omar in California."

Ah! The one who could presumably see into the future. The one who seemed to be able to walk through walls. He had come to kill Miriam?

"He was her protector. Now he will kill her? Do they think we have the minds of children?"

"They said his first objective is to take her out of the country, but if he is unable, he will kill her. They say he is in love with her."

So, if he could not have her, then he wouldn't allow another man the same privilege. This Omar might do, but not an American.

"I urge you to consider this threat, Sheik Al-Asamm," Al-Hakim said.

"Why didn't they tell us this earlier?"

"Perhaps they weren't ready to show their hand. If they'd told us earlier, we would've had enough time to deal with the situation. Now, with just over an hour to go, we are forced to reconsider our plans. It's good strategy on their part, bluff or not."

The sheik stepped out of the tent, alarmed, and breathed deeply. The sun was setting, a large orange ball in the horizon. He'd always taken Miriam's safety for granted for the simple reason that she was too valuable to kill. But he'd never considered that the Americans might kill her to preserve the status quo. A shaft of fear impaled him. Would they really do it?

If Miriam was killed before she bore Omar a child, the sheik's agreement with Khalid would be worthless. His daughter and his dreams of royalty would be smashed in one blow! The Americans could be as ruthless as anyone when they chose to be.

The sheik whirled around and strode into the tent.

"I must talk to Omar!" he said. "Tell Khalid that I will not move until I am assured of my daughter's safety."

MIRIAM WATCHED OMAR, unnerved by Seth's stalling tactics. "I won't play your bluff," he said. "Your time is finished. You may come willingly, or I will take you by force, the choice is yours."

"If you try to take me by force, Seth will kill me," Miriam snapped.

"Don't be absurd! This fool is incapable of killing you," Omar said. "This charade is finished."

"Is that so? Why am I incapable of killing her?" Seth asked.

"You don't have the backbone."

"You mean that I love her, don't you? You've been watching us and now you see that I have what you'll never have. Love."

To Miriam's surprise, Omar didn't object.

"But you're right," Seth said. He rotated the knife in his hand and flipped it through the air. The blade embedded itself in the tabletop and quivered like a spring.

Miriam stood immobilized. What was he doing? Seth had just given them up!

"I couldn't bear to hurt any woman, much less the woman I love," Seth said.

"And that is why you don't deserve this flower," Omar said. "Today you will die."

"But that's not what you believe, is it?" Seth said. "A good Muslim would say that I will die only if I am meant to die, isn't that right? Neither of us knows that yet, do we?"

Seth was taking this whole faith and fatalism thing too far! Or did he have something else on his mind? Could it be that he was seeing the futures?

Omar plucked the knife from the wood. "You stand unarmed, surrounded by twenty of my men, and you continue with this nonsense? Without this gift of yours, you're nothing but a babbling fool."

"My lack of sight doesn't make the future any less real. If I could see all of the potential futures right now, I would undoubtedly see one in which both Miriam and I survive. Just because I don't see that future now doesn't mean it doesn't exist."

Omar was right, the game had come to an end. A lump rose into Miriam's throat. Seth surely wouldn't have the stomach to kill her, but just as surely she didn't have the stomach to return with Omar.

What if she made a break for it now? She might be able to reach the door and run into the desert before Omar could stop her. But they would come after her. She would kill herself before allowing herself to be taken by Omar again.

Omar flipped open his phone and calmly pushed two keys. He lifted the receiver to his ear and locked his gaze on Miriam. "We are coming out," he said. "If the American makes a move, tell Mudah to shoot him in the head. Under no circumstances is the woman to be harmed. And make no mistake, the American is in a black abaaya, and she is wearing Western clothing." He snapped the phone shut.

He motioned to the door. "Go."

Miriam's heart pounded like a piston. Seth wasn't moving.

"Are you deaf? Out!" Omar boomed. His cell phone chirped in his hand. "If you don't move, I'll have you shot in here."

"I'm not moving. Not yet."

The phone chirped again. Omar snatched the phone to his ear. "I'm coming, you fool!" He took a step and then paled. Listened, motionless. Turned to Miriam.

"Forgive me, Abu al-Asamm. I thought you were one of my men."

Her father?

"Of course your daughter is alive." Omar spoke quickly, momentarily distracted by this intrusion. He took a step toward the window and glanced out, listening now.

Miriam caught Seth's eyes. They were steady, flashing with a determination she hadn't seen since California. He turned to her.

"No sir, you don't understand. I have your assassin!" Omar paused. "Yes, I have the assassin and I have your daughter here. They are both in my control, I assure..."

"Scream," Seth mouthed. And then again in an urgent whisper while Omar as distracted. "Scream!"

She understood immediately. Omar could not harm her while her father was on the phone. He had to know she was in danger!

She screamed, like bloody murder. Then again. "He has a knife to my throat!"

Omar spun to her, caught off guard, phone still pressed to his ear.

"Father!" she screamed.

"Don't be absurd!" Omar snapped. "There is no knife!"

A fist pounded on the door.

Seth moved then, while Omar's back was half turned, and his attention divided between her scream, the phone at his ear, and the knock on the door. He dove for Omar and slashed his arm down on the man's right hand. The knife clattered to the floor, but hadn't yet come to rest before Seth scooped it up.

In two long strides he was behind Miriam, knife at her throat.

"Now there is. Tell them to leave or I will kill her!" Seth shouted. "I will kill the sheik's daughter!"

Omar blinked several times. The fist pounded again, accompanied by a muffled yell this time. "Sir?"

Omar finally came to himself. "Leave us!" he yelled to the men outside. "Get in your cars and wait for my call!"

A garbled electronic voice squawked over the phone from across the room. Her father, loud now.

"No, Abu al-Asamm," Omar spoke into the receiver. "I assure you that there's no danger to your daughter. My men have this place surrounded. I have the situation under control."

"Scream," Seth whispered again.

"Father!" She put her full emotions into it now, tapping the pent-up horror of facing Omar alone again. "Father!" Agony and terror rolled into one cry.

Seth's ploy, however daring, probably still only delayed the inevitable, Miriam thought. Seth would not kill her, and once his empty threats played themselves out, her father would understand that. Once the sheik satisfied himself that her life was not in the balance, Omar would kill Seth and take her captive.

Miriam put the grief of this realization into her next wail. She sounded like a wounded jackal.

"Shut up!" Omar screamed.

Miriam took some small comfort in his momentary desperation. She winked at him.

"I assure you, Abu al-Asamm, there is no... Yes, he is here, but he's bluffing! Your daughter's screaming because she is with him! Speaking to her will prove nothing!"

The sheik was yelling at Omar.

Omar pulled the cell phone from his ear and glared

at Miriam, lips flat and trembling. "You will prove nothing by this!" he snapped. Dropping his voice, he said, "You will both pay before you die." He shoved the phone toward them. "Your father wishes to speak to you."

"No!" Seth said.

That stopped him.

"What do you mean no? She will not speak to her own father?"

"No," Miriam said softly. "I will not."

Omar lifted the phone. "She will not speak to you."

"Father!" Miriam cried. "I am dying!"

"She is not dying!" Omar said. "They are playing with us!"

"Father!"

THE TRUTH WAS now as clear to Seth as any algebraic equation. He'd seen enough of how futures worked to know that such an unlikely event as the sheik calling when he had, for the reason he had, was not necessarily arbitrary or without purpose.

The events of life were neither wholly random nor predetermined. Purpose and choice drove them. Simple, one might say, but not so simple in the mind of one who understood the ramifications as clearly as Seth did.

The call did nothing but stall Omar. But if there was a future in which Seth and Miriam survived, and if Seth could facilitate that future by stalling Omar, he would stall the prince some more. But stalling meant getting the knife back, a prospect that filled him with dread. Then again, his boldness paid off thus far.

He still didn't know how they were going to survive, only that he desperately wanted to.

"Father!"

And then Seth did know how they were going to survive, because without warning his mind opened up, as if the roof above their heads had been blown off.

He gasped.

Miriam gasped. "Ouch."

He'd inadvertently jerked the knife against her throat, but it took a moment for him to mentally organize the streaming images and relax his grip.

The sudden immersion into potential futures felt like diving into a clear, cool pool after being left to die in the desert. Seth lowered his arms. Now the stalling made perfect sense. Something had caused the sheik to call.

Miriam turned to him, no longer concerned with screaming. One look at his face and she knew.

"Of course she will talk to you. Please, please calm down!" Omar said. He, on the other hand, had no clue that anything had changed.

Seth spun through possible futures as if they were photos on a wheel. There—a future in which both he and Miriam survived. But it was only one of many. And it wasn't one he especially liked.

Seth winked at Miriam, who was grinning, of all things. He took a deep breath and stepped forward.

"Change of plans, my friend."

# 42

MIRIAM TOOK ONE look at Seth's face and knew that he was seeing the futures.

Her knees weakened, relieved. She'd been here before with Seth, staring into what appeared to be a box canyon without escape. Yet what once terrified her now delighted her. A silly grin nudged her lips.

Seth winked at her, took a deep breath, and stepped forward.

"Change of plans, my friend."

Omar lowered the phone. Her father's voice sounded distorted through the small speaker. Seth lifted the knife awkwardly, only mildly threatening. "Phone, please."

"You think your knife threatens—"

Seth snatched up the phone before Omar could finish. He brought the device to his mouth.

"I'm terribly sorry, Sheik, but I have to terminate this call for a few minutes. The prince will call you back momentarily, and I promise you he'll straighten everything out then. Your daughter will be fine. I love her, you know. Crazy but true. And I wouldn't storm the palace if I were you. Not just yet."

He flipped the phone closed.

The silence in the room hummed. Omar stood motionless and unsure what to make of Seth's commandeering.

"Checkmate," Seth said. "Your current thoughts aren't technically futures, so I don't know what you're thinking, but I know dozens of things you would try given the chance. If I'm right, one thing you will do is jump me. And although you're slightly stronger than I, I know what your moves might be, and I know exactly how to hurt you despite the fact that I've only thrown a few punches in my life. I may even kill you."

"You're bluffing," Omar said, doubt weighting his words.

"I assume you're hoping that your men will come crashing through that door about now, but I can assure you that there's no possibility of that for some time. You sent them packing, and they fear you. Terribly sorry."

Omar's hands gathered to fists. "You think this frightens me? That you can manipulate me with this nonsense?"

"I would be careful," Miriam said, surging with confidence. "I've seen Seth at work. He can defeat you with one hand." The words tasted delicious in her mouth.

Omar's face twisted, and for an instant she wondered if her taunting had been unwise. What if there were no future in which they survived?

"Miriam," Seth said. "As much as you're enjoying this, we're running out of time. As I see it, we have about thirty seconds. Do you mind turning away? This will get ugly."

Ugly? "You don't want me to watch?"

"Exactly. If you don't mind. I'm not normally given to violence, and I'm not sure I like the idea of your watching."

The scene felt surreal, Seth facing off with Omar, announcing that he was about to hurt him, taking the time to insist she hide her eyes. But that too was part of what he saw.

"Just turn around," he said.

She backed up.

"Maybe a quick kiss first," Seth said.

Omar snorted and lunged.

"Stay!" Seth said, shoving the knife forward. Omar paused, struggling to maintain his control.

"Kiss, princess," Seth said.

She looked at Omar. Yes, why not? With Seth, nothing was by accident, including a kiss. This was her part in delivering justice. She broke eye contact with Omar just long enough to kiss Seth tenderly on the cheek, then smiled at Omar. It was a pleasure to play her part.

Seth slipped the cell phone into her hands. "Hit the callback button when I say."

Omar roared. Miriam took the phone, turned from them, and walked to the corner.

"I don't want to hurt you, Omar," Seth said. "So I apologize in advance. There are two ways we can do this. You can attack me, or I can attack you. And if you're wondering, I'm talking matter-of-factly like this to unnerve you. It'll work to my advantage, even though you already know that I'm manipulating you. Foresight is such a wonderful thing."

"One call and my men will be here. Do you think you can overcome twenty men?"

"I don't know. It's not in the futures so I haven't seen it. They won't come. Unfortunately for you, they're in their cars. A Mercedes is amazingly well insulated. I'm afraid you're stranded with me, lover boy."

Omar did not respond.

"Well, should I run at you?" Seth said. "Or should I just provoke you into—"

A loud grunt made Miriam flinch. She glanced around and saw that Omar had thrown himself at Seth. Omar was a trained warrior. He looked like a demon descending on Seth, who stood without defending himself. She averted her eyes, like a schoolgirl caught peeking.

The cabin filled with sounds of heavy breathing and crashing, followed by a tremendous thump and a grunt. Silence.

Miriam could contain herself no longer. She turned.

Omar was on his belly, face pressed into the floor-boards, one arm twisted behind his back. He was gulping for breath. Seth's knee pinned Omar's back. He'd bent the man's arm at an unnatural angle with one hand, and with the other he pressed the tip of the knife into Omar's spine, where his neck met his shoulders.

"Now you listen to me!" Seth snarled. "The world doesn't need killers like you. Saudi Arabia doesn't need killers like you. Miriam doesn't need or want you." Seth bent over so that his mouth was close to Omar's ear. He applied pressure to the blade and the man groaned.

"And I know it comes as a shock to you, but women are not dogs. Most of the people in your country know that, it's time you learned as well."

A bead of sweat dropped from Seth's chin.

"I'm not a violent man, I'm really not, but I swear..."

He ground his teeth. Seth took a deep breath, calming himself.

"Call your father, Miriam."

She lifted the phone and pressed the callback button.

"You forced Miriam to marry you against her will," Seth said. "Now I'm going to force you to divorce her against your will. As far as we're concerned, she's not married, but we're going to make it official."

He looked at Miriam. "You aren't supposed to be looking."

She loved him more in that moment than ever before. The phone rang on the other end.

"This blade is very close to your spinal cord, Omar," Seth said. "If you turn or lift, it will sever your nerves and leave you a quadriplegic. Do you want to spend the rest of your days in a wheelchair?"

The sheik answered the phone.

"Father?"

"Miriam! What's the meaning—"

"I will never give Omar a child, Father. Never! I have refused him, and if he ever tries to touch me again, I will kill him!" She knew where Seth was headed and decided to assist.

"Omar despises me and wishes to divorce me," she said.

Silence.

"That's right, Omar," Seth said quietly. "You will divorce Miriam now. You will speak it into the phone and the sheik will be your witness. If you hesitate, I will drive the knife in. Do you understand? You'll never touch another woman as long as you live."

Omar moaned again and Miriam wondered if he might pass out from the pain.

"Omar cannot divorce you!" Her father had come to himself. "It will ruin everything!"

"It will not ruin me!" Miriam said.

Omar groaned.

Seth nodded at the phone, and Miriam held it to his ear. "If Omar doesn't divorce your daughter, he will leave here an invalid. There will be no son. Either way. Accept the will of God, Abu al-Asamm."

Miriam lowered the phone to Omar's lips. The man's eyes were round with terror. His nostrils flared with each breath, and a string of spittle ran from his mouth to the floor.

"Say it!"

Omar closed his mouth and then opened it, speechless.

"Have it your way," Seth said.

"I divorce you," Omar said in a barely audible groan.

"Again," Seth said. "I divorce you, Miriam."

"I divorce you . . ."

"Miriam."

"Miriam."

"Again. I divorce your daughter, Abu Ali al-Asamm."

Miriam heard her father's voice objecting on the cell phone's speaker.

"I divorce your daughter, Abu Ali al-Asamm."

A wave of relief flooded Miriam. Three times in front of witnesses. The law was fulfilled. She was free. The only way for Omar to reclaim her was to go through another ceremony. She snapped the phone closed on the sheik's protests.

Seth hesitated, staring at the back of Omar's head. He withdrew the knife, flipped it, and brought the butt down on Omar's head, hard. The man relaxed.

"Sorry about that," Seth said to the unconscious figure.

He jumped up. "They're coming out of the cars now. When they see me, they'll fire. Count to five and then run out to our car. They won't fire on you."

"They won't hit you?"

"In three out of four futures they miss."

"The car's out of gas!"

"We have enough for what we need. You just keep moving. They'll go for the tires, but that's not where our danger lies. Just do exactly what I say."

"So there is danger? Real danger?"

"There's always danger." Seth kissed her firmly on the lips. "I love you, princess."

# 43

SETH JERKED THE door open. "Remember, count to five," he said. He bolted from the hut.

Miriam dropped to a knee and began to count. Gunfire filled the desert air. Several rifles and at least one automatic weapon. How could he escape that?

In three out of four they miss, he'd said. What about that fourth?

Miriam rushed the last three counts, gathered herself, and then sprinted through the door. The black cars were lined up in a half-moon. At least six of them had their doors open, weapons trained on the shanty.

"Stop firing!" The driver from the car on the far left, Omar's driver, ran toward the hut. "It's the woman!" The gunfire ceased.

Miriam slipped at the corner, scrambled to her feet, and tore around the hut. Then she was at the car, panting. Seth sat behind the wheel, waving her in.

"Hurry!"

"I am!" Miriam clambered around the back, threw the front door open, and dove in. "Go!"

"When we get to the Mercedes on the far left, I need you to get out," Seth said. "They still don't know that Omar has divorced you. You'll be safe. I won't be—"

"I understand," she said. "It's Omar's car. His driver's in the hut now. Drive!"

"That's right. Don't worry about the tires—"

"Go! Hurry!"

Seth threw the stick into reverse. The car shot backward, throwing sand. They cleared the shack. A dozen rifles spun their way.

"We're cutting it close," Seth said. "Omar's up."

He jerked the stick into drive and roared for the abandoned Mercedes. Gunfire popped across the sand. Metal pinged and one of the tires blew. Miriam was sure they would slam into the hood of the car.

Seth hit the brakes at the last moment, and they slid to a stop, inches from Omar's car, nose-to-nose.

Miriam shoved her door open and stumbled out.

Immediately the gunfire stopped. Once again, the men's fear of Omar worked against him. She leaped to her feet, swung around the open door, and ran for the driver's side of Omar's Mercedes.

Seth ran for the other door, protected by the heavy car.

Miriam slid into the driver's seat. Seth piled in beside her.

Omar and his driver spilled out of the hut.

Beside her, Seth was smiling. "Take us out of here, honey."

She pushed the accelerator to the floor. They slammed into the car they'd just vacated.

"Sorry, I saw that coming," Seth said. "Other way."

She dropped the gearshift into reverse, and they spun backward in a tight loop. Something thumped into the car. Two more. Bullets! Then a whole row along the rear windshield. She glanced at Seth and saw that he was still grinning.

"Any other car, we'd be dead," Seth said. "This one's bulletproof. Literally. Omar's parting gift."

"The tires?"

"No chance."

"Ha!" She slammed the steering wheel in elation. They roared over the sand, leaving the circle of cars behind in their dust.

"Left or right?" she asked.

"Left, back to the highway. Then south, toward Jidda."

Miriam pushed the car to a breakneck speed. For a full minute neither spoke. She glanced at the rearview mirror—a plume of dust rose from the dirt road.

"They're following!"

"Don't worry, we have an ace behind the wheel," Seth said. "I told you your driving would come in handy."

"We were nearly killed back there!" she objected. "What if they call ahead and have the road blocked? We're in Omar's territory now, not the United States."

"Omar may try to block the road. But your father will withdraw his support now. The coup will crumble. King Abdullah will regain the upper hand. Khalid and Omar will be forced to run for their lives. Think about it, Miriam, they have no use for you now. Neither does King Abdullah. You are no longer their pawn."

She thought through his analysis. It made perfect sense.

"You see all this?"

"No. I don't see anything now. It's gone."

She looked at him, alarmed. "Then how can you be so sure?"

"Because I saw enough when I did see to know how this works. My days of seeing maybe be over—if so we'll have to wander around in the dark, but I'm not sure that's so bad, are you? Have a little faith." He grinned. "We're free, princess. Trust me, we're free."

Seth pulled Omar's phone from his pocket and dialed a long number. He looked at her and let it ring.

"Clive? Hello, Clive—"

Seth listened for a moment.

"Easy, my friend. Omar's divorced Miriam. The sheik is withdrawing his support. The coup is history. I have Miriam now and we're headed for the embassy in Jidda. Yes. Please have it open for us. I'll explain later. In the meantime, tell the State Department to call the sheik. He'll confirm everything."

Seth cut the connection.

They drove in silence for several long minutes. The plume of dust still hung on the horizon behind them, but if she wasn't mistaken, it was farther behind than it had been a few seconds ago.

They reached the highway and Miriam turned south toward Jidda. Seth was right; Omar would have more on his mind than chasing down a woman he'd just divorced. He would be fortunate to survive the night.

It occurred to Miriam that she and Seth had begun their relationship like this, in a car fleeing south over miles of pavement. A Saudi princess and an American outlaw. Bonnie and Clyde. Stranded between two cultures. When would the running stop? Where were they running to? What future awaited them? Only God knew.

Emotion swept over her like a tide. The road blurred and she blinked her sight clear.

"I don't think I can live without you, Seth."

"As long as I'm alive, you won't have to," he said. "I swear it. I won't let them take you back. Do you hear me?"

Miriam wasn't sure why, but she began to cry softly. It was the sweetest thing anyone had ever said to her.

"I love you, Seth. I love you very much," she said.

"I love you, Miriam. I will always love you."

# Epilogue

SAMIR STOOD AT the mosque's entrance, gazing over the floods of men who milled about after prayers, talking in low tones and nodding in agreement. Sheik Abu Ali al-Asamm stood near the front, discussing matters with several lesser Shia leaders here in Dhahran. Soon the sheik's day would pass, and one of the lessers would rise up to be the voice of the Saudi Shia. And what would be the word of that leader? Would it be a word of love and peace or a word of the sword?

Two weeks had passed since the failed coup attempt. Samir could not have imagined such soul-searching as had plagued him in these last fourteen days.

A lump rose to his throat. He had not discerned the sum of the matter yet, but he was confident the answers would not elude him for long—God would never indefinitely withhold the truth from any diligent seeker. In the meantime, several observations had presented themselves to him, none of them particularly welcome.

The least welcome of these was that he had lost Miriam's love forever. She had been and still was the only woman he ever loved, and he'd sacrificed her for a misguided ideal.

"Forgive me, dear Miriam," he mumbled. He turned from the entrance and walked down the steps to the street.

How could a good Muslim reconcile the militants' ideals with true love? How could a good Christian kill Muslims in the name of love?

How could he have turned Miriam over to a beast like Omar?

Samir held no ill feelings toward the American, Seth. In a strange way he was thankful that a man of such obvious character had taken her into a new life. How many men would have risked what Seth risked to rescue Miriam?

The American wasn't Saudi, of course. Nor Muslim. The pair would endure a host of cultural challenges if they were to wed, but in the end, Miriam would be happy with Seth. If there was anything Samir could do for Miriam now, he could wish her happiness.

"Afternoon, Samir."

Samir turned to the voice. It was Hassan, a fifteen-year-old son of the sheik.

"Afternoon, Hassan."

"God is great."

"God is indeed great."

The boy smiled and hurried off.

Yes, God was great, but those who swung the sword on his behalf were not, Samir thought.

Omar was dead, killed trying to escape the day after the coup. Killed by the sheik's men, no less. A kind of poetic justice. Khalid still hid somewhere out of the country. As long as the House of Saud remained in power, Khalid would be on the run. Ostracized, but not powerless. Others expelled from the kingdom had wreaked havoc throughout the world. Samir expected no less of Khalid.

The sheik had not only been spared but commended for his reversal of loyalty in the eleventh hour. Though he'd been one of the plotters, he was still more valuable to the king as a friend than as an enemy. It was the way of the desert.

The world's religions had engaged themselves in a great struggle. A struggle between those who wanted to fix the world with the sword and those who wanted to fix it with love. One day they would all understand that the world was tired of the sword.

Like most, deep in his heart, Samir was a lover, not a fighter. One day, if he would be so fortunate, he would find another woman to love. This time he would love her as he only wished he could love Miriam now, with all of his gifts and all of his gratitude. She would be free, and if she was not, he would set her free. Like a bird.

"Fly, my dear. Fly free, dear Miriam."

Samir walked down the street, vaguely comforted.

An Excerpt from

# FORBIDDEN

### Ted Dekker
### and Tosca Lee

Available in Hardcover August 2011.

# ROM

# 1

THERE WAS NEVER A BODY.

Not even at a funeral. Mourners sat angled toward one another in the stiff pews to avoid looking directly at the empty casket and the destiny hanging over them all. They all knew that only one of two things happened when the body died, one outcome more likely than the other.

The terrible outcome, of course.

Rom, the twenty-four-year-old son of Elias Sebastian, sat in a back pew by himself. He was a plain man by any measure. Not unattractive, but neither was he truly beautiful by the standards of the Order, which reserved true beauty for royalty.

He'd sung earlier in the service in homage to the dead man's life. It was a humble yet noble job, singing for the dead. Humble because any artist's life was humble—only by the grace of Sirin, who'd written about the educational merits of the arts, did artisans find work at all in a world unmoved by creative gifts. Noble because being near the dead was fearful business for most. But Rom didn't mind. He needed the work, and the dead needed their service.

Finished with his job here, he folded the funeral program lengthwise as he waited for a good moment to slip away. There, on the upper flap, was the name of the deceased: Lucas Tavor. Rom folded it again. There was Tavor's age: sixty-eight. Not so old in this advanced world where one might live to 110 or 120.

He glanced at the man's empty coffin lying atop its metal carriage between the front pillars of the great basilica. It was one of the finer basilicas in the city, in Rom's opinion—not because of its size, as it was far from the largest, but because of the intricate stained glass above its altar.

All basilicas boasted their treasures, but this depiction of Sirin, the martyred father of the Order, was more exquisite than the rest. The numbered, compass-like marks of his halo spread like a fractured sunburst above his head, even on a dull day. It was the universal picture of peace, an inspiring image of the man who had preached freedom from the excesses of modern life and from the snares of emotion.

Sirin's right hand cradled a dove. His left rested on the shoulder of a second man: Megas, holding the bound Book of Orders, canonized under his rule. Every basilica housed the same image, but none as intricate as this.

The priest stood behind the altar, the ordinal rays of Sirin's halo reflecting faintly upon his shoulders. Two clerics flanked him on the dais as he smoothed the pages of the Book of Orders upon its stand.

"Born once, into life, we are blessed."

"We are blessed," echoed the assembly, perhaps fifty

in all. Their murmurs rose like specters to the arched vault overhead.

"Let us please the Maker through a life of diligent Order."

"Let us please the Maker." The mouths of the clerics moved with the congregation. Beyond them on the dais, the silver censers that exhaled incense through normal assembly hung empty upon their chains.

"We know the Maker exists by his Order. If we please, let us be born into the afterlife, not into fear, but Bliss everlasting."

Bliss. The eternal absence of fear—or so it was said. Though Rom was less given to fear than most, it took some abstract thinking to imagine being forever untouched by at least some tinge of it.

It was said other emotions existed before the human race evolved, but they, too, were difficult to imagine. These sentiments of a baser age, like excised tumors, never reappeared; humanity finally resisted the black plague that had almost destroyed it.

Rom wasn't sure he even knew the words to describe them all. And those he did know were meaningless to him. That archaic word *passion*, for example. Try as he might to grasp this thing, he could only conjure up thoughts of varying degrees of fear. Or another: *sorrow*. What was sorrow? It was like trying to imagine what his life would be like if he'd never been born.

No matter. Humanity's one surviving emotion granted Order in this life and the possibility of Bliss beyond. Trying to imagine such a future, though, was enough to make his head hurt.

In front of Rom, a curly-haired boy turned around in

the pew. Sticking his fingers in his mouth, he stared bug-eyed as Rom continued to fold the paper program. Rom held up the small project so the boy could see the thing taking shape between his fingers.

A eulogist approached the podium, printed page in hand. The heads of those assembled were now fixed on that empty coffin, no longer able to look away.

"Lucas Tavor was sixty-eight years old," the man read.

"He fell," a young woman two pews up whispered. The basilica's unrestrained acoustics carried her words to Rom. "Broke his hip. One of his children found him a day after it happened."

It was easy enough to surmise the rest of the story. Society had long embraced the custom of transferring the infirm, the severely injured, and the feeble to an asylum under the auspices of the Authority of Passing. There, humans closer to death than to life might live out the minority of their days, sparing their peers the caustic reminder of death's inevitable pall. Thus, there was never a body at a funeral, because the one for whom the funeral was held often had not yet died.

Not technically, at least.

Rom stood and adjusted the strap of his shoulder bag. Slipping from the pew, he handed the finished paper crane to the boy, who accepted it with wet fingers.

Outside, on the steps of the basilica, the city spread out before him, concrete-gray beneath the ominous clouds of late afternoon. On each of the city's seven hills, the spires and turrets of centuries-old buildings stabbed at the heavens like so many lances piercing a boil.

This was Byzantium, the greatest city on earth, population five hundred thousand, home to three thousand of the world's twenty-five thousand royals, who had come from every continent to serve in her government and state-run businesses. It was the center of the earth, to which all eyes turned in matters politic and religious, social and economic. It was the seat of power to which all earthly dominions had deferred since the end of the Age of Chaos five centuries before, when the world had bowed to the great powers of the Americas and Russia.

Chaos. It had nearly killed them all. But humanity learned from her mistakes, and Null Year had signaled a new beginning for a new world cleansed of destructive passions. Peace had ruled in the 480 years since, and Byzantium was the heart of it all.

The city was more crowded than normal as it prepared to host the inauguration of the world Sovereign—Feyn Cerelia, daughter of the current Sovereign, Vorrin, of the royal Cerelia family. Never before had a future Sovereign been the direct descendant of a ruling Sovereign, and yet the random hand of fate was about to change history. And so Feyn Cerelia's inauguration was considered a particularly auspicious event, one that would swell Byzantium's population to nearly one million for days.

Her image had already graced the banners on streetlamps and city buildings for months. For weeks, train cars had brought construction equipment, barricades, and food from all parts of the world to supply Byzantium for the occasion. The black cars of the Brahmin royals and those in service to them had become a common sight on streets unaccustomed to motorized congestion. There had been no mass production of automobiles since the Age of Chaos, and no roadways beyond the city were intact enough to justify the vehicles' exorbitant cost. Businesses carried out their trade by rail, subway, rickshaw, or private courier. Rom himself had never driven a car.

Rom glanced up the street to the west. In five days, all traffic would be blocked within a one-mile radius of the Grand Basilica near the Citadel. Construction crews had already spent a week erecting the high stands on either side of the Processional Way, which the new Sovereign would travel atop one of the royal stallions. All other attending royals and citizens alike would approach the inauguration in sedate order, on foot.

Beyond the city to the east, the hinterland stretched all the way to the sea. The territory had been reshaped by the fallout of the wars, testament to Chaos. What was once a land of agriculture was now arid and unsuitable for producing the food Byzantium's population lived upon. Erosion had etched new canyons on the barren face of a countryside once lush and fertile. And so the city relied on the provisions of Greater Europa to the north and her more fertile sisters—Sumeria, to the east; Russe to the northeast; Abyssinia, to the south. These ancient territories, once better known as Europe, the Middle East, Russia, and Africa, provided willingly for Byzantium, the city once called Rome. Their imports were the tithe of Order, a small price to pay to live in peace.

To the south of Byzantium lay the industrial towns that nearly reached the coast, connected only by rail, her roads as broken as the landscape itself.

Only in the last century had the land shown signs of true recovery. Trees grew along scraggly creek beds, and in some places grasses had reclaimed the soil. Today the countryside was sparsely dotted by the estates and stables of royals wishing to escape the confines of the city for a scrubby patch of green. It offered only meager peace, but anything that reduced fear was a welcome respite.

Rom had heard the city was a place of light at one time, of sun by day and city lamps by night, like sparkling gems strewn against a backdrop of velvet. Televisions and computers connected everyone. Planes crisscrossed the sky.

Citizens owned weapons.

Now personal electricity was rationed. Televisions existed in public spaces and for state use only. Computers were restricted to state use. Planes, reserved for royal business, were a rare sight in Byzantium's overcast sky. And the only firearms in the world existed in museums.

A streetlight sputtered overhead, and Rom turned his head to the sky. No, not a streetlight, but lightning, striking out toward the Tibron River. Rom snugged his bag close and hurried down the sweeping steps to the street.

By the time he reached the underground, it had begun to rain. He hurried down the concrete stairs into the stale subterranean warmth and was greeted with the electric light of the station, the shuffle of foot traffic, the squealing brakes of an oncoming train.

His route home included a five-minute ride to the central terminus, and then a twenty-minute journey southeast. It was enough time to take out his notebook, lay pen to new lyrics for the funeral he was to sing at next week. But even after he had returned the pen to his pocket, they seemed inadequate, too similar to the song he had sung today—as creative as he knew them to be.

That was to be expected. If there was one thing that had not evolved since Null Year, it was art. Art and culture. As an artisan, Rom understood that the creativity of both had been squelched by the loss of their emotional muses. Even the subtleties of language had remained relatively unchanged. A small price to pay for Order. But a price, nonetheless.

He exited the underground six blocks from home and made his way past the distracted, worried expressions of those descending. Above was the steady drizzle of a lighter gray sky; to the north, the hard edges of the skyline he had just left were obscured by the veil of a proper downpour.

Foot traffic was thin. Those who were out darted to their destinations beneath umbrellas and newspapers. In the street, the lone dark car of a royal sped by, sending an arc of water toward the curb.

Rom ducked his head, rain already running off the wet spikes of his hair into his eyes, and pulled his jacket more tightly around him. He kept to storefront eaves before turning into a narrow alleyway between the broad brick backs of an old theater and an out-of-use hostel.

Today he had done his work diligently. He had earned his modest living. He had been in assembly three times already this week, but he would go tomorrow, a fourth time, for Avra.

Avra, his friend since childhood, who avoided basilica. Avra, with her quiet gaze and fearful heart. His attendance had been their pact for several years now, and why not? It cost him nothing to go for her, and though it might not be condoned by the priests, it might make a difference to the Maker. It was her only chance, anyway.

He was thinking of her troubled brown eyes when a voice sounded behind him.

"Son of Elias!"

The cry echoed against the lichen-spackled brick, over the patter of the rain. Rom turned and stared through the drizzle. A lean figure lurched through the alley's narrow file, his long, ragged coat flapping wetly behind him. His gaze was locked on Rom.

*Son of Elias.* Rom hadn't been called that in years. He squinted against the rain. "Do I know you?"

The old man was now so close that Rom could see his grizzled brows and sunken cheeks, the gray hair plastered to his head, and could hear his wheezing breath. The man closed the distance between them with surprising speed and seized Rom by the shoulders. The thin lids of his eyes were peeled wide.

"It's you!" he rasped between panting breaths. Spittle edged the corners of his mouth.

Rom's first thought was that the man had managed to escape the Authority of Passing and was fleeing the escorts of the asylum. He was certainly old enough. And obviously crazed.

But the man knew his father's name. A sliver of fear worked its way beneath Rom's skin. What was with this old fellow?

"It's you," the old man said again. "I never thought to lay eyes on Elias again, but by the Maker, you have the look of him!"

Two men rounded the corner at the end of the alley and sprinted toward them. In the dull splatter of the rain, it almost appeared that they wore the silver and black of the Citadel Guard. Odd. The jurisdiction of the guard was the Citadel itself—on the other side of the city. Perhaps because of the inauguration...

The man tore his gaze away to look over his shoulder.

At the sight of the two men, he tightened his grip on Rom's shoulders and spoke in a rush.

"They've found me. And now they'll come after you, too. Listen to me now, boy. Listen well! Your father said you could be trusted."

Rom blinked in the rain. "My father? My father's dead. He died of fever."

"Not from fever! Your father was murdered, boy!"

"What? That can't be true."

The man let go of him and fumbled with his coat, tearing at an inner pocket that didn't seem to match the rest of the garment. It bulged with a square shape the size of two fists put together. He tore it free.

"He was killed. As all the other keepers were killed. For this." He shoved the parcel at Rom. "Take it! There's no one else now. Take it, or your father died for nothing. Learn its secrets. Find the man called the Book. The Book, do you hear me? He's at the Citadel—find him. Show him you have this!"

Displays of fear were not uncommon, but the old man was obviously demented with it. In reaction, the sliver of Rom's own fear wormed its way to Rom's heart.

A third man had appeared at the entrance to the alley. One of the first two shouted back for him to go around. And now Rom could see that they did indeed wear the colors of the elite Citadel Guard. All for an old man?

Rom felt his fingers close around the parcel, damp and still warm from the man's body.

"Swear to me!"

"What—"

"Swear!"

"I swear. I..."

The guardsmen were no more than twenty paces away, running far harder than their aged quarry warranted.

The old man's voice rose to an unexpected roar. "Protect it! It's power and life—life as it was—and grave danger. Run!" The guardsmen were only a dozen steps away. *"Run!"*

The sound of that scream startled Rom so much that he took five or six long strides before he faltered. What was he doing? If the guard was after the man, for whatever reason, he should stop and assist them. He should give them the bundle, let them sort it all out. He pulled up hard and spun back.

They had the old man, sagging in their hold. Something flashed in the rain. The serrated blade of a knife. Not the ceremonial variety Rom was accustomed to seeing in pictures, but a weapon strictly forbidden.

"Run!" the man screamed.

As one guardsman held the flailing old man, the one with the knife ripped the blade across his wrinkled throat. The old man's neck opened with a dark, yawning gush. His last cry devolved into a gurgle as his knees gave way.

And then the gaze of the restraining guardsman locked on Rom. The old man was no longer their quarry.

*He* was.

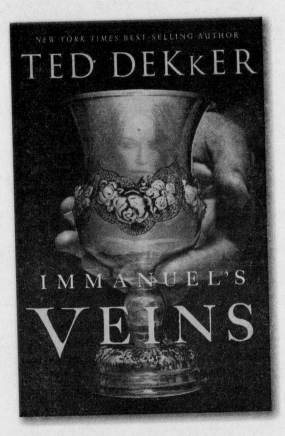